The Thunder Girls

At fifteen years old Melanie Blake was told by her high school career advisers that her decision to do work experience at a local record shop was an 'embarrassment and a clear example that she wouldn't go far in life or her career'. They were wrong. By twenty-one she was working at the BBC's iconic *Top of the Pops* show and by twenty-seven she had built a reputation as one of the UK's leading music and entertainment managers, with her own agency and a roster of award-winning artists who had sold more than 100 million records.

After a decade at the top, Melanie decided to manage a smaller client list and concentrate on her other passion, writing – first as a columnist for a national newspaper, then as a playwright and now as a novelist. They say write about what you know, and having lived and breathed every aspect of the music and entertainment industry, in *The Thunder Girls* she certainly has.

For more information on Melanie visit her Twitter account, @MelanieBlakeUK, or her website, www.melanieblakeonline.com.

The Thunder Girls

MELANIE BLAKE

PAN BOOKS

First published 2019 by Pan Books
an imprint of Pan Macmillan
20 New Wharf Road, London N1 9RR
Associated companies throughout the world
www.panmacmillan.com

ISBN 978-1-5290-1743-4

1 3 5 7 9 8 6 4 2

A CIP catalogue record for this book is available from the British Library.

Typeset in New Caledonia by Jouve (UK), Milton Keynes
Printed and bound by CPI Group (UK) Ltd, Croydon, CR0 4YY

This book is dedicated to true Thunder Girls all over the world who, despite the odds stacked against them in whatever way, shape or form, always fight their way through the negativity and somehow let their lightning strike! You go, girls.

All I ever heard nearly my whole life was no, no and no – the day I stopped looking for approval was the day I started getting what I wanted, so do the same and never let anyone put you down or make you believe you are not good enough to live the life you want, whatever that is and whoever you are.

We only live once – twice if you are really lucky – so make it count!

Legal warning . . . In my own career in the music industry I've been up close and personal with some of the biggest bands in the world, so although I'm legally bound to tell you that *The Thunder Girls* is entirely fictional (and whilst my own acts truly were delightful), trust me when I say that what you read in this book is just a peek behind the celebrity velvet rope – because, if anything, some real pop stars can be way worse than Chrissie, Anita, Roxanne and Carly. Life on the pop rollercoaster really is like this . . . So settle in and enjoy the ride – it's a white-knuckle one.

Lots of love,

Melanie Blake xx

The Thunder Girls

Prologue

November 1989

Carly Hughes stepped from the back of the limousine at the entrance to Shine Records. She was wearing a short kilt and leather jacket. Lacy tights with biker boots; big hair, kooky-looking shades and an oversized designer bag worth thousands.

Every inch the pop star.

Her driver, Dale, threw a protective arm around her as he steered her past thousands of screaming Thunder Girls fans, Carly stopping to scribble her name on the autograph books and tour programmes being thrust at her. Some of the fans were hysterical. A young girl clung to her, sobbing, burying her tear-streaked face in her idol's new jacket.

Without taking his eyes off her, a handsome lad was snapping endless pictures on a battered Instamatic whilst staring at Carly intently. Dale let Carly know it was time to move. She detached herself from the crying girl and escaped into the building.

As they waited for the lift she inspected her jacket. 'I think I've got snot on my sleeve. First time I've worn this, as well.'

Dale frowned and handed her a crisp white hanky. She dabbed at the damp leather.

'I keep telling you not to be so touchy-feely,' he said. 'You don't know where they've been.'

'Harsh, Dale. They're just kids—'

'Bunking off school, most of them,' he grumbled.

'—hanging about in the cold for hours, hoping for a word.'

'You're way too trusting. They could pull a knife, anything.'

Dale was ex-military. Special Forces. Decorated for bravery. Secretly hoping someone would step out of line one day so he could show what he was made of.

'They're our *fans*, they'd never hurt us.' Carly gave him a dazzling smile. 'Anyway, that's why you're here.'

He shook his head. 'That weird one taking pictures . . . I wouldn't trust him as far as I could throw him – his eyes don't look right.'

She giggled. 'Don't be mean. He's the Mad Fan – goes everywhere we do, just likes to look at us and take his pics, bless him.'

'Yeah, well that's odd as well, the quiet ones are always the worst.'

On the fourth floor of Shine Records, Roxanne Lloyd was in the glass-fronted executive meeting room – the think-tank, as it was known. She examined her reflection in the glass. Mussed-up dark hair tumbling over her shoulders, leopard-print T-shirt. Killer heels she could hardly walk in. Debbie Harry meets Joan Jett.

She checked her Swatch watch.

A good five minutes had passed, no one had even bothered to ask if she'd like a drink, and there wasn't even so much as a bottle of water on the table. What she really wanted was a rum and ginger ale but she knew she shouldn't have one.

Annoyed, she paced up and down. Number one in the charts and not even a bloody cup of tea on offer, this was outrageous, she thought to herself. Glancing at the corridor window she saw one of the junior A & R girls in the open-plan office gawping at her. Roxanne made a face. The girl went pink and looked away. Roxanne sighed. Where were the others? She felt like throwing a proper pop star strop just for the fun of it – flinging open the door and demanding someone be sacked for not bothering to even check on her while she waited.

Tempting, but, no, she would wait until the others arrived and kick off in numbers, that would really cause a reaction.

Restless, she perched on the table in the centre of the room. Piled her hair into a messy bun, the way she'd worn it for the *Melody Maker* cover shoot. As she gazed around the room it struck her the think-tank looked different. Bare. She could have sworn a picture of the girls on the red carpet at the Brits once took up most of the back wall. Weren't there a couple of Thunder Girls gold discs on display as well last time she was there? And where was their Record of the Year award?

Carly stepped from the lift to see a familiar figure coming out of the loo. Anita Owen, in an off-the-shoulder dress and spiky heels, rummaging in her bag for something.

Carly bellowed at the top of her voice. 'Hey, you – what do you think you're doing?'

Anita shrieked and dropped her bag, sending her make-up, purse, perfume and keys onto the wooden floor, scattering in different directions.

Carly doubled up. 'You should see your face!'

'Silly cow! I nearly died!' Anita scrabbled about, picking up her belongings, as Carly hunkered down next to her, retrieving a lipstick poking out from under a vintage jukebox, still laughing.

Roxanne saw them interacting down the corridor – Carly, always dazzling, and Anita, always making the biggest scene. Impatient as ever, Roxanne yanked open the door of the think-tank to join in the laughing and bickering. 'Thank God! I'm about to die of boredom here. I was starting to think I'd got the wrong day.'

Carly hugged her. 'Where's Chrissie?'

'No sign of her yet,' Roxanne replied, plonking herself down on the edge of the table.

Anita placed her bag on the floor and rummaged around

till she found a coconut lip balm. She started smothering it on with her fingers whilst mumbling, 'That's weird, she's always here first, and I had her driver this morning. Gorgeous George.'

'So, who's driving Chrissie?' Carly said.

'Search me.'

Roxanne looked perplexed. 'George *always* drives Chrissie – she usually won't let anyone else have him – there must be a hot new driver on the team and she's nabbed him first.'

'Poor George! He must be gutted – he barely spoke to me,' Anita said, flopping into a seat and fishing a compact from her pocket. She checked her reflection and frowned, slipping on a pair of shades. 'Someone needs to have a word with Rick about dragging us in for these early meetings. How are you supposed to look your best at the crack of dawn?'

Carly laughed. 'It's midday!'

Anita peered at her over the top of the shades. 'Exactly, and this is the music biz. We don't operate on normal hours.'

Carly dug a magazine out of her bag. 'Anyway, we've made it onto the cover of *The Face*. We are officially cool.'

Roxanne rolled her eyes. 'Like we need that lot to tell us. None of those mags wanted anything to do with us when we started, now they can't get enough.'

Carly gazed at the bare back wall. 'What's happened to our picture?'

Roxanne shrugged.

Anita grabbed the magazine. 'Remember them doing that piece on manufactured bands being the death of the music industry? That snooty woman who said we had "zero credibility" and ripped us to shreds, saying we wouldn't last five minutes.'

Carly shrugged. 'She must have felt sick when the single went to number one in the midweek charts the same day her piece hit the stands. And now we are on their cover!'

They'd had a bumpy start but in the course of two crazy years the Thunder Girls had proved the critics wrong with a string of number one singles, triple-platinum albums, record-breaking tours and award-winning videos. Not to mention several impressive performances on live TV that proved the girls could actually sing. Silencing the critics once and for all. The icing on the cake was a Brit award.

Now, on the brink of the new decade, they were ready to go even bigger.

Anita studied the cover of *The Face*, her expression darkening. 'What have they done to my nose?' she asked. 'That's not my nose. Tell me that's not my nose.'

Without looking, Roxanne said, 'It's definitely been tweaked.'

'They've made it bloody smaller, the racists – why have they only altered *my* pic!' Anita was indignant. 'There's nothing wrong with my nose, is there?' she said, touching her nostrils.

Carly took the magazine from her. She really did look

stunning in that photo. 'No, it's lovely as it is! I don't know why they have done that but don't let it spoil the moment, it's still a great picture.'

'A great picture of *you*,' Anita said.

'Of *all* of us,' Carly told her.

Roxanne was now peering at the image. 'Apart from the fact they've put Chrissie at the front and made the rest of us look like backing singers.'

Carly snatched the magazine back and stuffed it into her bag. 'So, anyway . . . can't wait to see what Rick's got lined up for us next,' she said, changing the subject. 'Come on, Roxy, you must have some idea. He's *your* boyfriend.'

Roxanne held up her hands. 'I swear, he hasn't said a word.'

'Something amazing, I bet, knowing Rick,' Carly said. 'I reckon our darling manager is lining up a world tour. Stadiums. Course, we'll need to knock out a new album first but that's no big deal.'

Anita looked up and saw Jack Raven, head of Shine Records, coming their way, sporting his usual faded jeans and leather bomber over a David Bowie T-shirt. His PA, Susan Fox, in checked trousers and a sloppy jumper, trotted along beside him. Under one arm she carried an enormous diary. The sight of the two of them sent a ripple of excitement through the office.

'Stand by your beds,' Anita said.

Roxanne followed her gaze. 'Wow, we must be doing

even better than we thought if we're getting an audience with the actual big boss.'

'Must be something huge for him to show up.' Anita whipped out her compact again and touched up her lippy.

Jack strode into the room. 'Morning, girls.' He locked eyes with Carly, holding his gaze on her for a moment longer than the others before looking down to check his watch. '*Afternoon*. Sorry to keep you waiting. Things are cray-zee, as you can imagine.'

'We've been here ages,' Roxanne said. '*Hours*. And no one's been in to offer us a drink.' She aimed a pointed look at Susan.

Carly gestured at the bare wall. 'And what's happened to our picture from the Brits?'

'We're having a bit of a change around,' he replied. 'We've got something else coming in here.' He gave Susan a questioning look. 'Remind me.'

She consulted the diary. 'Kylie at Hyde Park Festival. With the crowd behind her. Everyone with their lighters in the air.'

Anita gasped. '*Kylie!*'

Carly interrupted. 'What about *our* picture – what have you done with it?'

Jack ignored her. 'Let's take a seat and get started.'

Carly opened her mouth, but Anita spoke first. 'Where's Rick? We're meant to be having a strategy meeting – the Thunder Girls in the Nineties. Whole new era. New festivals, concerts, Wembley Stadium!'

'Wembley . . .' Carly echoed dreamily.

'Chrissie's late but let's start and we'll fill her in when she finally gets here,' Roxanne said.

'I think you'll find she's not just late – she's a no-show,' Jack said with a strange smile that made him look even more odd than usual.

Carly glanced at the others. 'Okay, we'll do it without her and tell her what's happening later.'

The girls sat at the conference table, across from Jack and Susan. There was an awkward pause.

Jack said, 'Ah, this is difficult.' He waited a moment. 'Just wondering how best to put this so no one gets upset.'

The girls exchanged a look. 'How best to put *what*, exactly?' Roxanne asked. 'Put what? What's wrong with her – is she ill or something?'

'Ill? No, nothing like that. The thing is . . .' He sighed. 'There's been a slight change of plan in terms of . . . *strategy*. As you all know, Chrissie's a bit special.' The others bristled. 'She's always had that certain *something*. What my A & R guys call *charisma*. Stardust. An *aura*, if you like. Not that I need to tell you girls. You already know all about the magic of Chrissie. I mean, you've bathed in it.'

'We've *all* got charisma,' Roxanne told him, 'which is why we're the world's number one girl band.'

Jack ignored her. 'Suffice to say, it's highly unusual for someone of Chrissie's calibre to be in a band. We'd expect someone with that level of star quality to be an artist in their own right, not part of a line-up. Think Annie Lennox, Stevie Nicks . . .'

Anita's jaw dropped. 'Chrissie's not in their league.'

Jack pressed on. 'Which is why we've been looking at how we might re-brand . . . maximize potential.' A puzzled look passed between the girls. 'And, after a good deal of thought and one or two confidential planning meetings involving a handful of top people, we've worked out a way forward.'

Roxanne started to say something but he put up a hand to silence her.

'We're launching Chrissie as a solo artist.'

Anita stared at him. 'What? *What* did you just say?'

Roxanne had a sudden sense of dread. 'You're not making sense,' she said.

Jack gave her an icy smile. 'Really? I thought I'd been clear. Which bit of "solo artist" don't you understand?'

Carly shook her head and stared Jack dead in the eye. 'I don't believe it. She'd have told us if all this was going on – and she hasn't said a word.'

Jack looked at Carly sympathetically. 'That's because I asked her not to. Sorry.'

Roxanne thought back to the last time they had all been together. Two nights ago at her place. Drinking, eating pizza. Anita making some crazy speech about the Thunder Girls and world domination. Carly getting emotional, saying they were like sisters and she loved them to bits. Saying wouldn't it be awful being a solo artist, going it alone, not having your best friends with you? Chrissie had sat there and said nothing.

Roxanne turned on Jack. 'This is bullshit! We're a *band*. In it together. There's no way Chrissie would walk out and drop us without a word. Not at the top of our game. We *know* her. She wouldn't do it.'

'You might not know her as well as you think.' Jack made a face. 'Look, I can see it's awkward for you girls, a lot to take in, and I wish you'd had more time to process things. Roxy, I'd have thought *you*'d have had a heads-up from Rick – pillow talk, and all that.'

Carly and Anita stared at Roxanne, who was now a ghostly shade of white, as Jack continued. 'Anyway, we can't afford to twiddle our thumbs while you lick your wounds. It's about timing. We have to launch Chrissie now, while the band's at its peak. This is her moment.'

Carly stared at Jack, a dumbfounded look on her face.

Anita erupted. 'It's *our* moment, you prick!'

He spread his hands in a gesture of helplessness. 'Believe me, girls, if I could think of something to soften the blow, I would.'

Carly jumped up. 'Okay, here's what you can do. You can tell her she is *not* going solo. You can also remind her it's not all about her – she is *one-quarter* of a band, not bloody Belinda Carlisle, or whoever she thinks she is. Then you tell her to get her arse in here *now* and forget this selfish, self-obsessed idea about being the frigging star of the show and dropping the rest of us – her *mates* – in it.' She held his gaze, defiant. 'That would be a start.'

Jack shrugged. 'Sorry – no can do.'

Carly stared at him again. For a moment everyone was silent, then she spoke.

'Look, there's obviously been a mix-up,' she said, softly this time. 'We need to talk to Rick. He'll get this sorted.'

Jack looked away from her towards Susan and then back.

'I was coming to that,' he said. 'Rick has done an amazing job with you girls. I didn't think he had it in him. Before the Thunder Girls he'd never had a proper hit. Rick made it happen for you, and all credit to him.

'Anyway, as I'm sure you'll appreciate, Chrissie needs a steady hand. Someone who understands what you might call her *foibles*. She's an artist, she's sensitive, so we need the right person to guide her.' He looked at the girls, as if to make sure they were following. 'We can't just palm her off on anyone. In my opinion, Rick – your *old* manager – is the right man for the job. So he'll be taking the helm on this.'

Roxanne clutched her stomach, looking as if she was about to be sick. 'No, you're lying,' she almost whispered. 'He wouldn't do this to me, to us.'

Jack smiled. 'Scout's honour, I'm not – he would and he has.'

An awkward silence filled the room, before Anita broke the spell. She could hardly contain herself. 'He's *your* fella – how could you not know?'

Roxanne shook her head. 'I didn't know, I swear.'

'So what about us then?' Anita turned on Jack. 'How are we supposed to keep going as a three-piece when you've made Chrissie look like the lead?'

'You won't be a three-piece.'

'So you're bringing someone new in?'

'It's a bit more straightforward than that,' Jack told her. 'As of now, we're not moving forward with the Thunder Girls—'

Anita gasped. 'What are you talking about? We're the biggest girl band in the world.'

'So you keep saying,' Jack said with an eye-roll. 'It's the perfect time to stop. Quit while you're ahead then. There's nothing sadder than a band dragging things out to the bitter end.'

'We're nowhere near that point, Jack, and you know it!' Anita shouted as Roxanne looked out of the window to see the whole office looking in at them.

'It's too late,' Jack continued. 'It's been decided and if you check your contracts you'll see Shine owns the Thunder Girls – the name, the rights, the lot. Course, you're free to go solo . . . although we all know how that works out for the back-up.' He rubbed his hands. 'Right, there's a press release ready to go out, soon as I give the word: "Thunder Girls are *No*-Go!"' He looked pleased. 'I came up with that.'

Anita felt like punching him.

'Your cars are waiting to take you home. Susan will show you out through the loading bay, in case our friends in the press have somehow got wind of any of this. We don't want to be . . . *insensitive*.' He looked at Roxanne, who was in tears, her face streaked with mascara. 'You might want to clean yourself up before you go.'

Susan held the door open. In shock, they stumbled out.

Jack caught hold of Carly before she left the room.

'This is it,' he said, lowering his voice. 'This is our chance.'

She stared at him in disbelief. 'Our chance for *what*?'

'Now we can be together for real. A proper couple, a family. Put the past behind us, get married, the works.'

She gave him a searing look. 'You think I'd want anything to do with you after what you've just done?'

Now it was Jack that looked shocked as he hung on to her. 'But I did it all *for* you, Carly.'

She yanked her arm free. 'You did it for me? Yeah, right. If the band's over, so are we. I never want to see you again!'

Turning on her heel, she ran after the others.

1

Thirty years later

'Don't get me wrong, Tony, it was a wonderful honeymoon, but I'm glad to be home. Four months is a long time to be away, and Miami plays havoc with your hair.' Chrissie Martin stretched out in the back of the car and smoothed the front of her Stella McCartney dress, a flowing white number designed to show off her tan. Chunky gold bracelets slid down her slender wrist. She examined her nails, no longer convinced by the fancy artwork that little Korean girl had persuaded her to have. Lilac wasn't really her colour, even if it was supposed to be the current hot shade, and the design – whatever it was meant to be – looked cheap. Like something a trainee who hadn't quite got the hang of it would do.

She managed to catch her driver's eye in the rear-view mirror before he looked away.

'Have you ever been to Miami?' she asked.

Tony grunted.

'You really must go,' Chrissie continued. 'I can tell you all the best places. The hotel was amazing. Private plunge pool on the terrace, overlooking South Beach – which is gorgeous, by the way.' She decided not to say they had never actually ventured onto the beach. Too many lithe young girls in thong bikinis for her liking. She went on, 'Still, there's only so much over-the-top luxury a girl can take. You get to the point where you long for something ordinary.'

Tony glanced at her in the rear-view mirror and frowned. She gave him a sweet smile. Nothing about her life was ordinary.

'But the last few days, I've been dying to get back home, because . . .' She paused for dramatic effect and made a face. 'Total dis*aster* – I only ran out of tea!' His frown deepened. Braking, he indicated left and turned onto a narrow road leading to an exclusive estate. 'Can you imagine? My special miracle tea, the one I get shipped in from Nepal. Yak butter and some kind of secret stem-cell thingy.' She caught his look. 'Totally cutting-edge, which is why it costs the earth. Worth every penny though.'

Tony gave another grunt.

'You'd think you'd be able to get it in the States but that backward lot at the FDA are still arguing over the health benefits. Which, by the way, are proven – all the supermodels swear by it.'

In front of them was a sprawling walled property. The

gates opened and the car inched forward, tyres crunching over gravel.

Chrissie gazed at the house. It had an odd, shut-up look about it. On the plane, she had imagined arriving home and the front door flying open before the car had quite come to a stop. Scott running towards her. Scooping her up and carrying her over the threshold, the way he had when they were married a few months earlier, the pair of them laughing and kissing like teenagers.

Just thinking about it made her go gooey inside.

For several moments she sat in the car, waiting. Where was Scott? In the front seat, Tony cut the engine and undid his seatbelt. Chrissie noticed the Range Rover was missing and smiled, another image coming to mind: Scott in the Italian deli on the high street, picking up olives, smoked salmon and the artisan bread she liked. Well, she would have something special of her own waiting for him when he got back.

Tony got out and unloaded her luggage. Six pieces of matching Louis Vuitton and an old-fashioned trunk she had found in a vintage shop in Coconut Grove on her last day in Miami. A present for Scott. The excess baggage charges had been horrendous. Not that she cared. Some things she refused to do, and scrimping on luggage was one of them.

'Leave the bags, if you like,' she said. 'Scott can bring them in when he gets back.'

Tony gave her a peculiar look. 'Might be best if I do it.

Since I'm here and Scott's, well . . .' He left the words hanging in the air.

What on earth was wrong with him? He had given her the silent treatment all the way home. Jealous, probably. She watched him struggle with the bulky trunk. It had taken two porters to lift it at the hotel, she remembered. And they'd had a trolley.

'Careful with that,' she snapped, as he manoeuvred it up the steps. 'It's for Scott.'

He opened his mouth, about to say something, before changing his mind.

Chrissie winced as the precious trunk struck the edge of the stone balustrade. 'Watch out!' She bent to inspect the damage, rubbing at an imaginary mark, aiming a filthy look at her driver. 'I'd like it in one piece when I give it to him, if it's not too much trouble.'

He gazed back at her with what looked like pity. 'I'll put a bit of dubbin on if you like,' he offered. 'Soon have it right as rain.'

Chrissie waved him away. 'Just bring the rest of the stuff in. Before my husband gets back.'

Again, he seemed about to speak, before going to retrieve the other cases and stacking them neatly in the hall.

'Will you be able to get them upstairs?' he asked.

'I'll leave that to Scott,' she said.

Another pitying look.

'For goodness sake, Tony, cheer up. It might never happen.'

As she turned away, he muttered something she didn't catch. She let it go. It had been a long flight and she wasn't in the mood. Still, something in Tony's demeanour bothered her. The way he had looked at her, it was definitely odd.

She swept through the hallway and into the kitchen, where the blinds were still down. As she yanked them up light poured into the room. At least the place was tidy. Suspiciously tidy, considering it wasn't one of her cleaner's days. Chrissie was impressed. Scott was in the habit of leaving dirty dishes on every available surface but there wasn't a thing out of place. Even the ludicrously pricey espresso machine he insisted he couldn't live without sparkled. She guessed he had persuaded the cleaner to come in that morning and sort out his mess ahead of Chrissie's return.

So like him to be thoughtful.

The answering machine blinked at her. Forty-two messages. The perils of being popular. She would check them later. A pile of mail sat on the windowsill. She began to leaf through it. Some for her, some for Scott.

She put the kettle on and checked the special tea situation. Relief. She had a month's supply, at least. The phone started ringing. She ignored it. The machine cut in and a few seconds later she heard Rick Davies' voice. 'Chrissie . . . where are you? And why isn't your mobile on?' Wanting to know why she hadn't returned any of his calls. She didn't like his tone. Demanding. Accusing. Who did he think he was? 'Tony told me your flight times and I know you landed ages ago. I thought you'd be coming straight home . . . under the circumstances.' He sounded peeved.

Under what circumstances? Chrissie had never been the sort to get off a flight and jump straight into a waiting car, preferring to go to the first-class lounge first for a blow-dry and a green smoothie. Rick, of all people, should know that. 'Look, I need to speak to you. *Now.*' A pause. 'If you're there, just pick up, will you?'

Chrissie smiled and opened the fridge to check the contents. Almond milk, going off, a piece of pecorino that had seen better days. A solitary bottle of champagne and a decent bottle of rosé.

Just as well Scott was at the deli.

In the background, Rick was saying something about going through some figures. *Urgently*. She made a pot of tea, letting him drone on. Couldn't he at least give her time to settle in? He was still speaking when she poured a cup of the special rejuvenating stem-cell brew and went upstairs with it.

She undressed and put on a robe she had bought while she was away. Oyster-pink. Shawl collar. Glamorous. According to the shop assistant, an exact copy of the one worn by Marilyn Monroe in one of her films. *Some Like It Hot* or *Gentlemen Prefer Blondes*, or the one with the white dress and the air vent. The girl wasn't sure.

She sat in front of the mirror in her dressing room, the silk robe cool on her bare skin, and redid her make-up.

Dabbed a little Chanel No.5 behind her ears and on her wrists. Slipped on a pair of strappy heels.

Scott was taking his time.

Downstairs, the doorbell went. Typical – so like Scott to forget his key! She leapt up and took the stairs as fast as she dared in the towering heels, her gown gaping, and flung open the door, ready for her gorgeous husband to take her straight to bed.

Rick faced her.

She knotted the belt of the gown, folded her arms and gave him an icy look. 'What the hell are you doing here?'

'So you *are* home. I've just tried calling – why aren't you picking up?'

'What's so important it can't wait? I've been *away*, as you know. And yes, I had a nice time, thanks for asking. Now, if you don't mind, the flight was long and very tiring, and I'm jet-lagged.'

He brushed past her. 'This can't wait. Believe me, I haven't driven all the way out here without good reason.'

'It's not a good time. Scott's on his way.'

Rick ignored her. 'How come you've not returned any of my calls? I've left about a hundred messages. Including one a few minutes ago.'

'Make it quick. And you'd better hope Scott doesn't get back and find you here. He'll hit the roof.'

Rick gave her a funny look. He sat at the kitchen table and began pulling papers from a file, putting them in order, catching Chrissie's look of disdain. 'I know how much you hate anything to do with money so I'll come straight to the point.' He picked up a bank statement. 'Current account – empty.' He tapped another document. 'Investment account – nothing there. Same with the high-interest one you opened just before you and Scott got hitched.' He gazed at the papers in front of him, selected one, and waved it at her. 'This is the one allocated for tax liabilities – the one you're not supposed to touch under any circumstances. Zero.'

Chrissie did her best to grasp what he was saying. Her stomach felt peculiar. When she spoke her voice sounded strained. 'What exactly are you saying?'

Rick held her gaze. 'I've been through everything with the accountants. I'm sorry, but it's better to be straight with you. All the money you had – which, as you know, was a lot – has gone.'

She steadied herself against the worktop. Her head was spinning. Someone had hacked her bank accounts and stolen her money? You heard about those things all the time. Identity theft. People losing their life savings. *Oh. My. God.* 'What's the bank doing? You've reported it? Told the fraud squad? They can track money these days, see where it's gone, can't they?'

'In some cases I guess so, but on this occasion there's been no fraud,' Rick said.

'Don't be thick! My money's gone! You just said so!' She studied his expression. 'One of those burner rooms—'

'Boiler rooms.'

'Or the accountant's helped himself. You hear about that going on all the time.'

Rick was silent for a moment. 'When did Scott come back?'

She was thinking about the accountant, a tubby little man with a fondness for bow ties and waistcoats. She had never liked him.

Rick asked again when Scott had returned home.

'Something came up – that's why he had to catch an earlier flight.' She remembered him complaining, saying it was a pain in the backside but he was going to have to leave early. It was the only time a particular investor would be in London. He had insisted she stay on and book as many spa treatments as she liked – it was all on him. The entire honeymoon was his treat, he'd said. She hadn't had to pay for a thing. 'He came back last week,' she said, distracted. 'Some business deal.'

Rick muttered something. 'And where is he now?'

'At the deli. Getting some bits and pieces.'

Rick shook his head. 'You've seen him – since you got back?'

'Not exactly.'

He was perplexed. 'Either you have or you haven't.'

'The Range Rover was gone when Tony dropped me off so I just assumed, you know, he'd nipped out to get a few things.' She waved in the direction of the fridge. 'There's nothing in.' She flung the door open, as if to demonstrate the sense of what she was saying. They were both silent.

Chrissie grabbed the bottle of rosé and sloshed some into a glass, gulping it down. 'Maybe he's just moved things to different accounts for better interest rates.'

'Oh, I think we can safely say he's done that, to better his interests . . .' Rick was sounding tetchy. 'Don't you get it yet? He's stolen your money!'

'Don't be ridiculous!' she snorted. 'We've just had the most amazing honeymoon – which *he* paid for.' She held his gaze. 'I don't expect you to understand. After all, we didn't have a honeymoon when *we* got hitched – you said we were too busy!'

Rick jabbed a finger at her. 'I'll tell you who paid for the honeymoon – *you* did! I've been trying to get hold of you for weeks but not once did you answer your phone. No tweets, nothing on Instagram, which you are normally never bloody off. Silence. It's like he's had you locked away.'

It had been Scott's idea to stay off social media while they were away (which wasn't easy for Chrissie, an online addict, who posted on every platform several times a day), but when he said he wanted her all to himself just this once, she gave in. Sod Instagram! He had actually taken her phone off her and, to her surprise, she *loved* how bossy he was being. It was a real turn-on. The fact he loved her so much he couldn't bear to share her did wonders for her ego. She told Rick they'd been too busy on honeymoon, if he got her drift, to bother with social media.

'The whole time you were away he's been taking your money,' Rick told her. 'The whole frigging lot.'

An idea came to her. 'Let me call him.' Scott never went anywhere without his phone, which was never switched off. She picked up the landline. 'There'll be an explanation. You'll see.' She held the phone to her ear – then disconnected and dialled again and got the same message. *The number you have dialled is no longer available*. Her face drained of colour as she dropped the phone.

Rick got to his feet. 'What is it?'

She turned away as he picked up the handset. The message was still repeating itself. Rick cut the call. 'I've been trying to tell you, he's gone. Ripped you off and done a runner.'

No. She could not believe it. She poured more wine. Her hands were shaking.

'There's been a mistake,' she insisted. 'We've only just got married. We've just spent four idyllic months together on honeymoon. I *know* him. He *loves* me. We're *soulmates*.'

Rick sighed. 'From what we've been able to piece together the money transfers happened while you were in the States. The whole thing took four months, start to finish – while you were having your *idyllic* time.'

Chrissie shook her head. 'No. It's not possible. We were together twenty-four-seven.' She thought back, picturing the two of them on the terrace, taking cooling dips together in the plunge pool. Then another set of images flashed through her mind. The times she had walked in on Scott doing something on the laptop, and the abrupt way he had shut it down the moment he saw her. Scott, nipping out of restaurants to make what he said were important calls.

She fiddled with her engagement ring, a showy square-cut diamond.

Rick nodded at it. 'You paid for that as well. I've seen the bill.'

She felt sick.

'Did I not advise you *not* to put everything in joint names?' Rick scolded.

She gave him a furious look. 'Don't you dare say another word. Bet you couldn't wait to leg it round here and dump all this on me. Point the finger at my husband. There's *no proof* he's done anything wrong yet.'

Rick stared at her in disbelief. 'Are you actually listening? Scott has transferred all the funds from your existing accounts into new ones. And you're right. Strictly speaking, he hasn't done anything wrong because everything was in joint names, so the money was his as much as yours.'

Chrissie was silent, taking this in. Is that why Tony had been looking at her strangely? Did everyone but her know?

After what felt like an age, she said, 'What's left?'

'Just this house, but you won't be able to stay here because he's taken out a massive mortgage on it, so you'll have to sell it, buy something smaller, and that will free up a small amount of cash but not much . . .'

Chrissie couldn't believe it. She shut down again, in another wave of denial.

'No, no, *no*! I am *never* leaving this house.' He went to

put an arm round her and she shrugged him off. 'I'd like you to go now, please. Give me time to think things through.'

'You've had one hell of a shock. I don't think you should be on your own.'

'Don't tell me what to do!' She gave him a murderous look. 'And don't act like you care, when you're loving this.'

'I promise you, I'm not.'

She turned her back. 'Close the door on your way out.'

'Chrissie . . .'

She kept her back to him. 'I'm not really thinking straight after the flight, so if you don't mind.' A single tear ran down her cheek. *Shit*. She would not fall apart in front of Rick, her gloating, pitying, told-you-so, ex-husband.

Eventually, he gathered up his stuff and left.

Chrissie waited a moment before grabbing the wine bottle and storming into the hall. On the side table was the photo taken a few months before, on her wedding day. Scott, gazing at her as if he couldn't believe his luck. She swung the bottle and smashed it against the frame, sending it flying. Splinters of glass went everywhere.

Breathing hard, she ground her high heel into Scott's grinning face.

2

Roxanne was in the cramped waiting room at the tiny Speedy Motors garage waiting to collect the Porsche after its service. She loved the car, an elderly white 911 convertible, but it was a drain on funds. Jim, who had been her mechanic for as long as she could remember, and had helped her find it in the Nineties, now advised her to get shot, as he put it.

It was costing too much to keep it on the road, and the rattle coming from the big end was a worry. Roxanne hated the idea of parting with her dream car but Jim was adamant and wanted her to look at a used Mini Cooper he had just taken in part-exchange. Good little runner, he said. Practical. Nowhere near as expensive to maintain as the Porsche.

She sighed and picked up a copy of *Hello!* magazine from the pile in the waiting room, Meghan Markle on the cover, looking stunning and giving Kate Middleton a run for her money, next to *This Morning* presenters Ruth and Eamonn, posing for wedding anniversary pictures.

She spotted an old *OK!* from a few months back, and at once a wave of annoyance went through her. Chrissie Martin's wedding, to a man half her age, plastered all over the front cover. *This time I know it's for real*, ran the headline. *How the gorgeous pop diva found true love at last*. Roxanne turned it face down. As if that fake bitch would know the first thing about being real – or true love, for that matter! Roxanne felt like getting on the phone and telling bloody *OK!* what Chrissie was really like . . . a scheming, hatchet-faced, self-obsessed, man-stealing bitch! Her heart was thumping. One of these days that surgically enhanced old witch would get what she deserved, Roxanne told herself.

Jim appeared. 'So what do you think?' he asked. 'How about a test drive in the Mini?'

Roxanne hesitated. She could not bring herself to part with the Porsche, a car she had fallen in love with the moment she saw it. Low mileage, one careful owner. Getting on a bit, the salesman had said, but still a head-turner. That had made her laugh.

You and me both, she reckoned.

She gave Jim a smile. 'I'll think about it,' she said.

Carly Hughes wasn't really listening to what the woman was saying. Something about deciding on a single-colour palette and sticking with it. Grey was popular, the woman said. Not that anyone called it grey anymore. It was Dove. Shadow.

Slate. Rock Salt. And not nearly as stark as you might think. Depending on the shade, the effect could be warm and comforting, or modern and clinical. She had just done a house top to toe in Cloudy Haze, she told Carly, which, for a shade on the grey spectrum, was positively uplifting. That was the thing with colour – it was all about how you used it. The woman smiled, showing teeth that were too white and slightly too big for her mouth. Carly forced herself to pay attention. She could not imagine a grey house being uplifting in any shape or form. Grey made her think of girders and concrete. Construction sites.

So far, her meeting with Kitty Bright had proved depressing. Carly had not even wanted to meet the woman, it was Dave who insisted they needed to cheer the place up, as he put it, insisting there was no one better than Kitty. He had promised to be there but when it came to it had disappeared into his snooker room with instructions not to be disturbed. Carly was livid.

According to Kitty Bright's website, her clients were almost exclusively famous. Footballers, celebrities, minor royals, *Love Island* contestants, soap stars. In other words, the kind of people who could be hoodwinked into thinking grey was somehow *the* colour to have, Carly decided.

It had been tricky getting an appointment with Kitty. The rising star in the world of interior decor was in demand. Once she realized who her potential new clients were, however – the former world snooker champion and his ex-pop star wife – she managed to squeeze them in at short notice.

Kitty was rake thin with porcelain skin. Tawny, shoulder-length hair, and one of those uneven fringes that looked as if she had cut it herself with blunt scissors. Wide-legged trousers, baggy blazer. Sharp elbows. Confident to the point of being overpowering.

'Let me show you this.' Kitty swiped the screen of her iPad and inched closer to Carly.

'Here's an example of how you can change the entire character of a place.' She flashed a terrible smile.

The screen displayed a cavernous space. Sterile. Hard surfaces. No carpet or curtains. Bare walls. Not a single knick-knack. A sofa that brought to mind the kind of hard benches in railway stations. A room that would never feel snug, Carly suspected.

'You should have seen it before we got our hands on it,' Kitty said. '*OMG*. *Full* of clutter. Swags and tails. Chandeliers. Bookshelves.' She shuddered. 'Simple, clean lines, that's the way to go. The guy we did it for – a footballer, between you and me – *loves* it.'

Carly looked around her own sitting room with its cushions and curtains and rugs, and elaborate light fittings and matching gilt-framed mirrors. Photos and candles and odds and ends occupying every inch of the mantelpiece. The chaise-longue with its fancy gold legs. All of it, the kind of stuff Kitty Bright was on a mission to consign to the tip. The idea of letting her loose on her precious home filled Carly with horror.

'Can I think about it?' she asked. 'Get back to you once I've run it all past my husband?'

Kitty flashed her another dazzling smile. Those teeth. 'Of course. Just don't take too long. I'm almost all booked up for the rest of the year.'

The rest of the year. Carly smiled, relieved.

She watched Kitty clamber into a chunky SUV that looked too big for her and reverse, just missing the stag sculpture – that would go too, if Kitty Bright had her way – before driving off.

Carly went looking for Dave, still closeted in the snooker room, supposedly practising for his series of exhibition matches. She listened at the door for the sound of balls being struck, cannoning into pockets, but all she could hear was a strange voice yelling, 'Holy smoke!'

She went in and found Dave slumped in a chair, glued to his favourite fishing show. On the screen a bulky man in a windcheater and baseball cap was reeling in a monster fish.

Dave had already started on the whisky, Carly saw.

'I thought you were practising,' she said.

'Give me a break.' He chuckled. 'See what I did there? Give me a *break*. The old ones are the best.'

She watched him drain his glass. His T-shirt was on inside out again. He hadn't bothered with a shave or put a brush through his hair, by the look of things. Probably hadn't had a wash. The roomy felt stuffy. She swallowed her frustration. 'How did you get on this morning?' she asked.

He took his time answering. 'The thing about snooker,

you have to play it day in, day out, to be any good. Spend hours, days, *weeks*, of your life hunkered over the green baize perfecting your shots. Preparing for every eventuality. It takes discipline, routine. Sheer slog.'

'I know. That's why you need to keep at it.' She glanced at the table where the reds were in their triangle, the colours on their spots. Cues lined up in the rack on the wall. Nothing to suggest anything had been touched. 'Just do a couple of hours. Pot the colours – that trick you do with the black. Something.'

He threw her a look of contempt. 'What would you know about it?' His voice was thick. She wondered how much he'd had to drink. It was only just midday. 'What is it you do again?' he asked. 'Ah, that's right . . . nothing.'

'I run this place, don't I? Shop, cook, clean. All the boring domestic stuff you can't be arsed with, so you can focus on your snooker.' Dave yawned. Had another slug of scotch. She wanted to shake him. 'I've just met with that awful decorator woman because *you* fancy a makeover. Wasted an hour of my life listening to her talk crap about grey being the hot new colour. Grey! God help us if she gets her hands on this place.'

'I thought it would give you something to do. A little project. Stop you getting bored.'

Carly stared at him. How had it come to this? When they had first met, Dave was smart and sharp, at the top of his game. Quirky sense of humour, a gift for mimicking people.

The way he carried on cracked her up, which was just what she had needed back then.

The Thunder Girls had broken up and she was still putting herself back together. To have had everything snatched away without warning, and hurtle from world-famous pop star to nobody in the blink of an eye, had sent her over the edge for a while.

She had hidden away in her flat and stopped taking care of herself. Got by on whatever she had in. Coco Pops. Crackers. Cheese slices. Pickled beetroot eaten straight from the jar. It didn't matter since she was hardly eating anyway. For almost two weeks she stayed indoors, shuffling about in her dressing gown. Not taking calls, not answering the door. Crying herself to sleep.

She was in mourning.

For the passing of the band.

And something else.

Jack had tried to get through to her but she wouldn't see him. It was his fault, all of it. She didn't want him anywhere near her. And the fact he couldn't understand that? Delusional.

Her mother had got her well again. Stephanie Hughes had hammered on the door until the neighbours came out onto the landing to see what the fuss was about. Kept her finger on the doorbell until Carly had to let her in. Once inside, she went from room to room, opening blinds and windows and straightening things up, while Carly sat on the floor, hugging her knees to her chest.

Stephanie changed the bed, ran a bath and put her daughter in it. Washed her hair, put her in a pair of fresh pyjamas, then nipped to the corner shop and got some essentials in.

Slowly, Carly got well again.

Then Dave came along with his cheery, seize-the-day attitude, and proved to be just the tonic she needed.

She gazed at him now, slouched in the chair, as if he might slide all the way onto the floor. One-time golden boy of snooker, Dave 'The Destroyer' Dixon, a victim of his own success. He had done too well – made so much money he didn't need to keep playing – and it made him lazy. Once he retired, his days had no structure or purpose. Picking up a cue to keep his hand in was too much effort. He had not played properly for years and now was about to make a comeback playing for a prize pot of millions.

The way he was going, it would be a complete disaster.

'How about some lunch?' Carly suggested.

He held up his glass. 'I'm okay with this, thanks.'

'I've made soup and there's some nice crusty bread, strong cheddar.'

He looked her up and down. 'Bread and cheese. That explains it.' She gazed at him, perplexed. 'Carbs and fat. I mean, *I* don't mind a fuller figure. Plus-size, or whatever they call it.'

Her mouth flew open. '*Plus*-size? I'm a size bloody *12*.'

'Babe, don't get me wrong. I think you look great with a bit more meat on the bone. It's normal to pile on a few pounds once you hit the forties. And big bums are all the rage now, aren't they?'

She stared at him. 'Why do you always do this?'

He tipped the rest of the whisky down his throat. 'Do what?'

'Be so nasty to me.' She felt tears well up. 'You never used to.'

'I've always had a mouth on me. You knew that.' He made a face. 'Any case, you were tiny when we got together.'

'That was nearly thirty years ago! And I'd been ill.'

'Okay, keep your hair on. I'm only joking.'

She wanted to tell him where to go. Run upstairs, pack a bag and leave. Only trouble was, she wasn't sure what she would do then, or where she would run to. At one time, it would have been home to Mum, but she had passed away years before.

Dave sighed. 'Sorry, babe. I'm probably a bit stressed about the match, that's all. If I'm taking it out on you I don't mean to.' He gave her another appraising look. 'You look hot. Same as always.'

It was what he always did. Had a go, then pretended he didn't mean it. She was fuming.

If only the sponsors could see him in his tatty old things, doing anything but pick up a cue. She glanced at the whisky bottle. It was probably only half the story. 'Pull out,' she told him. 'Tell them you've changed your mind.'

He laughed. 'Not that simple. I've done the deal. Now I've got to do the deed.'

'Say you're ill.' Looking at him, it wasn't much of a stretch.

He sank lower in the chair. 'I'll be fine. I'm The Destroyer.'

Anita Owen took off her flip-flops and walked along the beach, keeping close to the shoreline. The sand was damp and warm, the sea cool, the sun not quite up. In the distance figures moved about in the half-light on the jetty, fishermen getting ready to take their boats out.

This was the time of day she liked best, when the place was quiet, before most people had woken up.

Most days she was up and out before sunrise. On the beach, relishing the peace. Watching crabs scurry in and out of the sea, writing her name in the sand. It was her thinking time. How she had become such an early bird when she practically had to be dragged out of bed in her younger days, never ceased to amaze her.

Her old life seemed a million miles away.

She stood for a moment, gazing out at the horizon, casting her mind back to the days of the Thunder Girls when the schedule was so frantic there seemed barely time to breathe. Every minute taken up with meetings, signings, sessions with stylists, recordings, promo tours, rehearsals. TV and radio . . . endless interviews. When the diary came through each week, Anita scanned it for early starts. They were *all* early. She loathed the hair and make-up calls for breakfast TV, the video shoots when the car came at some ridiculous hour, four in the morning, usually. She was never ready.

Her driver had a key so he could let himself in and get her up. Poor Trevor, having to put up with all that. He was an angel, she remembered, getting coffee down her and tucking her into the back of the car, still in her pyjamas. Handling her like precious cargo, while she huddled under a hoody, complaining, wanting to know why they couldn't just shoot videos at a civilized hour. Was there a law against it or something? Trevor catching her eye in the rear-view mirror, nodding, sympathetic.

God, she had been such a little cow!

Carly never seemed to mind the early starts. She was the youngest, full of life, bouncing around like a puppy. Except at the very end, when something knocked the stuffing out of her. Anita frowned. The band had fallen apart before she had had a chance to find out what.

As for Chrissie, always bitching about something – usually to do with wanting more time in the make-up chair, or a different outfit – she also took the punishing schedule in her stride. Whatever it took to get to the top and stay there was fine by her. As if she knew the band was nothing more than a springboard, a means to an end – the ride that would take her all the way to being a star in her own right.

Roxanne, though, was no early riser, constantly moaning about the early starts and taking it out on Rick. Saying she needed her sleep and how were they supposed to look anything other than shit on no shut-eye? Not that they ever did, thanks to Liz, their miracle-worker make-up artist.

Rick used to go mad, saying they had no idea how lucky

they were, and to be grateful for every moment – early starts included – because one day it would all be over.

He was right about that.

The sun sparkled on the water. Anita slipped off her cover-up and waded in, feeling the shock of the cold, forcing herself to keep going as a wave broke and drenched her, making her shiver.

She swam parallel with the shoreline. After a few strokes, she stopped feeling cold and dunked her head under the clear water, seeing a flash of something bright as a fish darted away. When she surfaced again, gulping in air, the sun was up and the first of the night boats was in, landing its catch. A dog wagged its tail, going hopefully from one person to the next, while by the jetty a small wooden boat started up its engine and chugged out to sea.

Anita kept swimming, using the palm trees on the beach to mark out lengths. One or two tourists had appeared. A man who came to the village from Ohio every year and liked to paint was setting up an easel. She returned to the shore and dried off in the sun.

Coming to Brazil had been a good move. When she first arrived she was as good as on the run, the press hounding her after what had happened. She had needed a bolt-hole, somewhere she could get her head straight. Where no one knew who she was.

It wasn't as if she intended to ditch her old life and disappear for good. Not for a moment had she dreamed she would put down roots so far from home.

Not until she fell in love, anyway.

The tiny fishing village of Sao Miguel was home now.

No going back.

It still hurt to think about the night everything fell apart. The timing was wrong, her head in a bad place. Too much partying. Way too much coke. She was paranoid, volatile, all over the place. What she had really needed at that point was a stint in rehab, not *Eurovision* – the biggest show of her life! – yet Rick seemed to think she would walk it. Maybe she could also make it as a solo artist after all, follow in Chrissie's footsteps after the band's break-up. All Anita had to do was learn one song, do one big show, and that was it. For someone as experienced as she was, how hard could it be?

No pressure.

The way he put it made it sound easy, and the coke she was shovelling up her nose made her think she could take on the world. After all, she was a Thunder Girl – twelve top-ten singles, eight consecutive number ones. A show known for its joke performers and novelty acts and terrible styling was no match for her. Losers, all of them!

And yet, somewhere in the back of her mind, a nagging doubt had gnawed away. A small, annoying voice warning her she was making a terrible mistake. The world would be watching, the voice said. She should have listened. Told Rick it wasn't for her. Owned up about how much coke she was doing – admitted she was terrified of performing live in front of an audience of millions and messing up.

She should have, but she didn't.

She left the beach and cut through a dusty street, waving to an old woman busy sweeping sand off the porch of a lop-sided house. The Sea View Bar was one street back from the ocean. Strictly speaking, the name was misleading, but Anita had insisted on it because it brought back memories of the B & B she had stayed at in Blackpool on family holidays as a child. That didn't have a view of the sea either.

She went up the steps at the front and onto a wooden veranda. The scent of baking was in the air, sunlight spilling onto tables and chairs painted a mishmash of bright colours.

'Maria – I'm back,' she called.

The beaded curtain at the side of the bar parted and a woman in a vest top and denim cut-offs appeared. Barefoot, dark hair twisted into a braid that fell almost to her waist.

'The beach was amazing,' Anita said. 'No one about when I went down, just a couple of guys on the jetty getting the boats ready. Perfect.'

'Of course no one was there.' Maria spoke with an accent. 'You swim in the dark, like some kind of mad woman. Stealing away in the dead of the night. You know you are the talk of the village. They call you Crazy Ingles-ee.' She put her head on one side, perplexed.

Anita laughed. 'I've been called worse than that, believe me.'

'I ask myself, what could be so attractive that you would swap your warm bed for the chilly ocean every morning.'

Maria went behind the bar and began grinding coffee beans, making strong espresso, frothing up milk.

When Anita had first arrived in Brazil and headed north up the coast from Rio, not knowing where she was going, booking into the first ramshackle inn she liked the look of, she was in a bad way. Falling apart from the inside out was how she felt. She spent her time sleeping and swimming, doing her best to blot out bleak thoughts of her TV debacle. Trying not to think about the press laying into her, the awful headlines. Swimming made her strong. Gradually the horrible spectre of it all began to fade and she began to heal.

'Remember how we met?' she said.

Maria brought the coffee over and they sat at a table bathed in sunlight. 'I will never forget.'

Anita had been for an early swim and headed for the beach bar, a shack on stilts that was popular with fishermen. Inside, a bunch of them occupied a corner, drinking beer, smoking, having some bad-tempered discussion that sounded as if it could become a brawl. The smell of cannabis hung in the air.

Maria had stepped out from behind the bar. Lean, golden limbs. Attitude. Piercing green eyes. She steered Anita to a shady table on the balcony, away from the noise, and brought her a slice of juicy papaya.

'You were in one of those little ra-ra skirts.' Anita sipped her coffee. 'Hair scraped back. Bangles up to your elbows. Those guys. Every time you went anywhere near the volume dropped.'

'And you . . . like an exotic sea creature with your hair wet, a sprinkle of sand and salt on your skin.' She frowned, thinking back. 'And those shells you used to wear.'

The shells that littered the beach had fascinated Anita when she first arrived in Sao Miguel. She had gathered them, along with bits of driftwood, and fashioned them into pieces of rustic jewellery. 'I made all that stuff myself,' she said, proud of her efforts.

Maria raised an eyebrow.

'You said you liked them!'

'I liked *you*. The shell business I never understood.'

She reached up and stroked Maria's cheek. 'I gave you a shell bracelet. As a token of my love.'

'And I kept it. I still have it in the box where I keep my most precious things.' She planted a kiss on her hand. 'Just don't ask me to wear it.'

Anita finally felt her life was on track. She was happy. The only times she felt anxious were when the past came back to haunt her as she slept, waking her with a start, sending her from the bed she shared with Maria to the beach, where the sea seemed to wash away her worries.

She had grown to love her new life – and one of the best things about it was that no one from her old life knew where she was.

3

Chrissie was at home. Waiting for a call. She checked her phone for messages. It was a whole day since she had been in touch with Chloe about getting in for a facial, saying she had to see her *urgently*, and she still hadn't heard back. She rang the therapist's mobile and left another message, not quite as friendly as the first one, then she rang the salon.

The call was picked up by a girl with a sing-song voice asking how she could help.

'It's Chrissie Martin,' she said. 'I'd like to speak to Chloe.'

'She's in the middle of a treatment at the moment. Can I take a message?'

'I've already left one. Two, actually.'

'I can ask her to get back to you.'

'That's okay, I don't mind holding.' She tried to keep the irritation out of her voice. Actually, she did mind. Very much. She was Chloe Booth's best client, after all.

Over the years, Chrissie had spent thousands getting her

face done, not to mention plugging the salon in interviews, giving Chloe rave reviews. It was thanks to her that Skin Guru was doing so well. The place was buzzing. You couldn't move for pop stars and actresses, the reality TV crowd. Chloe even had a duchess on her books now and a waiting list for appointments. It was practically impossible to get in if you were a mere commoner. Not that it affected Chrissie, since Chloe was always happy to bump someone aside – the duchess included – to fit in her star client.

On the other end of the line, the girl was saying something about Chloe being with an important client. 'I'll take your number,' she offered. 'What name was it again?'

Chrissie could not believe what she was hearing. What *name* was it? Who the hell did the jumped-up little bitch think she was talking to?

'Do you like your job?' she asked.

'I love it,' the girl chirped. 'We get some amazing people in.'

'And have you given any thought to what you might do next?'

'Oh, no, I'm really happy working for Chloe. She's *so* lovely. And she's training me, showing me the ropes, so I won't be going anywhere for at least two years.'

'I wouldn't bet on it,' Chrissie snapped. 'Once I speak to her you'll be out the door before you can say anti-ageing.'

She cut the call and sent Chloe a text. *Call me. Urgent.* No niceties, no kisses. What was the woman thinking, employing some brainless bimbo with zero social skills on reception?

Chloe was one of the first people Chrissie had gone to see after getting back from Miami, when it was only just sinking in that Scott really had done a bunk and cleaned her out. Wanting sympathy, she had confided in Chloe, told her she was up to her neck in it. Chloe, always a good listener, made all the right noises, and by the time Chrissie swept out of the salon, plumped-up and dewy and loaded down with expensive products – promising to settle up once things got back to normal – she was feeling a lot better. Thank goodness for loyal friends like Chloe.

Chrissie gazed at the phone, willing it to ring. If Chloe knew what was good for her she would be in touch ASAP with a grovelling apology. She gave the screen an impatient tap. Oh God, the state of her nails. Those cuticles! She peered at them. The girl who'd talked her into having those awful gels in Miami deserved to be shot. Chrissie's rage towards Chloe's receptionist spread in the direction of the Dolce Vita nail bar thousands of miles away in Florida. She had a good mind to get onto them and let rip. A rant would make her feel better – a warm-up for when she gave Chloe what-for. Then again, she didn't much feel like making an international call when money was tight and there was no guarantee the person at the other end would give a damn.

The phone remained silent.

She continued examining her nails. Shocking. She was

desperate for her personal manicurist, Bobbi, to do a rescue job. When it came to nails, Bobbi was an artist, the best in the business. Rumour had it half the guests at Harry and Meghan's wedding had gone to her. Chrissie couldn't wait to tell her all about that shitty little girl Chloe had working for her. Get her to spread the word, make sure no one else took her on.

She frowned. Funny. She had left messages for Bobbi too and she hadn't got back to her either. And she was still waiting to hear from Jordan, her personal trainer. Why was no one available? Was it London Fashion Week, or something? No. That wasn't for months.

Her phone beeped with a text from a number she didn't recognize. Chloe must have changed her phone and not got round to telling her. The message began: *Hi! You're now on the Skin Guru waiting list. We will be in touch when an appointment becomes available*. Chrissie blinked and read it again.

It had to be a mistake.

She was about to send a terse reply straight back telling them where to stick their waiting list when a horrible thought occurred. Chloe knew Chrissie was broke, that she would need everything on tick until she got back on her feet. With shaking hands she tried calling the salon again. The message service picked up. She sent another text to Chloe's mobile, a nice one, with kisses.

Silence.

Gradually, it came to her – Chloe had cut her dead. She

must have done. Because Scott had cleaned her out. Chrissie felt sick. They had known each other *years*. They were *friends*! Chrissie had given her (pricey) Swarovski crystal earrings for her birthday. A Kate Spade make-up bag for Christmas.

With her stomach in knots, she tried calling Bobbi again. Left a cheery message, trying not to sound as desperate as she was beginning to feel. Nothing came back. Panicking, she called Vince, who looked after her hair. Vince always answered his phone, no matter what. Voicemail.

The awful truth began to dawn. Chloe was friendly with Bobbi, who did the odd magazine shoot with Vince . . . who had put Chrissie in touch with her personal trainer. They all knew each other and clearly word had got round. Now that she was on her uppers, the very people she thought of as her closest friends were blanking her. She put her head in her hands. People she had nurtured and promoted . . . spent thousands on. Blocking her calls! Just when she needed them more than ever.

Chrissie Martin – social outcast.

Her expression darkened. Scott had done this to her and one way or another he was going to pay.

Arthur Sullivan accepted Chrissie's offer of a coffee. He squeezed his portly frame onto a seat at the breakfast bar while she hunted around for a jar of instant and one of the Portmeirion mugs she had never liked.

'I need absolute discretion,' she told him.

'Understood.' He produced a sheaf of papers and pushed them towards her. 'Here's a bit of background for you. I was twenty-five years in the police force, did a stint in SO14, the unit that looks after the Royals, and I've had my own private detective agency for almost ten years. Covered everything from cheating partners to fraud.' A film of sweat had formed on his brow. He dabbed at it with a handkerchief. 'It's all in the folder.'

Chrissie gave the coffee a stir. 'How are you with tracing missing persons?' she asked.

He nodded. 'It's relatively straightforward these days. We've got access to various databases. Disappearing under the radar for any length of time isn't easy.'

'It's my husband,' she said. 'Scott Monroe.'

'What can you tell me about him? Where does he work, for instance? What kind of person is he?'

She hesitated, not sure how best to describe Scott. Low-life. Scumbag. Rip-off merchant. In the past, she would have said he was a model but his last campaign, for some cheap catalogue, was too embarrassing to mention. 'He doesn't have a job as such – he does different things.' Sponges off his wife, mainly, she thought. She held up her phone. 'That's him.'

Arthur peered at the picture. 'What sort of age is he?'

Chrissie gritted her teeth. 'Twenty-seven.' He wrote it down without comment. 'You think you could find him?' she asked.

'Oh, I can find him. I'll just need a few more details. Date of birth. Relatives. Any bank accounts you know about. That kind of thing.'

She liked his confidence but had one more private investigator to see. 'Okay,' she said. 'I'll be in touch.'

When Andy Flint arrived, Chrissie got out her favourite mugs. Andy had short dark hair and bright blue eyes. A winning smile. While Arthur had been in a suit, all very formal, Andy wore jeans and a T-shirt; a Belstaff jacket and proper cowboy boots. Chrissie was a sucker for all things cowboy after recording an album in Nashville and having a wild fling with a married country star. She was also married at the time, she remembered. To Rick.

She made espresso and steamed the milk. Broke open some fancy Italian biscuits.

Unlike Arthur Sullivan, Andy didn't have a CV complete with sample case files to show her. Instead, he produced an iPad and guided her to a stylish website with a bio pic that made him look like James Dean. Not that she said so. Andy Flint might not have known who she was talking about.

He pulled his chair up close to hers to run through a few highlights. Chrissie, suddenly experiencing the same kind of tingly feeling inside she used to get with Scott, took in only a fraction of what he said.

When she told Andy Flint about Scott leaving, he put a sympathetic hand on her arm, and it was as if electricity went through her.

'You sure he left and wasn't kidnapped?' he asked, not

taking his eyes off her. 'Because he would have to be out of his tiny mind to walk out on a gorgeous woman like you.'

Her stomach flipped over. She blinked at him, glad she had bothered with false eyelashes. 'Can you find him?'

He placed a hand on his heart. 'Hundred per cent. No need for you to worry your pretty head. Just leave everything to me.'

That was good enough for her. God, those eyes!

She didn't ask about previous experience. She had no need. When it came to important decisions Chrissie preferred to rely on gut feelings. And her feelings were telling her that while Arthur Sullivan was undoubtedly the more experienced of the two, when it came to something so personal – *intimate*, almost – it was crucial to work with somebody she felt in harmony with. She was definitely in harmony with Andy.

'The job's yours,' she said.

'You can count on me.'

She cracked open a bottle of bubbly.

As she poured his drink, all giddy and girly and flirty, she accidentally-on-purpose brushed up against him.

'Oops,' she said.

He gave her a hungry smile.

For a moment they locked eyes, then his hands were on her, expertly undoing the buttons on her top, as she clawed at his back.

4

Jack Raven lounged on the white leather sofa in his office on the top floor of Shine Records. On the screen he was watching Eighties heart-throb Jason Donovan, reflecting to the TV show's interviewer on how it felt to have a number one album and sell-out tour after so many years out of the spotlight. Coming across as humble, grateful. Chuckling about how eating kangaroo anus in *I'm A Celebrity* had certainly been a challenge but having a hit again had washed away the bitter taste, and saying of course he would be playing his old hits when he toured.

'Quite right,' Jack told the TV. 'That's what the fans want. Nostalgia. Stuff they can sing along to that takes them back.'

It seemed that all of a sudden everything Eighties had gone mental. Reunion tours wherever you looked. Rewind festivals. Conventions. Cruises. Bands who'd gone through horrible, bitter break-ups and couldn't stand the sight of each other, patching things up once the price was right.

Funny, that.

He stretched and put his arms behind his head, his Stray Cats T-shirt riding up to give a glimpse of firm flesh. Jack took pride in how he looked. He watched what he ate, drank in moderation – vodka and soda, a squeeze of lime – and worked out most days. High Intensity Interval Training and yoga in mind-blowing heat. Worth it to keep the six-pack and snake hips he'd had as a twenty-year-old. Same as Mick Jagger, he liked to think, although the wrinkly rocker was a good ten years older.

He continued to gaze at the TV. Old Jason was looking pretty good too. Trim, the awful mullet hairdo gone. Less . . . *fluffy* than Jack remembered. Pity some of the artists who came to Shine wanting a career in the music business didn't have the same discipline. Just kids, some of them, and already gone to seed. Junk-food junkies. The week before, one of his A & R guys had brought in a boy band for him to look at. Good, catchy sound. Writing their own stuff. Promising. The only problem was – and there was no easy way of putting it – they were *fat*.

Jack liked his pop stars pocket-sized. Lean and lithe. The Minogue sisters. Cheryl Tweedy. Little Mix. The boy band hopefuls were utterly crestfallen when he said the only thing standing between them and a deal at Shine was their obesity. That might have been putting it a bit strongly but they needed to understand; the music industry was ruthless. No one wanted tubby pop stars. They had stared at him, open-mouthed.

In a business that was full of bullshit, Jack had never shied away from telling it like it was. It had earned him the nickname Jack the Knife, which he took as a compliment.

His second in command, Rick, appeared in the doorway. 'Knock-knock,' he said. 'You ready for me?'

Jack waved him in. 'Shut the door and pull up a pew, mate.'

The choice was between a stool in the style of a turntable or a bucket seat that swallowed you up. Rick chose the bucket seat, sinking into its depths. Jack hooked an ankle over the end of the sofa and aimed the remote at the TV, freezing the picture. He was silent for a moment, thinking.

'Old Donovan's doing well for himself.'

'He played a packed-out gig at the Royal Albert Hall last week,' Rick said. 'Still got the voice. Smoking-hot band. Did half a dozen tracks from the new album, then wrapped it up with "Too Many Broken Hearts".' His first solo number one in 1989.

'This Eighties thing, it's interesting, don't you think? Just seems to get bigger.'

Rick nodded. 'Definitely.'

Jack sat up straight. Rick attempted to do the same. The chair sucked him back down.

'There's a monster gig in the offing. Strictly entre nous, understand?' He gave Rick a conspiratorial look. 'The whole thing is under wraps while they nail down the line-up and get contracts in place, so not a word.'

Rick gave another nod. 'Course.'

'They're calling it *Rock Legends*.' Jack looked thoughtful. 'More *pop* than rock if you ask me, but who cares? It's got a ring to it. Did I say, it's Wembley Stadium?' He caught Rick's look. 'It's the dog's bollocks. TV audience of millions. *Billions*, probably. They've done some crazy global deal on the broadcast rights.'

Rick leaned forward excitedly. He could see where this was going.

'Rick, this is strictly hush-hush for now,' Jack continued, 'but it's going to be bonkers massive. All the Eighties crowd – the mega stars – will be there. And I mean *all* of them, including the ones who swore they'd never set foot on stage together again. Argy-bargy swept nicely under the carpet.' He grinned. 'Saw the pound signs and, wallop, they're just about *fighting* to kiss and make up. Mate, I tell you, money talks, and this is a biggie. No one's going to be stupid enough to turn it down.' He nodded at the screen. 'Our friend Jason will definitely be on it, going platinum with his comeback album at just the right moment has secured him a place – jammy bastards at his label must be lapping it up.'

Rick had another go at sitting up.

'You're thinking, where am I going with this?' Jack leapt to his feet and crossed to the other side of the office, perching on the expanse of African blackwood that was his desk. 'Now here's the really interesting bit. This is where you come in.'

Rick heaved himself out of the chair and went to sit on the turntable stool. It gave a precarious wobble.

'I've set something up with the *Rock Legends* office,' Jack said. 'For one of our bands to open the show.' He leaned forward, fixing Rick with steely grey eyes. 'Go on, who do you think it is – a band that said they'd never work together again?'

Rick frowned. 'Not The Smiths, surely.'

Jack clapped his hands, delighted. 'You'll kick yourself,' he said.

'Help me out,' Rick pleaded.

Jack did a drumroll on the desk and pulled out a gold disc. 'The Thunder Girls!'

Rick blinked. 'But . . . we . . . they . . . you . . .'

Jack was on his feet again. 'I know! Insane, isn't it? Who'd have thought there was any mileage left in them? With this gig, though, they could actually be hot again.' He looked at the girls' image on the disc and focused on Carly's face for a moment, but then, casting his eye over the other three, he wrinkled his nose. 'Well, not exactly *all* hot. I mean, it's thirty years on. Age can take a toll.' His gaze landed on Rick's middle. His number two seemed to be developing a bit of a paunch.

Rick sucked his stomach in. 'But the Thunder Girls? I mean . . . I don't get it – you ended them.'

'And now I'm saying we re-boot them again for this gig. Shine will make a fortune off the back catalogue.' Jack smiled and rubbed his fingers together in a way that reminded Rick of Fagin in *Oliver Twist*.

'Like I said, this is massive. We're talking top dollar here. I'm telling you, mate, a deal like this doesn't come along every day and no way are we turning it down.' Jack rubbed his hands together. 'I've already said we're doing it.'

Several beads of sweat had appeared on Rick's brow. 'It's just . . .'

Jack gave him a sharp look. 'What?'

'Well, we'll never get them back together. I mean, the break-up was bad. Beyond bad.' Not so much a break-up, Rick thought, as a deliberate dismantling.

'There's always a way. Look at the Spice Girls. No one thought they'd tour again – albeit without Posh – but still filling stadiums.' Jack waved a hand in the air. 'Rick, please, do *not* go all doom and gloom on me. This is *exciting*. An *opportunity*. Never-to-be-repeated. No one in their right mind would say no. Am I right, or am I right?'

Rick gripped the stool in an effort to stop it spinning. 'All I'm saying is, you know, when the band came apart it was ugly. Chrissie shafted the others. Big time. They hate her and they hate me! The whole thing was nasty. Bitter. So with the best will in the world—'

Jack cut across him. 'Remember how bad things got with Fleetwood Mac?' Rick nodded. 'Well, after all the wife swapping, drugs and debauchery even they're *back together*—'

'Minus Lyndsey Buckingham after that nasty lawsuit they just went through,' Rick interrupted.

Jack stared at him dismissively. 'The point is, as soon as a wadded promoter came along dangling a juicily paid tour in front of them, the rest of them are best friends again.' Rick sighed as Jack continued. 'This is one offer they *cannot refuse*. A chance to finally play Wembley Stadium!' His brow furrowed. 'I remember how they were always banging on about that.'

Rick nodded, remembering.

'Wembley-this, Wembley-that and on and on they droned. Well, now you can tell them their chance to finally do it is here.'

Rick stared at him open-mouthed. 'You want *me* to talk to them?'

'Who else could do it? Rick, mate, you're *their* man. I'm counting on you.' He smiled a terrible, chilling smile. 'You've already managed the old bags once, you know how all the bits and pieces fit together – literally in at least two cases, eh, you old dog!' Jack winked as Rick continued to take in what he was saying. 'Look, it's got to be you, mate. Don't let me down.'

Back in his own office, Rick sat slumped at his desk, unable to think straight. Sweat trickled down his back. He shrugged off his suit jacket and loosened a button on his shirt. His armpits felt clammy. A copy of *Q* magazine caught his eye, Noel Gallagher on the cover, leering up at him. *Laughing* at his predicament, it seemed. He turned it face down and waited for his heart rate to return to normal. Perhaps he should resign. Before Jack sacked him. Which he would when he went back to tell him he had, indeed, let him down.

A Thunder Girls reunion! The one thing he could never have predicted, bizarrely handy for Chrissie's current predicament but totally impossible. He had never been able to read Jack. No one could. All those years back, with timing that made no sense, his decision to pull the plug on the Thunder Girls had caught everyone off guard.

Rick, the girls, the fans, the world.

Only Chrissie took it in her stride.

There was a tap at the door. Susan, the PA he shared with Jack, hovered. 'I've brought you a coffee. Everything okay?'

Rick gestured at her to come in. He wasn't sure he trusted himself to speak without his voice cracking.

She placed the coffee on the desk in front of him and sat down. 'You look as if you've had a shock,' she said.

He shook his head, waited a moment. Took a deep breath. 'Jack. He wants me to get the girls back together.'

Susan's brow furrowed. 'Oh. You mean . . .'

He squeezed his eyes shut for a moment. 'He's done a deal for the Thunder Girls to play Wembley. Opening act for some kind of Eighties super-gig. Not a word to me about it until today. It's all been agreed and now I'm supposed to make it happen.' He threw up his hands in despair. 'How? There's no way. For starters, I haven't a clue where Anita is, or how to find her. No one's set eyes on her since . . .' He gave Susan an awkward look. 'The others hate me as much as, if not more than, they hate Chrissie. And as for Roxanne, I'd be amazed if she'll ever speak to me after what I did to her . . .' He shrugged, uncomfortable. 'Well, you know . . .'

Susan nodded, sympathetic. She knew only too well, having been on the inside track of the Thunder Girls from the beginning.

'Look, I know it was a rough choice at the time, but you *really* dodged a bullet by not being in the band,' Rick said, rubbing his temples to try to kill his headache.

Susan shrugged. If things had worked out differently, she could have been a Thunder Girl herself. 'I don't really think about it anymore. The shift to PA worked out so well for me – I love what I do,' she said. 'How does my thirty-year career alongside Jack compare to a few years in a band?' Her job title of PA told only part of the story. Everyone knew she had Jack's ear, and that when it came to the workings of the label she understood what kept the wheels turning better than almost anyone else.

'God knows how I'm going to do it. What an almighty mess.' Rick gave her a helpless look.

She waited a moment. 'I assume this is the *Rock Legends* gig you're talking about.'

He was taken aback. 'You *knew*?'

'I knew about the gig, that's all. Not about the girls, but I can see why – it will be monster money.'

Rick was silent for a moment. 'But I'll never be able to

get them together again – too much has gone on. I'll just have to tell Jack it's not possible.'

Susan gave it some thought. 'Don't do that. I can think of at least one way round it. What you need to do is get someone else to take the first bullet for you . . .'

5

Rick decided to do as Susan suggested and make Chrissie reach out to the others first. It would keep her busy, he reasoned, and take her mind off the Scott business. He arrived at the house just before noon to find her floating about in her dressing gown. From the look of her, still sleepy-eyed, she hadn't been up long. He steeled himself for a rant about Scott and precisely what she would do when she got her hands on him. It had to have 'sunk in' by now, he reckoned. But to his surprise, when she greeted him, it was like nothing had happened at all. She seemed in overly good spirits, making coffee and offering him a croissant; moving around the kitchen humming to herself, as if she hadn't a care in the world. Nothing about her suggested she had almost lost everything. Nor did she look in the least bit broken-hearted.

Rick wondered if she was still in denial.

Or perhaps she was having some kind of breakdown.

'Love is in the air,' she sang along to the radio, pouring the coffee.

He watched her, wary, as she perched on a stool at the breakfast bar facing him. 'Is it?' he asked.

She gave a slight shrug and produced a bright pink lip gloss from the pocket of her robe, slapping on a generous dollop, then rearranged some white roses on the countertop.

'So, how are things?' Rick said curiously as he watched her.

'I'm coping. You know me,' she breathed, almost melodically, whilst topping up the vase with water. 'In the words of Destiny's Child . . .' She belted out part of the chorus of 'Survivor' before collapsing in a fit of giggles.

Rick stared at her. Had she taken something? 'Has there been any news?' he asked.

'Concerning my *runaway* husband, you mean?' She narrowed her eyes. 'Still missing. Presumed dead. Or he will be, once I find him, which won't take long now I've got a detective on the case.'

Rick raised an eyebrow. No wonder she was so perky. Nothing galvanized Chrissie like the prospect of taking revenge. He knew all about that. When their marriage was in its dying throes and she (wrongly) suspected him of having a fling with one of the marketing girls at Shine, she had put all his clothes on a bonfire, including the new Versace suit he hadn't had a chance to wear, and the handmade shirt from Savile Row, still in its box. The girl at Shine – the one he wasn't seeing – had got a box of stinking pig's innards in the post. (He didn't want to know how she'd arranged that particular present.)

For a moment he almost felt sorry for Scott.

'It's good you're doing something,' he said carefully.

She nodded, absent-mindedly slathering on another layer of lip gloss. It was a gesture familiar to Rick. Something Chrissie did when she was feeling less sure of herself than she was willing to let on. Despite the tough exterior, he suspected she was hurting badly over Scott's betrayal. She probably still even wanted him back. It couldn't be much fun rattling round that big house on her own. Just then the kitchen door opened and a dishevelled figure in a *Fast & Furious* T-shirt and boxers wandered in, took a carton of juice from the fridge, and drank down half of it. Rick shot Chrissie a bewildered look.

'This is Andy,' she said. 'How's it going, babe?'

Andy wiped his mouth with the back of his hand. 'Getting there, babe. Getting there.' He gave Rick a mock salute and sauntered out, taking the juice with him. Swiping a banana from the fruit bowl on his way past.

Rick stared.

'What?' Chrissie gave him a coy look.

'Who the fuck is that?'

'My P.I. Hot on the trail of Scotty. And you needn't look at me like that. He's highly qualified.'

'Qualified in what? Don't you ever learn? You've just

been ripped off something rotten by a toy boy and what's the first thing you do? Shack up with another one!'

'Oh, get stuffed, Rick. Don't come all high and mighty with me. As if you never put a foot wrong.' She gave him an accusing look. 'He's helping me, and so what if I have a little fun along the way? Don't I deserve it? Or would you rather I went round crying, feeling sorry for myself? Oh, yes, you'd love that, so you could come charging to the rescue. Well, for your information, I will do as I please. Whether you like it or not. And if you *don't* like it, you can bugger off.'

'I am *trying* to look out for you, Chrissie. I have your best interests at heart. I'm still your manager, remember.'

'Well, do some managing then! Go and earn me some dosh instead of hanging around here getting all narky about something that, frankly, is none of your business.' She glared at him. 'Seriously, why am I not guest hosting *This Morning*? Or doing a beauty slot on *Lorraine*? How come I'm not a regular on *Loose Women*, putting the world to rights on a daily basis? Or guest judging on *X Factor*? I could do it all standing on my head.'

'Now is not the time. You'd be put on the spot about Scott. Is that what you really want?'

Andy padded back into the kitchen and left the banana skin on the worktop. 'All okay, babe?' he said.

Chrissie shot him a brilliant smile. 'Perfect. We're just finishing up here.'

Rick waited until he had gone.

'Babe?' he said sarcastically.

She gazed at him, defiant. He rolled his eyes. 'You never learn, do you?'

'Isn't it time you were leaving, Rick? I've got things under control, go and get me some work,' Chrissie said, gesturing towards the door.

Rick didn't move. 'Actually, I came here today to discuss a bit of business,' he said. 'An offer's come in.' He waited a moment.

'I'm not going on *I'm A Celebrity*,' Chrissie said indignantly, 'and before you say it's made Jason Donovan hot again, I don't care!'

'A gig,' he said.

Chrissie looked relieved.

'A big one. Wembley Stadium.'

Chrissie blinked in what looked like shock; she'd had so much Botox it was hard to tell but Rick was sure it was as close to shock as her face would allow.

'*Wembley*?' she breathed.

'Yep, Wembley.'

Chrissie thought for a moment. 'What's the catch?'

'No catch.'

'There's always a catch.'

'Crazy line-up. Every big name from the Eighties. *Rock Legends*, they're calling it.' He waited a beat. 'The scale of the thing is mind-blowing. Everyone you can think of wants a place on that bill.'

She looked taken aback. 'And you're sure they want me? It's a solid offer?'

'Rock solid – pardon the pun. They want *you*.' Rick gave a bright smile. 'And – here's the amazing thing – they don't *just* want you . . . they want the Thunder Girls to open the whole frigging show!'

Her jaw dropped.

'It's a massive opportunity, a one-off,' he said, quoting Jack. 'And you always said you wanted to play Wembley.'

'Yes – on my own!'

'Well, now's your chance.'

She worried away at her pout with the lip gloss, slathering on enough to create a gooey, sticky slick.

'We're talking big money,' he went on. 'Enough to save this house and get you back on your Manolos again.'

Chrissie sat shaking her head.

Rick tried another of Jack's lines. 'No one in their right mind would turn it down.'

She gazed at him, incredulous. 'I'll give you three people who will – Roxanne, Carly and Anita. There's not the slightest chance in hell. We both know the Thunder Girls are no more.'

He remembered what Susan had said. *Be tough. Make Chrissie do as she's told, for once*. 'That's where you come in,' he told her.

'I don't see how—'

Rick cut across her. '*You* need to talk to the others. Get them on board.'

'Me?! Are you out of your mind? No. Forget it.'

He fixed her with what he hoped was a steely look. 'I'm not running this past you, as in you have a choice. This *is* happening. The deal is *done*. The Thunder Girls *are* going to open the *Rock Legends* show. Simple as. You'll be the only female act on the bill.'

'Are you mad? I can't! The others hate me – even though the way things ended for the band was all down to Jack.'

Rick held her gaze. They both knew that wasn't true. Chrissie had been a complete cow and leapt at the chance of going solo, even when Rick spelled out that it would mean disaster for the others. Without as much as a backward glance she had ditched her bandmates – her friends. Sold them down the river. Rick had made a last-ditch attempt to stand up for the other girls, even suggested bringing in someone new to keep the band going, but Jack wouldn't have it. For Roxanne's sake, Rick had felt torn, but for Jack it was strictly business. The choice had been simple – fall into line or walk.

It hadn't taken Rick long to make up his mind. He took the coward's way out and dumped Roxanne, dropped her like a stone. Chucked his lot in with Chrissie. He hadn't even had the decency to talk to Roxy properly. It was the worst thing he had ever done, and he still regretted it.

'Five hundred grand, minimum. Each,' he said.

She stared at the floor. 'I'm not going crawling to the others. You can't make me. And besides, once Andy works out where Scott is I'll get my money back, so I won't need your shitty plan.'

He gasped. 'Are you for real? For one thing, I'd be amazed if Boy Wonder knows the first thing about detective work – if he manages to find Scott I'll open the *Rock Legends* gig myself.' She refused to look at him. 'For another, what part of being broke don't you understand? You have *nothing* left in the tank. Zilch. You're only ticking over because I'm subbing you . . .'

'Oh, I wondered when we'd get to that! Well you can have your lousy money back! Take it. See if I care.' She threw her peach-blush calf-skin Prada purse at his head. Rick ducked, and she winced as it hit the floor. Rick continued as if nothing had happened – he was pleased it wasn't the vase.

'Do you have *any idea* how close you are to losing this place? The upkeep isn't cheap and there's no way I can keep bankrolling you for ever.' He was livid. 'You're not married to me anymore – which was your choice, remember – so I don't need to do any of this. So, yes, I'll help you out on a personal level for old times' sake but I am *not* responsible for you, and I am warning you that if you don't make this happen you'll have the bailiffs on your back quicker than that so-called "PI" was on your front.'

Chrissie glared at him as he continued. 'Oh yes, they'll be taking all your designer this and that. Gucci frocks, Dolce & Gabbana, Versace . . . God-knows-who-else handbags, shoes, the lot, and flogging it at auction.' She kept glaring at him.

'You'll lose this house and everything in it without some serious money coming in, and then what – you'll be begging to eat kangaroo balls at that stage!' Chrissie steadied herself against the worktop at the very thought, as Rick went on. 'So believe me when I say, the sooner you get used to the idea that Scott has gone – *and* your money – the better.'

'Do you have to be so horrible?'

Rick ignored her. 'This is your only chance. Make *Rock Legends* happen. Go and see the other girls, sell the idea of the gig and get them on board. Chances are they could do with the money too.'

'Does it have to be me that asks them? Why can't you?'

Rick gave her a steely look. He was proud of himself for coming up with this one. 'Because if they can't put aside their differences with you, this will never work. Better you all make peace, or as close as you can, together and at the start and then I will take over. Repairing this has to begin with you, not me.'

Chrissie looked flustered. 'I wouldn't know what to say.'

'Start with a big slab of humble pie. Grovel. Do whatever it takes.' He waited until she looked at him. 'And ditch Super Sleuth upstairs.'

Rick eased the car out of the drive. He was worn out. For the best part of an hour, Chrissie had done all she could to make him change his mind. Begged and pleaded, turned on the waterworks. Stamped her foot. Hurled one of her favourite china mugs at the wall in frustration (he had got the blame for that). Said she would go to the press with a salacious kiss-and-tell about their marriage. By then she was scraping the barrel. Rick knew the last thing she wanted was some nosy journalist asking how things were going with Scott. Wondering why no one had seen him and Chrissie together since the honeymoon.

Rick had remained impassive in the face of threats and insults and emotional blackmail, letting it all wash over him until in the end she caved in.

The gates swung shut behind him and he stopped for a moment to search through the glove box for the kind of music that would make him feel less like he'd just gone ten rounds with Anthony Joshua. He flipped through the CDs, feeling like a dinosaur. He didn't know anyone else who still had CDs. He preferred to think of it as nostalgia. Something caught his eye and when he looked up he spotted a tall figure with a bulky bag, the kind paper boys carry. Delivering leaflets probably. A bicycle was propped against the hedge. Rick rolled a window down.

'There's a box on the side, there,' he said.

The delivery man swivelled round. Tall, well built. Piercing blue eyes. He looked vaguely familiar. Rick wondered if he'd seen him before, hoped he hadn't once been in any of his bands that had failed. He'd read that one of the lead singers of Eternal was working as a receptionist these days – music was a fickle world, it could happen to anyone, he mused as blue eyes looked back at him.

Rick pointed. 'It's over there, mate – the mail box.'

The man nodded and reached inside the bag for something as Rick slid Deep Purple into the deck and accelerated away.

6

Back in the office a few days later, Rick watched Jack beat out a tune on the desk with his pen. His eyes were blazing. Rick thought he looked wired, dangerous. In full-on Jack the Knife mode. 'Thinking caps on, people,' he said. 'Give me your best ideas. Shoot.'

He leaned back in his chair, looking straight at Rick, who pretended to be absorbed with scribbling something in his diary. Rick had tried everything to get out of the meeting but Jack insisted he needed his A-team round the table, hammering out a strategy to promote the newly reformed Thunder Girls. Rick wasn't feeling well. The girls were nowhere near back together so he had nothing to say. In fact, as far as he knew, Chrissie had still not even talked to either Carly or Roxanne, nor did she have a clue where Anita was.

He doodled something, feeling anxious, willing Jack not to pick on him; pressing down with such force his pen went right through the page.

Jack kept on tapping. Rick knew the tune but couldn't quite place it. 'Under Pressure'? 'Paranoid'? 'Match of the Day'?

A mash-up of all three, by the sound of it.

The office was stuffy and Rick felt as if he couldn't get enough air. The back of his neck was damp. If only he could open a window. Open it and throw himself out. He gazed longingly at the sliding glass doors that opened onto the balcony overlooking the Thames, and imagined floating through the air and landing in the river. Going under before coming to the surface and swimming away in the direction of Hammersmith Bridge. For a few delicious seconds he allowed himself to fantasize about pulling off a daring escape, worthy of 007. Not that he could get anywhere near the window. Not with Rebecca, the marketing chief, in his way. He would have to vault over her.

Rick was wary of Rebecca. Wide and lumbering, with a love of billowing clothes in clashing colours, usually set off with some kind of headscarf-cum-turban affair, she was gruff and outspoken and prone to saying, 'with all due respect', by which she meant the exact opposite. Rick had lost count of the times she had told him he was talking bollocks – 'with all due respect'. Privately, he was surprised Jack hadn't come up with some reason to let her go since he made no secret of his distaste for obesity. Rebecca was good at her job, though. Bloody brilliant.

Rick could feel Jack's eyes on him as he drummed 'I Should Be So Lucky' on the desk.

'Come on, mate, you kick us off,' Jack said, smiling one of his sinister smiles.

Rick said the first thing that came into his head. 'Well . . . I was thinking a *Greatest Hits* album. Some of the old favourites re-mixed, given a new twist. A couple of featured artists . . . Katy Perry, maybe. Adele.' Adele! Who was he kidding?

'With all due respect, Adele will never do it,' Rebecca said. She was wearing some sort of shawl that could have passed for a wall hanging. As she hurled it across her shoulder it whacked Rick on the side of the face.

He flinched. 'No, I mean, it doesn't have to be Adele . . .'

Rebecca made a snorting sound.

Jack was nodding. 'Yeah. Collaborations. They're big. Look into it. See who's a fit. None of Ed Sheeran's leftovers, mind. And we'll need a catchy title. Spare me the dreary *Thunder Girls are Go* bollocks. Or anything that screams thirtieth anniversary. That'll turn the kids off right away.'

Rick, on the point of suggesting *Thunder Girls are Go* and *30* on the album cover, clamped his lips shut.

He wondered if he was getting too old for all this. He was fifty-five, still young if you believed *Men's Health*, but some days he felt thoroughly past it. Going out night after night checking out new bands, something he used to love, had become a chore. As for all the launches and showcases and after-show parties when he had to work the room, he had started to feel like a dinosaur. The only one who wasn't on Snapchat.

A couple of nights earlier he had been cornered by some hyper young woman talking excitedly about bands he hadn't even heard of. Was it his imagination or were all the rising stars in the music industry ex-public school these days? Not only did he feel old and out of touch, he also felt like a bit of a dunce. He sneaked a look at Jack. No one knew how old he was but Rick reckoned he had to be sixty-something. Not that you'd ever guess from the way he bounced around. All that boundless energy. Maybe the disgusting-looking daily green smoothie he swore by really did put the spring in his step.

Rick was the only one wearing a suit. Jack was in his usual drainpipe jeans and T-shirt combo. Hari from the press office, fresh out of university, in an embroidered tunic and matching trousers, might have walked straight off the set of a Bollywood movie. Carrie, from A & R, was in a see-through blouse missing its shoulders, and a pair of geeky specs. Were they some kind of fashion statement? As far as Rick knew, she didn't need glasses.

Tucked away in the corner, quietly making notes, was Susan. When Rick first knew her she wore short skirts and clumpy boots and flamboyant bows in pink-streaked hair. Now she stuck to conservative tops and trousers and shiny brogues. Kept her ebony hair in a severe, jaw-length bob.

'There wasn't a proper Thunder Girls book, was there?' Hari asked.

Rebecca frowned. 'No, only a picture book made up of concert pictures of them, aimed at young girls, nothing revealing, mainly make-up tips and song lyrics. A few pages at the back where you could cut out figures of the band and dress them up. Like *Bunty*.' She saw Hari's face. 'A *comic*,' Rebecca explained. 'Very popular in its day. Before you were born.' She turned to Jack. 'With all due respect, shouldn't we have a *senior* press officer here? Preferably someone who actually remembers the Thunder Girls.'

'I've seen the cuttings – I get it,' Hari said, undeterred.

Jack stretched. His Taylor Swift T-shirt rode up, revealing the waistband of his Calvin Kleins. 'No harm getting a range of views, Becky.' He was the only one who dared call her Becky.

She gave a mild snort.

'So, we could think about a real book then,' Hari went on. 'Like, I mean, a band biography. All the stuff no one knew at the time. We're talking the Eighties. It was pretty wild, right? You just have to watch *The Tube* to know that.'

'You watched *The Tube*?' Rebecca asked, incredulous.

'Seen the clips online. They were crazy wild. Did the whole thing live, you know.'

Rebecca gave him a withering look. 'Yes, thanks, Hari. With all due respect, I was in the studio every week.'

His eyes widened. 'Shit. For reals?'

Jack had stopped drumming. He banged the table, making Rick jump. 'Genius! That's it. A book, something edgy. The uncut inside story of the band. What's that word everyone uses these days?' He clicked his fingers, thinking. '*Authentic*. I mean, let's face it – how much does anyone really know about the Thunder Girls? Hari, you've read the cuttings. What do you reckon?'

'To be honest, there's not a huge amount of depth. It's all pretty . . . safe.'

Rebecca bristled. 'With all due respect, that's because we marketed them as *safe*.'

Jack looked gleeful. 'And now it's time to lift the lid. A proper exposé. Warts and all. What *really* made the girls tick – tears, tantrums, bitching, backstabbing.' He shook his head, thinking back. 'God, I can think of a few stories myself. Remember that trip up north, Doncaster or somewhere, for tour rehearsals?' Rick sank as low in his seat as he could, guessing where Jack was going with this. 'So, Roxanne was out on the lash the night before and in a bad way the next morning. Still drunk, probably. The driver kept having to come off the motorway and find a lay-by so she could throw up at the side of the road. Five, six times, at least. Took hours longer than it should have done to get there. Crew sitting about at the other end twiddling their thumbs, first day of rehearsals down the drain *and* she was fronting a responsible drinking campaign for the government with some of the *Grange Hill* kids . . .'

'No!' gasped Carrie.

'It's true. And I remember now. It was her birthday and *someone* thought it was a good idea to pour tequila shots down her throat.' He gave Rick a sly look. 'Isn't that right, *Rick*?'

Rick felt five pairs of eyes on him. Susan, frowning.

Carrie, looking at him with what could have been admiration or disgust, it was hard to tell which. Hari, mildly curious. Rebecca, with her oh-my-God face on. Jack, smiling his terrible smile.

Rick tried to look as if he didn't mind. 'I don't remember that,' he lied.

Jack threw his head back and roared with laughter. He dabbed at his eyes as he calmed down. 'I know just the person to do it, too,' he said. 'Kristen Kent. She's bloody good.'

Kristen Kent was a hack with a reputation for getting her story. What she couldn't find out she made up. Everyone was talking about the tell-all book she had just co-written with a former pop star. Explosive was putting it mildly.

Not so long ago she had done a hatchet job on Chrissie, Rick remembered. What was meant to be a cosy profile piece ended up peppered with insults. Chrissie's house was 'neat to the point of suggesting the occupant had borderline personality disorder'. Kristen had sneaked a look inside the kitchen cupboards and found cans of tomato soup, all carefully lined up with their labels facing out, indicating, she decided, some kind of 'creepy obsessive mindset'. As for Chrissie, she was 'plastic', her smile 'more witchy than bewitching'. She had been as withering about Scott. He had offered her champagne – 'proper Italian stuff', he said, which she found hilarious.

Not surprisingly, Chrissie had gone ballistic.

Rick could not see the Thunder Girls taking to the idea

of spilling the beans to Kristen Kent. 'Are we sure she's the right person for this?' he asked.

Jack rounded on him. 'Absolutely. A *hundred* per cent. Why, you don't think so?'

'No, it's just . . . I'm thinking, when she met Chrissie . . . well, they didn't exactly hit it off.'

Jack was dismissive. 'That's not an issue. Chrissie won't need to speak to her.'

Rick didn't follow. 'So who *is* she going to speak to? I mean, where's she going to get the info?'

Jack tapped the side of his nose. 'Leave that to me.'

7

Carly stood beside the bed surveying the chaos. It looked as if there'd been a break-in. One of those mean burglars who can't just steal stuff, they have to trash the place at the same time. The wardrobe was empty, doors open, everything off the hangers and flung across the bed, the floor – even the dressing table. The culprit who had turned the place upside down? Herself.

All afternoon she had been looking for something suitable to wear for the Sporting Heroes dinner at Grosvenor House that evening, and growing increasingly desperate when nothing she tried on looked right.

She should have gone shopping, as Dave suggested. Splashed out on something new. After all, it was a big night. Dinner with the sponsors. The same people who had stumped up millions to get Dave 'The Destroyer' to make a comeback. Dave had got himself a new suit, something well cut in the kind of fabric that looked navy in one light, almost purple in another. Not cheap, but worth every penny, he said. One of his trademark snazzy waistcoats was also getting an airing.

Carly had been instructed to pull out the stops. Dress to impress.

Her gaze landed on the bedside table where an embossed card was propped up. Its arrival that morning had left her intrigued. An invite from Chrissie to have dinner. *It's time to talk*, Chrissie had written. Really? After all these years, what was there to *talk* about? she wondered.

Carly had not set eyes on her old bandmate since the Thunder Girls break-up. In the early days she'd tried to get in touch and heard nothing back. No wonder. Chrissie had really dropped them in it when she trampled all over them. Carly was dying to know what would make her resurface after a gap of thirty years. When she had looked up the address on Google Earth she got a glimpse of a stunning white mansion behind wrought-iron gates.

What could she possibly want with Carly?

She stepped over an Alexander McQueen dress. Short, off-the-shoulder. She had only worn it once. In the days of the Thunder Girls, she only ever gave clothes a single outing. Otherwise, the magazines wanted to know if she was on an economy drive or just plain lazy. She picked it up and put it back on its padded hanger. It wasn't right for a formal do and, anyway, it was a bit shorter than she liked these days. The last time she put it on Dave said something about her knees, that there were ways of having saggy skin tightened up – hadn't he read somewhere about Demi Moore having it done? You couldn't go wrong with wide-legged trousers, he said.

She bent to retrieve a Balmain dress she had once loved. Black, floor-length and backless. High-necked. Slit up the side. The cut was incredible, everything in proportion. The fabric was amazing too, a kind of slinky silk chiffon that never creased. She held it up. The last time she had worn it was to the *Sports Personality of the Year* award show, going back a few years. It had got her onto a best-dressed list. Whether she could still carry it off now was another matter. All that skin on show! She wouldn't even be able to wear a bra. Well, there was only one way to find out.

She peeled off her T-shirt and leggings and put the dress on, pairing it with crystal-embellished Giuseppe Zanotti heels. When she studied her reflection in the full-length mirror, she blinked, taken aback. The woman looking back at her seemed poised and elegant, self-assured. She felt a rush of confidence. The dress was wonderful, the fabric like a second skin. Perhaps a teeny bit clingier than when she had last worn it. As for the side slit, it was not exactly subtle. An image came to mind of Angelina Jolie in a similar dress at the Oscars, being taken to task for what the papers called her leg-baring antics. If Angelina got stick, Carly suspected she could well be torn to pieces. Oh well, sod the lot of them. It had been a while since she felt this good about herself.

She crossed to the far side of the room and began walking towards the mirror, checking her posture, keeping an eye on the exposed leg, watching for any tell-tale wobbles. No cellulite that she could see. She positioned the mirror on the inside of the wardrobe so she could see how she looked from behind as well as in front. Pretty good, as far as she could tell. No unsightly back fat and the kind of shapely bum the *Daily Mail* would call peachy. She giggled, turning this way and that, checking for likely wardrobe malfunctions. In a dress like this she would probably make the *Mail*'s infamous Sidebar of celeb pics.

The bedroom door opened and Dave appeared, tumbler in hand, not quite sober. He did a comic start when he saw the mess of clothes scattered everywhere. 'Blimey, have they taken much? Quick, dial 999!'

Carly faced him in her posh frock. He took a few tentative steps, picking his way through the pile of clothes with exaggerated care, as if stepping into a minefield. 'Thieves have raided the home of the former snooker world champion Dave "The Destroyer" Dixon and his retired popstar wife, "Thunder Girl" Carly,' he said, putting on a silly newsreader voice.

'Ha ha, very funny. I'm picking an outfit for tonight.' Carly waited for him to say something about the dress.

He gave her a long look. 'Give us a twirl, then.'

She did an awkward little turn, the spiky heels catching in the thick pile of the carpet. 'I haven't decided if I'm wearing this yet.' She was suddenly self-conscious. 'What do you think?'

He was nodding and frowning at the same time. He finished what was left of his drink. 'Doesn't bother you, then, the split-thing at the front?' He let out a sigh. 'I mean, the dress is *hot*. It's just not everyone can pull off the barely-there look. Rita Ora, maybe. Kylie Minogue.' He gestured at her to do another twirl, eyes narrowed in concentration as she shuffled around, no longer feeling confident. 'Have you worn it before?'

She reminded him of the awards do and making it onto the best-dressed list in one of the tabloids the following day. Dave listened without comment.

Finally, he said, 'You know it's a big deal tonight? I mean, these are the *sponsors*. This is when they find out who they're involved with.' He looked nonplussed. 'I'm not sure giving them an eyeful sends the right message.'

Carly was crestfallen. 'So what *is* the right message?'

'That they're dealing with serious people. *Decent* people. The kind of people whose involvement will enhance the image of their brand. That's what it's all about. *Perception*. If my wife's dressed like a hooker . . . well, it sends out the wrong signal straight away.'

At Grosvenor House, Carly got stuck with a small sweaty man whose hair had been carefully arranged to conceal his bald patch. The chairman of the company sponsoring Dave's comeback, it turned out. He ran a hand up and down her arm as he told her in a broad Black Country accent they were expecting great things from her husband. She did what she could to shake him off but the stroking persisted. She glared at him. He gave her a sickly smile and took his hand away. Dave, in conversation with another of the sponsors, caught her eye and gave her a sharp look. A look that told her to play nice. She gritted her teeth and smiled. The chairman's wandering hand landed on her hip.

Out of the corner of her eye she could see Dave knocking back champagne, laughing uproariously. She drained her own glass and grabbed another from a waiter circulating with a tray. They had only just arrived and already she wanted to go home.

She felt sure people were staring at her. Maybe she should have worn something else – the long dreary number with a high neck and full sleeves that Dave suggested. It sent out that all-important right message, he said. Carly had decided to stick with the revealing Balmain. She had seen similar dresses on a host of celebs: Alexa Chung, Daisy Lowe, even the Duchess of Sussex. Somehow, they had managed to carry them off. Suddenly, the dress felt all wrong. As if it was too revealing. She felt horribly self-conscious.

'Excuse me,' she said, removing the chairman's hand, which had migrated from her hip to her bottom, and headed towards the powder room.

Before she got there a hand grabbed her by the elbow and yanked her behind a pillar.

'What the hell do you think you're doing?' Dave hissed.

'I need the loo,' she said.

'That bloke you've just managed to insult happens to be the big boss, the one who's stumping up the cash for the exhibition matches.'

'He can't keep his hands to himself.'

'He's being friendly, that's all. Would it kill you to be polite?'

'I *was* polite. If I'd wanted to be rude I'd have slapped his sweaty face.'

Dave grabbed at a passing waiter, took a drink from a tray and necked half of it. 'I've just had to say you've got a migraine.'

'Good. I'll go home then. Lie down in a darkened room and wait for it to pass. If you think I'm going to spend the rest of the night smiling at that little pervert while he feels me up you've got another thing coming.'

Dave snorted with derision. 'Get you, Little Miss Whiter-Than-White. Who do you think you are? We *need* these people. When did you last bring home some bacon that you didn't fry and eat?' Carly felt her eyes sting as he continued. 'So I'll tell you what's going to happen. We are going back over there and *you* are going to turn on the charm and hang on to our new friend's every word.' He gripped her arm. 'You are going to let him put his hand on your arm, your bum, or anywhere else he fancies.' He finished his drink, deftly plopped it onto a passing tray and grabbed another as he steered her back towards the promoters.

8

Roxanne parked the Porsche at the back of Heaven & Hell and let herself into the club through an unmarked door, leaving it on the latch for Jamie. She trudged along a narrow corridor, switching on lights as she went, feeling weary, ready to throw in the towel. It had taken all her willpower to come in, to face reality. How much longer she could manage to keep the place limping along was anyone's guess.

For years the club had been struggling. As the takings dipped, Roxanne told herself it was a phase; that every business had its tough times. She kept going, not wanting to face up to how bad things really were, but now there was no more avoiding it. Heaven & Hell was practically on its knees, haemorrhaging money at an alarming rate – money she did not have.

It would take a miracle to save it.

And now she had been forced to use money set aside for

corporation tax to keep the suppliers at bay. It was as if at every turn she found herself in a deeper hole.

At the end of the corridor, she unlocked a door that led to the dance floor. The place was even more depressing when it was shut. No atmosphere. Then again, it wasn't exactly buzzing when it was open anymore. The night before, there hadn't been a single person in the VIP section and, for the first time ever, Roxanne opened it to what she called civilians. For a price, a minimum £200 spend, anyone could take a private booth in the once-exclusive roped-off area. It had helped boost takings but she couldn't help thinking it signalled another nail in the coffin.

At one time, the idea of letting just anyone into the hallowed VIP area was unthinkable.

The club had always pulled in celebs like a magnet, mainly because Roxanne had gone out of her way to make them feel special. Ploughed money into getting the mezzanine just right. The kind of lighting that took about ten years off; booths and private rooms and balconies overlooking the dance floor. Perfect for hiding away as well as a spot of posing and preening. There was also a well-used hidden staircase leading to the exit at the rear for anyone who wanted to make a discreet getaway without being photographed.

Those were the days.

Famous faces milling about, queues stretching along the street, people being turned away. Something going on pretty much every night – top DJs, bands, launch parties, secret gigs, catwalk shows. The gossip columns loved the place. What made it unique was having Roxanne at the helm. People were still playing Thunder Girls hits back then and she was all over the papers. *She* was once the star attraction.

That felt like a lifetime away.

At the bar, she pulled out her stock list and perched on a stool opposite a wall plastered with photos of sporting legends, supermodels, pop stars and actors. Posh society girls. Some of the biggest names on TV – many of them now dead, she realized – were all regulars, back in the day.

She heard footsteps and looked up to see a woman cutting across the unlit dance floor.

'We're not open yet,' she called.

'Hello, Roxanne.'

She froze. It was a voice she had not heard for thirty years but would know anywhere. Chrissie Martin. Roxanne turned towards her, her hands gently shaking. 'What the hell are you doing here?'

Chrissie stood in the middle of the dance floor. 'I just saw the club and—'

'Don't tell me this is a coincidence.'

She advanced a few steps. In the gloom, Roxanne couldn't quite see her face, just a cascade of blonde hair, killer heels and a floor-length coat. 'No, it's not.'

Roxanne snorted. 'Then I repeat – what the hell are you doing here?'

'I just wanted to say hello.'

'Well, you've said it, so now try goodbye.'

'I wanted to talk.' Chrissie hesitated. 'That's why I wrote to you. I . . . I want to put things right.'

The invitation had dropped through the letterbox a few days earlier. Expensive stationery with gold edging and elegant script. Its arrival had taken Roxanne right back to that terrible day at Shine Records in 1989. Now Chrissie Martin, the last person on earth she wanted to see, was summoning her to dinner with a curt, 'It's time to talk.' Did she *really* think all she had to do was click her fingers and Roxanne would drop everything? That she would be grateful to hear from the old witch after so many years? Well, she had another think coming. In a fit of rage she had ripped it up – which took some doing since the card was unusually thick – stuffed the pieces into the envelope and sent it back.

'I assume you got my reply,' Roxanne said.

Chrissie sighed and took a few tentative steps, edging towards the bar. Close enough for Roxanne to get a good look. She took in the fur coat, open over a loose shirt and cigarette pants. Snakeskin peep-toe boots. Chanel tote. She studied Chrissie's face, which was unlined and expertly made-up to appear make-up free – apart from the glossy red slick on a suspiciously full pout. Chrissie never could survive without half a ton of lip gloss. Some things never changed.

'It's been a long time, Roxy,' Chrissie murmured.

'Not long enough.'

'There's something I need to run past you. You, and the other girls. It's important. Please, Roxy. If we could just sit down together, have a glass of Cristal, talk things through in a civilized manner.'

Roxanne shook her head. 'You really are pathetic, you know that?' Chrissie looked confused. 'You think that's all it takes – the offer of some fizz? I run a *club*, I can drink Cristal whenever I like.' That wasn't entirely true. Heaven & Hell no longer stocked Cristal. There was no call for it with her 'more common' clientele. 'You come marching in here – *trespassing*, by the way – thinking you can twist me round your little finger, when the truth is *I don't care*. I'd rather poke sharp sticks in my eyes than sit down with you. *In a civilized manner!* Do you even know what that means? There was nothing *civilized* about what you did when you broke up the band.'

'That wasn't me, it was—'

'You just don't get it, do you? You ruined everything. *You*. So nothing you have to say could possibly be of any interest to me now – *I do not want to know!*'

Chrissie was silent for a moment. 'I just thought it would be nice to come and see you.'

'Oh, please. Lie to someone who cares!'

'You're as direct as ever, I see.'

'And *you're* still having problems telling the truth, I see.'

Chrissie turned to go.

'Bye then,' Roxanne called after her.

Chrissie stopped and exhaled loudly. Roxanne watched expectantly.

'Look, I'm sorry,' Chrissie said, turning back to face her.

Roxanne raised an eyebrow. 'Yeah? Sorry for what?'

'For whatever the reason you're being so hostile to me is.'

'This is a joke, right?' Roxanne spluttered.

'What is?'

'Was I supposed to be pleased to see you?'

'No, well . . . this isn't easy for me either.'

Roxanne went up to her. 'Go on, then – I'm listening.'

'I've been approached about re-forming the band.'

Roxanne gave a hollow laugh. 'So this *is* a joke!'

Chrissie threw up her hands in frustration. 'Forget it. I knew you'd be like this. *Difficult*.'

'What did you expect – a hug and a warm welcome?'

Chrissie gazed at her. 'Sorry to have bothered you. I can see you're *terribly* busy. I just thought you might have been interested in the deal I was offered, but since you're obviously happy running a morgue these days I'll leave you to it.'

Roxanne's teeth clenched. 'Who the fuck do you think you are, turning up here and speaking to me like that?'

'The same person I've always been; someone with ambition. But don't worry, I'm leaving. I can see I'm wasting my time. I knew this was a bad idea when the label suggested it but I thought, no, give her a chance. Maybe time's mellowed her, softened the jealousy. Obviously, I was wrong.'

'I'm not jealous of you, you bogus bitch!'

Chrissie gave her a haughty look. 'My mistake, of course you're not.'

Roxanne shook her head. 'You're as deluded as ever.'

'I'll let you get back to your stock-take . . . although I wouldn't bother adding it up – I'm sure it's all still there.'

'Hang on, oh my God! Chrissie, you're so right, it's all coming back to me – of course I'm jealous of you . . . Now let me think what it is I'm most jealous of . . . so much to choose from . . . hmm . . . now was it your marriage to my ex? Oh no, that failed, didn't it? Maybe your career? No, can't be that because if you still had one you wouldn't be here begging for a reunion. And it can't be your looks because, let's be honest, you haven't aged well.' She gave Chrissie a withering look as her eyes narrowed. 'Still, I know you're *always* right, so if it makes you feel better, off you go with the knowledge that I, Roxanne Lloyd, am overwhelmingly jealous of you.'

Chrissie gave a slow handclap. 'Very dramatic. Maybe you should have pursued a career in acting when the gravy train ended. Who knew you had such theatrical talent.' She sighed. 'You know though, *back in the day*, I always thought if anyone from the band was ever going to give me a run for my money it would have been you – but I was so wrong: you really did amount to nothing.'

Roxanne stepped towards her. 'It was a murky business, music, *back in the day*. Not all of us were interested in offering the special kind of "overtime" you were so good at, to get those contracts,' Roxanne spat. Chrissie flinched – they both knew who Roxanne was referring to. 'I've got no regrets it didn't happen for me again – I moved on and found a *real* life. Maybe now's the time for you to do the same.'

'I've *got* a real life,' Chrissie hissed. 'And it's a hell of a lot better than yours.'

'If it's so good why are you raking up the past? What was it you used to say in interviews? Oh, yes, I remember – "I'd rather die than go back to the Thunder Girls!" Changed your mind now you're no longer in vogue?'

'Does it really have to be like this, Roxanne? We did used to be friends, you know. Doesn't that count for anything?'

Roxanne gave a derisive snort. '*You're* talking to *me* about friendship – you don't know what the word means! Carly tried keeping in touch with you for years after the split and never heard back. And I don't remember a word of congratulations when I gave birth.'

They glared at each other.

The back door swung open and Roxanne's son, Jamie, came in with takeaway coffees.

'Oh, sorry, didn't realize you were busy,' he said.

Chrissie looked him over. 'Oh, you must be—' she started, before Roxanne marched over and stood between them.

'She was just leaving.' Roxanne gave Chrissie a mild shove towards the exit. 'I'm sure you can appreciate we have work to do, so if you'll excuse me.'

Chrissie tried again. 'At least think about what I said.'

Jamie put the coffees on the bar and gave Roxanne a questioning look.

Chrissie gave up. 'You know where I am if you change your mind. And I really hope you will.'

Roxanne gave her an icy smile. 'I appreciate the offer but it's a no from me.' Her words dripped with sarcasm.

Chrissie held her gaze for a moment before striding away, her heels making a rat-a-tat sound on the dance floor.

Jamie said, 'What was that all about?'

Roxanne ignored him and went back to checking the stock behind the bar.

When she got in her car, Chrissie screamed at her dashboard and slammed the steering wheel. What had Rick expected would happen? Why did she agree to this? It was ridiculous. She couldn't help but wonder again if there was a voicemail at home waiting for her from Scott, or maybe she'd wake up in the morning and find him in the shower like Pam Ewing did with Bobby in *Dallas* . . . finding it was all a bad dream. She was kidding herself and she knew it.

There had been no reply from Carly, no sign of Anita and now a flat-out *fuck you* from that bitch Roxanne. How the hell was she supposed to get the band back together?

And what would happen to her if she failed?

9

'This is the Rome trip we're talking about? October 1987, when "Wicked Way" was at number one in the UK?' Kristen Kent made a note to dig out the cuttings and double-check everything. 'You're saying they came to blows in the dressing room – proper fisticuffs?'

'Full-blown catfight. Blood and everything.'

Kristen Kent raised an eyebrow.

'Chrissie had just had a root perm, even though she'd been told not to. The trend back then was big hair, the bigger the better, but perms were tricky to get right and once you'd had one, you were stuck with it. I mean, it was *permanent*. The girls had someone – Amy – who did their hair. She *hated* perms. You could get the same effect with a bit of backcombing – hairpieces, heated rollers, that kind of thing. So, Amy told the girls to *never ever* have one. Course, you couldn't tell Chrissie anything. She did what she wanted and to hell with the consequences. I mean, Amy was only the hair stylist – what did she know? Chrissie always knew better.'

'She was . . . *superior*, if you know what I mean. Thought the world revolved around her. Didn't care who she trampled on, who got hurt, as long as she got what she wanted.'

Kristen Kent smiled. It was what people said about her.

She had agreed to do the interviews for the Thunder Girls book at her place since Jack, paranoid about the project leaking out ahead of publication, and determined to protect the identity of his secret source, had vetoed using a room at the record company. Nor was the home of the source any good. 'Too risky,' Jack had said. 'Someone might see you coming and going.'

In the end, Kristen reluctantly suggested her own apartment. Located on the top floor of a riverside block in south London, access was via an underground car park and a lift that could only be operated with a code. Perfect for anyone not wanting to be seen.

She'd eyed up the woman lounging across from her on the sofa, feet tucked under her bottom. No make-up, long hair that looked like a wig. Tracksuit pants. Oversized sweatshirt. Glasses with thick black frames. In contrast, Kristen was in her usual pinstripe trousers and crisp white shirt. She sat ramrod-straight and formidable-looking in a high-backed chair.

When Kristen first saw her, she had felt a wave of disappointment. Somehow she had expected the Thunder Girls' secret mole to be more . . . dramatic. If the woman's unremarkable appearance was anything to go on, the book was going to be pretty boring, she decided.

'Call me Kimberley,' the mole said. If that was the best fake name she could do, Kristen thought the book was doomed.

But Kimberley was now beginning to change Kristen's mind.

'So, she had the perm,' Kimberley was saying. 'Disaster! She was stuck with all these tight little curls that wouldn't drop.' She giggled. 'She looked like a poodle. A proper Kevin Keegan! Poor Amy had to rescue it. So, in Rome, Anita was going to have her long-awaited fringe done. Then Chrissie got to Amy first and once she was in the chair she wouldn't shift. Anita went mental. So, eventually she was sorted, but by then there was no time left for Anita. She had a few heated rollers bunged in and had to make do. Course, she had a right go at Chrissie, who said it didn't matter because no one would be looking at Anita anyway. Said something like, "What's the big deal? You're the *drums*, get over it." The way she said *drums* made it sound like a dirty word. That's when Anita flipped. Got hold of her – by the *hair* – and pulled her off her feet. Landed a couple of slaps, gave her a bloody nose, before Rick waded in and pulled them apart.'

She smiled at the memory.

Kristen Kent checked the red lights on her recorders, keen to make sure she was getting it all. Well, well. The Thunder Girls were proving to be quite a revelation.

Kristen had never been a fan of the band. They struck her as a bit on the tame side. Not edgy enough. She preferred The Bangles. Heart. From what she remembered – and the press clippings from the record company archive seemed to back her up – the girls had a wholesome, best-friends-forever image. Going on about how they were there for each other. More like sisters than bandmates. Family, blah, blah. And even after the split none of Carly, Roxanne or Anita had done any interviews to confirm the speculation that Chrissie's exit had fucked them all over. Her own personal experience of Chrissie had proved she was as fake as her press releases. But according to this blow-by-blow account – literally – of someone who was there and saw it all, the hype was nothing like the reality and the dirt much darker.

She finished her coffee. 'What happened next?' Kristen asked.

'Well, it was a live telly show, lots of bands performing, but the bust-up meant the girls weren't ready to go on when they were supposed to, obviously. They had to get Chrissie cleaned up first – make-up redone, hair. New outfit, since the one she was supposed to wear had blood all over it.' She looked thoughtful. 'It was on loan from some designer and the stylist who'd borrowed it practically had a breakdown. We've got stills of the girls on stage and you can tell the styling's all wrong, that Chrissie's the odd one out. Liz, the make-up girl, gave her a white Adam Ant-style stripe across her nose to try and hide the swelling.' She had another think. 'Anyway, they had to push the girls further down the running order, which meant Bros had to go on early. Carly took over lead vocals and the director was told to avoid close-ups of Chrissie, due to her "nosebleed". It was Rome, luckily, so the UK audience didn't see it and nothing ever got out.' She shrugged and tucked a stray piece of hair behind her ear. 'There were quite a few fights, if you're interested. Like the time Chrissie gave Carly a split lip when they were rehearsing for *Top of the Pops* . . .'

Kristen Kent could hardly believe what she was hearing. Who'd have guessed life behind the scenes with the world's number one girl band was a total bitchfest? And to think, she had worried *Thunder Girls Uncut* would be dull.

When Jack Raven first approached her about doing a tell-all book Kristen was sceptical, questioning how good the material could possibly be. How much did Kimberley have to say – and would any of it set the world alight? She had her doubts. Kristen was picky about the projects she took on. She was at the top of her game and intended to stay there. Anything that wouldn't get her front page exclusives got the elbow. When she voiced her concerns to Jack he told her not to worry. Kimberley was the real deal, he said. She had the inside track as well as an axe to grind. When it came to spilling the beans she would not hold back.

Even so, Kristen had not expected so much from the first session.

Already, she was thinking about how she would take the Rome punch-up and embellish it. Ripped clothing. Clumps of hair yanked out, that sort of thing. Expletive-filled dialogue. Thanks to her source, she now knew that, in private, the clean-cut Thunder Girls certainly lived up to their name.

'I almost forgot,' Kimberley said. 'There was a barney over one of the dancers as well. Anita had her eye on this guy, Desi. Amazing-looking – Michael Hutchence meets the good-looking one from Brother Beyond, if you can imagine that. He was paired with Anita and they were all over each other in rehearsals. Everyone knew she fancied him. So, when they got to Rome and checked into the hotel she got the girl from the record company to put her in the room next to his. She had it all worked out.

'You could see her over dinner eyeing him up, practically drooling. Enough to put you off your food. She went to the loo and when she got back he wasn't at the table. No one really noticed until Chrissie slipped out and didn't come back. Desi was still missing. Eventually, Anita went looking and found the pair of them in the restaurant's linen cupboard – Chrissie was enjoying her main course and it wasn't vegetarian, if you catch my drift.'

Kristen Kent's jaw fell open.

'I know. Everyone goes on about Boris Becker bonking in a broom cupboard but I'm pretty sure Chrissie was the first. No one ever found out, though, that's the thing.'

Kristen blinked. The light on one of her recorders was

flashing. She put up a hand to stop Kimberley for a moment and changed the batteries.

'You're okay putting all this on the record?' she asked.

Kimberley shrugged. 'Why not? It's my chance to get my own back.'

10

Chrissie's heart hammered in her chest. She was half awake, half asleep, dreaming about Scott. The two of them in bed, Chrissie in the saucy lingerie he had bought her for her birthday – the front-fastening bra and lacy knickers. Stockings. Scott had a thing about stockings. He was on his side facing her, stroking the bare skin at the top of her leg, telling her he had never seen her look so beautiful. Her insides were liquid. As his hand slid across her middle she held her breath. Seconds ticked by. Nothing happened. She reached for him and he pulled away. She woke with a start to find Andy beside her – one arm flung across his chest, snoring. Despite what Scott had done, she missed him. Bastard that he was. For a moment, she lay watching Andy, his chest rising and falling, making small grunting sounds.

Her dream had put her in the mood for some serious shagging; reverse cowgirl would be a nice way to start the day but her randy thoughts were soon derailed by her phone emitting a high-pitched whistle alerting her to message after message, no doubt from Rick. He'd been breathing down her neck constantly, wanting updates on the Thunder Girls. It was infuriating. And a real passion killer. How was she supposed to be seductive with all that going on?

She flung back the duvet and got up.

Rick had left a series of messages, each one more impatient-sounding than the rest. 'I could do with an update, Chrissie,' he said. 'Where are you with the other girls? Have you spoken to Roxanne yet? What about Anita – do you know where she is? I keep coming up blank. Dig deep, think back to the last time you heard what she was up to. I need an update, as fast as you can. Just get back to me, will you?'

She made a face at the phone and deleted the messages. Almost at once, it started ringing. Rick. He might as well have her tagged.

'Don't you have anything better to do than suck the life out of me?' she snapped.

'Trust me, there are plenty of things I'd rather be doing with my time,' he told her. 'What's happening with the girls?'

Chrissie groaned. If she told Rick of her lack of progress – especially the meeting with Roxanne – he'd only be on her case even more. 'I'm on it.'

'I'd like to think so but something tells me you're doing bugger all – dossing about with that so-called private eye.'

She was indignant. 'How dare you!'

'Are you even dressed yet?'

'How I spend my time, and who I choose to spend it with, is none of your business. You don't get to tell me what to do.'

His patience was running out. 'You need to get off that self-obsessed peachy arse of yours right now and make this reunion happen.'

Chrissie gasped. 'Who the hell do you think you're talking to?'

'It's time to grow up, Chrissie. You're a woman of fifty, not some wet-behind-the-ears kid – so stop acting like one.'

'I can't believe you said that.' Chrissie's voice shook.

'Said what?'

'The *F-word*.'

'I didn't!'

'*Fifty*. You said I was *fifty*!'

'You *are* fifty! You should think yourself lucky. Some people don't make it that far. Now listen to me. At the risk of repeating myself, this is a once in a lifetime – and pretty bloody well-timed – opportunity here to reform the Thunder Girls and save yourself from this mess you have got yourself into. So get on with it.'

Silence.

'Rick,' she said eventually, her voice small, 'do you really think I've got a peachy arse?'

Chrissie swept through Spitalfields Market, on a mission, in her Prada fur-trimmed coat (rabbit, she discovered, after she had bought it). It was a risk wearing the coat. The last time she was out in it some girl with piercings on her face and a DIY haircut had hurled abuse at her for wearing real fur. Called her a callous old bag.

It was the old bit that had bothered Chrissie.

A few months earlier she had been at the market, shopping at an organic skin care stall that had got rave reviews in a couple of the glossies, and as she handed over her credit card someone tapped her on the shoulder, making her jump. Spinning round, she found what she thought was a homeless person standing a bit too close for her liking and fumbled in her purse for some loose change.

'Hey, Chrissie,' the homeless man said. 'I thought it was you. God, you still look amazing.'

She blinked. 'Oh . . . thanks.'

He put his head on one side. Scruffy beard, nice teeth, clear grey eyes. Something about the eyes was vaguely familiar.

'You don't remember me, do you?' He looked amused.

She was thrown. 'Sorry. I'm hopeless with names.'

'Brett. We met in Glasgow, 1988. When you girls were on tour.' He gave her a sheepish look. 'I was with Anita.'

The penny dropped. Glasgow Brett. Chrissie gave him an uncertain smile. God, he had really gone to seed. 'Yes!' She tried to sound pleased. 'Of course, I remember. What are you up to these days?'

He gestured vaguely behind him. 'I've got a stall here selling vintage stuff. Doing really well, actually. I live round the corner.'

Not homeless, then. She chatted for a minute or two. He wondered if she ever heard from Anita. She had gone quiet since she took off after *Eurovision*, he said. Just the odd postcard. Chrissie, keen to get away, wasn't really listening. When he had suggested she have a look at his stall she made an excuse about being late for a meeting and then fled. Glasgow Brett! Shit. As she fled, memories of the girls playing two nights in Glasgow came back to her. Anita turning up with Brett, a struggling muso. Chrissie bumping into him on the tour bus later when no one was about and shagging him. It was nothing, a quickie, and Anita never found out, although she definitely had her suspicions. To think she'd slept with someone who looked like he should be begging made her physically retch.

Now, as she prowled the length and breadth of Spitalfields, searching for Glasgow Brett's vintage stall again, she tried to put the memory out of her head and remember exactly what he had said about Anita. She wished she had paid more attention now. Been a bit nicer. Rick was always saying it cost nothing to be nice. Personally, she had never seen the point.

As she scanned the stalls it struck her that Chloe Booth's Skin Guru salon was not a million miles away. Once she had finished with Glasgow Brett she might just make a detour and drop in. Throw a massive strop in reception. Complain that one of Chloe's products had sent her skin haywire and she'd been in hospital for weeks having her face repaired by a top dermatologist. A *proper*, *qualified* expert. With luck, one or two of her precious A-list clients might be about. The Duchess, perhaps. Ha! She smiled. Tempting. One day she would see to it that Chloe got her comeuppance. Just not today.

She had examined almost every inch of the market and was beginning to wonder why people were always going on about how wonderful Spitalfields was. It was a bit too – what was the word? – *gritty*, for her liking. As she wandered on, an old-fashioned stereo stack system caught her eye. Like the one she'd had in the Eighties. She took a closer look and a voice she recognized said, 'Chrissie!'

She turned and flashed Glasgow Brett a dazzling smile. 'This takes me back,' she said, at once regretting her choice of words. God, she sounded ancient!

'Lovely, isn't it? Everyone had these at one time. Hard to believe how long they've been around.' He smiled, apologetic. 'Course, you probably know more about the iconic Sony system than I do, being a pop star and all that.'

She shrugged, not interested in getting into a tedious technical discussion.

He gave her a shy smile. 'It's good to see you again. You look incredible. You really haven't changed a bit.'

She gave him a suspicious look but as far as she could tell he was being genuine.

'Seriously, what's your secret? Whatever you're on, I want some of it,' he said.

She considered recommending the yak butter tea, the only thing she ever owned up to. As for the skin peels, laser treatments, fillers, Botox, oxygen facials, endless tweaks and surgical procedures she relied on – not to mention the bio-dynamic whatnots she got from a sweet little man on Harley Street – she never divulged any of it.

'I look after myself,' she said.

'I can see that.' He gazed at her in awe. 'Anyway, what brings you to this neck of the woods? I always had you down as more of a Westbourne Grove girl. Primrose Hill. Hampstead. Sloane Square.'

'I cut through here sometimes,' she said. 'I'm glad I bumped into you. I was thinking it would be nice to catch up. Properly. Any chance you could leave the stall for a bit and we could grab a drink somewhere?'

A minute later they were on their way out of the market and heading for Shoreditch House. Chrissie had her fingers crossed the Prada coat would be enough to get them in, because, even by hipster-London standards, practically everything about Glasgow Brett, from his scruffy sneakers to his dropping-to-bits denims, violated the dress code.

11

Kristen Kent made coffee and tipped a few Hobnobs from the biscuit tin onto a plate. Kimberley had a sweet tooth, she had discovered.

In the living room, the Thunder Girls mole stood at the window gazing at the river, where a cruiser chugged past in the direction of Westminster. A rowing boat crewed by a team of eight in identical blue vests was going the other way, oars slicing the water in unison. 'Reminds me to tell you about the time Carly nearly died in the Thames,' she said, when Kristen came into the room.

'You're kidding.'

Kimberley got comfy on the sofa and helped herself to a Hobnob. 'On the South Bank, not far from where the Design Museum used to be. It was a photo shoot for the cover of the second album, one of those mad early calls, not quite light, no one about.'

'Christ Almighty, what happened?'

'Chrissie kind of bumped her and . . . splash, she was in.'

'On purpose?'

Kimberley raised her eyebrow. 'An "accident", Chrissie said. One of the photographer's assistants went in after her. Did I say – she couldn't swim?' She brushed crumbs from the front of her top and reached for another biscuit. 'So, the two of them were bobbing about, Carly thrashing, dragging the poor lad under, the pair of them swallowing mouthfuls of filthy river water, the rest of us on the side, gawping. No one had the faintest idea what to do. Rick chucked a lifebuoy in but they couldn't get hold of it. I remember thinking, *They've had it*. I mean, it was March, and the water was freezing.' She gave Kristen an odd smile. 'I really thought they were goners.'

'Didn't anyone dial 999?'

'God, no. No one wanted to get the police involved. The press would have been all over it. Jack would have hit the roof.'

'But she might have drowned! The lad as well!'

Kimberley nodded. Through a mouthful of biscuit she said, 'Then someone dangled one of those pole things in the water and managed to drag them out.' She sank back into the sofa.

Kristen glanced at the recorders on the coffee table. Reached over and pushed them closer to Kimberley. The sudden mournful blast of a horn on the river below made her jump.

Kimberley looked pointedly at the empty biscuit plate.

Kristen paused the recorders and went into the kitchen.

Something about Kimberley bothered her. She was . . . *creepy*. Dead behind the eyes, almost. The way she had described Carly Hughes landing in the Thames and almost drowning, without a trace of emotion, was borderline psychopathic. Even Kristen, who prided herself on being tough, had shuddered at the thought of a non-swimmer fighting for her life in the icy river.

The kettle boiled and she warmed the coffee pot, took clean mugs from the cupboard and opened a fresh packet of biscuits.

When she turned round she almost dropped the tray. Kimberley had come into the kitchen without a word and was in front of the fridge peering at the photos and paraphernalia that decorated it. She looked up. 'Sorry, did I give you a fright? My mum said I was like a cat, padding about, not making a sound. Always creeping up on her, I was. It freaked her out.' She went back into the sitting room. Silently.

Kristen was having serious second thoughts about doing the interview sessions at home. She guarded her privacy and in the past had been adamant her place was off-limits. For the same reason she never accepted invitations to stay over with whoever she was working with. For both parties, it was important to have boundaries, she reasoned.

Going back a few years, a pushy actress rattling around on her own in a mansion miles from anywhere had insisted Kristen take the guest room rather than booking into a hotel. It turned out to be a mistake. The next morning, the woman came into Kristen's room before she was properly awake and got into bed with her. The memory still made her shudder.

By letting Kimberley into her home, she had broken her own cardinal rule.

'I love your place, by the way,' Kimberley said, nestling back into the sofa. 'I looked at something similar before I bought my flat. Wish I'd gone for that one now. There's something soothing about the river. Maybe you could let me know if anything comes on the market here . . .'

Kristen fiddled with the recorders. She would speak to Jack. Say it wasn't working out doing the sessions at home. He would have to think of somewhere else.

'Right,' she said, sounding brisk. 'That day on the South Bank, was Carly drunk? On drugs?'

Kimberley shook her head. 'Definitely not drugs. She never touched them.' She snapped a biscuit in two. 'Anita was the druggie.'

Kristen blinked. She had not anticipated such a seamless switch from drowning to drug-taking and scribbled a note on her pad to come back to the Thames episode later.

'It was on one of the Berlin trips when she lost the plot,' Kimberley explained. 'We were there for one of those TV specials – mostly European bands, a couple from the UK.' She shook her head. 'You could see something was up. Anita was wired, moody as hell – all over the place. Some poor journalist from one of the German rags asked if it was true she was seeing the drummer from Curiosity Killed the Cat, which was fair enough since she'd been snapped the week before coming out of a club with him – but Anita went mental. Remember Björk and that photographer a few years back? Well, that was nothing. Anita *broke* the poor girl's front teeth, she had to be dragged off her. Minutes before, she'd been holed up in the plane loo for an hour. Of course, it's obvious now, all that locking herself in the loo stuff, that she was on cocaine . . . but at the time we just thought the whole fame thing had gone to her head and turned her into a bit of a diva.'

'So what happened?' asked Kristen.

'Well, later that day, the girls were in the wings, waiting to go on, when Anita said she needed the loo again,' Kimberley said. 'Rick told her she'd have to wait but Anita had claimed she was on her period, to which Chrissie had made some comment, in front of the whole crew, about Anita being the only woman she knew who shoved white things up her nose instead of *downstairs* when Mother Nature called. Humiliated, Anita locked herself in the toilets again and refused to come out. When she failed to come back the others went on without her.'

'Wow.'

'Rick made up some story, claimed she'd been ill all day, throwing up,' Kimberley said. 'Nasty stomach bug. The executive producer was muttering about legal action until Rick pointed out she'd been fine until she scoffed a prawn cocktail from the buffet backstage. That shut the guy up.'

Kimberley continued to recount the events of that day to Kristen. It had taken Rick a while to track Anita down. She wasn't in the Thunder Girls' dressing room, nor in any of the dressing rooms on their corridor. He checked the entire backstage area before going into the yard where some of the tour buses were parked up. It was quiet, no one about, just a few roadies smoking weed, one in a Bon Jovi T-shirt leaning against the wall. He jerked his thumb in the direction of another band's tour bus.

'The blinds were down – that dark glass you can't see through,' Kimberley said. 'But the bus was rocking ever so slightly, a sight Rick knew only too well. He presses the door-release button and goes in. Gets to the top deck and the little lounge bit at the back and finds a heap of bodies – Anita starkers in the middle of a group of roadies. I mean, it was an orgy! Lines of coke everywhere.' She started laughing. 'Priceless.' Her face darkened. 'Not that drugs are a laughing matter. I wouldn't want to give that impression.' Her voice took on a mocking tone. 'Kids, do not try this at home.' Another peel of hideous laughter.

Kristen Kent scribbled on her pad, underlining it with a fierce stroke that almost went through the page. *Mad bitch*.

She didn't mean Anita.

12

'I'm not going,' Chrissie said. 'I can't do it.'

Rick held her gaze. 'You have to.'

'What's happened to you? When did you get so narky and nasty?' She yanked a lever on the espresso machine. 'Are you having some sort of mid-life crisis – going through the *man*opause? There *is* such a thing, you know. It's well documented. I was reading about it in one of the glossies not so long ago, men bleating on about falling testosterone levels and feeling less virile. Apparently *some* men, once they realize they're no longer the strong and powerful creatures they once were, become vile bullies.' She gave him a pointed look.

Rick flushed. He wasn't about to tell her that the notion of a mid-life crisis had gone through his mind only the week before when he placed an order for the Harley-Davidson he had always wanted.

Chrissie dumped a cup of coffee on the counter in front

of him, slopping it in the saucer, and plonked herself on a stool. Everything about her radiated indignation.

'Aren't you having one?' Rick said.

'I'm having tea,' she snapped. 'A special de-stressing blend.'

He sniffed the air. 'I wondered what that horrible smell was.'

She gave him a poisonous look. 'I've done what you asked and tracked down Anita. And believe me, it wasn't easy. Or pleasant, for that matter.'

She had suffered two of the most boring hours of her life with Glasgow Brett in Shoreditch House. Been stared at by members appalled to see such a scruffy-looking oik in their midst. It was utterly humiliating. Just getting him into the place was a nightmare, Chrissie having to bung the girl on reception a massive tip to look the other way. Still, at least it was Rick's money. Glasgow Brett definitely had the wrong idea of why he was there. The way he carried on it was clear he was hoping for a repeat performance of the memory that made her shudder. She felt bile rise in her throat as he kept pawing her – enjoying a drink, when all Chrissie wanted was to find out where Anita was hiding and get the hell out of there. Preferably, before one of Chloe Booth's A-listers came in and saw her. That really would have been the icing on the cake.

Glasgow Brett seemed to need to put a hand on her arm for emphasis whenever he told her something. It was all she could do to refrain from punching him in the face. Every time she brought up Anita and where she was living these days he steered the conversation back to Chrissie and what *she* was doing. Had he not paid any attention to the (still positive, thankfully) coverage about her and Scott?

Presumably not, because then he asked if she was single. Oh God, he thought he stood a *chance* with her! By the time she managed to drag it out of him that Anita was running a bar in some remote spot on the coast in Brazil – a place Chrissie had never heard of – she was losing the will to live. The moment she got what she wanted, she went to the loo, tapped the info into her phone and emailed it to herself, then left without bothering to say goodbye to Glasgow Brett.

She slapped a Post-it note on the counter in front of Rick and tapped it with a bright pink nail. She'd had to make do with a nail-bar manicure but the girl had done a reasonable job. 'Here,' she said. 'Anita's in some beachy spot miles from anywhere. We're not talking Marbella or Capri, or even Ibiza. No – bloody deepest, darkest, off the main tracks Brazil.' She peered at the note. 'Miles from anywhere, apparently. There's no way I can go. You know I can't cope with mosquitoes.'

Rick studied the address. 'I know this place,' he said. 'I went not far from there once on a Sting tour. You can fly to Rio and then a small boat takes you up the coast.' He smiled. 'Think of it as a holiday.'

'I've just *got back from my supposed honeymoon* – and a small boat trip?! You know I get seasick on anything less than a five-hundred-foot yacht.'

He gave her a searing look. 'Chrissie, *you* have to go and see her.'

'Why can't you go?' Chrissie snarled, losing her cool. She knew they kept having the same argument, but she hoped each time the answer might be different.

'Because it's got to come from *you*. I know I played my part but it's not me they want to hear an "I'm sorry" from – it's you and you know it.'

She swallowed. She knew he was right but after crawling to Roxanne she was in no mood to go down the begging route with Anita. Especially when it meant flying halfway round the world.

Arguing with Rick wasn't working so she tried a different tack. She concentrated, sniffed and worked really hard to conjure up a tear. Nothing. She was a singer, not an actress. Frustrated, she shook her head dramatically. 'I can't, I'm at breaking point. What if Scott comes back and I'm not here?' She gave him a pleading look.

'Scott. Isn't. Coming. Back,' Rick said slowly.

Neither of them spoke for a moment.

'What about Randy Andy? Have you got shot of him yet?'

Chrissie stared at the floor. She wasn't about to tell Rick she had walked in on Andy FaceTiming some little slut for sex – in *her* bed! – when he was supposed to be checking the Automatic Number-Plate Recognition database (whatever that was) for clues to Scott's whereabouts. She had dragged him down the stairs in his boxers and chucked him out. Hurled his stuff onto the drive then burst into tears as soon as she had slammed the door. Why was she such an easy touch for men these days? She'd always been the one in control; suddenly she felt every one of her years. Rick softened his tone.

'Look, if I thought it would help I would come with you but I can't get away,' he told her. 'I've got too much on my plate here. You've no idea how much has to be done to make this reunion happen. Jack's listed it as our top priority. He keeps hauling me into the office for meetings about a new album, merchandise, you name it. And apart from the Thunder Girls, right now he's also got me working on some charity collaborations – he wants one of Little Mix, Claire from Steps, and . . .' He frowned. 'And someone from McBusted to do a song for some injured whales – and I'm not even joking.' Chrissie rolled her eyes.

'So, trust me, he does *not* want to hear about problems – just that the Thunder Girls are back together. Trust me, I am not trying to bring you down but *you* need to do this.' He sighed. 'Remember, I'm paying your bills, and that's based on the reunion dosh. So no *Rock Legends* gig and you lose the house. It's as blunt as that.'

Chrissie stared at him. 'You'd make me homeless?'

'I didn't get you into this mess, Chrissie. Remember I paid for half this house originally and since it was you that got to keep it when *you* divorced *me* I think I'm being pretty bloody good trying to keep you afloat.' He looked around, his gaze drawn to an enormous display of fresh flowers. One of several dotted around the house. 'And while we're down to brass tacks, when I said I'd cover essentials that did not extend to flower arrangements courtesy of some overpriced London florist.'

'Those *are* essential – for my well-being. And for all you know, Scott *might* still come back.' Despite herself, she clung to the flimsy hope his disappearance might be down to unexplained memory loss, like an old episode of *Dynasty* she remembered. Or perhaps an accident, right after he had invested all of their money somewhere brilliantly lucrative.

A wave of defensiveness over Scott surged through her. She glared at Rick, who was shaking his head in frustration and anger.

'For God's sake! How many more times? Scott. Is. Gone.'

She hated the fact that she knew he was right.

Rick was tapping away on his phone. 'Now, I've had just about enough of this so you listen to me – you're going to Brazil and you *will* persuade Anita to come back and join the re-formed Thunder Girls for the Wembley gig and that's that.' More tapping.

She gazed at him. 'You could at least look at me,' she muttered.

'I'm busy sorting your flights,' he said without looking up. 'Right, all done. I suggest you pack. You leave tonight.'

She folded her arms. 'Fine, have it your own way. But if I come back with Ebola or Zika or something, I'm blaming you. And I am *not* flying economy.'

13

The taxi pulled up in front of a small clapboard hotel on the corner of a dusty street. Chrissie gave it a dubious look and fished her travel itinerary from her bag. Beach Drift. Going on the name, she had imagined somewhere modern. One of those swish boutique hotels with in-room spa treatments and access to a private beach. Rick knew her needs, after all.

Yet this place looked to be on its last legs. Paint peeling off, lopsided shutters, garden like a jungle. And nowhere near the beach, as far as she could tell.

Reluctantly, she got out of the car and was met with a steamy, sticky heat. She knew straight away her blow-dry was fucked. And she had a crick in her neck from the flight. That bastard Rick *had* put her in economy, after all.

On either side of the hotel were dilapidated houses, one with a half-built extension choked by weeds. Further along the street, gaudy beach dresses and straw hats hung from a rail outside a shop. Opposite, music boomed from a bar where a noisy game of cards was underway. In among shouts and whoops came the sound of a bottle breaking. She caught a whiff of marijuana.

She considered getting her driver, a cheerful sort with gold teeth and broken English, to take her to the nearest Hilton or Marriott, or whatever Brazil had, but he was already dumping her bags at the side of the road. No pavement as such, she noticed. A scruffy dog ambled over from the bar, stopping every couple of steps to have a scratch. She was going to kill Rick – if she survived this.

'Is this the right place?' she asked, trying not to sound as desperate as she felt, but the driver was already back in the car starting the engine, and didn't answer.

She didn't dare leave her belongings in the street so lugged them up the steps and into the hotel, sweat trickling down her back. She was regretting wearing one of her good Self-portrait dresses. The heels had been a bad idea too.

She found herself in a dimly lit lobby. Wood-panelled walls, an old-fashioned grandfather clock. Fishing nets hanging from the ceiling. A ship's figurehead. No one about. She banged the brass bell on the desk. It emitted a faint ding. Cursing, she whacked it several times. 'Bloody dive! Service!'

From below the desk, a head bobbed into view. An imperious-looking woman in a green and gold turban and floaty kaftan fixed Chrissie with large brown eyes. She was holding a screwdriver.

'Can I help you?'

Chrissie jumped. 'Sorry, I didn't . . . were you there the whole time? I . . . I didn't think anybody . . .'

'Hmm. English lady.' The woman ran a finger down the page of a thick ledger. 'Room 1. Top of the stairs.' She produced an old-fashioned key and placed it on the desk.

Chrissie glanced at her luggage. She had brought too much and the bags were heavy. Rick had told her to travel light and she had done her best but, as far as she was concerned, two suitcases *was* travelling light. She started to ask if there was someone to help with her bags but when she looked up the woman was no longer there. She leaned over the reception desk. Called out a tentative 'Hello . . . ?' No reply. Defeated, she hauled the cases up two flights of stairs, one at a time.

She showered and changed into a pair of wide-legged Joseph trousers and a Victoria Beckham T-shirt. Put on the flip-flops she had bought at the airport and ditched her favourite Cartier shades for a pair of tortoiseshell Ray-bans. Her idea of dressing down. Slinging a few things into a Chanel tote that had cost more than her plane ticket and was the closest thing she had to a casual bag, she slicked on a gooey layer of lip gloss.

Downstairs, the woman in the turban was back behind reception, dismantling what looked like a radio. Chrissie asked if she could phone for a taxi to the Sea View Bar. The woman laughed. 'Go left, left and left,' she said, gesturing with the screwdriver. 'Two minutes.' Chrissie looked dubious. 'Go, go,' the woman said, coming out from behind the desk and propelling her towards the door.

Chrissie turned left, as instructed, feeling several pairs of curious eyes from the bar across the road on her. Someone whistled. Laughter. More whistling. The scrawny dog she had seen earlier got to its feet and trotted beside her. She hurried along. Two women on a veranda, chopping up what looked like a carcass of some kind, stopped what they were doing and stared as she went past. A skinny boy in a football shirt came skipping up and tried to hold her hand. She batted him away. At the corner she turned left again and was relieved to find the Sea View up ahead. Thank God. A few more yards. Before she got to where she was going, two guys appeared out of nowhere, one after another, and hit on her.

By the time she reached her destination she was thoroughly frazzled.

The only customer in the bar was a gnarled man in a paint-spattered shirt and baseball cap who gave her a wink. She swept past without acknowledging him and went to sit at a table on the other side of the room. To her annoyance, the dog settled itself at her feet. She took in her surroundings. Rickety wooden tables. Hard chairs. Everything painted in clashing colours. What a dump. The worst bar she had ever been in. It didn't even have four walls! An open-air bar? The sea breeze could only be so refreshing and it had to wreck your hair. If Anita was holed up here, she had to be in a bad way. No one would choose to live in such a place. Chrissie had a horrible sinking feeling. What if she had come all this way for nothing? From what Glasgow Brett had said, it was a while since he'd heard from Anita. She could be anywhere by now.

Feeling depressed, she reached into her bag for her phone and started a text to Rick, saying she'd had a wasted journey and was coming straight back. *Assuming I make it out of this hell-hole alive*, she wrote. She went to click send but had no signal, so she threw her phone into her bag and was looking for her lip gloss when she felt someone standing over her.

'Hi, there. Can I get you a drink?'

She looked up to see Anita. At least it *looked* like Anita. Not the manic, coke-addled version who'd shown herself up on telly, which was the last time Chrissie had seen her. This version was a picture of health. Masses of hair in soft beachy waves. Not a scrap of make-up. Short shorts, bikini top, golden limbs. Strings of shells around her neck. Like some kind of sea nymph. All of a sudden, Chrissie, head to toe in designer gear, felt a touch overdressed. The new Anita was peering at her uncertainly. Chrissie took off her shades. The glossy lips parted in a wide smile and Anita's hand flew to her mouth. Beneath the tan she seemed to go pale. As if she had seen a ghost.

'Chrissie?' She took a step back. 'Shit! How the . . . what on earth are *you* doing here?'

'I've come to see *you*, of course!' She got up and planted a sticky kiss on her cheek. 'God, Anita, I'm so pleased to see you – I can barely believe it!'

Anita was shaking her head. 'I don't understand. No one knows I'm here.' She looked ready to do a runner.

'And I haven't told a soul,' Chrissie lied. 'Hand on heart. No one else knows where you are and I'm not about to blow your cover, I promise. I just had to see you. Something amazing has happened.'

Anita frowned.

'Let's sit down and I'll tell you all about it.' Another dazzling smile. 'It is *so* good to see you. You've no idea how much I've missed you.'

Anita blinked. 'Yeah, right!'

'I mean it. I've always wanted to get in touch with you, but at first I thought I'd let the dust settle after the Thunder break-up and what happened to you at . . . well, you know.' Anita looked away. 'But, well, by the time I tried to reach out you'd disappeared. Gone, in a puff of smoke. No one knew where you were – you vanished.' Chrissie reached for her hand. 'I understand why, of course, as a fellow performer, I know how awful you must have felt. I couldn't help thinking what I'd have done if . . . well, that, you know, had happened to me, on live telly. All those people watching. I felt for you, really I did.' She caught Anita's look. 'Anyway, that's all in the past so let's not dwell, because here you are, living the dream in your own little corner of paradise – and looking phenomenal, by the way.'

Anita was watching her closely. 'Thanks. I'm happy. No stress. All that pop star bullshit we went through nearly killed me.'

Now Chrissie was frowning. 'It wasn't all bad though, was it? I mean, we had some good times, didn't we?'

Anita held her gaze. 'Did we? And what's with this Thunder Girls *break-up*? I seem to remember it was actually just you fucking us all off so you could go solo. No warning, no apologies, no Thunder Girls break-up, as you just put it – just you flouncing off leaving us in the shit.'

'Look, I don't—' Chrissie started to say but Anita cut her off.

'So, when I think back – which I try not to – it's not so much good times that come to mind as a whole heap of shitty stuff, including that time you humiliated me in front of everybody when you knew I was struggling with my *problems*.'

Chrissie was going to have to work hard to talk her round. 'I'm sorry. I know a lot of bad things went on back then but it is thirty years ago, I'm a different person. It's not too late to rewrite our memories,' she said.

'You can't change the past.' It was what the therapist had told Anita after the TV debacle.

'No, but we *can* learn from it,' Chrissie countered. She had got that from a self-help book. 'Do things differently.'

'Definitely. Which is why I'm living here, in the middle of nowhere, about as far away from the whole crazy fame thing and *the past* as it's possible to get.'

Chrissie took hold of her hands. 'I get it, I really do, but wait for this. We've got a chance to play *Wembley Stadium*! Remember, we always talked about it – *dreamed* of it? Well, there's a monster gig coming up, a big Eighties revival thing, and they want *us* to open. Anita, *babes*, this is a one-off. We'll never get a chance like this again. We *have* to do it.'

'I don't follow. What exactly are you saying?'

Chrissie gave her a broad smile. 'A Thunder Girls reunion, of course. The four of us back together. The only all-girl act on the bill. It's huge.'

Anita smiled. 'You're asking me to be part of the Thunder Girls again?'

'We can't do it without you.'

Anita laughed. 'Chrissie, you're asking the impossible. My life is here. I'm happy. I don't need all that shit.'

Chrissie was nodding. 'I know, I get it. I felt the same.' Another lie. 'But we owe it to ourselves, and the fans. One last show. A biggie. Plus, we're talking big money.'

Anita shrugged. 'I've got enough to get by on.'

'Please. Come back with me. We need you – all of us. You're the one who held things together. Think about it, at least – the Thunder Girls is all four of us – don't make us do a Spice Girls and go on without our Posh.'

Anita laughed. 'Me, the missing Posh? Now I know you have lost your mind.'

Chrissie felt annoyed at her choice of analogy – Anita would have preferred to be likened to Geri. Damn. She could sense a *no* coming and tried to head it off. '*Forget* about that for now. Let's have a drink, catch up and hang out together. I'm here for a few days anyway. I'm doing a photo shoot for a magazine on the other side of the island tonight, so maybe tomorrow.' Chrissie hoped Anita couldn't tell she was lying about the shoot – she hated feeling desperate, but hated looking or sounding desperate even more.

'Oh, where are you shooting?' Anita asked.

'Some hotel, you know the type, all palm trees and marble, but anyway, forget that, just think about it overnight.' She stroked her hair. 'I can see being here suits you. You look fab.'

Anita grinned. 'You haven't changed.'

A slender woman with waist-length hair burst through the beaded curtain at the side of the bar. Anita turned towards her. 'Maria, this is—'

'I know what she is,' Maria shouted in a thick Brazilian accent. 'Another of your *putas*.'

She looked Chrissie up and down, eyes blazing. Chrissie looked confused as Maria stormed towards them. Anita went to stand up but Maria was over the bar and between them before she could speak.

'Bitch!' she screamed.

Anita jumped up. 'Maria!' She shot a panicky look at Chrissie.

Chrissie gave the woman a cool look. 'I think you've got the wrong end of the stick, whoever you are.' She shot Anita a questioning look as she said the words with a raised eyebrow and continued, 'Anita and I go way back. We were just about to have a drink. Two Mojitos, if you can manage it.'

'*Escoria!*' Maria shouted, as she grabbed a pitcher of rum punch that was on the bar and emptied it over Chrissie's head. Bits of fruit landed in her hair. Something cold and slimy went down the front of her VB top. She gasped. At her feet, the dog stretched and shook off a pineapple chunk.

Chrissie was reeling. 'What the . . . ?'

Anita jumped between the two women. 'Maria, stop it, it's not what you think—' Before Anita could finish, Maria was trying to wriggle free to have another lunge at Chrissie, whose mouth was still wide open in shock: who was this crazy woman attacking her and what was she to Anita?

'Just go, run, I won't be able to hold her long,' Anita shouted and shot Chrissie an urgent look. 'And please don't come back, Chrissie – I want no part of it.'

Chrissie thought about trying to reason with Anita one more time but as she saw Maria wriggling free of her hold she bolted for the door. She shouted to Anita as she ran. 'I'm at the Beach Drift for the next few days. Come and find me!'

Outside in the street she could still hear Maria shouting. Chrissie surveyed the damage done to her outfit, running her hands through her sticky hair.

'Fuck!'

14

Roxanne had spent half the day in the salon having extensions put in. She couldn't get over how natural they looked. Her hair was fuller, more . . . *swishy*. Like something off a shampoo advert. She tossed her head and the newly luscious locks bounced and fell into tousled, glossy waves. If she'd known how good extensions were she'd have had them done ages ago. The downside was how much they had cost. She almost passed out when she got the bill. Just as well she still had her platinum Amex, although the thought of having to clear the balance at the end of the month was already giving her a headache. Still, she couldn't think about that now.

Her hair wasn't the only thing to have had a makeover. She now had a pair of strong, straight brows. Kelly, who'd done them, claimed shaping and colouring your eyebrows was the equivalent of a mini facelift. Roxanne had been sceptical but the effect really was dramatic. Kelly had done her make-up too. Individual eyelashes, the works. Transporting Roxanne back to the days of the Thunder Girls, when having someone there to ensure you always looked your best went with the territory.

She put on a white shirt tucked into tailored trousers and her best diamond drop earrings. A pair of red Manolo Blahnik slingbacks. It was a look that suited her. Stylish and understated. Not in-your-face designer everything, like a certain someone she could mention. She applied lipstick in a subtle nude shade, dabbed Miss Dior on her wrists and the back of her neck, and checked her reflection in the floor-length mirror.

All of a sudden she felt deflated, certain she was about to walk into a trap.

Something told her the evening was bound to end in tears.

She peered at herself. 'Are you sure you want to do this?'

On the dressing table was a bottle of Prosecco in an ice bucket. She poured herself a glass and swallowed some down.

Another of Chrissie's posh invitations had arrived, this time complete with grovelling handwritten note. *I know I've been a complete cow and I'm sorry. I don't expect you to forgive me but please come to dinner, where we can at least talk. I know the other girls really want to see you.* PLEASE, *Roxy.*

The second *please* was in capitals and underlined several times for emphasis. Roxanne felt briefly tempted to tear the thing up and send it back again, this time with her own handwritten note. Something along the lines of, *What part of NOT INTERESTED don't you understand?* Those few scribbled lines of Chrissie's had got her thinking, though. What could be so important she was willing to beg? And what did she mean about the other girls? As far as she knew, no one had seen or heard from Anita since . . . that dreadful night. Was Chrissie saying they were back in touch? Or was she simply playing games, knowing full well which buttons to press in order to reel Roxanne in? Her stomach tightened. She felt gullible, played. Chrissie always was a manipulative bitch, willing to do whatever it took to get her own way, and here she was, back to her scheming best, making Roxanne dance to her tune.

Well, she could take a running jump.

'Sod it, I'm not going,' she said, reaching for the fizz.

Jamie appeared in the bedroom doorway. 'Just to say the car's coming at quarter-past. And, wow, you look incredible.'

She gave a tight little smile. 'I've changed my mind. I'm not going.'

His face fell. 'Oh, Mum, you can't bail out. You said you'd be there.'

'Well, now I won't, after all. I'll say something's come up. It's all probably a big scam anyway. You don't know Chrissie Martin like I do. There's only one reason she'd come crawling back – because it suits *her*, no one else. Trust me, there's got to be a catch.'

'What if there isn't? At least find out, hear what she's got to say. *Then* decide whether you want to see her again.'

She put a hand to her brow. 'I can't believe I nearly fell for it. God, I must be getting soft. Chrissie Martin clicks her fingers and I go running. I need my head examined.'

The doorbell went. Jamie checked his watch. 'If that's the car, I'll get him to wait.'

'Tell him not to bother.'

She knocked back her fizz and poured another glass.

Jamie called up the stairs. 'Mum, can you come down? Someone to see you.'

As she clattered down the stairs she half expected to fling open the door of the sitting room and find Chrissie waiting there. All that Prosecco had made her light-headed. She imagined telling her exactly what she could do with her pathetic invitation – chucking it in her face. Damn! She had left it upstairs. By the time she strode into the sitting room she was pumped-up, ready to give her old bandmate what-for.

Finding Rick waiting for her was so unexpected she almost passed out. Her legs buckled and she steadied herself against the wall. Rick gazed at her and ran a hand through his hair, the way he always did when he was nervous. She took in the well-cut suit. Shirt, open at the neck. Stray lock of dark hair falling over one eye. Her stomach turned inside out.

He cleared his throat. Another sign of nerves. 'Roxy, it's

good to see you. Sorry to show up without warning, it's just . . .' He gave a helpless shrug and one of those shy, heart-melting smiles that had always made her weak at the knees. 'I thought if I told you I was coming, well, you might not want to see me.'

Jamie appeared with a mug of coffee and handed it to Rick. He gave Roxanne a questioning look. 'Can I get you anything, Mum?'

She shook her head, still not sure she was capable of speaking.

'Okay, I'll leave you to it.' He glanced from Roxanne to Rick and back again. 'Nice to meet you, anyway.'

'Yeah, you too.' Rick waited for him to leave. 'Nice lad. A credit to you.'

She held his gaze. 'Best thing that happened to me, having him.'

He dug his hands into his pockets. His expression was serious. 'Look, the reason I'm here . . . I wanted a word before you go to Chrissie's.'

'I'm not going.'

'I had a feeling you might be having second thoughts.'

'I don't know what game she's playing, and I don't care. She can count me out.'

Rick nodded. 'Okay. I get it.'

She gasped. 'Do you? Do you really?' She gave a hollow laugh. 'You've got some nerve coming here after what you and that scheming, cold-hearted bitch of a so-called friend did.' That was stretching a point. She and Chrissie were never exactly close. 'You didn't even have the decency to tell me yourself that you were going. I had to hear it from Jack! Any idea how that felt? No, I don't suppose so. While you and Chrissie went skipping off into the sunset, doing her solo shit – then getting *hitched* – the rest of us were putting our lives back together. Some more so than others.' She glared at him and he looked away. 'Oh, don't flatter yourself – it didn't take me long to get over you. It's not like I was crying myself to sleep at night.' It was a lie. Her heart had been broken into a thousand pieces. 'I met someone a hundred times better.' Another lie. Pete had turned out to be a useless good-for-nothing – a hundred times *worse*, really. 'And, as you can see, I ended up with a gorgeous son. So, all in all, life's pretty good.'

He looked puzzled. 'I thought you and your bloke had split. Isn't he with that artist, the one with the show at the Saatchi gallery?'

How did he know? Had he been checking up on her? 'I don't see what that's got to do with you.'

'No, course not, it's just . . .' He gave her a peculiar look. 'Never mind.'

An awkward silence followed.

He crossed the room and stood in front of her. She stared into green eyes framed with thick dark lashes, and her heart did an unexpected somersault. 'Roxy, you have to go tonight.'

'I don't *have* to do anything. And you're the last person who gets to order me about.'

'I didn't mean . . .' He made an exasperated sound. 'God,

you're stubborn, you always were.' As she opened her mouth to say something he placed a finger on her lips, silencing her. She swallowed. 'Do you remember what you always used to say – the one venue you wanted the Thunder Girls to play?' His finger was still pressing lightly against her lips, stopping her from answering. She gave a mute nod. 'Wembley Stadium. It was the same for all you girls. Well, between you and me, that's what Chrissie wants to see you about. I'll let her explain.' He took his finger away. Roxanne seemed unable to speak.

'And try not to be too hard on her,' he said. 'She's having a tough time of it right now. That toy boy husband of hers only went and did a bunk. Right out of the blue. She didn't see it coming.' Roxanne's eyes widened. 'She needs this reunion.'

'She can't need the money – not after everything she robbed off me and the others.'

The look on Rick's face told her she just might. 'Look, I can't go into details. But he's done her over, and it's bad, but what I've told you is strictly between us, so don't repeat a word.'

Outside, a car horn sounded. 'Is that your cab?' She nodded. 'You're going, right?'

Roxanne suppressed a smile. After what he had just told her she wouldn't miss it for the world.

15

Carly could barely contain herself. For days, all she had been able to think about was Chrissie's invitation and now the moment had come. Dave had been vile about it when she told him, said it was fit for the bin and that seeing the rest of the women, who were bound to be much thinner than her these days, would only depress her. She pushed his cruel words to the back of her mind and checked her watch. The car was due in an hour. Her stomach flipped over with a mixture of anxiety and anticipation. She couldn't wait! This was her chance to put Chrissie on the spot, get some answers. She intended to make the most of it. Find out what happened to her Brit award, for starters. The one Chrissie had offered to 'look after' when Carly went clubbing on the night. It had never been seen again. Not by Carly, anyway. Well, if she spotted it, she was having it back.

Then there was the interview in *Hello!* not so long ago. Chrissie spouting on about body image in the music industry, telling some story about the time one of the Thunder Girls had been hauled over the coals by the record company for piling on the pounds during a promotional trip to the States. This particular Thunder Girl – more thunder thighs, really, Chrissie had said – was put on a strict juice fast and daily colonics until she lost the chunk. Carly had no recollection of that. What she did remember was her own brief flirtation with juicing and colonic irrigation. Not that she was ever fat. Was Chrissie taking a swipe at her? she wondered.

She put a dot of concealer in the corner of each eye and swept highlighter across her cheekbones. For once, she knew exactly what she was going to wear, a gorgeous little Pucci dress, all splashy sequins and beaded at the hem. She had got it the year before, spent a small fortune, and never been out in it. The first time she put it on, for one of Dave's gala dos, he claimed it looked like something a cheap showgirl would wear and made her get changed.

Since then the dress had languished at the back of the wardrobe.

Now, though, as she slipped it over her head, she knew the real reason Dave hadn't wanted her wearing it. He was *jealous*. Couldn't stand the thought of her in something sassy and bold and guaranteed to turn heads. Not when he always had to be the centre of attention. Well, she was sick of playing the obedient wife, blending into the background. Being second fiddle. Those days were gone. Tonight was about *her* and the dress was a mark of defiance, as much as anything. Her way of saying, 'Look at me – I've still got it.'

For the first time in thirty years she was about to catch up with her old bandmates. The girls she had thought she would be close to forever. Carly knew this was not a night to dress down, not when Chrissie would be pulling out the stops.

She did a twirl in front of the mirror and felt a surge of joy. The dress was amazing, showing off bare legs that gleamed with just the right amount of fake tan.

She knew there could only be one reason Chrissie wanted to get the girls together after all these years. It had to be a Thunder Girls reunion. Why else bother?

For Carly, on the brink of starting a new life away from her moaning, drunken excuse for a husband, the timing could not have been better. Not that Dave knew she was about to leave him. He was too busy practising for his precious exhibition series, saying he wished he had never agreed to do it. Getting hammered and taking his frustrations out on her.

Well, not for much longer.

Ever since the horrible, humiliating Grosvenor House do, Carly had harboured a secret. The following day, while Dave was still sleeping off his hangover, she had gone to see a solicitor. A straight-talking woman with shark eyes and a filthy laugh whose speciality was securing record-breaking divorce settlements for her celebrity clients. Dave's behaviour was abusive, the woman decided. Coercive control, she called it. When Carly mentioned Dave's forthcoming multi-million-pound exhibition series, her face lit up. Carly could expect to get a hefty slice of that, she said. If she played her cards right, she would never have to worry about money again.

She had skipped out of the office feeling better than she had for years and gone straight to view a property in Hampstead.

As she twirled in front of the mirror, Dave shuffled into the bedroom, glass in hand, in tracksuit bottoms that had lost their shape and a Rolling Stones No Filter T-shirt. The same outfit he'd had on all week. He tugged at the saggy pants, hitching them up. 'Is that new?' he asked, aiming a hostile look at the sparkly dress.

'I've had it ages.'

He tipped scotch down his throat, making a slurping sound. 'I can see why you've never worn it.'

She ignored him and bent to fasten the strap on a pair of ludicrously high shoes.

'No wonder they keep upping the limit on my credit card, the amount you spend on clothes,' he grumbled.

Carly straightened up. The dress shimmered in the light. 'You want me looking nice, don't you?' He didn't answer. 'Anyway, I told you, I got this ages ago, and it wasn't even expensive.' It was actually two grand, she remembered with a smile.

She hoped he wouldn't notice the shoes were new, an impulse buy the day before from a hideously expensive shop in Mayfair. They had cost almost as much as the dress. Worth every penny, she decided, liking the way they made her legs look longer. All being well, by the time the bill landed and Dave got to see it, she would be long gone.

'So you're actually going to Witch's Manor tonight then?' he said. 'And after you said you'd never speak to her again – blimey, how two-faced are you? It wasn't all that long ago you were defacing her wedding pictures in *OK!*'

On and on he went.

She knew what he was doing. Goading her. Trying to make her feel weak for accepting Chrissie's invite. He would needle away until she caved in and said she wasn't going after all. For too long she had put up with his bullying. Being made to feel worthless.

Not anymore.

She straightened her shoulders. 'Don't worry on my account,' she said. 'I can handle Chrissie Martin, and I'll be asking for my *award* back,' she smiled.

'Yeah, yeah, how much money have I wasted on that old story? Okay, suit yourself. Just don't come crying to me when it all goes wrong. Which it will.'

Her phone pinged with a text. The car was outside. She breezed past him, not bothering with a goodbye kiss.

'I think *you'll* be the one crying to *me*,' she said under her breath as she flew down the stairs in the fancy shoes. 'A lot sooner than you think.'

16

The car drew up in front of a set of ornate wrought-iron gates. The driver wound down his window and reached for the call button on the intercom. Carly peered through the gates at the sprawling mansion with its pillars and white stucco walls. Bigger than she had imagined. Her own place seemed small by comparison. She had a sudden attack of nerves and fished her compact from her bag to check her make-up. A voice crackled through the intercom and the driver gave Carly's name. As the gates swung open it was clear to her Chrissie was running the show here. She had choreographed the entire evening, made sure it was on her terms. Carly was going to have to watch her step.

Candles flickered on either side of the driveway. She looked around at the manicured lawns and ornamental pond; fairy lights flickering in the trees. She took a breath as the car went back down the drive, its tail lights disappearing into the night.

'Well, this is it,' she said, making her way up the steps to the front door. She waited a moment. In the silence, she thought she heard a faint clicking sound behind her but when she looked there was no one in sight. She took a deep breath.

When the door opened, she did a double-take. The woman facing her in a stylish black dress, hair done up in a sleek bun, was none other than Susan Fox, their old PA at Shine Records.

Carly couldn't hide her surprise. 'Susan – is that you?'

'Hello, Carly.' Susan stepped aside and ushered her in. 'You look nice. If you'd like to follow me I'll show you where you can wait. Chrissie won't be long.'

She led the way through the entrance hall, past an enormous, sweeping staircase. Carly trotted along behind, her heels making a racket on the marble floor.

'Am I the first to arrive?' she asked Susan's back. 'What about the others? Are *all* the girls coming?'

Susan threw a polite smile over her shoulder and pushed open the door into a vast space dotted with oversized sofas and side tables, the occasional rug. Floor-to-ceiling windows faced onto the extensive garden at the back. Carly gazed about her.

On either side of the fireplace were over-the-top arrangements of fresh flowers. Jo Malone candles burned on the mantelpiece, giving off a heady rose scent. A series of Andy Warhol-style pictures, identical headshots of Chrissie pouting in glorious, saturated colour, took up most of one wall.

There was a dining table, big enough to seat at least twelve comfortably, and a sleek marble-topped bar, crowded with bottles of champagne on ice and bowls of olives and nuts; a bucket of cheesy Wotsits. Carly smiled, remembering Roxanne had always preferred them to what she used to call poncey nibbles. She glanced up at the funky chandeliers, wondering if Chrissie was out of sight, watching from the mezzanine level.

Susan poured champagne into a flute and handed it to her.

'So, how are you?' Carly asked, flashing her a bright smile.

Susan gave a polite nod. 'Oh, you know, still Shining.' Carly waited for her to elaborate. 'Sorry, would you excuse me? I need to check on something. Make yourself at home.' With that, she turned on her heels and left.

Carly watched her go, then wandered over to the dining table where four places were set. Did that mean all the Thunder Girls were expected – or that Susan was joining them?

Her eye went to the far corner of the room and an alcove cluttered with photos and keepsakes. In pride of place was the gold disc the band had got for their first album, *Midnight Madness*. Carly had always loved the cover. The four of them at their best, she reckoned.

There were photos of Chrissie with various celebs – Carol Vorderman, Simon Cowell – and a Rear of the Year trophy. Next to it was the gong she'd got from Shine when her debut solo single, 'Me', topped the UK singles chart and stayed there for an unprecedented fifteen weeks. To Carly's amazement, amid the clutter was a framed certificate from a charity recognizing Chrissie's unique contribution as an ambassador. She stared at it, dumbfounded. The idea of Chrissie doing charitable work of any sort was beyond belief. A closer look revealed it was one of those marathon TV fundraising things. 'As long as you got on telly, eh, Chrissie?' she muttered, feeling distinctly *un*charitable.

Tucked away, behind a photo of Chrissie cosying up to Tom Jones before he went grey, was a familiar-looking statuette. Carly snatched it up and read the inscription: 'Thunder Girls: Songwriting, 1988'. Carly had been the songwriter in the band – it was her missing Brit! Well, she was having it back. Just as she was stuffing it into her bag a voice yelled, 'Gotcha!'

She spun round to see Roxanne at the other end of the room. 'Roxy!'

Roxanne grinned. 'Anything else worth taking? Might as well help ourselves. Let's face it, she owes us.'

Carly held up the Brit, triumphant. 'She definitely owes *me*. She got her claws on this thirty years ago and every time I asked for it back she made some excuse. Never thought I'd see it again.' She shoved it into her bag and beamed at Roxanne. 'Oh my God! You're *tiny*. I'm so jealous!'

'Stress diet.' Roxanne hugged her. 'It works but I don't recommend it.' She went to the bar, poured a glass of champagne and took a handful of Wotsits. 'Anyway, you look incredible. I *love* the dress. Those legs!'

'Well, there's a bit more of me than there used to be. Not that I mind my curves now. Thanks to the Kardashians, my arse passes as practically minute these days.' She caught sight of herself reflected in the floor-to-ceiling windows.

'Nothing wrong with a few curves.' Roxanne gave her a long look. 'You look pretty good in *all* departments, I'd say. What's the secret – is that what being happily hitched does for you?'

Carly looked away. 'Well . . . not sure I'd put it down to that. I do look after myself and I've had a bit of help – Botox, facials every week . . . teeny bit of lip filler now and then to keep the pout in place. No actual surgery, though.' She nodded at Chrissie's picture and said, 'I know where to draw the line. Unlike some.'

Roxanne shook her head vigorously. 'I couldn't do it. Just thinking about surgery frightens the life out of me. I mean, what if it went wrong? You hear horror stories all the time. Some poor cow goes under the knife – bit of lipo, bum lift, bigger boobs . . . something she doesn't even need – and never wakes up.'

Carly nodded. 'I know. I was sitting there with the surgeon the other day while he was trying to flog me a proper cut-you-open-and-stitch-up-the-slack facelift jobbie and I thought, sod it. I look after myself as best I can, have the odd injection here and there, but why should I have to try and look twenty-five just because we live in the kind of crazy world that seems to think women aren't allowed to age?'

Roxanne shuddered. 'It's Jamie I think about. I'd never forgive myself.'

'Jamie! He must be all grown up now,' Carly said.

'He is and he's bloody gorgeous. Clever, too. He's working in fashion – pattern-cutting for Vivienne Westwood.'

'Wow, that's fabulous.'

'I know. He's amazing.'

'Well, if you ask me, you're still amazing – you haven't changed a bit.'

'Kind, but not true, sadly.' She gave Carly a squeeze. 'I love you for saying it, though. When the cabbie pulled into the drive just now he asked me if I worked here. *Worked* here! It's only because you can get banned from Uber for saying rude things to the drivers that I didn't tell him where to go.' She went to the bar and helped herself to more fizz, topped up Carly's glass. 'Have you actually seen Her Highness yet?' she asked.

Carly shook her head. 'Susan let me in, said Chrissie would be right down, but she hasn't shown her face.'

'I almost fainted when I saw Susan was *still* around. Didn't even recognize her now she's gone all Stepford Wife-looking. Like a cross between a zombie and a fembot.' Roxanne chuckled. 'Mind you, spending time with Chrissie would have that effect on anyone.'

'She's still at Shine, she said.'

'Can't say I'm surprised. For reasons I never understood she idolized Jack. Worshipped him. Utter shit that he was.'

Carly thought that was an outright understatement. They were silent a moment.

'I wonder if Anita's coming,' Carly said.

Roxanne shrugged. 'Weird, isn't it – the way she went off-grid?'

'You can't really blame her after what happened,' Carly said. 'If that had been me *I'd* have gone into hiding too.'

'Poor Nita, I hope she's okay. I know that whole experience was mortifying but so what? People forget.'

'Not when it's on YouTube for all time.' Carly shuddered. 'One of our old make-up girls reckoned she ran into her on holiday somewhere. Said Anita would never come back to England – *ever*.'

'Typical Anita. Life goes pear-shaped so what does she do? Surround herself with hunks in trunks.'

They both laughed.

'Remember that bass player she had a thing with?' Carly said. 'Love-Bite Gary. God, he was gorgeous.'

'I seem to remember we *all* had a thing with him.'

Carly shook her head. 'What were we like?'

Roxanne took another handful of Wotsits. 'Not nearly as well behaved as most people thought.'

'So, any idea what Chrissie wants with us?' Carly asked. 'I mean, it's got to be a reunion, don't you think?'

'She definitely wants us to think that. But who knows with Chrissie?' Roxanne said, knocking back her champagne.

'Maybe she's dying and wants to apologize for being such a bitch,' Carly said before going quiet for a moment. 'Did you see that interview she did a while back? Talking about body image?' Roxanne looked unsure. 'She said one of us had got a bit tubby. Turned into a real thunder *thighs* was how she put it. You don't think she was having a go at me, do you?'

'I remember her calling *me* thunder thighs once.'

'But you were always dead skinny!'

Roxanne gave a shrug and helped herself to another handful of Wotsits. 'She came to see me, you know.' Now Carly looked surprised. 'Turned up out of the blue and practically begged me to come tonight. Actually, she *did* beg. Grovelled like you wouldn't believe. So, I'd say, one way or another, she's desperate.' She went to the bar and opened a second bottle, sending the cork shooting up to the ceiling. 'Shit, nearly brought the chandelier down.'

'She didn't come to see *me*.' Carly sounded put out. 'I just got an invite.'

'I got one too but I sent it back. In pieces. Told her where she could stick her gold-edged, la-di-da invitation.'

'What is she up to?'

Roxanne shrugged. 'I guess you need to ask her. *If* she ever shows one of her many faces.'

17

Chrissie paced around the bedroom. A jabbing pain dug into the side of her temple. She scrabbled about in her bedside drawer for painkillers and washed them down with a glass of champagne, before sinking into the chair in front of her dressing table. God, she was looking pale. She swept blusher on her cheeks, giving them a healthy glow. Better. Downstairs, Carly and Roxanne were catching up and, no doubt, ripping her to shreds. She'd seen them arrive on the CCTV. She was dreading going down but she knew that sooner rather than later she was going to have to face them.

First, though, she had to deal with Rick. Tell him the truth.

He had already been on the phone twice, checking up, wanting to know if the others had arrived and how it was going. So far, she had managed to palm him off but he was no fool. Before long he would twig that his precious reunion was not going entirely to plan.

How she was going to own up about Anita was anyone's guess.

It wasn't her fault he was under the impression she was coming. Chrissie had tried her best to tell him. Dropped endless hints. All he did was sweep her concerns aside. That was the trouble. He wasn't listening.

As far as he was concerned, Anita was on board. A done deal. Okay, perhaps Chrissie had misled him a teeny bit. Not actually said in so many words that Anita had rejected the idea of a Thunder Girls reunion out of hand whilst Chrissie nearly got a battering from her crazed girlfriend. Anita had come to see her before she left but she was clear she wasn't going to change her mind. Despite Chrissie nagging, cajoling and even grovelling, to try and make her cave, nothing had worked. Defeated, she flew back and as soon as she stepped off the plane from Rio, Rick was all over her, telling her she'd done a great job, *assuming* she had persuaded Anita to come back. She hadn't dared put him right. Not after upgrading to business on the return leg, using his card. Anyway, it was his own fault for jumping to conclusions. Not that he would see it that way.

The phone rang again. Rick.

'How's it going?' he asked.

'I'm on my way downstairs now,' she snapped.

'What? You haven't been down yet?'

'I haven't had a chance, not with you on the phone every two minutes.'

'Okay, sorry. What about Anita – is she there?'

Tell him, Chrissie thought. Pain drilled into her skull. She could not speak.

Rick said, 'Hello? You still there? Hello?'

'Everyone's here,' she said at last, feeling weary. It was true. Everyone who was ever going to show *was* there. What she couldn't bring herself to admit was that there was not the faintest possibility of Anita turning up.

'Great! I'm proud of you.' Chrissie felt like being sick. 'You've done a brilliant job. Always knew you would. Last hurdle, now. Keep me posted – and good luck!'

She hung up.

It would take more than luck to magic Anita out of thin air.

She slathered on half a tube of Candy Kane shimmer lip gloss. 'Chin up,' she told her reflection, aiming a brilliant smile at the mirror. 'Showtime.'

Chrissie swept into the room in a red Valentino dress, floor-length with a deep slash, almost to the navel. Thanks to her various boob jobs she still looked good without a bra.

Carly saw her first and nudged Roxanne.

Chrissie smiled at them from across the room, hands on hips.

'Good to see you, girls,' she breathed. 'Looking well, both of you.'

'And you're looking well . . . *upholstered*,' Roxanne fired back. 'Is that as close as you dare come? Worried we'll see the joins from all the nips and tucks? I've got a needle and cotton in my bag – if anything comes undone you can use it to repair yourself.'

Chrissie aimed a haughty look at Roxanne as she sashayed closer. Susan followed and put a glass of champagne into her hand. Chrissie took it without acknowledging her. She held up her glass as she reached them.

'Here's to us – the Thunder Girls.'

Carly looked perplexed. Roxanne scanned the room in an exaggerated fashion. 'Erm, weren't there *four* of us?'

Chrissie sipped her drink. 'I've spoken to Anita.' Carly's eyes widened. 'Don't worry, she's been invited.'

'It *is* a reunion!' Carly said out of the side of her mouth towards Roxanne. 'I knew it.'

'And there was me thinking you'd invited us over to celebrate your birthday. The big Six-O, isn't it?' Roxanne said.

Chrissie gave her a cold look. 'I'm nowhere near sixty.'

'No? The *Mail* must have got it wrong then. Probably just a typo.' Chrissie looked rattled. 'Not that there's any shame in hitting a big milestone birthday. I mean, if I look as good as you when I get to your age I'll be chuffed. Not that there's much chance I will, since I don't go in for the sort of pickling and preservative treatments you seem to rely on.' She put her face up close to Chrissie's. 'Can you still move anything? You look very unnatural, sort of embalmed, does your surgeon double up as a taxidermist?'

Chrissie's jaw was clenched. She looked ready to fly at Roxanne. Instead, she took another drink of champagne and attempted a sweet smile. 'If you think I look dead perhaps I should come back to your club – I'd fit right in, I mean, it is a graveyard.'

The two women started walking closer to each other but Carly slipped between them. 'Now stop it, both of you! Can't you just be civilized for once?'

Roxanne turned on her. '*Civilized*! Get you, Miss Prim and Proper. When I showed up you were busy robbing the place.' Carly flushed. 'I'd do a bag search if I were you, Chrissie. God knows what she's got stashed away in that thing. No wonder she won't put it down.' Carly's hand tightened around the tote slung over her shoulder. 'Clearly, she came prepared. Why else bring a swag bag to a dinner party?' She started laughing.

'At least I'm not drunk,' Carly snapped.

Roxanne drained her glass. 'Neither am I. I'm having what's called a good time. You should try it.'

Chrissie held up her hands.

'Can we *please* stop bickering and calm down? I didn't get you over here so we could fight.'

'No, we could do that anywhere – go on, get on with it then,' Roxanne cut in.

'The reason I invited you was to talk about the *Rock Legends* gig.' She looked from one to the other. 'You've heard about it?'

'Everyone's heard about *Rock Legends*,' Carly said, interested.

'What's it got to do with us?' Roxanne went to the bar for another drink. The champagne frothed and fizzed and went everywhere. Susan appeared with a cloth and began mopping up.

'They want us to open the show.' Chrissie let this sink in. '*Us*. As in the Thunder Girls.'

18

'I'm not interested,' Roxanne said.

Carly looked thrown. 'Are you sure? I mean, that whole *Rock Legends* thing is massive. They never stop talking about it on the radio. Isn't it being broadcast all over the world?'

Chrissie nodded. 'And we're the only girls on the bill. The offer's on the table. A cool five hundred thousand each, minimum.'

Carly's mouth fell open. 'You don't think we're maybe a bit . . . *old* to be prancing about on stage singing pop songs?'

'Age doesn't mean a thing,' Chrissie told her. 'We're in our prime, and if you ask me we look a lot better now than we did years ago – let's face it, a hell of a lot better than most of the blokes on the bill. Plus, we get to play Wembley Stadium, like we always wanted to. And earn a big chunk of money in the process.'

Roxanne snorted. 'Well, that would be a first. Don't know

about you, Carly, but I seem to remember making barely a fraction of what she got from the Thunder Girls.' She gave Chrissie a poisonous look. 'You robbed us blind.'

Carly nodded.

'That's ridiculous, you got paid for what you did and I got paid for what I did – I just did more, that's all,' Chrissie snapped as Roxanne rolled her eyes. 'But let's just talk about the present – this is an amazing offer,' she continued, forcing a smile in Carly's direction and turning her back on Roxanne.

'But why would they want us?' Carly said, looking genuinely perplexed.

'We've got Jack to thank for that,' Chrissie replied. 'He had a go at the promoters for thinking an all-male line-up was acceptable in today's #MeToo era, apparently. Said they'd be savaged for it. When he offered them a Thunder Girls *reunion* they apparently bit his hand off!'

'I don't know. It would bring a lot of attention on us.' Carly was looking dubious.

Chrissie ploughed on. 'Look, we were bloody *amazing*, remember? And it's a fantastic opportunity.'

'And what about Anita?' Roxanne said. 'Shouldn't she be part of this?'

'Anita knows all about it and was invited tonight.'

'Somehow I doubt that. No one even knows where she is.'

'I went to see her, actually.'

'So how come she isn't here? Told you where to go, did she – can't say I'm surprised!'

'Roxanne,' said Chrissie sternly – anything to dodge answering *that* question at this delicate stage of negotiations. 'Let's concentrate on the now . . . this is Wembley! Wasn't that always the big dream? Well, now we can do it.'

Roxanne blinked her eyes dramatically and said, 'Look, we've played this game for long enough now and I'm bored of looking at your waxwork face, so why don't you just speed things up and tell us the *real* reason you're so desperate to make this happen?'

Chrissie looked nonplussed. 'I just did.'

'Oh, yeah. *Wembley*.' Roxanne sneered. 'Pull the other one. A little bird told me you and Scott aren't on such good terms these days.'

'I don't know where you got that from . . .'

'In fact, from what *I've* heard, the fairy tale is well and truly over,' Roxanne ploughed on. 'And so soon after the wedding, too.' Chrissie gave her a stony look. 'That's what you get for selling your wedding pictures to a gossip magazine. Kiss of death. And what were you thinking, hiring one of those Cinderella carriages at *your age*? Talk about mutton, not even dressed up as lamb, more Spam.' Roxanne gave a slow shake of the head as Chrissie bit her lip. 'So embarrassing to poor Scott – what must all of his young friends down the youth club have thought of him marrying some granny! I guess it was only ever a matter of time before he woke up and realized he'd got hitched to the Wicked Witch of the West.'

Chrissie glared at her. 'For your information, things are fine between me and Scott.'

Roxanne gave a hollow laugh. 'Does memory loss come with the menopause?'

Carly intervened. 'Please, Roxy. This isn't getting us anywhere.'

At the other end of the room, Susan slipped unnoticed from behind the bar and went out.

'How come you ended up with a child-groom anyway?' Roxanne was getting into her stride. 'Didn't fancy *stealing* another man from one of your *mates*, like you usually do?'

'Oh, here we go!' Chrissie shook her head. 'I wondered when you'd bring Rick into it. Do you have any idea how pathetic you sound? It was *thirty* years ago, Roxy. Your boyfriend fancied me more and left you for me, it's not exactly a crime. Move on, stop feeling sorry for yourself. It's ancient history that no one cares about, and talking of ancient, you really could do with having some work done, you look haggard – I bet Rick counts his blessings he doesn't have to wake up to that old face every day.'

Roxanne's eyes flashed with rage as Chrissie downed her drink and went to refill her glass.

'I think we should all sit down and—' It was as far as Carly got before Roxanne took aim and hurled her drink in Chrissie's face.

Chrissie gasped. Her hair hung in stringy strands. 'You crazy cow – that's considered assault, you know!'

'No it isn't, but this is, you toxic bitch!' Roxanne shouted and grabbed her round the throat, knocking them both to the floor as Chrissie screamed out, 'Get her off me, Carly, help!' The two women tussled and rolled around the floor, each aiming blows back and forth as Carly shouted at them to stop and called for Susan, who was nowhere to be seen. Roxanne smashed Chrissie's head against the floor, grunting, as Chrissie fought back, kicking out, legs in the air. The Valentino dress rode up, exposing a tiny flesh-coloured thong and a creamy expanse of bare bottom. Chrissie got hold of Roxanne's hair and yanked. An extension came out in her hands and she laughed, which made Roxanne hit her even harder. Shocked, Carly thought about trying to prise them apart but didn't want to get too close in case she got hit herself, so she continued to shout for Susan.

Suddenly there was a terrible ripping sound, bad enough to stop both women in their tracks. Roxanne's spiky heels had ripped through what looked like an antique silk rug that the girls were tussling on. 'This is sixteenth-century, you stupid bitch,' Chrissie squealed whilst still underneath Roxanne, who was breathing hard with the effort of pinning her down. Chrissie's eyes flashed wildly, her glossy lips were parted, perfect white veneers bared in a snarl, hair plastered to the unnaturally smooth brow. A sudden urge to laugh took hold of Roxanne.

'Oops,' she said, shaking with mirth, yanking the heel free, causing another stomach-churning rip. Chrissie howled and clawed, trying to grab Roxanne by the throat. 'You'll pay for this,' she screamed.

'Bill me!' Roxanne said, still grappling with her.

A few feet away, Carly continued to hover, wincing.

As Chrissie's hands tightened around her rival's throat, a familiar voice cut in.

'And slugging it out in tonight's All-Star Bitch Fest . . . in the red corner, Chrissie "The Mauler" Martin, and in the blue corner, Roxanne "Let-Me-At-Her" Lloyd. Ding-ding, seconds out! Let's give these two seasoned sluggers a *thunderous* reception!' Slow handclaps echoed around the room.

Chrissie let go of Roxanne, who crawled away, retching and clutching her throat.

A figure stood silhouetted against the doorframe. 'Well, well, ladies. Nothing changes, I see. There was me thinking the old Thunder Girls spark was gone for good!'

The women struggled to their feet. Chrissie's dress was in tatters, while clumps of Roxanne's extensions were all over the floor.

'OMG, Anita!' Carly squealed, running over and hugging her tight.

'That's my old name, so I'll let you use it! I take it the reunion's on, then?'

19

'To say I was surprised when Chrissie tracked me down and said there was a plan to get the band back together is an understatement,' Anita said, almost deadpan. 'I didn't think anyone knew where I was. I've done my best to stay under the radar, as you know.'

'How *did* you find her?' Carly asked.

Chrissie gave a shrug. Her face was streaked with mascara. 'I got lucky.'

'So where *have* you been hiding?' Roxanne said, trying to smooth her hair, which now had several obvious gaps.

'Brazil. A beach bar in a little fishing village. Let's face it, I had to get away after . . . you know.' She fiddled with the stem of her glass. 'As far as the press was concerned, I was the pissed-up Euro flop who'd let the UK down. *Nul points, Anita*. Every time I went out some pap was on my tail hoping for more pictures of me making a fool of myself.

'I was sick of it, I'd had enough. So I sold my flat, got rid of all my stuff, and changed my name. Which wasn't difficult, by the way. Then I went into a grotty little travel shop on a dodgy high street, somewhere I knew no one would recognize me, and booked a flight to Brazil. I travelled around the islands for a while before I stumbled on Sao Miguel. All of a sudden I felt more at home than anywhere else I'd ever been.'

'I wish you'd told us you were going,' Carly said. 'At least let us know where you were. It was as if you vanished into thin air.'

'Erm, that was the idea. And it's not like we were exactly close by then.' Carly looked away. 'Plus, I wasn't thinking straight. My head was all over the place. I just wanted to do a runner, the quicker the better.' She held up her empty glass. 'Any chance of another drink? I'm dehydrated after the flight.'

'Course. I've got more chilling in the orangery,' Chrissie said.

Roxanne snorted. 'The *orangery*! Could you *be* more fake? You're from Salford, Chrissie, remember?'

Chrissie gave her a withering look and limped away, wearing just one stiletto.

Anita watched her go. 'I'm guessing the two of you knocking lumps out of each other had something to do with Rick?'

'She couldn't wait to rub my nose in it over him,' Roxanne said.

'I don't think it was quite like that, Roxy,' Carly said.

Roxanne gave her a filthy look. 'You knew what he meant to me.'

'It's a hell of a long time ago,' Anita said. 'Seriously, are you *still* hurting over that?'

'You have no idea,' Roxanne said. 'I don't trust her and I don't trust Rick. I'm surprised you do after the way he stitched you up over *Eurovision*.'

'He didn't,' Anita said. 'I never should have agreed to it in the first place. The pressure not to mess up is unbelievable – I'm no solo performer; I only ever wanted to be in a band. Still, I was flattered Rick wanted me to do it but once I'd said yes it was like being on a horrendous rollercoaster ride that I couldn't get off. I had a horrible sick feeling in my stomach that wouldn't go away. On the night, waiting in the wings, I was shaking so much I knew I couldn't go on. Remember that bloke I was seeing – Love-Bite Gary?'

Carly and Roxanne exchanged a look.

'He said he'd get me something to calm the nerves.' She made a sheepish face. 'I'd already had a fair bit to drink . . . I'd also had a line of what I thought was coke.' She paused. 'Turned out to be ketamine.' Carly's jaw dropped open. 'Anyway, Gary came back with a triple shot of tequila laced with Valium. I knocked it back and the nerves went away but all of a sudden my insides were gurgling and my legs were like Bambi. When Rick saw me he tried everything to persuade me not to go on but the Valium had kicked in and I decided I was fine.'

Chrissie reappeared with more bottles of champagne, all

signs of the brawl erased. Make-up redone, lip gloss gleaming, not a hair out of place. She had changed into a slinky sleeveless jump suit.

Roxanne said, 'Rick tried to talk you out of going on?'

Anita nodded. 'I wouldn't have it. I was off my head – invincible, so I thought. Convinced I was going to bring it home for the UK – that I'd succeed where Sonia had failed. So the band strikes up, I open my mouth to sing the first line, next thing I'm hurling everywhere. All over the orchestra.' She shuddered. 'God, even now I can barely begin to think about it. Still, what doesn't kill you—'

'Makes you change your name and drink something stronger!' Chrissie chipped in.

'Exactly! Cheers!'

Carly was shaking her head. 'And all this time I've been blaming Rick.'

'He was pretty good to me, actually,' Anita said. 'Told me to lie low, said the tabloids would be after me, digging up as much dirt as they could, and it was bound to come out I was gay.'

Carly blinked. 'Gay!'

Chrissie smirked. 'Didn't you know?'

Anita laughed. 'My other half in Brazil happens to be a woman. Gorgeous, hot-blooded Latin type. Bloody possessive, mind you. We definitely have our moments.' She grinned at Roxanne. 'Your and her ladyship's set-to isn't a million miles away from what happens at home from time to time.'

'When did you change sides, then?' Carly asked.

'Once she finally worked out all men are shits,' Chrissie said.

Anita laughed. 'Oh I always knew that.' She held out her glass to Chrissie for a refill. 'Didn't stop me having fun with them though! But I always knew I wouldn't settle down with a bloke. I mean, it's not like I woke up one day and *decided* I liked women. I always knew, I just didn't share it. Remember Liz, who did our make-up? Pretty little thing. Redhead.'

'You *didn't*.' Carly looked taken aback.

'I did.'

'How come you didn't tell us?' Roxanne asked, puzzled. 'It's no big deal. My Jamie's gay and no one cares.'

'I don't know. It seemed more of an issue then, I suppose. The kind of thing the papers would have loved to make a fuss about. I can see it now: *Thunder Gay*! Rick thought I'd be better off keeping it quiet, anyway.'

Chrissie seemed surprised. 'Rick knew – way back then? He never said anything to me.'

'He was always good to me.' Anita caught Roxanne's look. 'Sorry, babe, but he was. He saved me from so many scrapes. If I'd listened to him, that whole embarrassing chucking-up on telly fiasco could have been avoided.'

There was an uncomfortable silence.

'Sounds to me like you were having some kind of breakdown,' Chrissie said at last. 'I mean, did you *really* think you could do better than Sonia?'

20

Susan listened to the four of them from the adjacent room, where even more booze and snacks were on standby. A mighty feast – not that Chrissie could afford it. Since Rick had volunteered to fund this get-together, no doubt hoping to get a huge payday in the long run, Jack was happy to send Susan to help him out.

'Give me the blow-by-blow on those bitches,' Jack had said. 'I need Rick to pull this off, but odds are on it being an utter catastrophic shit show.'

But, for Susan, the dinner was full of unexpected turns: Anita had *actually* shown up, and Chrissie and Roxanne had only had a minor tiff – well, minor for them. Like Jack, Susan had expected a bloodbath.

Anita announcing that she was gay wasn't news to Susan. Sure, she'd had fun with men as much as Carly and Chrissie back in the day, but anyone with eyes in the Thunder Girls era would've seen that her tastes were varied. But the other three bandmates were too self-obsessed to notice anything about anyone else. Not Susan, though – she'd kept an eye on everyone.

She peeked into the next room as the girls, still a little tense but fairly civilly, all things considered, took seats around Chrissie's living room. Susan had made a £1,000 bet with Jack they wouldn't even reach the sit-down-for-dinner stage. Jack expected they would, before one of them stabbed Chrissie with a crystal fork. Neither might win after all.

Jack was right to be hopeful: Shine stood to make a fortune from royalties with the Thunder Girls opening the *Rock Legends* gig. But if the band was too 'happy families' to the outside world, the *Thunder Girls Uncut* book that Jack had commissioned from Kristen Kent wouldn't seem as juicy or fly off the shelves the right way. As for the 'special guests' she had let into the grounds at Rick's request – who the girls knew nothing about – well, she felt obliged to put on a good show for them.

Susan looked across to the fridge and pulled out a couple of Cristal champagne bottles with a smirk. The ladies would wash these down quickly – it was always their drink of choice back in the day. A refill should help bring more arguments bubbling back to the surface. After all, the reunion couldn't go *too* smoothly.

That wouldn't be according to plan.

21

The Thunder Girls were all sitting in Chrissie's living room, freshly poured Cristal champagne in hand thanks to the eager-to-help Susan. The glint in Roxanne's eye reflected the bubbles.

'Well, this is all very cosy, isn't it?' Roxanne said in a chipper tone. 'Is that it – we're all best friends again? After everything she did?'

'It's business, Roxy,' Chrissie said. 'A job. Cold, hard cash, not some nostalgic love-in. Hate me as much as you want, but this is the best offer you'll ever get.'

'I don't see the point of holding a grudge after all this time,' Carly said.

'No, I don't suppose you do, what with your perfect life and your millionaire snooker star husband and your two-grand shoes,' Roxanne said. 'You got off lightly.' Carly flinched. 'What I still don't get is, how come Queen Bitch over there's suddenly all in favour of a reunion after decades of silence? Telling journalists how much she loved being a solo artist and she'd never work with her old bandmates again. *Ever*. *She*'s the one who blew the band to bits in the first place, so she could go off and be a star – and sod the rest of us.'

Chrissie looked at her feet.

'She's got a point,' Anita said. 'You didn't even tell us what was going on. Left us to hear the bad news from Jack the Knife.'

'That wasn't my idea. I wanted to tell you but Jack said it was better that way.'

'Better for you, maybe – not for the rest of us,' Anita said. 'You should have told us.'

Chrissie hung her head. 'I know and I'm sorry,' she whispered.

'Well, that's a start,' Anita said.

'Do you have any idea what it was like for the rest of us?' Roxanne said. 'The whole thing came crashing down, no warning. And the fallout lasted years. Even when I was taking Jamie to nursery I was being hounded by photographers.' Roxanne reached for the bottle. Chrissie swiped it away.

'I think you've had enough.'

'Oh, I'm just getting started.'

'Are you surprised I bailed out?' Chrissie was frustrated. 'I'd had enough – of *you*, Roxy, drinking yourself to oblivion. Stumbling about on stage. Forgetting your lines. The rest of us having to cover for you night after night when you missed your cues.' Roxanne stared at her open-mouthed as she continued. 'If it wasn't for you hitting the bottle, making us look like rank amateurs instead of the world's hottest band, we'd have cracked America. *You* blew it.'

For a moment no one spoke.

'Did it never occur to you why I was drinking?' Roxanne said at last, her voice cracking. 'I was miserable, that's why. Crying myself to sleep. My heart was breaking. You really think I didn't know you had your sights set on Rick? He was *my* boyfriend, we were in love, and *you* were all over him, you slag.'

'I never went near him!' Chrissie did her best to sound outraged.

'Well . . . that's not quite true,' Anita said. 'We all knew you had a thing for him. It didn't exactly come as a shock to any of us when you went off with him.'

'It did to me! I *loved* him! He *said* he loved me! I thought we were in it for the long haul.' Roxanne sloshed more champagne into her glass.

Another awkward silence followed.

'Look, Roxy, it's not as if I'm asking you to like me,' Chrissie said. Roxanne made a loud noise that was either a laugh or a sob. Or both. 'And I don't have to like *you* either,' Chrissie continued. 'Just do the *Rock Legends* gig, take the money and then go our separate ways. You'll never have to see me again.'

'I can't believe I'm saying this after all my years hiding out – but, fuck it, I want this dosh to do up our bar and I don't have a pension, so what the hell – I'm in,' Anita said. 'How about you, Carly?'

'For me, it's not about the money – more about getting out there and doing something with my life again after years of playing second fiddle to Dave. The timing's perfect, actually.' She took a breath. 'I'm thinking of leaving him.'

There was a shocked silence.

'I feel like I missed out, settling down so young.'

'But you've been together forever. I thought you were smitten,' Roxanne said. 'Head over heels.'

'I always thought that long hard thing in his hand was why you fell for him,' Chrissie said, chuckling.

'It's true, Dave's wood was a legend in its own right,' Anita chipped in.

'No wonder he was able to sink the pink!' Chrissie added.

They collapsed in laughter.

Carly rolled her eyes. 'Ha ha. Don't get me wrong, we had some good years. I always thought we'd have kids once the snooker side of things quietened down, but when it did and I brought the subject up, it was always the wrong time. Well, it's too late now. Since he retired all he does is drink and moan and slag me off – he said I looked ridiculous in this dress *and* called me fat. I'm sick of it. I feel ready to spread my wings again. So I'm up for the gig.'

'Shit, he sounds awful,' Anita said. 'No wonder you want out. Don't worry – we'll make sure this reunion's a right laugh.'

'So that's three of us in,' Chrissie said. All eyes were on Roxanne. 'How about it, Roxy?'

She stared into her drink.

'Come on,' Carly said. 'Like Nita says, it'll be fun.'

Roxanne turned to look at Chrissie. 'What's the *real* reason you want to do this?'

'I've already said. Wembley.'

'We were booked to play Wembley before, right before you swanned off on your solo jaunt – funny how it didn't seem important to you then,' Roxanne said. 'Isn't the real truth here that it's *you* that needs the money from this gig more than any of us—'

'Don't be ridiculous. Do I look like I need the money?' Chrissie gestured around.

Roxanne gave it some thought. 'That's the thing about being on your uppers. It's not always obvious. Appearances can be deceptive. I mean, I drive a Porsche and I've just spent more getting my hair done than some people earn in a week, and yet . . .' She shrugged.

Carly looked confused. 'What are you getting at, Rox?'

'You don't actually believe she wants to get the band back together out of the goodness of her heart, do you? So we can play our dream Wembley Stadium gig like we always wanted to. Get real, Carly! When did she ever do anything that wasn't all about her?'

'You're wrong,' Chrissie said. 'This is about all of us.'

'Bollocks! The only reason we're here is because your precious husband's left you high and dry.' She caught the look in Chrissie's eyes. 'Go on, ask her.' No one spoke. Roxanne went on, enjoying herself. 'She's broke. And now she *needs* us to save herself. Isn't that right, Chrissie darling?'

Chrissie's jaw was rigid. 'Who told you that?'

Rick might have pointed her down this line of thinking, but Roxanne wasn't going to rat him out to Chrissie. Not yet, anyway. 'No one – I sort of guessed it but thanks for confirming. There had been rumours Scott's already left you – so him taking you for a financial ride would certainly make sense of why he was with someone old enough to be his mum in the first place, and the *real* reason behind this whole "reunion" nonsense.' Chrissie's eyes welled up as Roxanne knocked back her drink with a smirk. 'And just so we're clear, I didn't come here tonight because I thought there might be some money in it, even though I could do with it. No, I came to see the look on that frozen face when I said I knew about Scott – some small semblance of the pain and humiliation I suffered when you went off with Rick.' She raised a glass. 'Oh, I do love to kick an old dog when it's down.'

'You spiteful bitch.' Chrissie looked furious. 'It's no secret *your* husband walked out on you, you know. And everyone knows he's shacked up with a younger, prettier woman.'

'She's welcome to him,' Roxanne laughed. 'And at least *my* husband was out of nappies when we got together. Cradle-snatcher.' She gave Chrissie a look of disgust and got to her feet, unsteady. 'So, you can forget your reunion. I couldn't care less about the money – I'm not interested in helping you save your lipo'd arse at any price.' And with those words she stumbled triumphantly out of the room.

22

Rick poured himself another drink. He was having second thoughts on his strategy for tonight. Not about Chrissie running the reunion: facing the wrath of a united Roxanne and Carly still frightened him senseless. Best let Chrissie calm them down and bring them back into the fold first. No, he was nervous about her doing it without back-up.

Should he be there in the next room, ready to pop out when it was all happy smiles and back together? Maybe. Or maybe that'd be too much. Best to see them tomorrow, let them bond first.

He took a big swig of the G&T. 'Needs to be stronger,' he muttered, adding more G to the T.

No, Chrissie would be fine. She'd got Carly and Roxanne there after all. And *Anita*. Rick was really proud of her for that. It had been so long since he had seen her. Ashamed of her televised disaster. Terrified of people knowing who she really was, who she really wanted to love. Some trashy tabloid would bring up the *Eurovision* debacle for sure, but her being gay wouldn't faze anyone these days – it hadn't harmed Samantha Fox. The world had changed so much. It might actually be a great talking point for the media. A good news angle. Something fresh to talk about, to take focus off any whispers about Chrissie and Scott.

Chrissie, Carly, Roxy and Anita back together. What would that be like? The thought of seeing them together again was becoming less of a nightmarish chore, more something . . . exciting. It might even be fun.

Rick wondered how Roxanne would feel about him. Their first meeting in years hadn't gone too badly. He threw back the rest of his drink.

He gave himself a virtual pat on the back for secretly organizing the paparazzi to photograph the reunion at Chrissie's. With them not knowing about it, they wouldn't be preening or posing like most of those tacky fake pap reality-star shots the tabloids were always full of. No, these would be charming, natural, classy. He couldn't wait to see the pictures: he visualized them drinking champagne together, laughing, hugging, and smiled . . .

23

'Just the two of us.' Anita sang a line from the famous Stevie Wonder song whilst stretching out on one of the sofas. 'Let's hope Carly manages to get Roxy home without her puking all over the back of the cab. I hear they charge for that kind of thing these days.'

Chrissie closed her eyes for a moment, her head pounding. 'What a night.'

Susan came into the room, checked the patio doors were locked, peered into the garden, and drew the blinds.

'I've cleared up,' she said. 'My car's outside. Okay if I go?'

Chrissie waved a hand at her. 'Yes, of course. And thanks.'

Susan gave a nod. 'No problem.'

They waited for her to leave.

'I have to say, you really blew it with Roxy tonight, babe. I doubt she'll change her mind now,' Anita said.

Chrissie looked taken aback. 'Me?! She's the one who won't let the past go, Nita. But when she wakes up tomorrow with the mother of all hangovers and it hits her that she said no to five hundred grand, she'll come crawling back. Trust me, she'll be begging at the gates – and she'll be lucky if I let her in. If I do, you will have to be on security duty, cos if she starts another fight with me, this time I won't let her win.'

Anita raised her eyebrow. They both knew Roxanne was way stronger than delicate Chrissie, but she ignored the lie. 'Well I wouldn't put a bet on it, babe. You heard her – she doesn't care about the money.'

'She needs it more than anyone – that club of hers is dying and it's killing her with it. That money would be a lifeline for her – I'm really doing her a favour even inviting her to take part.' She caught Anita's look, which was sceptical. 'Okay, she's not the only one. I admit I need it badly too; if we don't make this gig happen there's a chance I'll go bankrupt.'

'Shit! It's really that bad?'

'Worse. I'm hanging on by a cheap manicure.' She shot a look of disgust at her hands. 'Can't afford Margaret Dabbs-style pampering treatments at home anymore. Forced to rub shoulders with civilians. Go cap in hand to Rick for loans. Can you imagine?' She gave an exaggerated shudder. Anita suppressed a smile. Chrissie said, 'I could never do what you did – go and live in the middle of nowhere where you can't even get a blow-dry, let alone a decent facial.'

'Actually, there's a woman in the village does some kind of clay and papaya treatment that's brilliant. I go every few weeks and slap the mask on at home in between. Sets like concrete but seems to work.'

Chrissie gave her a curious look. 'Really? Well, whatever you're doing, it works. You look incredible.'

Anita waited a moment before asking, 'What happened with Scott?'

Chrissie looked down. 'He ripped me off, like Roxanne said. No warning signs at all. I mean, we were *so* happy. Proper in love – so I thought – yet all the time the thieving bastard was robbing me blind and planning a midnight flit with everything I had apart from this house – which he also took nearly all of the equity out of. And I didn't even have a mortgage, Anita! – I owned this outright. And I was absolutely *clueless* until I came back from honeymoon to find Rick here telling me I'd been a fool to think anyone as young as Scott could ever have wanted me for anything other than my money.'

'I can't believe Rick would have said that.'

'He didn't exactly use those words. But it was written all over his face.'

Anita looked at Chrissie, her face full of pity. 'How come you didn't mention any of this when you came to Brazil?'

'No one's supposed to know, that's why. I kept hoping Scott would come back, say he'd lost his mind – had a breakdown, or something – and it was all a horrible mistake. Beg me to take him back.' She sighed. 'Part of me still would take him back. But I don't suppose there's much chance of that now.'

'Can't you get him for theft or fraud, or whatever? Report him, get the police onto him.'

Chrissie gave a sad shake of the head. 'Nothing they could do; I didn't sign a pre-nup, so his name went on everything I owned.' She covered her face with her hands. 'What was I thinking?'

Anita sighed. 'That's the thing about being in love. It's a form of madness, you know, tends to make you do crazy things.'

Neither one said anything.

'What about you?' Chrissie asked, keen to change the subject. 'Maria seems . . . a bit of a handful.'

Anita laughed. 'That's putting it mildly. She's the jealous type, with what you might call trust issues. Goes off the deep end if she thinks I'm about to stray. As you know.'

'I never did get the stain out of my top,' Chrissie said.

'Yeah, sorry about that. What can I say? My wife's a hot-blooded woman. Passionate. Fiery. Crazy about me.'

'She's crazy, all right.'

'It can get a bit much, being with someone who's so . . . *explosive*. Right now, it's probably not a bad thing for us to spend some time apart.' Anita tipped the last of the champagne into their glasses.

'I could bloody strangle Rox,' Chrissie said frustratedly.

'Er, when I walked in last night you *were* doing just that!' Anita laughed.

'Wembley. We'll never get a chance like this again at our

age. But she's not over Rick dumping her for me all those years ago. We're talking prehistoric times, practically.'

'You wanted him and he went. That's what's hard to bear.'

Chrissie threw up her hands. 'Oh, for God's sake, she needs to get over herself. I seem to remember any bloke was fair game back then.'

'Is that why you all had a crack at Love-Bite Gary?'

Chrissie looked surprised. 'We didn't think you knew about that.'

'Remember the cover shoot we did for *Smash Hits*, all of us stripping off, trying on different outfits? Every single one of you had one of Gary's trademark love bites.'

Chrissie had been about to mention her quickie with Glasgow Brett. She decided not to. 'You never said anything.'

'No, well, I got my own back with a bit of a fling with that photographer bloke you were seeing . . . As well as the soap actor Carly had a thing for. Robert or Richard, or whatever his name was.'

Chrissie stared at her.

'C'mon, we were all at it back in the day. What goes around comes around, so to speak.'

Chrissie laughed.

Anita's look turned serious. 'But some guys were off-limits, Chrissie – you knew that. I'd never have gone anywhere near Rick, nor would Carly, we knew how Roxy felt about him. It was obvious he was The One.'

'Oh, come on. They were never serious.'

Anita gave her a long look. 'I always worried she was heading for a fall with Rick. Poor thing was *besotted* but it was like he saw her as the warm-up act – someone to fill in until he got with you, his forever girl.' Chrissie seemed taken aback. 'It's true, I remember talking to Carly about it. We both felt the same. Shame after all that it didn't work out for you and Rick. Seems like once you got him, you didn't want him – so I guess everyone lost out in the end.'

'We were married for fifteen years, Anita, so I'd hardly say I didn't want him, and it's not like I set out to hurt her – it just happened.'

'Not directly on purpose, maybe. But you knew what you were doing, though. Admit it, every move you made was calculated.'

Chrissie paused, thinking, then her expression softened.

'Look, I'll admit I knew what I wanted and I went for it.'

Anita smiled at her honesty. 'Actually, I always wanted to be more like you . . . ruthless.'

Chrissie looked pleased. 'Thanks.'

'You knew how to make things happen. Still do. Which is why you're going to have to talk Roxanne round if you're serious about this Thunder Girls reunion.' Chrissie opened her mouth to object but Anita put up a hand to silence her. 'Apologize, for a start.'

'I've *tried*.'

'Try harder. And mean it. It all rests on you two now.'

24

Rick stared at the tabloids spread out on his desk. Damning paparazzi pictures on every front page of Chrissie and Roxanne at each other's throats – literally. Lurid headlines swam before his eyes: *THUMPER GIRLS! THUNDER BRAWLS!* One rag had come up with *THUNDER GIRLS AND LIGHTNING . . . very, very frightening!* He felt sick. It was a catastrophe. A PR disaster.

Jack would kill him.

Sack him, *then* kill him.

This was not the story Rick had expected when he'd tipped off the paparazzi. It was meant to be a way of getting the girls on the front pages, without revealing exactly what they were up to. And he had decided not to tell them the snappers would be there, thinking that way the pictures would feel more authentic.

What he had failed to anticipate was a full-blown brawl breaking out.

Susan appeared and put two paracetamol and a cup of coffee in front of him. 'Double espresso,' she said soothingly. 'I got some of those Java beans you like. How are you feeling?'

He pushed a lock of hair off his brow. 'Awful, that's how I'm feeling.' He picked up the cup and slurped the scorching liquid. 'I've got palpitations.'

Susan peered at him, concerned. 'You might want to go easy on the coffee in that case. It's blow-your-head-off strong.'

'I don't understand.' He pushed the papers aside and let his head fall into his hands. 'How could this have happened?'

'Well, it *was* your idea to get the paparazzi along . . . I just did as you said,' Susan said calmly.

The frown lines running down the centre of Rick's brow deepened. 'I don't mean how they got the pictures, I mean *this*.' He swept a hand over the front pages. 'How come Chrissie and Roxanne were scrapping on the floor – you were there, couldn't you have stopped it? It was supposed to be a *reunion*. They were *supposed* to be toasting exciting new beginnings – Wembley – not have a wrestling match! How did it descend to this?'

Susan cocked her head on one side. 'Don't take this the wrong way,' she began. 'I'm trying to think if there's a delicate way of putting it . . .'

'Never mind about that – just tell me.' Rick sounded desperate.

'It was about you. The fight.'

'*Me?*'

'Roxanne was winding Chrissie up over Scott. What she actually said was that it made a change for Chrissie to be with a bloke she hadn't stolen from one of her friends, like she did when she got with you. And *someone* had told her Chrissie was having some financial issues, so she came well-armed for battle . . .' Rick groaned, knowing what he had done. Susan continued, 'Chrissie obviously defended herself with a slew of revelations of what she knew about Roxanne's troubles and next thing it turned into some sort of high-heeled mixed martial session.' Susan smirked. 'Always were feisty, those two.'

Rick was pale. 'What's Jack going to say?'

'Actually, that's what I came in to tell you. He wants to see you. Soon as.'

Rick swallowed down the rest of the coffee, burning his mouth.

Jack was at the window, gazing at the river, and didn't bother to turn round when Rick tapped at his open office door, just said to come in.

Rick hovered, not sure what to do. The TV was on, the sound right down. He found himself face to face with Britney Spears in a schoolgirl outfit. She mouthed 'Oh Baby, Baby', causing Rick to look away. It wasn't the first time he had been summoned to see Jack, only to find this exact music video playing in his office. It could hardly be a coincidence.

He aimed a hostile look at his boss's back.

A mess of newspapers lay on the African blackwood desk, pages strewn everywhere. Rick had no idea how to begin explaining. If Jack asked him directly who was responsible for tipping off the paparazzi he would have to own up.

Jack turned to face him. He had one of his hard-to-read looks on. As if able to see inside Rick's head, he said, '*How* did the paps know the Thunder Girls were gathering at Chrissie Martin's house?'

Rick opened his mouth to speak. Nothing came out.

'Take a pew, man,' Jack said, indicating the stool that looked like an old turntable. Reluctantly, Rick sat down. He had hoped to avoid sitting there since it had a tendency to swivel unexpectedly. Rick suspected it was just one of Jack's many tricks for making visitors to his office feel inferior. In his more paranoid moments, he pictured Jack putting the turntable on a fast spin at the touch of a concealed button on his desk.

Nothing would surprise him.

Jack remained standing. He was in his usual skinny jeans and a Status Quo T-shirt that was supposed to be ironic, Rick guessed. Jack hated Status Quo – one of Rick's favourite bands, as it happened.

Rick cleared his throat. Jack strode across the room, flung himself into the enormous leather chair behind his desk and pointed the remote at the TV. The screen went black. For a moment he gazed at Rick without speaking, using a button on the arm of the chair to tilt it up and down.

Jack rubbed his chin. 'I've had Big Becky in here this morning already, bleating on. Not happy. Not happy at all.' His voice changed. 'With all due respect, I don't remember discussing a full-on tabloid *assault*, pardon the pun,' he said in a mocking Estuary accent that was clearly a dig at the marketing chief. 'She said this had to be down to you.'

'It was meant to be shots of the four of them meeting up again. I didn't mean . . .' Rick began.

Jack scrabbled among the papers and pulled out the *Daily Post*. Chrissie, legs in the air, bare backside on show, took up half the front page. The headline was: *MENO-PAUSE MADNESS! CHRISSIE TELLS RIVAL ROXY: YOU'RE NOT* A PATCH *ON ME!* The paper had enlarged part of the photo and ringed something on her bottom. Jack peered at it. 'What *exactly* is that?'

Rick leaned over the desk. He hadn't a clue. 'One of those flesh-coloured plasters, I think. She might have had a tetanus jab.'

Susan, who had come into the room without Rick noticing, sidled up to Jack's elbow. 'It's an HRT patch,' she said, matter-of-fact. 'Hormone Replacement Therapy. You know – for the *menopause*.'

Jack threw his head back and roared with laughter. Rick felt a rush of sympathy for Chrissie. She would be devastated. He shot a panicky look at Susan, now arranging the tabloids into an orderly pile, placing the *Post* with Chrissie's bare bum on top. Jack was still laughing, showing rows of sharp white teeth in a gaping mouth. A single gold filling.

Rick waited for the awful laughter to subside, knowing that when it did he would be fired.

Jack wiped his tears and fixed Rick with cold, pale eyes. 'Mate, this is genius. We couldn't buy this kind of coverage. It's priceless. You've got everyone talking about the Thunder Girls. Brilliant.'

Rick blinked. He hadn't expected that reaction. 'But it's . . .' he searched for the right word. '*Mortifying*. For the girls. Chrissie, especially.' HRT. She would never forgive him.

'They're not *girls*, are they? As we all now know, at least one's menopausal. Just shows, all the fillers and Botox and tweaks in the world can't halt the march of time. On the outside, plastic fantastic, but on the *in*side . . .' He thought for a moment. 'More like a shrivelled old crone. Or am I being unkind?'

Rick stared at him. He had long suspected Jack of being a secret woman-hater. Not so secret, in fact. He felt like punching him, wiping the self-satisfied smirk off his reptile face.

'Still, it's done the trick. Stirred things up,' Jack went on. 'The *Rock Legends* people are talking about a tour, all kinds of shit.' He glanced at his watch. 'Sorry, mate, got to go. Conference call, and all that. Keep up the good work, eh?' He got up and slapped Rick hard on the back, almost sending him flying. 'Oh, and do give the *girls* my best.'

25

Kristen Kent had spoken to Jack about using an office at the record company for the remaining interview sessions for the Thunder Girls book. He said no. Having the mole at her place wasn't working out, she said. Doing the interview sessions there felt too intrusive.

'She's opening up to you? You're getting good material?' Jack wanted to know.

She was, but that wasn't the point. What was bothering her was the oddness of Jack's secret source, who was seriously weirding her out. Finding a tactful way of saying so was tricky, however, so she simply said, 'Actually, some of what she's telling me is pretty raw.'

'That's rather the point, isn't it?' He sounded annoyed. 'The feedback I'm getting is that she loves you.' Kristen's heart sank. The sort of love that came to mind was of the *Single White Female* kind. 'Correct me if I'm wrong but wasn't the whole point of doing the sessions at your apartment to guarantee privacy – so no one would find out what you were up to? It would never work here at Shine. Word would get round in two seconds flat.'

She gave up.

The lights on the recorders glowed red.

Kristen, who'd had a weight problem when she was younger and never ate biscuits anymore, was now on her third digestive. A sure sign she was feeling stressed.

On the sofa, the mole, Kimberley, fiddled with the cuff of her shirt. She was wearing wide-legged navy trousers with a broad pinstripe. Not unlike the ones Kristen had on. Her hair was shorter too. Sharper. A bit like Kristen's, in fact.

'Did you know Anita's gay now?' the mole asked.

Kristen looked surprised. 'I always thought she liked men. When I went through the cuttings it seemed she had a different bloke every week. In fact, there were so many it was hard to keep track.'

'She did like men. She just liked women more. People weren't as relaxed about sexuality then. I mean, obviously there were tons of gay pop stars.' She looked thoughtful. 'Men, mostly, I seem to remember. Anyway, Rick seemed to think if Anita came out she might get a bit of hassle from the press. Even now, some of the tabloids can be cruel.' She gave Kristen a long look. 'You only have to look at what the *Post* did with those photos of Chrissie's HRT patch. Anyway, Anita played the straight card and secretly had her flings with women. She's married now, you know. To a woman.'

'Whoa, hang on. You're sure about that?'

Kimberley nodded. 'I know all about it. Some crazy Brazilian. Jealous as hell. They're having a trial separation while Anita's here for the reunion gig.' It wasn't really a trial separation, but never mind.

'She was pretty good at covering up her . . . dalliances, you might call them,' the mole went on. 'No one suspected a thing. I certainly didn't until I walked in on her with the make-up girl one day. Liz. Freckles, red hair. Very pretty. They were so involved they didn't even see me. I left them to it. Didn't tell a soul.'

Kristen reached for another biscuit. Before she knew what she was doing she had dunked it in her coffee, something she used to do when she was a junior on a paper in Hertfordshire. Everyone dunked then. These days she considered it common.

'Ooh, I love to dunk,' Kimberley was saying, following Kristen's lead, cramming the soggy end of the digestive into her mouth. 'One of life's great pleasures.'

Kristen winced. 'The thing about Anita's sexuality – who cares these days?' she said. 'You can be who you want.'

'True. Except Anita had a way of getting into trouble. We were on a trip to Cannes, performing on a yacht at one of those TV festivals they have, and there was this gorgeous girl. Exotic-looking. Huge violet eyes, short hair.' She gazed at Kristen. 'Bit like yours, actually. Unusual name – Desdemona or Persephone or something. They "ended up" together in one of the cabins. It was nothing to Anita, a fling. Until the girl got all lovesick and tried to stay in touch. Turned out her dad was some record company big cheese in New York. Not a man to mess with. He went ballistic. Threatened to get them dropped from their American label.' She shook her head. 'That nearly brought the whole band crashing down. We had to pay him off. It was all hushed up.'

'How did you find out?'

'Rick.' A smug smile spread across her face. 'He never could keep any secrets from me.'

26

Rick wasn't taking calls. His phone kept ringing so he switched it to silent. By the time he summoned the strength to look at it there were thirty-eight missed calls, almost all from Chrissie. A personal best for her. Or worst, depending on how you looked at it. He knew he would have to speak to her sometime but wanted to let her cool off first. It was a risky strategy since ignoring her could simply send her anger levels to new and more dangerous heights. By early evening she'd stopped ringing. He closed his eyes, counted to ten and took a few deep breaths.

Then he dialled her number.

'Where've you been? Have you *seen* the papers?' Still furious. 'Who *did* this? *Who* tipped the paps off about the dinner? Who let them *on my property*?! No, don't tell me. I already know.' Rick's heart rate shot up. 'I bet it was Jack! I'm right, aren't I?'

'There's no point . . .'

'And just to set the record straight, I am *not* on HRT!'

'No, I never thought . . .'

'It's an energy patch. To rebalance my chakras.'

'Right . . .'

'I am nowhere *near* menopausal.' She let out an anguished scream. 'I daren't even look at the *Mail Online*. You can bet the trolls are having a frigging field day.'

'Chrissie, listen. The message boards are going crazy.'

'Course they are! At my expense! Oh, it's all right for *you*. You're a *man*. I don't expect *you* to understand.'

'I do, I promise.'

'When I get my hands on Jack he is dead, trust me.'

Rick swallowed. It didn't bear thinking about what she would do if she found out he was the one who'd tipped off the paparazzi. Their divorce came to mind, Chrissie daubing his classic Aston Martin DB5 with graffiti. Letting everyone at Shine know what she thought about the size of his manhood – even though she was the one who dumped him! He'd had the car resprayed but it was never the same again.

'Chrissie, listen to me – it's all good. Everyone's saying pretty much the same thing . . . that you look bloody amazing. They couldn't care less about the HRT thing—'

'How many times? I am NOT on HRT!'

'Listen to this: "What's Chrissie Martin's secret – the woman's got legs to die for." And: "That has to be the peachiest bum on the planet." Here's another: "Not so much as a hint of cellulite – how does she do it?"'

'Skin-brushing.'

'Sorry?'

'That's why I don't have cellulite. Skin-brushing. I'm fanatical about it.'

'We should be thinking about a beauty book. Some kind of health and fitness manual.' Aimed at older women, he was about to say, stopping himself just in time. 'Once the Thunder Girls are up and running.'

'I'd forget about a reunion, if I were you. Roxanne's *out*. Told me in no uncertain terms where to stick the gig . . . somewhere in the vicinity of my energy patch, as it happens.'

Roxanne was inside the club, changing an optic behind the bar. They weren't due to open for another couple of hours. She heard the empty bar echo with footsteps coming down the stairs. She looked up and saw Rick.

'Oh, spare me. You're not here for sentimental reasons. You've come to try and change my mind. Well, forget it,' she said.

'Just hear me out.'

'Why should I?' She slapped a copy of the *Post* on the bar. 'That's a pretty accurate reflection of the state of things between me and Chrissie. To say we hate each other wouldn't be putting it nearly strongly enough.'

Rick sighed. 'Roxy . . .'

A voice said, 'Oh, sorry, didn't know you had company,'

and Jamie appeared from the far side of the dance floor. 'Can I get you a drink?'

'He's just going.'

Jamic saw thc *Post* on thc bar's countcrtop. He chuckled. 'We had a good laugh at the papers this morning. Never knew Mum had such a good left hook.' Roxanne shot him a warning look. 'What? It's funny. Hilarious, if you ask me.'

'Chrissie says you don't want to do the gig,' Rick said to Roxanne.

Roxanne snorted. 'Can you blame me? It's for the best, we're not safe around each other. We won't just come to blows next time, we'll probably actually kill each other and I'd rather be poor and free then rich and banged up.'

Rick held up his hands. 'I get why it's so hard for the two of you to get on. And if there's anyone you need to have a go at, it's me. I'm the one who let you down.'

Jamie saw the way Rick was looking at Roxanne. 'I'll be in the office, if you want me,' he said, retreating.

'What do you want, Rick?' Roxanne sounded weary.

'To say sorry. For what I put you through. What I did . . . it wasn't fair. I was a prick.'

'You got that right.'

'I should never have dumped you like that. I was too bloody selfish to think about what it would do to you. Thinking back, I'm ashamed of how I treated you. I don't know what got into me.'

'I do. I know who you got into, anyway.'

He looked sheepish. 'I mean it, Roxy. I didn't mean to

hurt you. If I could go back and do things differently, I would.'

She looked away.

He took hold of her hand. 'Look, I know you're struggling with this place.'

'I suppose that'll be all over the papers next.'

'Not if I can help it.' He was still holding on to her. 'I want you to do the reunion. It's what you need.' She opened her mouth to object but he silenced her with a look. 'I don't just mean the money. You're a Thunder Girl. This is another stab at stardom and, thanks to all the stuff in the tabloids, the stakes just got much higher. It's not a one-off gig anymore, there's a tour on the cards and there's interest in a fly-on-the-wall TV series.' Roxanne raised an eyebrow. 'Channel 5, who love the idea of four strong women—'

'Three,' Roxanne corrected him. 'I told you, I'm not doing it.'

Rick gritted his teeth and tried again. '*Four* strong women making a comeback.'

'Comeback to what? I have a business to run.'

Rick looked around the empty bar and gave Roxanne a despairing look. 'You'd give up another chance at fame, money, everyone wanting you again, for an empty, failing bar?'

Roxanne took in the empty room they stood in. Seeing it so bare tore her up. Not because of the bottom line, but because she loved this place. It had been her sanctuary for *years*. And now it was dying, for no other reason than it had gone out of fashion.

'Say that again,' Roxanne said.

'You'd give up fame and fortune for this place?'

'No – the everyone wanting a piece of me bit.'

'Well, that comes with the rock star territory, doesn't it . . .' Rick replied, raising one eyebrow.

Roxanne grinned.

'There would have to be a big relaunch party, right? A media blitz to celebrate the return of the Thunder Girls ahead of the Wembley gig?'

'Of course.'

'Okay. The relaunch party will be here.'

Rick looked taken aback. 'Here? The place is *dead*, Roxy.'

'And so is your reunion without me. I don't want to do the bloody gig, but if it gives me the chance to make Heaven & Hell *the* place to be seen again, then it will be worth it.'

Rick nodded. 'If that's what it takes.'

'And Shine will agree to this? It's not an empty promise that you agree to and then suddenly it's not *feasible*?' she said, using her fingers to make quote marks around 'feasible'.

Rick stared her dead in the eye; she felt her stomach do a little flip of excitement. 'You have my word,' he said.

'I've heard that before.'

They both stood looking at each other in silence for a few moments. Rick breathed deeply and looked away, gesticulating around the space.

'It's a deal. We'll pull in all the press . . . put this club back on the map again, in exchange for one last ride on the Thunder ship,' he said and winked.

Roxanne leaned towards him. 'I want it in writing that the launch is here, and if it gets pulled I am released from my contract.'

'Absolutely,' Rick said, smiling.

'*And* I want Jamie on board designing the stage outfits and a deal that gives him full credit. Make that happen, and keep that crazy bitch away from me as much as possible during this road back to hell, and you've got a deal.'

27

It took Carly ages to get ready. She couldn't decide what to wear. The black dress and ankle boots were all wrong. As for the bangles on both wrists . . . she looked like one of the Bananarama girls circa 1983. She put on jeans and a cashmere sweater. Too dressed down. From the restaurant's website it was hard to tell what kind of crowd went there. It looked pretty rustic to her. What seemed to be sawdust on the floor, which couldn't be right. She checked the time. She was going to have to get a move on. Didn't want him to think she had stood him up.

It was a week since she had left Dave, telling him she needed her own space. Since the night at Grosvenor House they had barely spoken and a couple of times he had bunked down in the spare room. On at least one occasion he had not gone to bed at all. Worried, she had crept down and put her ear to the door of the snooker room, hearing the sound of balls sinking into pockets. At least he seemed to be practising seriously, at last.

He was in the snooker room when she told him she was leaving and waited for an outburst, something sarcastic and belittling, but nothing came. He seemed, literally, thrown off balance and she thought he might be about to pass out. The colour left his face and he lost his footing, did a little stagger (which might have been the drink), before steadying himself on his cue.

'No problem,' he said. 'We've got a freezer full of M&S ready meals and if I run short of anything –' he nodded at the drinks cabinet – 'there's Ocado.' He made a silly-me face. 'I mean, it's not like you do much shopping or cooking or *anything* really these days. So, fine, run along and play pop stars, or whatever it is you're doing. You'll soon be back.'

He chalked his cue and effortlessly potted the black.

Carly stood for another few seconds, trying to think of some witty put-down, not managing to come up with anything, before storming out and giving the door a good hard slam.

She was renting her own place now on a six-month lease, to give her time to think through her options. The terraced house, not far from Brick Lane, was one of the first properties she had looked at. Cosy sitting room. Modern, spacious kitchen that led to a courtyard full of greenery at the back. She wasn't the only person who'd wanted it, though. Someone from one of the big City firms was also keen. A broker by the name of Adam Smith.

The estate agent had arranged for them to view at the same time. When they both said they'd take it Carly couldn't hide her disappointment but, before she knew what was happening, her rival bowed out. Said there was an apartment at Butler's Wharf he could have another look at.

She had taken him for coffee as a thank you.

Now they were meeting for lunch.

She spotted Adam as soon as she got to the restaurant, perched at a stool at the bar. He got to his feet when he saw her.

'Wow, you look gorgeous,' he said, kissing her on both cheeks.

She wasn't sure she had got the dress code right. Everyone looked so formal. Suits and tailored shirts. Cufflinks. Shoes polished to within an inch of their lives. The women as well as the men. Carly was in a floaty print dress that looked more garden party than boardroom.

'I didn't know what to wear,' she said, sounding apologetic.

'I love it. You look sensational.'

She smiled at him, grateful for the compliment. It was a long time since Dave had told her she looked good.

Adam poured her a glass of champagne. He was in a light grey suit, white shirt and what could have been an old school tie. She glimpsed a pair of rose-gold cufflinks. Rolex watch. He was a couple of years younger than her, she had discovered. Dark wavy hair. Slim, strong-looking. A sudden image of the two of them in bed took hold and she felt light-headed. He held up his glass and gave her a thousand-watt smile. Twinkly eyes. They clinked glasses and she gulped down some of her champagne, hoping it wasn't obvious what was on her mind.

She knew she would sleep with him.

Dave had already checked out the address. Why Carly would choose to live in a terraced house on a scruffy little street was beyond him. Clearly, she had gone a bit bonkers. Her age, most likely. He had seen the pictures of Chrissie Martin in the *Post.* Carly wasn't that much younger but Chrissie looked amazing, he thought begrudgingly. A bit of HRT obviously worked wonders; perhaps that's what Carly needed too.

He went to the pub on the corner – not a bad boozer, a few addled-looking City types already getting stuck into the wine – and took a seat at the window where he could keep an eye on the house. Just before midday, the red front door opened and Carly came out all dressed up. As if she was going to the races or some posh wedding. She had those ridiculous shoes on again, the ones she had worn the night of the Thunder Girls reunion dinner. Well over the top, in his opinion.

At the side of the road, a black Mercedes was waiting. She got in and it pulled away, heading towards Bishopsgate. Perhaps she had a meeting at the record company. Or some press thing. That would explain the fancy outfit.

He waited a few minutes before getting up and going out

into the street, approaching the house from the back. The gate leading into the courtyard was unlocked and he let himself in. Through the patio doors he could see into the kitchen with its gleaming black fridge and copper pans hanging from the ceiling. A mug was on the table, a jacket slung over the back of one of the chairs.

When the car pulled up again in front of the house a couple of hours later he was back in his window seat at the pub. A bloke he didn't recognize got out of the Mercedes. Dave studied him. Well-cut suit. The kind of unruly hair that doesn't happen by accident. Designer stubble. He came round the back of the car and opened the door on the passenger side, and Carly emerged in her floaty dress. Looking happy. A lot happier than Dave had seen her look for a long while. The bloke slung his arm around her and the two of them went into the house together.

Dave felt a pounding in his chest. A deafening whoosh inside his head. The room started to gather speed and his glass slid from his grasp and smashed on the floor. He wanted to run into the street and hammer on the red door but he didn't trust his legs to hold him up. Instead, he stayed where he was, struggling to take in what he had just seen. The flash motor. Stubble man. And Carly, radiant, in her floaty frock. The whole thing playing over and over in sickening slow motion.

His wife with another man.

Cheating little slut.

28

Jason Naylor's house was the tidiest on the street. Bright white nets hung behind sparklingly clean windows. Two planters either side of the front gate were filled with neatly trimmed conifers – they looked out of place in a street where all the other houses were rather unkempt. In the front garden a neat square of lawn was perfectly manicured. Two robin redbreasts were nibbling at a nut stick laid on top. Behind them a curtain twitched as Jason watched them contentedly. Suddenly his handsome face looked twisted as the birds flew away, having spotted a grey squirrel climbing the post to steal the nuts.

Inside, Jason reached for an air rifle he kept by the front door. He opened the window slowly and aimed it at the squirrel – with one finger click, a pellet shot through the window right into the squirrel's head and it fell onto the grass. 'Got you,' he smiled. He went outside, took a pair of rubber gloves out of his pocket, picked the squirrel up by its tail and carried it to the bin. 'That's what you get for stealing,' he said, still smiling, then made a whistling sound towards the sky and called out, 'You can come back now, birdies, it's safe again.'

Back inside he washed the gloves in the sink and laid them out to dry on the side. The house was as spotless inside as it was out, even the furniture had plastic coverings; his mother had always said that was the best way to keep things pristine and Jason liked things just so. He loved being inside his bolt-hole, a place of refuge, where he could escape from an ugly world he had never fully felt part of. At home, he felt capable, confident and in control. As if he could do anything he set his mind to. He smoothed down his crisp linen trousers and took a seat again by the window, smiling as he saw the birds return. He looked around the living room. All the cushions were in a perfectly neat row and all the tiny Murano glass animal ornaments were lined up with perfect symmetry across the fireplace.

At one time, his mother saw to the cleaning. Made sure the place was spotless. It had only been a few months since she finally died, after a two-decade battle against motor neurone disease. After her condition had deteriorated and made housework too challenging, he had made sure that he kept the house just as she liked it. He tried not to think about his mother. It got him down. He was on his own now but he had a plan to change that. He ran a finger along the shelf and, finding no dust, smiled once again to himself. Perfect. Now he had done his daily ritual of making the house spotless and protecting his friends in the garden it was time to devote more time to his new mission. A file on the kitchen table had the words 'special investigation' neatly stencilled across it.

Sitting down at the little kitchen table with four red stools and a setting for one, he opened the file and poured himself a glass of water from a jug; no tea for him, as Mother said it was full of sweepings from dirty floors. As he raised the glass to his mouth his teeth sparkled pure white. He cleaned his teeth at least four times a day.

Over on a shelf by the fridge sat a Thunder Girls mug he had bought in 1987 after their debut single had just gone to number one and there was a signing at HMV on Oxford Street. He had queued overnight to make sure he would see them. There were thousands like him, mainly hysterical girls, huddled on the pavement behind crash barriers, desperate for a glimpse of their idols. He was just fourteen and his mother had tried to stop him going. Usually he did what he was told, but not that time. His mother didn't understand – he *loved* the girls and nothing was going to stop him meeting them.

As he had got near the front of the queue and caught a glimpse of them he almost passed out. Close-up, they were incredible, a million times better than the posters he had on his bedroom walls. Other-worldly, it seemed, with their perfect skin and glossy lips. He had fought for breath. There had already been a few fainters, girls carried off by security, never to be seen again. Sent straight to the back of the queue, he suspected. Well, not him. A few more steps and he would be within touching distance.

He could remember every detail of that day.

Carly's sweet smile. Roxanne winking cheekily. Anita saying she loved his passion for the band. 'I'm mad about you all,' he managed to say, his cheeks flushing bright pink. Anita smiled. 'Well we'll call you our Mad Fan, then!' she said, laughing – he took it as a compliment, no one was madder about them than him. The other girls were pretty, but Chrissie was The One. Drop. Dead. Gorgeous. Everyone said she was the bitch of the group but he didn't believe it. She was the one he had clicked with. Asking his name and where he was from. Saying how lovely it was to see a boy there. A good-looking lad, she called him. *Flirting*. He was horribly tongue-tied but managed to stammer that she was his favourite. 'Well, you're *my* favourite, Jason,' she said, signing her name and adding three kisses and the words *To Jason, our Mad Fan! – we love you!*

At that moment, he fell in love for the first and only time.

He had stood rooted to the spot, staring at her; his pupils seemed to dilate and became like dark moons. Eye to eye they stood until one of the security blokes appeared next to him saying he was holding up the queue and yanked him away. At the merchandise table he spent all his birthday money buying the mug, which was still in its original packaging after all these years; he'd have loved to use it but that would have made it dirty, and it had to stay perfect. Upstairs he still had his *Midnight Madness* T-shirt, plus a wrist band that snapped before he got it back home, but he had repaired it carefully with glue and kept it in his bedside drawer.

He finished his water, washed the glass and dried it, then went upstairs to the bedroom he had slept in all his life. Against one wall was a single bed with a white duvet cover and pillows.

On a large chest of drawers were framed pictures of the girls neatly lined up. A set of Thunder Girls dolls posed along a bookshelf, all still sealed apart from Chrissie's – her packing was open and the doll was laid next to it – he had to play with her, he couldn't help himself. Just that one meeting had confirmed that Chrissie would forever be the love of his life. His big regret was that looking after his mother for so long had kept him from seeking her out. He loved his mother, but he had his own life to live too. Now there were no more reasons to keep them apart. He'd kicked himself for not telling her before Mother became ill. There had been so many opportunities. Backstage meet and greets, all those times he had bagged front row seats at their concerts when Chrissie had clocked him gazing up at her. All he had to do was scramble up on stage and throw himself at her; declare undying love. Other fans got on stage but at the last moment he always lost his nerve.

Over the years, whenever he saw Chrissie pictured with another man it cut him up inside, although he told himself that mostly they weren't real relationships, just fake dates arranged by the record company. The cynical workings of the publicity machine were well known and he was no fool, he knew what they had – a true connection.

It almost destroyed him when she married Rick. If he'd been on the ball he'd have seen it coming but he read the situation completely wrong, thinking Rick would go back to Roxanne eventually, leaving Chrissie free once again.

Even though it pained him, he kept all the stuff from the papers about the wedding to Rick, telling himself that one day he and Chrissie would look back at the cuttings together and laugh. The pain of her marrying Rick had prepared him for the eventual marriage to Scott too.

For a whole week he couldn't eat, couldn't sleep, and refused to go to school. Missed two of his mock exams, not that he cared. What good were qualifications if he couldn't have the woman he loved?

Over the years Jason had learnt to bide his time. He was a firm believer in things working out the way they were meant to once the timing was right. Chrissie was his soulmate. As long as he was patient, destiny would bring them together at precisely the right moment.

He turned and gazed at his reflection in the mirror on the wardrobe door. He lifted his shirt to reveal perfect abs, the result of the fastidious one hundred sit-ups before bed routine that he never missed. His skin was clean and clear and his hair smoothed back with the lightest touch of Brylcreem. Yes, he thought to himself – Chrissie would approve.

He went back downstairs to what he thought of as the operations room – what his mother had quaintly called the parlour and only ever used on Christmas Day, when Jason lit the fire and the two of them settled down on the plastic-covered settee with a small sweet sherry each to watch the Queen's speech.

All over the walls were neatly pinned notes and pictures. Scraps of paper and photos were lined up all over the room with Post-it notes on each. There were hundreds of pictures of Scott, all pinned to one cork board at the end of the room. Jason had been monitoring him ever since he first started seeing Chrissie, instantly knowing he was trouble.

A sequence of photos showed Scott arriving back at Chrissie's place by cab and loading bags into the Range Rover. He had looked furtive, Jason thought. Shifty. Up to no good. Jason heard him make a call before driving off, telling whoever was on the other end 'the deed was done, mate', and that Chrissie was 'completely in the dark, stupid cow'. Jason didn't like the sound of that. 'So if it's all right with you,' Scott had said, 'I'm getting out of here quick as you like, before it all hits the fan.'

Jason had upped the frequency of his visits to the house and happened to be there, watching from inside a rhododendron bush, when Chrissie arrived home – after an extended honeymoon in Miami, according to the papers.

He witnessed Rick arriving soon after, looking grim. The discreet listening device Jason had attached to the outside of the kitchen wall, neatly concealed by a drainpipe, came in handy that day, revealing to Jason the true extent of Scott's betrayal. The man in the spyware shop hadn't lied when he said it would pick up conversations through solid brickwork.

While he couldn't help feeling pleased that Scott was now out of the picture, Jason didn't like to think of Chrissie being dumped. Dumped and fleeced. Ever since, he had taken it upon himself to get to the bottom of things. This was his chance to be Chrissie's knight in shining armour. To take revenge on Scott for his despicable behaviour.

That meant finding him.

Jason was glad now that he had attached a tracking device to the underside of Chrissie's Range Rover. It made locating Scott a whole lot easier. He also had access to something called Automatic Number-Plate Recognition, which confirmed Scott had spent the night in Devon after leaving Chrissie's (handily, the hotel also used the ANPR system) before heading into Cornwall.

Sitting in front of a white laptop, he tapped in some details. A map appeared, showing exactly where the Range Rover had gone. Across the River Tamar and down through Cornwall on the A38, veering off eventually at Marazion, along twisty narrow lanes as far as Karenza Cove, close to Land's End. For a few days it was parked up, before going back the way it had come, stopping at Truro, which was where it was now. It had hardly moved since then, just short hops here and there.

He felt pleased with himself. He already knew plenty about Scott – while Scott hadn't the foggiest he was under surveillance. That was the thing about covert work. The best operatives were the ones you didn't see. Unremarkable-looking individuals you wouldn't look at twice. Under the radar, carrying out their vital work undetected.

It was how he thought of himself.

He typed in the Truro coordinates, which he now knew by heart. Google Earth's street view allowed him to poke around the town centre location and make a few calls. It was amazing what people would tell you. He now knew Scott had sold the Range Rover – it was featured on the website of a local garage – and was driving a powder-blue Fiat 500.

He was living at Karenza Cove, a tiny village with a few houses, a pub and a shop. Parts of it looked familiar, similar to scenes he'd seen on *Poldark*, which he only watched for Eleanor Tomlinson, whose feisty Demelza character reminded him of Chrissie.

He wondered if Scott had run off with another woman, although it hardly seemed credible – who in their right mind would leave Chrissie?

He studied the series of photos he had of Scott going in and out of the house in Surrey. Loading up the Range Rover, looking over his shoulder. Guilty as hell, and no wonder. Jason felt a surge of sympathy for Chrissie. Scott could only have ripped her off because she was too generous. Too trusting. He had always thought so.

She deserved better.

He picked up a Sharpie and began defacing a picture of Scott's handsome face, drawing on the kind of droopy moustache sported by the Village People's Leatherman.

Annoyingly, that only made him look more attractive, so he gave him straggly, greasy-looking hair and made him bug-eyed. Jason was in no doubt what Scott really was. A sponger. A waste of space. The type to take advantage of a vulnerable woman. He attacked the photo, delivering a series of frenzied blows with the Sharpie, until every bit of Scott was obliterated.

Panting, he went to the mantelpiece, where a row of candles flickered beside framed photos of Chrissie. His shrine to her. Some of the pictures were ones he had snatched of her from one of his hiding places, as she came and went at the house. They were the ones he liked best. Not the most flattering, perhaps, but . . . *unique*. No one else had those.

On a screen, the video of the Thunder Girls on their first tour played. He had been there. In Reading, and at both shows in Hammersmith. He pointed a remote at the screen and cranked up the volume, singing along to 'Love You, Hate You', doing the moves. When the big close-up of Chrissie filled the screen he hit the pause button and gazed at the frozen image. It was as if she was in the room, watching over him, egging him on, as he worked tirelessly on her behalf. He laid some paper towel across the floor under the screen then stepped back and unbuckled his belt as the camera zoomed in on Chrissie blowing a kiss with her glossy red lips. He dropped his trousers and began to masturbate. 'I'm going to have to take a little trip, my love,' he breathed towards the screen. 'I won't be gone long, though, and once I get back we can be together.'

29

Carly was in the bedroom doing her make-up and watching what she still thought of as the *Matthew Wright Show*, even though Jeremy Vine had taken over. Anne Diamond was on, looking slim, Carly thought. The gastric band seemed to be working. It was a shame she'd had so many body battles in her later years – she'd been lovely to Carly when she'd interviewed her back in the day on TV-am, although Carly had found the Roland Rat puppet very annoying. On the show they were talking about a woman who'd reported her ex-boyfriend for leaving flowers and chocolates on her doorstep and generally getting in touch when she didn't want to hear from him. The police didn't seem to think it was stalking and, as a consequence, failed to take her complaints seriously. While they were still taking a softly-softly approach the ex went from bombarding her with unwanted gifts to attacking her.

Carly couldn't help thinking about Dave, seemingly on

his best behaviour now that she had left him. He was in the habit of sending flowers and chocolates and notes that said he missed her and most days called to see how she was, leaving concerned messages if she didn't pick up. It was starting to irritate her. Was that the same as stalking? she wondered.

On TV, a woman with a pinched face and poker-straight hair was saying her ex had gone a bit crazy when they broke up. Chucked a brick through her window. Turned up at her office screaming obscenities. Carly shook her head and combed mascara through her lashes. She was getting ready to see Adam. Dave was irritating but not the kind to throw bricks. Even if he wanted to, he'd probably think it was too much effort anyway. After thirty years there was nothing she didn't know about him. A troubling thought then went through her head: how much did she really know about Adam?

The doorbell went and she hurried downstairs. On the doorstep was a box fastened with black ribbon. She looked up and down the street but couldn't see who had left it. No note, unless it was inside. She took the box into the house and opened it at the kitchen table. A card was tucked inside, next to a simple arrangement of white lilies well past their best. Petals starting to shrivel and go brown, the stems showing the first signs of rotting, giving off a pungent smell. She wrinkled her nose and took the card from its envelope. *In deepest sympathy*. Carly flinched. The typed message inside offered condolences on the tragic death of . . . Carly Joleen Hughes. *Taken from us too soon*. She flung the card down, shaken. Who would be sick enough to do such a thing? The doorbell went again, making her jump. She half expected to find a delivery driver apologizing for leaving the wrong package.

Then again, it was *her* name on the card.

Dave was on the doorstep, an enormous bunch of roses in his arms, looking embarrassed. 'Sorry, I know I shouldn't just turn up without checking,' he began. Carly burst into tears and flung her arms round his neck. 'Whoa,' he said. 'What's wrong?' He held her while she sobbed. 'Steady on, you're squashing the blooms.' She pulled away, tears running down her face. Dave gazed at her. 'I have to say, that wasn't the reaction I was expecting.'

They went indoors and he read the card and examined the box. Nothing to say where it had come from. He asked if she wanted to call the police but she shook her head.

'It's just some crank,' he said.

'Whoever it was knew how to spell my middle name,' she said. 'Not many people get it right.'

Dave put the flowers in the bin and tore up the card. Made coffee and sat with her, squeezing her hand. 'I'm here if you need me. Whatever's going on with us, you know that, right?' She nodded. 'I'll always love you, babe, even if you . . .' He gave her an anguished look. 'Even if you don't want me.' Carly felt something pull at her heart. 'And I'm sorry it's taken a fight for me to realize that. You're the only one. I meant it when I made my vows. For better, for worse. Now and forever.'

She texted Adam and said she was running late. A text pinged straight back saying that was fine, he would push the car back half an hour, if that gave her long enough. She sent a couple of kisses back.

She left Dave finishing his coffee while she went upstairs and repaired her make-up. It felt good having him there. Already she felt a lot better about the flowers business. Dave had asked if it might be an obsessive fan. There had been a few of them when the Thunder Girls were at their height, so-called super-fans who followed them everywhere. One or two were a bit odd, Carly remembered. The lad they called the Mad Fan, who was fixated with Chrissie. The young girl who sent Carly love letters and kept trying to get backstage – their tour manager had caught her climbing through a window at the venue in Newcastle. She had even got into their hotel in Manchester and made it as far as the floor the girls had commandeered. It had taken a restraining order to put a stop to all that.

Now that Carly and the others were back in the public eye, everyone speculating about a Thunder comeback, all kinds of people could be taking an unnatural interest.

Dave stayed until her car arrived. Outside, he gave her a light peck on the cheek and told her to let him know if there was any more bother. She promised she would.

He watched the car pull away and once it was out of sight went to the pub over the road. There was a spring in his step, a self-satisfied smile on his face. He had earned a drink, he reckoned. Things had gone a lot better with Carly than he had dared hope. Who knew a few rotting flowers and a condolence card would send her over the edge like that? Lucky he turned up when he did. He congratulated himself. Right place, right time. Shoulder to cry on.

He sank his first pint in five seconds flat.

'You look like you're celebrating,' the barman said, pulling another.

'I am,' Dave said. 'That's exactly what I'm doing.'

Carly told Adam about Dave showing up at the house, making her late. She didn't mention the other business.

'Everything okay?' he asked. 'With the hubby, I mean.'

'There's a lot to sort out. Best to stay on good terms, if we can.' She had put the shark-eyed divorce lawyer on hold for now. No point stirring things unnecessarily, she decided, not with Dave being so good about everything.

Adam gave her hand a squeeze. They were in a cosy pub in the City. Low ceilings, candles, wood-panelled walls. Adam had booked a table in the restaurant upstairs. She had been worried her Isabel Marant dress was a bit much for daytime but it was obvious the place was posh. No prices on the menu, for a start, and more designer handbags in one place than in Harrods. She recognized a rake-thin blonde woman in a tight dress from one of the TV reality shows, drinking with a football pundit whose name was on the tip of her tongue.

Adam ordered pink Bollinger. They clinked glasses. The bubbles went straight to her head. After the first glass she felt light-headed, a bit jangly. Probably a bit too much caffeine earlier on. She excused herself to go to the ladies and Adam rose to his feet, easing her seat out for her. She caught the telly woman watching, taking in the pricey frock, the Goya bag. Perhaps she knew who Carly was.

As she strode through the bar to the powder room, feeling heads turn, she felt a surge of power. How she had let a few dying flowers and a spiteful card turn her into a sobbing wreck was a mystery. When you're in the public eye the odd nutty thing was bound to happen, she reasoned.

In the ladies' room, she reapplied lipstick and ran her hands under the cold tap. An elegant woman in a smart shift dress – the toilet attendant, Carly realized with a jolt – held out a fluffy white towel. From a selection of hand creams Carly chose one called Resurrection by Aesop. The attendant suggested a spray of Goutal Eau d'Hadrien, the light citrus fragrance a perfect match for the hand cream. Feeling reckless, and a bit woozy from the champagne, Carly tipped the woman a fiver.

Things were going her way, at last. A gorgeous new bloke. Hype galore around a Thunder Girls reunion – even before the official announcement had been made. She had lost a bit of weight as well. The fly in the ointment was Dave. She had expected him to play dirty, not declare undying love. What he'd said about meaning the vows they'd made had got her thinking.

Perhaps she had been a bit hasty.

The truth was she had no idea what to do for the best.

30

Life for Roxanne Lloyd sure had changed gear since the meeting at Chrissie's house, and the paparazzi aftermath.

The pictures of Roxanne and Chrissie slugging it out had sparked a media storm, with one of the tabloids running an entire page on what they called Roxanne's killer heels. Manolo Blahnik then reported a surge in sales of that particular shoe.

The paper rehashed what had happened with Rick thirty years earlier, calling him Roxanne's soulmate, and accusing Chrissie of pinching him from under her nose. Chrissie was portrayed as the kind of cut-throat bitch who'd stab you in the back soon as look at you, best friend or not. Definitely not a girl's girl, the paper concluded.

For good measure, they reproduced the bare bottom picture and one of their columnists wrote an opinion piece on why some women denied being menopausal. The columnist said Chrissie was ideally placed to speak out about The

Change but instead had chosen to let down millions of women by refusing to admit she was on HRT. As if the menopause – a perfectly natural event, the columnist said – was something to be ashamed of.

The irony was that Roxanne was also menopausal and taking bio-identical hormones. She had a good mind to go public about it and cast Chrissie in an even worse light.

To add insult to injury, the paper said Roxanne had always been the best singer in the band. Roxanne was gleeful, knowing how incensed Chrissie would be by the whole business.

Jamie had come up with the bright idea of having the pictures of the brawl blown up and put on screens all around Heaven & Hell. A friend of his edited the images into a fast-cut video starring Chrissie's bare bottom and the patch she continued to insist was *not* HRT. It played on a loop above the dance floor.

The club was suddenly buzzing. Takings were up. The queues were back and the VIP area crowded, mainly with TV reality stars and footballers. Roxanne had come up with a gin-based cocktail that packed a punch and called it the Slapper. It was proving popular. When the *Daily Post* gave it a five-star rating in a feature on the hottest drinks in the capital, sales rocketed.

Rehearsals for the Thunder Girls reunion show were about to get underway and Roxanne could hardly wait. Chrissie would be out for blood, not that Roxanne cared. She was looking forward to taking her on. For good measure, she might just turn up at the rehearsal room in the notorious killer heels – see if that got a reaction.

She spotted a couple from *Made in Chelsea* on their way up the stairs to the VIP area and was about to go and speak to them when a voice said, 'Any chance I can try one of the special cocktails?'

She turned to see Rick standing there. Her stomach did a funny little flip.

'Looks like business is booming,' he said, looking round.

'We're doing all right.'

'The Thunder Girls effect.' He gazed at a screen filled with an unflattering close-up of Chrissie – hair all over, face contorted in a snarl. 'Is there somewhere we can chat?' he asked.

Roxanne led him upstairs to one of the few unoccupied booths at the back of the VIP section. A waitress appeared and asked what they'd like to drink. Roxanne ordered two Slappers.

Rick was frowning. 'You know the other night, when I told you Chrissie was having a hard time, it was meant to be between the two of us. I didn't think you were going to use it as ammunition. Actually, I hoped you might understand, sympathize even, given you've had a rough ride.'

'I did what I had to.' Roxanne bristled. 'Yes, I certainly know how it feels to be turned over by someone I thought I could trust, although to be honest I don't think that's territory you should be going into.' She gave him a defiant look.

He sighed. 'I know what I did to you was wrong on every level.' He put a hand against his heart. 'I'm sorry. I really meant what I said when I told you that if I could go back and do things differently, I would, trust me.'

'It's that whole *trust* thing I'm struggling with.'

'If it's any consolation, it's not like things worked out the way I imagined,' he said. 'No happy endings – for me or for Chrissie.'

Not for me either, Roxanne thought. 'No, well, what goes around, and all that,' she said.

'Please, Roxy, I don't want any bad feeling between us. We're working together again, and it looks like the Thunder Girls are going to be huge. The last time there was this much hype around a band was when . . .' He thought for a moment. 'Well, when you girls were first in favour. You won't believe what's going on behind the scenes at Shine. The press office can't keep up. They're getting calls from all around the world. The whole Thunder Girls madness is taking hold all over again.'

The waitress appeared with their drinks.

Rick raised his glass. 'Here's to us.' Roxanne's insides did another flip. She touched her glass to his. Rick tried the cocktail. His eyes widened. 'Wow, explosive stuff! What's in it?'

'Funny you should say that. There's something in there called Pinhead Gunpowder.'

Rick looked dubious. 'Is that even legal?'

She laughed. 'It's a kind of green tea, silly. Full of

goodness. Chrissie might like it – it might help with her hormone problems.'

'You'll be telling me it's a health drink next.'

She shook her head. For a moment neither of them spoke. On the dance floor below, Jamie weaved his way through a mass of bodies, stopping occasionally to have a word with someone. A lanky blond boy, shirtless in ripped jeans, flung an arm round his neck.

'He's good with the punters,' Rick said, watching. Roxanne nodded. 'I take it his father's out of the picture?'

She gave him a sharp look. 'He walked out. Story of my life.'

'So you brought him up on your own? Well, you did a great job.'

Roxanne played with her drink, submerging slices of lime with a straw. 'Actually, Pete stuck around in a half-hearted way until a few years ago.' She shrugged. 'Worse than useless, to be honest. When he left, the press had a field day. Apparently, I'm the Thunder Girl who can't keep her man.'

Rick had seen the stories. 'I don't think anyone ever—'

She cut him off. 'Not that I care. When you've got a kid, that's your focus. All that ever mattered was making sure Jamie was okay.'

'So what happened with Pete in the end?'

She laughed. 'He took what money I had and, shall we say, invested it unwisely. Dodgy timeshare schemes. Left me up to my neck in it.'

'I'm sorry.'

'So now he's with that artist – if you can call chucking globs of paint at a canvas art. She's rolling in it; no wonder he likes her.' She gazed at the floor. 'And all these years later, I'm still cleaning up his mess, juggling debts he landed me with. If there's one thing I've realized it's that when someone shafts you the consequences can be far-reaching.' She looked at Rick. 'That's been my experience, anyway. Still, water under the bridge now. Onwards.'

He leaned forward and she got a whiff of Davidoff. 'You're amazing, you know that, don't you?' She felt her heart rate speed up. 'I mean it. And now's your chance to turn things around, once and for all.' His thumb stroked her wrist. Roxanne felt faint. 'There's a big pay day coming, more maybe than anyone knows, given the offers flooding in.' Oh God. She wanted to kiss him. 'Look, I don't need you to tell me I let you down big time, so let me make it up to you – prove I've changed. There's a hell of a lot riding on this. For all of us.' An image appeared on the screen above them, Chrissie, legs in the air. Rick glanced at it, then turned back to her. 'How about calling a truce?'

The spell was broken. She nodded and Rick looked relieved. What she didn't make clear was that the truce she was agreeing to was with him.

It did not extend to Chrissie.

31

Carly sat down on the floor of the rehearsal room. She was scrolling through her social media, only half listening as the other girls talked. After that last run-through, they all needed a recovery break.

'So, this is it, it's actually happening.' Anita, in loose jogging pants and a cropped top, slumped to the floor in the rehearsal room. Her face was pink. 'Considering I swim every day, I can't believe I'm so unfit.' She waited for her breath to return to normal. 'Just as well we're only doing a short set for the relaunch show at Heaven & Hell.' She glugged down some water and gave her face a spritz of Evian. 'Tell you what, Rox, you can really throw some shapes. You probably told me years ago but I don't remember much pre-1990! Did you have dance training?'

Roxanne stretched like a cat. The logo on her T-shirt said 'Star Struck'. 'Not really. Ballet when I was four, if that counts.' She did a perfect pirouette. 'Didn't keep it up, though. Too much like hard work. I just wanted to wear the tutu.'

'*I* had formal training,' Chrissie said. She was in a tiny mesh vest and spray-on leggings. As Lucy, the choreographer, had guided them through their routines, Chrissie had kept pace with ease, and despite the morning's exertions her make-up remained intact. 'Contemporary, a bit of jazz and tap,' she said. 'Street dance too. We did pretty much everything at stage school.'

Roxanne rolled her eyes. 'What happened – did they boot you out once they discovered your complete lack of natural rhythm?'

'At least I can follow the steps,' Chrissie snapped back.

'Sadly, not the steps we're actually doing. You're the Gary Barlow of the band.'

'He was also the lead. Are you the Jason Orange then?'

Anita held up her hands. 'Now, now, you two. No fighting.'

'How about you, Carly?' Roxanne said.

Carly was in the far corner of the room checking something on her phone. She looked up. 'Sorry, did I miss something?'

'You're not a bad dancer – where did you learn?'

'Blimey, your memory is bad, isn't it! I was at Sylvia Young, wasn't I,' Carly said.

'Oh yes, I remember now,' Anita said. 'Loads of famous people went to Sylvia Young, didn't they?'

Carly nodded. 'Emma Bunton, Billie Piper, the Appleton sisters. Danniella Westbrook, poor thing. I wasn't there long, though, before I joined you lot. I was glad to leave – I didn't really fit in,' Carly said.

Roxanne turned to Chrissie, who was in front of the mirrored wall reapplying lip gloss. 'Who went to your stage school? Anyone we've heard of?'

'Well, *I* did, obviously,' Chrissie said.

'Where was it – in Manchester? I'll look up the website, see who else went there.' She whipped her phone out. 'What was it called?'

Chrissie muttered something.

'What did you say – Strangeways?' Roxanne doubled up. 'Come on, tell us – give us all a laugh. Was Julie Goodyear from *Corrie* in your year?'

The door swung open and Susan appeared with a tray of drinks. 'Right,' she said. 'Flat white.' She handed it to Roxanne. 'Skinny cappuccino.'

'That's mine,' Anita said. 'Did you remember the hazelnut syrup?'

Susan nodded.

'Another cappuccino with soya milk – that's yours, Carly.'

Carly looked up from her phone, distracted. 'Oh, right, thanks.'

'And the kombucha . . . for Chrissie.'

'Come-what-cha?' Roxanne looked amused.

'It's a kind of tea. Incredibly good for you,' Chrissie said.

'Is it to do with, you know . . .' Roxanne looked conspiratorial. '*The Change*?' she whispered, loud enough for everyone to hear.

Chrissie thrust the drink back at Susan and turned away from Roxanne.

'Has it affected your movement?' Roxanne continued. 'I'm clearly a better dancer than you. And *I* didn't even go to stage school.'

Chrissie spun around. 'Shut it, Roxy, before I shut it for you.'

'Ooh, I'm shaking.'

'That's probably the booze in your system,' Chrissie snarled.

Susan stepped between them. 'I got everything you wanted from the beauty hall at Selfridge's,' she told Chrissie, pushing one of the store's distinctive bags at her.

Chrissie took it and peered inside.

'Is that where you get your patches?' Roxanne asked. 'The ones for *energy balancing* or whatever it is they're supposed to do.'

'Leave it, Roxy,' Anita said.

'Why? I'm enjoying myself. Anyway, she started it.'

'You did, actually,' Anita said.

Roxanne pointed at Chrissie. 'No. It was the tea bollocks that set me off.' Her shoulders shook. 'I wish someone had thought to mention that Gwyneth Paltrow herself would be joining us for rehearsals.'

'I'll take that as a compliment,' Chrissie said, making a mental note to check out Goop.com later.

Susan took hold of her elbow and steered her to the far

side of the room. 'Here, have some kombucha,' she said soothingly.

'Hey, Susan,' Anita said. 'Would you be able to get me some skin care stuff from that swanky salon on Sloane Square?'

Susan nodded. 'Course, that's what I'm here for. Just let me know what you want.'

Roxanne wandered over to Carly, who was still checking her phone. 'I see you're keeping out of things. Very wise.'

Carly looked up. 'Has your social media gone mad?' she asked.

Roxanne nodded. 'Several thousand more followers on Twitter.'

Carly was frowning. 'I'm getting some weird messages.'

'Oh, yeah, there are definitely some oddballs out there. Our fans, mostly.' She grinned. 'Remember the boy? The Mad Fan? Intense, always had his anorak zipped right up. Utterly potty about Chrissie, which tells you the poor kid must have been insane. Well, he popped up on Twitter and had a right go at me for coming to blows with the old trout. He must be – what? – forty-something and he's still following the Thunder Girls.' Her phone pinged. 'As I was saying.' She glanced at the screen. 'No, that's J to say he's ordering pizza for us tonight.'

Carly didn't want to say what kind of messages were appearing on her Twitter account. She was getting pornography, pictures of coffins, road kill. Someone had sent a series of disturbing photos of her Thunder Girls doll, tied up, a tiny piece of duct tape over its mouth. Pictures of the girls from way back, Carly's image manipulated to look as if she was drenched in blood, her face scribbled on. Every time something horrible popped up she blocked the sender but it did nothing to stem the flow of disturbing messages. Every day brought a fresh wave from a new set of trolls. The accounts were phoney, as far as she could make out, yet somehow the messages felt personal.

As if one person was out to get her.

If it was a stranger, she had no chance of figuring it out, or stopping them. But didn't they say a crime was most often committed by someone you knew? She wondered about Dave, but he was so hopeless with social media he relied on his manager to run his Twitter account. It was doubtful he even knew how to tweet, let alone what a hashtag was.

Adam, on the other hand, was on Twitter and Instagram, always posting updates.

There had been more unsettling stuff at home. Brochures from funeral parlours. A dead crow on the patio. Fortunately, Dave was due round that day and he had got rid of it.

So far, she had not told the other girls what was going on.

'I seem to be getting a lot of nasty stuff,' Carly said.

'Like what?' Roxanne asked.

'Oh, stuff from blokes. What they'd like to do to me.'

'Have you told Rick?'

She shook her head. 'No point getting worked up. It

probably just goes with the territory, although . . .' she hesitated. 'I can't help thinking I'm being stalked. There's some weird stuff going on at home. Like, the other night, I was on the sofa watching *Botched* in my jim-jams, and a tweet popped up: *I like your pyjamas*, it said.' She bit her lip. 'It was like they could *see* me.'

'That sounds personal,' Roxanne said, 'not some random weirdo. More like someone who knows how to press your buttons.'

'You don't think we're making a mistake?' Carly asked her.

'What do you mean?'

Carly shrugged. 'All this. Doing the reunion. I mean, we think it's wonderful, a fantastic opportunity and all that, but being back in the spotlight . . . there's got to be a downside. Don't you think?'

Roxanne looked puzzled. 'I don't see why.'

'It's horrendous out there these days. Online is like the Wild West. Everything laid bare.'

Roxanne chuckled. 'Like Chrissie's backside, you mean?'

'It's like being under surveillance.' Carly shuddered.

'You worry too much. Don't take things so seriously,' Roxanne advised.

Carly was silent. 'This reunion . . . playing Wembley. They say you should be careful what you wish for,' she said at last.

'Well, *they* are talking crap,' Roxanne told her. 'If you don't know them it doesn't matter, end of.'

32

Sitting in the corner pub, Dave refreshed the Twitter feed about Carly Hughes. The trolls were working overtime. Just what any knight in shining armour needed to save his damsel in distress.

He unlocked his phone and fired off a WhatsApp message. *How about turning the screw?*

He got the reply he was looking for.

'Tonight's my lucky night,' he chuckled to himself, polishing off his pint. He popped in a breath mint after. The New Dave didn't drink and always showed up right when Carly's online torment was at its worst, after all.

The one thing Carly hated about living alone was going back to an empty house. She let herself in and put all the lights on, hoping to make the place feel more cheerful. In the kitchen, she switched on the TV for company and put her phone on charge. Endlessly checking her social media accounts seemed to drain the battery in no time. She'd have to remember to take her charger with her in future.

On *The One Show*, Alex Jones was asking a cute young lad what he liked about Wales. Carly wondered who did her hair. It always looked amazing.

There wasn't much in the fridge. She poured a large glass of wine and opened a shop-bought superfood salad. After a couple of mouthfuls it went in the bin. She hadn't realized the red stuff was quinoa.

Her phone pinged with an alert. Voicemail. Adam. 'Hey, babe, hope the rehearsals went well.' At once she felt better. She would ask him to come over. They could order in something to eat and she could tell him what was going on with her social media. 'So, I'm at the airport, about to catch a flight to New York,' he was saying. She blinked. *What?* 'And, well, I just wanted to say goodbye.' The line went dead. A female voice invited her to listen to the message again. She put the phone on speaker and stared at it, a horrible sinking feeling taking hold, hearing him give her what could only be the heave-ho. *Just wanted to say goodbye.* Was that *it*? She had heard about people dumping their partners by text these days. Or WhatsApp. Or doing something called ghosting, which Carly thought was utterly heartless. Not Adam, though. He wasn't like that. She played the message over and over, hoping each time to hear something different. *Goodbye. Goodbye. Goodbye.* It didn't make sense.

She knew he had been based in New York before moving back to London – if indeed he *had* moved back. All the time she had known him he had been staying in a hotel. What if he was only ever going to be in town for a few weeks and wanted a casual fling? Maybe he'd been stringing her along the whole time while she was getting carried away, falling for him.

She went on Twitter to see if he had sent her a direct message. Nothing. A tweet caught her eye. *You suit your hair like that*. Sent a few seconds ago. She wheeled around and peered at the window overlooking the garden. Was someone out there, watching? The doorbell went, sending her heart rate into overdrive. She stood absolutely still. The bell went again, a longer more insistent ring, then a voice called through the letterbox.

'Carly? Carly? You in there?'

Dave! Relief went through her. She ran from the kitchen and opened the door, flinging herself at him.

'Hey, you nearly had me over,' he said, steadying himself on the doorframe.

'Thank God you're here,' she said, clinging to him.

'Why? What's happened?' She led him into the kitchen and drew the blinds. 'You look upset,' Dave said. 'Something go wrong at rehearsals?' Carly shook her head. She pointed at her phone. He frowned.

'I think someone's stalking me.'

Dave listened while she told him about the torrent of vile

messages. Thousands of them. How she kept deleting them and blocking the senders but more kept appearing.

'They're just sickos,' Dave told her.

'You don't understand. It's like I'm being watched. That's how it feels.' She went to the window and made sure the blind was as far down as it would go. 'Look. The message about my hair. I tied it up today for rehearsals. I never normally wear it like that. Whoever saw it *knows* that.'

Dave was giving her a peculiar look. All of a sudden, she felt foolish.

'Maybe someone saw you at the rehearsal rooms,' Dave said. 'Did you run into anyone there?'

She thought back. She had gone to the canteen where a couple of guys were hanging out. She had got chatting to a swarthy bloke in a leather jacket who claimed to be with Steps. Their driver, or tour manager, or something. She knew the band was in the building because coming back from the loo she had bumped into Claire Richards, looking phenomenal and so slim Carly was definitely jealous. She had always liked Claire. Before she knew what she was doing, she blurted out she was her favourite Step.

'It could all be dead innocent,' Dave was saying. 'Someone paying you a compliment. Loads of people get trolled. I've had a few since the big gig was announced.' He chuckled. 'Best off ignoring them, I say. You don't think you're maybe getting things a teeny bit out of proportion . . .'

She covered her face with her hands.

'Is there someone who could run your social media for you, just for the time being?' Dave suggested.

She could ask Susan.

'You going to be all right? You look pretty shaken up.'

She thought about being alone in the house overnight. 'You couldn't stay tonight?' she said.

Dave looked surprised. 'You sure that's what you want?'

Carly nodded. 'I'm going to have a bath, if that's okay. There's food in the fridge. Help yourself.'

She almost collided with him on the landing as she was coming out of the bathroom, wrapped in a towel.

'Oops, sorry,' he said. 'Just checking out the sleeping arrangements.'

She saw her bedroom door was open. 'The spare room is along the hall,' she said.

Dave put a hand on her bare arm. He was standing close enough for her to smell the wine on his breath. 'Come on, babe,' he said. 'We're married. We don't need to muck about with all that separate beds malarkey. You know me better than that.'

Carly pulled away from Dave. For a split second she could've sworn she felt his grip tighten, but almost immediately he took a step back, raising his hands.

'I get it, I get it,' he said, looking sheepish. Or trying to. 'No means no. Sorry, babe. I just love you so much, I want to be close to you. But if you're not ready yet, I understand.' He smiled charmingly and walked towards the spare room.

Carly watched in silence, not sure what to think. Was Dave her protector, or was he more of his old self than he was letting on?

33

Roxanne heard voices coming from the kitchen as she let herself into the house.

'I'm back, J,' she called, taking off her trainers and hooking her Moschino tote over the end of the banister. Her feet were killing her. Despite their protests, Lucy, the choreographer, had made them do the routines in heels.

She dug an old pair of battered Ugg boots from the cupboard under the stairs and put them on before padding along the hall to the kitchen. On the table was a bottle of red wine, half-empty. Pizza boxes. Olives. A bowl of salad. Jamie, his face flushed, beamed at her. Sitting across from him was Pete.

She stopped in the doorway. 'What's going on?'

Pete got to his feet. 'Hi, Rox, how's it going? I just called round to catch up with J.' Roxanne gave him a suspicious look. Catching up with Jamie was something he rarely did. She wondered if he'd fallen out with Lisa. 'He tells me he's got a big commission – designing the stage gear for the Thunder Girls comeback gig.' Pete grinned at Jamie. 'Good on you, son.'

'It's meant to be confidential,' Roxanne snapped, annoyed.

He put up his hands. 'You know me, soul of discretion. I won't breathe a word.'

She glared at him. Looking back, she was sure all the leaked stories about her in the press when the two of them had first got together had come from him, not that she had been able to prove it. 'I'm serious,' she said. 'There's going to be a press launch. I doubt they'll see the funny side if anything leaks out beforehand and ruins their big moment.'

'You can trust me,' Pete said.

She was tired. Looking forward to having some wine and a soak in the bath. Making small talk with Pete was not her idea of relaxation. For the sake of Jamie, though, who seemed delighted to have him there, she kept quiet.

'Have some pizza, Mum,' Jamie was saying, sliding a slice of pepperoni onto a plate. He handed her a glass of red. 'How did it go today?'

She shot him a warning look that seemed to go right over his head. She was not about to let Pete in on what was going on behind the scenes in the rehearsal room. 'Fine,' she said, tucking into the pizza.

Pete aimed a few mock punches at her across the table. 'No more fisticuffs?'

She chewed the pizza slowly. 'This is delicious,' she said. 'Franco makes the best pizza.'

Pete tried again. 'You and Chrissie cleared the air now?'

Roxanne started on another slice.

Jamie said, 'You should see the club. We've got pictures of the punch-up everywhere. The place is packed every night.'

Pete was looking at Roxanne. 'I might pop in.'

'Anytime. I'll sort you a VIP pass,' Jamie said, enthusiastic.

Roxanne pushed her plate aside. 'Think I'll finish this later. Right now, there's nothing I want more than a hot bath.'

Jamie jumped up. 'I'll run it for you, put some salts in. Great for aching limbs.'

Once he had gone, she turned on Pete. 'What do you think you're playing at?'

'I just want to draw a line under things,' he said.

'So now the papers are full of the Thunder Girls and the club's taken off again you think you can come swanning in like nothing happened? You must think I'm an idiot! Just fuck off, Pete, and don't come back – you're not welcome.'

34

Another day of bitching and rehearsals, for Carly another night of collapsing exhausted on the sofa. At least she had taken her phone charger with her to this one. Although she wasn't sure that was such a good idea after all, as it meant she'd had continuous access to the online hate.

The direct messages, tweets and other nastiness focused on some of the classics: from 'thunder thighs' to dick pics. And now some of the trolls were going on about what a prude she was, no fun and never up for a good time. Chrissie and Carly, from slut to nun, one predictable and one downright dull. Most of the accounts that had first popped up had focused on the usual topics, but now they were going on about her inactive sex life. Days ago they'd called her a whore – to the point she'd wondered if people somehow knew about Adam. She found it bizarre.

Dave had been an utter gentleman. He'd set the table for dinner, massaged her feet while watching TV and reassured her again over the trolls. He hadn't been this supportive in so many years. The more she thought about it, the less bothered Carly was by Adam skiving off. Perhaps Dave was good for keeps after all. She left him on the sofa as she went to take a shower. Almost a déjà vu of the night before, she emerged from the bathroom in her towel to find Dave standing there.

He smiled at her. 'I'm having a really good feeling about us, babe.'

'Yeah, it's been . . . good,' Carly said. Why was he being so weird?

'You and me, babe. We should let nothing – and *no one* – get in our way,' he said, taking a step towards her. He began to caress her bare shoulder, his fingers gliding down towards her towel.

Carly put her palm on his chest, as if to push him away. 'Things are improving, but we've got a long way to go, Dave.'

The caress down her shoulder turned to a gentle hold on her arm. Standing very close to her, Dave took in a deep whiff of his fresh-smelling wife.

'Carly . . .' he muttered.

'Dave, stop.'

His grip tightened on her arm and he moved even closer. Carly felt herself pressed against the wall, the dado rail digging into her back. She wriggled free.

'What are you doing?' she said. 'I thought you wanted to help. I should have known what you were up to, worming your way back in.'

'I am helping.' A film of sweat glistened on his top lip. 'And, well, I'm here now, aren't I? And you are my wife, which must mean something . . .' He gazed at her. 'You know, you definitely do suit your hair like that.'

She tried to push past but he blocked her way. 'Move,' she said.

'I bet you're not so coy with your posh City boy,' Dave said, whipping the towel away.

Carly gasped and struck out at him. He made a grunting sound and caught hold of her, hanging on as she fought to get away, the two of them bumping against the wall and the edge of the banister. When he let go without warning she stared at him, long enough to register his sudden startled look before she tumbled backwards and went crashing down the stairs.

35

At Chrissie's house, Anita was in the kitchen making dinner. Cheesy pasta bake for her and some kind of grain she had never heard of and didn't know how to pronounce for Chrissie. It bubbled away in the pan. She sniffed at it uncertainly. The smell was . . . wet dog. She put a lid on the pan and popped her pasta dish in the oven.

The bell on the gate went, the camera showing Rick in his Aston Martin. Anita buzzed him in.

'Well, this is a scene of domestic bliss,' he said, planting a kiss on her cheek. 'You've given me an idea – a Thunder Girls cookbook.'

'Just don't ask Chrissie to contribute,' she said, lifting the lid on the pan of slop. 'She's gone gut-friendly, whatever that means. Today, anyway.'

Rick screwed up his face. 'What the hell's that?'

Anita smiled. 'Search me. Some so-called super-nutrient from one of her dodgy woo-woo websites, probably.'

'Where is she?'

'Outside.' Anita smiled again. 'I'm not even going to begin to tell you what she's doing. I'll let her explain.'

'I hear it went well today and yesterday,' said Rick.

'Yeah, it did. We're not as past-it as we thought – but the bitching's as sharp as ever.' She rolled her eyes. 'Roxanne had a go at Chrissie again. Nothing serious. Smart move of yours giving us Susan as our PA, by the way. We're all loving having her run round after us, and she's a diamond when it comes to stroking Chrissie's ego. Clever you.'

Rick found Chrissie at the bottom of the garden. A fire was burning in an old metal dustbin, flames shooting into the air, Chrissie watching, swaddled in a Ferragamo wrap. As Rick drew near she tossed something into the flames.

'What's going on?' he asked.

'I'm burning some stuff.' What looked like a lace teddy went onto the fire. There was a whoosh as it went up. 'I never knew how flammable this stuff was,' she said. 'All those times making love in front of the fire. Anything could have happened.' A flimsy bra joined the teddy.

'You're having a clear-out?' Rick asked.

'A ritual bonfire, actually.' She gathered up several pairs of knickers and flung them into the flames. 'Apparently, when you have a break-up you should get rid of anything you wore when you were with them. The negative energy of the old relationship gets stuck in your smalls.' She shrugged. 'Makes sense to me.'

Rick wondered which wacky online blog she had got that from. 'How were rehearsals?'

'Easy for me. I've kept myself in shape. That heifer, Roxanne, though, she really struggled. She needs to lose about a stone. Barely any better today than yesterday.' She looked in the direction of the house. 'You might want a word with Anita, as well. She practically lives on carbs.'

'You and Roxy getting on any better now?'

Chrissie snorted. 'Leaving aside her constant sniping and bitching and the odd punch-up, we're best of friends.'

'Chrissie . . .'

'Don't "Chrissie" me! Where are you when I need you? Cosying up to that spiky little cow, probably.' To Rick's astonishment, she looked close to tears. 'I'm not made of stone, you know, despite what you – and the press – might think. I've got feelings too. I'm sick of being cast as the villain of the piece, the bitch of the band.' From a pocket in the wrap she produced her lip gloss and began slapping it on, the way she always did when she was upset. 'This is all your doing,' she wailed.

'*Me?*'

'You dumped Roxanne and went off with me but no one's saying a word about you.'

'It's not fair, I know.'

'No, it's bloody not.' She heaved more saucy pants and several pairs of stockings into the fire.

Rick went and put his arms round her. She buried her

face in his chest. He stroked her hair and tried not to think about getting lip gloss on his shirt.

Their embrace was disturbed by Rick's phone. Keeping one arm wrapped around the gently sobbing Chrissie, he used his other hand to put the phone to his ear. He listened to the caller's news, then turned back towards her looking worried.

'Something's happened to Carly.'

36

'I'm fine. A few bruises, that's all,' Carly said. 'No harm done.'

She was sitting up in bed wearing a nightdress the hospital had given her, Dave at her side, his face a picture of concern.

'Don't tire yourself out,' he told her, giving her shoulder a pat. Carly gave him a thin smile.

Anita and Roxanne, at the foot of the bed, exchanged a look. Chrissie, who had bagged the only other chair in the cramped room, and was barely visible beneath the extravagant arrangement of flowers she had arrived with, frowned. Rick was in a crisis management meeting with Jack about the situation, but said he was going to come by as soon as possible.

'Didn't they have a nicer room?' she asked through a froth of cellophane. 'We could get you moved. I know a really good private hospital.'

Roxanne rolled her eyes. 'It's a proper doctor she needs, not one of your cosmetic quacks.'

'They're not keeping me in,' Carly said. 'I'll be going home in a bit, once the doctor's done his rounds.'

'What exactly happened?' Anita was looking pointedly at Dave.

'I fell,' Carly said with a shrug. 'Came out of the bathroom, not watching where I was going, and, I don't know, misjudged where the stairs were and fell before I knew it. I'm not *quite* sure. Next thing, I'd bounced all the way down. It's one of those steep staircases, straight up and down. Everything happened so fast . . .' She shrugged again and caught the look that passed between Anita and Roxanne. 'It was my own fault. I wasn't watching what I was doing.'

'Sounds like this new place of yours is a death-trap,' Roxanne said. She, too, was looking at Dave.

An awkward silence followed.

'There's a cobweb on the window,' Chrissie said, making a face. Her faux fur jacket was in the same shade of shocking pink as her favourite YSL lip gloss. 'And heaven only knows how long it is since they decorated – the skirting boards are scuffed to bits.' She peered at Carly over a pair of enormous shades. 'Do they actually know who you are?'

Dave reached for Carly's hand. 'You frightened the life out of me. I thought you'd really hurt yourself.'

Roxanne caught a flicker of something in Carly's eyes as she slid her hand away. 'Lucky you were there,' Roxanne told Dave, not taking her eyes off him. 'Were you nearby when she fell?' *Fell* sounded as if it had quotation marks around it.

'Dave called the ambulance,' Carly said, giving him a look that might have been grateful, or something else.

'Handy,' Roxanne said, sounding unconvinced.

Another uncomfortable silence.

'They thought I might have concussion. That's why they kept me in overnight.'

'Did you lose consciousness?' Chrissie said.

Carly glanced at Dave. 'Not for long, I don't think.'

'She was out for a matter of seconds,' he said.

'I've not been sick, no headaches . . .' Carly mustered a bright smile. 'Right as rain, so stop worrying, all of you.'

'It *is* worrying, though,' Roxanne said, still looking at Dave. 'When someone falls down the stairs for no apparent reason.' *No apparent reason* was in quotes.

'Working too hard,' Dave suggested. 'She was in a right old state last night after rehearsing with you lot.' He aimed an accusing look at each of the women in turn.

Anita said, 'Come to think of it, you did look a bit peaky yesterday.'

'And you had hardly anything for lunch,' Roxanne said.

'For the last time, I'm *fine*,' Carly said, getting cross. 'Stop making it into such a drama.'

'As long as you'll be fit for the relaunch gig,' Chrissie chipped in.

'Trust you to bring that up,' Roxanne said.

'I'm only saying what everyone's thinking.'

Carly wished they would all leave her alone. She was worn out. It had been a long night and she had got no sleep. When the ambulance brought her into the emergency department she spent a couple of hours there before they moved her to her own room. Then Dave decided she needed a bigger room, so they moved her again. By the time she finally got settled it was gone four in the morning. She had told Dave to go home but he refused.

Afraid of what she might say behind his back, probably.

The only moment of peace she'd had was when she asked if he would mind getting her a coffee. A cappuccino, if he could find one. Soya milk, if that was no trouble. Almond, if he couldn't get soya. He went out, leaving his phone on the bedside cabinet.

Acting on a hunch, Carly checked his texts and emails. Nothing suspicious. She looked at his WhatsApp messages and saw he had disabled the 'last seen' feature. Weird. All that was there was a single thread with someone called Payback Prince:

Dave: *Genius, mate.*

Payback Prince: *Glad you're happy.*

Dave: *That one was spot-on.*

Payback Prince: *Cheers.*

Carly frowned. Was this 'Payback Prince' some kind of snooker contact? She scrolled down.

Dave: *You just smashed it.*

Payback Prince: *Always a pleasure.*

Dave: *How about turning the screw?*

Payback Prince: *No worries.*

Carly felt peculiar. What did it mean? She thought about how Dave had been with her lately. His tendency to show up just when she needed him. She typed a message in the chat:

Dave: *The hair thing freaked her out.*

She didn't have to wait long for a reply as almost immediately she got one.

Payback Prince: *Result!*

She stared at the screen. So Dave was behind her trolls. She deleted the last two messages and googled 'Payback Prince' on her own phone. A series of links led her to a creepy-looking website offering what it called 'rough justice'.

While she was still considering her next move, the doctor had come in with the results of her blood tests. What he had said left her reeling.

She gazed at her visitors. 'Actually, I'm feeling a bit wiped out,' she said. 'I might try to have a nap before the doctor comes back in.'

When no one showed any sign of leaving she did a theatrical yawn.

'I'll stay,' Dave said. 'Make sure you get home okay.'

'There's no need.' It came out sounding sharper than she had intended. 'I mean, thanks, but I can manage.'

'I can stay,' Roxanne said.

Anita was nodding. 'Me too.'

Chrissie checked her watch. 'Well, I'll have to go soon anyway. I'm having a gold-leaf facial with Sergei at eleven.

They're booked up for months but of course he fitted me in.' Ever since the Thunder Girls had hit the headlines, Chloe Booth had been bombarding Chrissie with messages, inviting her back for a facial and a catch-up. Chrissie was ignoring her.

Carly waved them away. 'No one needs to stay. How many times? There is *nothing* wrong with me.'

'You still need someone to take you home.' Anita was adamant. 'You shouldn't be on your own.'

'I won't be on my own,' she lied. 'I'll get Adam to come for me.'

Dave's face fell.

Chrissie got to her feet. 'Good. That's sorted, then.' She plonked the flowers on the bed and blew a kiss in the vague direction of Carly. 'See you in rehearsals tomorrow.'

Roxanne gave her a cold look. 'Let's see how she's feeling first.'

Carly had only just got rid of them when there was a gentle tap at the door. She closed her eyes and pretended to be asleep. Someone came in and tiptoed over to the side of the bed. There was a rustle of cellophane. Whoever it was had brought flowers. She lay completely still, hoping they would get the message and go away. She pictured Dave, hanging about until the others had gone, then buying the biggest bunch of flowers he could find and coming back, hoping to impress her. Well, she would tell him where to go. She had a good mind to report him – see what the police made of her 'fall'. Not that she was a hundred per cent sure he had actually pushed her. It was possible, as Dave insisted, that she had simply lost her balance. It might well have been an accident.

As for the Payback Prince and the online hate campaign, she would take her time thinking of how best to get back at him, the little toad.

Right now she had more important things to think about.

The figure in the chair at her bedside shifted position. More rustling. The vinyl-covered seat squeaked. Carly opened her eyes a fraction and sneaked a look. The sight of Elvis Presley's face inches from hers made her blink and sit up. Jack, in a Graceland T-shirt, sat hunched forward in the high-backed hospital chair gazing at her. Looking at her with what seemed a mixture of concern and something else. Desire, perhaps. A bunch of yellow roses lay on the bedside table. He leaned forward to give her a clumsy hug.

'Good to see you, Carly,' he said. 'How you feeling?'

She gave him a wary look. 'Fine, thanks. I took a bit of a tumble, that's all.'

'A little bird told me you weren't yourself at rehearsals yesterday.' He put his head on one side and frowned. 'A bit distracted, I heard. Didn't even eat your special sushi.'

She sighed. Susan, telling tales. That was the downside of having her at their beck and call. She was Jack's little spy. It was true, the day before Susan had traipsed all the way to some posh Japanese restaurant in Kensington for yellowfin sashimi, something Carly usually loved, only for it to end up in the bin. The raw fish had turned her stomach. She knew why now.

'Adrenalin,' she told Jack. 'I always lose my appetite when there's a lot going on.'

He was nodding. 'I get that, I'm the same.'

Neither of them spoke for a moment.

'You look amazing,' Jack said at last, not taking his eyes off her. 'I'm not kidding, you haven't changed one bit.'

He didn't look that different either. A few more lines than when she had last seen him, and a bit thinner; more sharp-featured. The way he was looking at her was making her uncomfortable. She feigned a yawn. 'I could do with getting some shut-eye,' she said at last.

He drew his chair closer to the bed. 'You're happy about everything – the Thunder Girls getting back together?'

She looked puzzled. 'Yes, of course. Why do you ask?'

He reached across the bed and took her hand. 'Because if you're not, I've wasted my time.'

She frowned – what was he getting at? – and tried to tug her hand free. 'We're all up for it,' she said.

'You get what this is about, right?'

Carly wished he would stop looking at her like that. As if he was about to jump on her.

'Sorry, Jack, I'm not with you.'

'This whole thing . . . I made it happen for you. *Us*.' He gripped her hand a bit tighter.

She shook her head. '*Us?* What are you talking about?'

He was so close she could see the tiny scar on his cheek,

the one he'd got falling off his bike when he was nine. His eyes blazed. Carly didn't remember him being this . . . *intense*.

'Do you ever think about . . . ?' His eyes stayed on hers. 'The baby. *Our* baby. How we were meant to be a family. Don't you ever wonder how different everything would be if you'd kept it?'

Carly struggled to speak as memories came flooding back. Chrissie going with her to the clinic. The casual way the woman who did the pregnancy test told her it was positive. Chrissie making the arrangements. She found her voice. 'Why are you bringing this up now? It's ancient history.'

'Not to me it isn't. I think about it all the time.'

She shook her head. 'You know full well having the baby was never an option. I was way too young, the band was on a high – and we weren't even together properly.' She gave him a helpless look. 'The timing was all wrong.'

'It's the one thing in my life I regret – and I know you must too.'

'I don't. It was the right thing to do. For both of us.'

'I could have had kids,' he went on. 'I've had my chances but I wasn't interested. You know why?' She shook her head. 'Because I always knew if I couldn't have kids with *you*, I didn't want them at all. It had to be the same for you, Carls – all those years with Dave and you never started a family. How come?' He didn't wait for an answer. 'You didn't *want* to, that's why. You knew it wouldn't feel right with anyone else.' He let his words sink in. 'How *could* it when what we had was perfect?'

Carly's head was spinning. He was wrong. About everything. She *had* wanted kids with Dave but it never happened and, deep down, what scared her was that the abortion she'd had as a teenager might be to blame.

'I love you, Carls,' Jack was saying. 'It's why I'm doing all this – the relaunch, Wembley . . . The whole thing's so we can be together again, have the family we always wanted – it's not too late. I wanted to bring back the Thunder Girls to remind you about us.'

'You ended the Thunder Girls in the first place!'

'That was a mistake,' he said solemnly. Carly stared at him as he continued. 'I thought you'd see it as a chance for us to be together. But I see now that I hurt you.'

'And you thought bringing back the Thunder Girls was the way to get close to me again?' Carly asked sceptically.

'Is that so wrong? Think about all the good times we had together, back in the day. It was the worst thing that happened to me losing you, losing the baby.'

'It would never have worked. We had nothing in common for starters.'

'I *loved* you – I'd have made it work. We'd have made great parents. Don't you regret not being a mother? I've learnt to forgive you for what you did – we can make it all right again.'

He leaned towards her for a kiss as Carly recoiled in horror.

She gasped. 'Are you out of your mind? I don't need forgiveness. I don't regret it – and for your information, I'm actually pregnant right now!' She registered the look of bewilderment on his face. 'That's right. Nine weeks gone. And I'm keeping this baby.'

Jack's head was moving from side to side. 'Pregnant? No. *No*. Don't you see? You can't be. If you have someone else's baby, you'll ruin everything.'

Carly glared at him. 'No – having *your* baby would have ruined everything, Jack. You weren't even there when I was faced with having to work out what to do.' She pressed the call button to summon a nurse.

'Yes, I know Chrissie was the one who convinced you to kill my baby!'

'She was there for me.' She kept pressing the call button.

'Oh, she was there for you all right – you're both murdering bitches,' Jack hissed, furious.

'I'd like you to leave,' she said. 'And take your flowers with you. I don't want them. I don't want anything from you.'

The door swung open and a nurse appeared.

Jack got to his feet, snatched up the bouquet and stormed out.

37

'I never knew Jack and Carly were an item. There's nothing in the cuttings.' Kristen Kent was taken aback. 'He's quite a bit older than her. All the other girls were too.'

Kimberley, the Thunder Girls mole, twisted a strand of hair around her finger. 'The age difference never mattered to them. They were mad about each other.'

'They kept it secret, though – why was that?' Kristen asked.

Kimberley gave a shrug. 'The press would have been all over it and Carly was the one who'd have had to bear the brunt. Jack was very protective of her. There was a ton of pressure around the band anyway – I don't suppose you know what it's like to have hacks hounding you, on your back the whole time; paparazzi everywhere you go. So-called friends selling stories on you.' She gave Kristen a critical look. 'Believe me, it's not easy.'

'I don't suppose it is.'

'Carly was young, a bit naive, and Jack didn't want her having a hard time. He knew if the press got wind of things they would twist it – play up the age gap, make out the only reason she was in the band was because the boss had done her a favour, when the truth was what Jack and Carly had was the real deal.'

'So, was that how they met – when Carly got in the band?'

'Actually, they were already seeing each other. They met in a club. The first time Jack saw her she was on a bar top in eight-inch stilettos, dancing while stepping over bottles and glasses. She lost her footing and he caught her.'

Kristen couldn't help smiling. It was quite a way to meet.

'They looked at each other and that was it,' Kimberley said. 'Love at first sight, for both of them. She literally fell into his arms.'

'Sounds magical.'

'It was.'

'So what went wrong?'

'Rick putting her in the Thunder Girls was the beginning of the end really.'

'How come? Didn't she fit in? Or did everyone resent the fact she was the boss's youthful girlfriend?'

Kimberley was shaking her head. 'Nothing like that. Jack loved Carly but he hardly paid attention to Rick or the Thunder Girls, or who Rick was putting in the band, until they really took off. He was only paying attention to Carly. He'd backed the band with Shine Records' money, but he was so unsure about their prospects he wanted as little professional ownership over it as possible, to save his skin if they failed. So he put all the key decisions on Rick's shoulders,' Kimberley said, biting her lip. 'That changed once the band was successful, of course.'

'So Carly was welcome from the start?' Kristen asked.

'Carly was perfect – great voice, she looked the part. We all thought she was the right choice. And at the time no one knew about her and Jack being together. They kept the whole thing under wraps.'

Kristen was surprised. 'That can't have been easy.'

'Trying to hold a relationship together when you're in a band isn't easy for anyone. You're working crazy hours, on the road, hardly ever at home. Meeting new people all the time. There's a lot of temptation out there. When you've got someone in your life and you're having to act like they don't exist . . . it's a recipe for disaster.'

'So who called time on things?'

Kimberley plumped up a cushion and tucked it behind her back. 'It all came to a head when Carly got pregnant.' Kristen's eyes widened. 'This was just before a big tour. The baby wasn't planned, obviously. Jack was in the States on business when Carly found out.' She frowned. 'I think she got scared and panicked, which wasn't surprising really, with Jack thousands of miles away; she was vulnerable. That's when Chrissie got her claws in.'

'Were she and Carly close?'

'Not until Chrissie put two and two together about the baby. Carly was distracted in rehearsals, not really pulling her weight – which wasn't like her – and one day Chrissie followed her into the loo and caught her chucking up. I was two cubicles down and heard everything! They didn't even know I was there. Chrissie put her on the spot, demanded to know what was going on. Carly started blubbing and said she thought she might be pregnant. Chrissie took control and arranged a test, then whipped her off to an abortion clinic.'

'Just like that?'

'More or less. It was all done on the quiet, the rest of us kept in the dark. As for poor Jack, he barely got a look-in.'

'Didn't Carly tell him?'

'By the time he got back, it was all over with. Jack had wanted the baby. *Begged* her to try for another one, but it was like the more he pleaded with her, the more she dug her heels in. She could be a stubborn little mare.'

'How do you know all this?' Kristen asked, her eyes as wide as saucers.

'Jack tells me everything,' Kimberley said, like it was obvious. 'Anyway, he asked her to marry him even though she'd done it. It broke his heart.'

Kristen turned all this over in her head. She had known Jack Raven a long while and considered him to be cold . . . *unfeeling*. The type to break hearts, rather than suffer a breakage himself.

She wondered now if he had been a different man before his affair with Carly and if losing her – and his unborn child – had changed him.

Jack had never married. He had no children. She had always assumed it was because he was too self-absorbed but perhaps she was wrong. What if it turned out he had never recovered from what he had been through with Carly half a lifetime ago?

From what she had just been told, Carly, the sweet young thing of the band, was a lot harder than she seemed. Heartless, some might say. Although, from what Kimberley had just said, Chrissie seemed to have been the driving force behind the abortion.

She glanced at Kimberley. 'So you reckon things might have been different if Chrissie hadn't been involved?'

Kimberley nodded. 'Hundred per cent. Carly would have stayed with Jack and they'd have had the baby, but Chrissie destroyed what they had.'

38

Jack paced about the office while Rick tried, unsuccessfully, to get comfortable on the turntable stool. The hard seat dug into his backside. Jack had requested a Thunder Girls update and Rick had arrived ready to deliver what he considered to be good news. Carly's fall had turned out to be nothing serious and the girls were back in rehearsals, which were going well. The feedback from the vocal coach and choreographer was positive. They had pretty much nailed the set for the relaunch gig at Heaven & Hell, and Chrissie and Roxanne were just about tolerating one another. Rick had been about to make light of their feud for Jack's benefit – say something about designer handbags at dawn, maybe – but looking at his boss's thunderous face, he decided to ditch the wisecracks.

So far, Jack had barely said a word, which Rick knew from experience was not a good sign. The TV was off. An even worse sign. He knew to sit tight and say nothing until his boss was ready to speak.

Jack swept past again, frowning in concentration. Stopping for a moment to check something on the iPad on his desk, making a sound that was something between a growl and a grunt. There was a kind of crackling fury coming from him that made Rick anxious. Had something awful happened? Jack swiped at the screen of the iPad, tutting, a gleaming lock of hair swishing in front of his face. Rick suspected he had his impressive mane blow-dried and pictured him in some fancy salon where everyone wore black, whether it suited them or not, and the complimentary drinks included a Cosmopolitan at the very least.

He studied Jack's outfit. Ripped Versace jeans, Western-style belt with a snake buckle. Biker boots with steel toecaps. (How he managed to drive the Maserati in those was anyone's guess.) Alice Cooper T-shirt. Rick, in his usual dark suit and white shirt, felt staid by comparison . . . *square*. Even the word 'square' was a sign of how out of touch he was, he suspected. He was probably the only person at Shine who still used it.

He gazed at the grinning skull on Jack's Alice Cooper top. Rick could never get away with wearing anything like that. Casual clothes didn't suit him. Even on holiday he managed to look dapper. *Dapper*. Another word that had fallen out of use, among the hip young things at Shine, anyway. *Hip*. That was probably another one. He sighed.

Jack was on the move again. Rick felt a rush of cool air on

his face as he stomped past. At the other end of the room, Jack muttered something under his breath and Rick swivelled around as best he could on the awkward little stool, almost losing his balance, to find his boss staring at a whiteboard covered with scribblings about the Thunder Girls. Grabbing at a red marker pen, he scrawled something on the board. Rick leaned forward. The writing was awful and difficult to read, but the word looked like *guilty*. Jack underlined it and stood back for a moment. He reached for a picture of Chrissie and stuck it next to *guilty*, drawing an arrow from the word to the picture. Then he got busy with a black pen. By the time he had finished, Chrissie bore a striking resemblance to Alice Cooper and the devil.

Rick braced himself.

Jack strode back to his desk and flung himself into his seat. Rick made an effort to sit up straight.

For what seemed like an age, Jack stared across the desk, saying nothing, while Rick did his best to smile pleasantly.

'I am not a happy bunny,' Jack said eventually.

Rick wanted to laugh. *Happy bunny* sounded worse than *square*. For all Jack's efforts to be on-trend (no one said trendy anymore, Rick decided), he too fell into the trap of using fuddy-duddy expressions. *Fuddy-duddy*. Another one! The corners of his mouth twitched and he clamped it shut. Jack gave him a cold look. Nothing got past him. 'Sorry, did I say something funny, mate?'

Rick shook his head. 'Twinge of toothache,' he lied. 'Whenever it comes on it makes me wince.'

Jack narrowed his eyes. 'So, the Thunder Girls – where are we at?'

'All going well,' Rick said. 'They're on top of the set for the relaunch and—'

Jack cut him off. 'I'm having second thoughts. I thought it would be fun getting them back together. Maybe even profitable. What I didn't count on was how much of a frigging headache the whole thing would be.'

'I know things got off to a bit of a bumpy start but—'

Jack wasn't listening. 'This whole thing has *grief* written all over it in big letters. You go out on a limb to bring a set of washed-up old hags back together – doing them the biggest favour of their lives, by the way – and do you get one bit of gratitude?'

'Well . . .'

'No. You do not. Not one of them has had the courtesy to thank me for making this whole thing happen.' He gave Rick an accusing look. 'You told me Wembley was their dream gig.'

'I know . . . it is.'

'You could have fooled me. And I'm just wondering how it's going to play when four knackered has-beens – and I'm being kind there – get on stage and make fools of themselves. The *Rock Legends* people cancelling the cheque, that's for sure.' Jack's face was rigid. 'I'm telling you, if I'd had the slightest idea what I'd be dealing with I'd never have gone near it.'

Rick swallowed. 'I think you're being a touch hard there . . .' he began.

'Have you *seen* the state of them? I'm not sure who's the biggest tub – it's a toss-up between Anita and Roxanne, although Carly's not much better, she's definitely let herself go. As for Chrissie – you can tell her from me the HRT patches, or whatever she's calling them, aren't working.' He stuck a foot on the desk. 'Fat, ugly whales. Out of shape, legs like tree trunks – I could go on. Every last one of them a disgrace to women.'

Rick stared at him. 'We're thirty years on, Jack. I mean, we've all changed.'

'Really? *Have* we? Don't look at me, mate. I look better now than I ever did because *I* have looked after myself.'

Rick wanted to say that Chrissie, slavishly working out, submitting to endless beauty treatments and what she called *work*, had done a pretty good job of holding back the years. He opened his mouth to speak, caught Jack's look, and shut it again.

'You know what's really pathetic,' Jack went on. 'The wax one. Whatever she gets done at the local funeral parlour isn't working – she looks like she should have a wick sticking out of her head. More ready for a coffin than a stadium stage.' He pointed at the wall behind Rick where Chrissie as Alice Cooper leered out. '*She*'s an embarrassment,' Jack said.

Rick had seen Jack in full meltdown many times and was used to him ranting, pulling people to bits. Never like this, though. This was Jack cranking up the vitriol to a whole new level. He was puce, his veins popping, as if he might burst into flames. Rick had no idea what lay behind the outburst. As far as he knew, everything was going to plan.

'How's the official book coming along?' he asked, hoping to change the subject.

Jack didn't bother answering him.

'I'm holding *you* responsible if it all goes tits-up,' he said. 'This is *your* gig. *You're* the one running it.'

Rick felt like pointing out that Jack was the one who had decided to reunite the Thunder Girls in the first place; Rick was simply doing his bidding.

'From now on I want sweetness and light in the media,' Jack told him. 'This isn't a game and it's about time that bunch of hatchet-faced bitches took things seriously. Tell them to stop taking the piss. That means doing as they're told. I don't want any more bad press. No more pissed-up bitch fights. I mean it, mate – one more bad story and that's it, I'm pulling the plug.'

He put the other foot up on the desk and sank deep into his chair, not taking his eyes off Rick. 'Am I making myself clear?'

Rick nodded and got to his feet with difficulty. The stool had given him backache.

Jack was smiling one of his terrible smiles. 'Good. Off you

go.' The TV seemed to come to life on its own. Cher began to sing her latest cover of an ABBA song.

Jack watched, impressed. 'See her? She's older than any of that lot and looks way better. *That's* what you can do with a bit of effort. Might want to show them this.'

39

Chrissie got out of bed and stretched. She put on her workout kit and did a series of squats followed by a hundred crunches. She had read somewhere that exercise was more effective on an empty stomach. After a few lunges she ran on the spot until she was out of breath. It was definitely working. Her stomach was nice and flat and she could see her ribs, although whether that was down to the early-morning exercise regime or the fact she had been on a cayenne pepper cleanse for two days, was hard to tell. One good thing about being single again was she could do as she pleased. When Scott was there she would never have been able to follow her early-morning exercise plan. Then again, the workouts they did together before getting up were pretty strenuous. Those must have burned a fair few calories before breakfast. She sighed.

She pulled on a robe and wandered downstairs. The tantalizing smell of coffee and toast told her Anita was already up. Chrissie had tried explaining to Anita why she'd be better off without bread. All those carbs! Not that Anita cared. As far as she was concerned, a life without toast was not worth living.

Chrissie filled the kettle. She was starving. Anita had left a bit of burnt crust on the breadboard. Chrissie eyed it. One little morsel couldn't hurt, surely. Her stomach felt hollow. The kettle boiled. No, she would not weaken. She dumped the crust in the bin, squeezed lemon juice into a glass and added hot water and a generous helping of cayenne. It tasted vile but it was definitely doing the trick. The weight was falling off, although Anita remained sceptical. Chrissie's dramatic weight loss was less to do with the so-called cleanse, she said, and more because she had stopped eating, basically. What Anita didn't seem to get was that the lemony drink was a way of boosting metabolism and, literally, dissolving stubborn pockets of fat. That was what Chrissie had heard, anyway.

She was finishing her drink, feeling virtuous, when Anita came into the kitchen carrying an armful of newspapers. She gave Chrissie a peculiar look. 'Sit down, babe,' she said, dumping the papers on the table.

'Why? What's wrong?'

'Rick called first thing.' Anita hesitated. 'No one knows how, but the papers have found out about Scott leaving.'

Chrissie put down her drink, feeling every bit of wellbeing drain out of her. Anita steered her to the table and sat her down.

'How bad is it?' Chrissie asked, feeling queasy.

'I won't lie, it's bad. Bastards seem to know all the ins and outs.'

Chrissie picked up the *Daily Post*. She was on the front page. *HE'S OFF – SCOTT-FREE! TOY BOY DUMPS THUNDER'S CHRISSIE!* She skimmed through the text. It was all there, every sordid detail. Scott doing a runner while she was still on honeymoon in Miami, and leaving her penniless. The story seemed to imply he had skipped off once she ran out of cash – not a word about him stealing her money. 'That's a lie!' she wailed. 'He ripped me off, the thieving little scumbag.'

What the paper called 'a source close to Ms Martin' revealed she was 'devastated, utterly broken', and that Scott's walking out couldn't have come at a worse time. 'She's at that stage in her life where she feels *old* . . . no longer attractive,' the anonymous source said. 'The sad thing is she really loved him but it looks as if all *he* loved was her money and once it was gone he was out of there faster than you could say unauthorized overdraft.'

The inside pages carried wedding pictures – Scott giving her his slimy, two-faced smile – and the now infamous shot of her bare backside complete with patch. A short piece written by Vanessa Feltz, claiming to be some kind of so-called women's health expert, suggested the reason Chrissie had attacked Roxanne was because 'her hormones were all over the place' following Scott's departure.

'She can bloody talk!' Chrissie exploded.

She went through the rest of the papers. The story was everywhere, all of them banging on about fifty being a difficult age for a woman. The *News* gave her age *five* times, the bastards.

Some snooty columnist had written a piece implying she should have seen the writing on the wall. What did she expect, tying the knot with a gorgeous model half her age? Wasn't it sad, the columnist went on, when an older woman tried so desperately to cling to her lost youth through a relationship everyone around her could see was a disaster from the off?

Chrissie leafed through the pages feeling furious and humiliated. How the hell had they found out?

'Who told them?'

Anita put a cup of coffee and a slice of toast dripping in butter in front of her. Chrissie bit into it. To hell with the bloody cayenne cleanse!

'Maybe it's not as bad as you think,' Anita said.

'No, it's about a hundred times worse!'

'Look, women hate reading this kind of stuff . . . the digs about age and hormones and all that. They'll be on your side. I bet loads of the comments online are positive.'

'I'm not going anywhere near online. You can bet the haters are in their element, chipping in. It'll be "no fool like an old fool" and "what first attracted the gorgeous young model to the ageing *rich* pop star?" What I want to know is where all this came from – who leaked it to the papers?'

Anita shook her head.

'Someone at Shine? Wanting headlines for the Thunder Girls and not giving a shit how they get them. Hanging me out to dry. Well, if they think I'm taking it lying down they've got another think coming.'

'Speak to Rick – he's as upset as you are—'

'Oh, I doubt it. Is *his* name being dragged through the mud? Is *he* being portrayed as some kind of hormonal nutcase? Is *his* age – he's older than me, by the way – plastered all over the papers? No, it bloody is *not*.'

Anita sighed. 'He told me Jack had him in yesterday and wiped the floor – said he didn't want any more negative press before the official launch. One more thing and he'd pull the plug, Jack said. Rick's seeing him again this morning, hoping to smooth things over.' She thought about it. 'Maybe someone at Shine's got it in for Rick. That place was always full of backstabbers.'

Chrissie was thinking. Her face was mutinous. It couldn't be Scott. He would want to keep well under the radar. So who else? It came to her . . . Andy. Claiming to be a private eye when he was nothing of the sort. All he had done was sponge off her. She covered her face with her hands. How could she have been so stupid?

She looked up. 'Andy – the prick who was meant to be tracking Scott down. I bet it was him.'

She took her mobile from the pocket of her dressing gown and found his number.

He answered with a cheery, 'Chrissie, babe! Good to hear from you—'

'Don't you babe me, you little vulture – I've seen the papers! A word of advice. You might want to think about changing your name – getting a whole new identity, even – because when I get my hands on you, which I *will*, your life is over. You are a *dead* man, understand? No one crosses me and gets away with it.'

'Where's your proof it was me? And anyway, there's no such thing as bad publicity . . .'

'I will rip you limb from limb, starting with that useless thing between your legs.' She was shaking with rage. 'And if you ever see that shit of a husband of mine you can tell him the same. I'll kill him for what he's done. Got it? Dead. Both of you. D-E-A-D.'

40

Chrissie was surprised how excited she was just by being here. The tour bus swept into Wembley Stadium through a scrum of several hundred fans being held back behind crash barriers. Some chanted and waved thirty-year-old tattered posters of the Thunder Girls. Others held up scarves. The sight of the bus set up a chorus of piercing screams.

'And to think this is just our reception for the dress rehearsal,' Carly said. '*Rock Legends* is going to be huge!'

'*We* are going to be huge,' Chrissie said with a grin.

The bus came to a halt.

'Looks like we're here,' Carly said.

Rick got up. 'Okay, everyone ready? This is it – the official dress rehearsal. Thunder Girls are go!' Chrissie rolled her eyes. 'So listen up. It's a big day and the hype is crazy. Mega press interest. We've got newspapers, magazines, telly for a mini press conference . . . and bloggers are coming to write up the actual rehearsal itself, give it good word-of-mouth buzz. From when you get off and until the press conference is over, you'll have more cameras on you than a Premier League game – just like the actual show night itself.' He swept a hand through his hair, a sure sign he was nervous. 'Think back to the scrutiny you were under thirty years ago – this time it's going to be a whole lot more intense. And I can't stress how much is riding on this. We *have* to get it right. That means pulling together, as a team.' He aimed a pointed look at Chrissie and Roxanne.

'I don't know why you're looking at me,' Chrissie said, sounding offended. 'She's the violent one.'

'Only when provoked by La Bitch over there.'

'Oh, really? Who threw the first punch?'

'I was defending myself.'

'If that's what you think you need your head looked at, as well as your extensions.'

Rick threw his hands up in despair. 'Enough! I want *no more* of this mud-slinging in public. Do you have any idea how close Jack is to calling time on this whole thing? He's pretty much had his fill of the drama and bad press – and all before the official launch! So, best behaviour.' He frowned. 'Where's Anita?'

Carly said, 'She went to the loo.'

Rick looked exasperated. 'She can't manage a half-hour bus ride without needing a pee?'

'She's been in there the whole time.'

He rapped at the door. 'Anita? We're here.' A muffled

reply came back. Rick knocked again, harder. 'Get yourself out here.'

The door opened and Anita squeezed out. 'Okay, keep your hair on.' She stumbled as she went past, standing on his foot, her stiletto spearing his big toe. Rick winced in pain. 'Oops, sorry. It's being on the bus. That weird motion thing you get. Makes me lose my balance.'

He stared at her. 'We've stopped.'

'I know we've *stopped*. Not got my land legs back yet, that's all.' She teetered off, giggling to herself.

They followed Rick through the backstage area to a green room where Susan was waiting, wearing an Access All Areas pass.

'There's coffee, if anyone wants one. Water?' she said.

Roxanne went straight to the fridge in the corner, peered inside, and held up a bottle of champagne. 'Bingo!'

Anita punched the air. 'That's more like it.'

Rick took the bottle from Roxanne and put it back in the fridge. 'That's for after. Assuming we're still in the mood to celebrate once you lot have been let loose on the world's media.' He looked at his watch. 'We're on in five minutes, so do any last-minute checks and get yourselves ready.'

'Just nipping to the loo,' Anita said.

Rick gave her a suspicious look. 'Susan, can you go with Anita?'

'I'm perfectly capable of finding the toilet, you know,' Anita said, sounding huffy.

'This place is a maze. Don't want you having a Spinal Tap moment and getting lost on the way back, do we?' Rick said.

Anita gave him a blank look.

Chrissie went to check her reflection in front of the full-length mirror. She was in an off-white semi-sheer dress she had bought in Miami and rhinestone-studded boots. She gave her lips a final, unnecessary slick of gloss. Carly came and stood beside her. She was in a pastel pink playsuit. Bare legs, skyscraper heels.

'I feel like a whale,' she said, tugging at the hem of the playsuit. 'Is this too short, do you think?'

'You look fab for your age,' Chrissie sniped, too busy studying her own reflection to give Carly so much as a cursory glance.

On the other side of the room, Roxanne straightened her Gucci leather maxi dress and ran a hand through her hair.

Rick looked at his watch again. 'That's it, we have to go. Go out there and slay them.'

The door opened and Susan came in, Anita trailing behind. Her face was flushed. 'Come on, Thunder Girlies! Let's *do* this!'

Chrissie went over to her. 'You've got your dress tucked in your knickers.'

Anita giggled and tugged at the hem of her dress, a floaty little number by Rixo. 'Thanks for telling me. Imagine the shame of having your bare bum plastered all over the papers . . .' She clapped a hand to her mouth in mock horror.

'What am I saying?' Chrissie gave her a sharp look, making Anita double up. 'Don't be such a poker face – I'm only teasing!'

Roxanne caught Carly's eye. 'High as a kite,' she mouthed.

Rick and Susan exchanged an anxious look.

'Any chance of a drink before we go on?' Anita said. 'Just a teeny-weeny one.'

'There's no time for that.' Rick peered at her. 'Are you feeling all right?'

'I might have to change my shoes.'

'It's too late!'

'Well, don't blame me if I take a tumble.' She fiddled with the strap on a pair of gladiator sandals she had borrowed from Chrissie. 'I can hardly walk in these. I hope a certain *someone* isn't trying to sabotage me.'

Chrissie looked about to say something but Rick stepped in. 'Let's just get out there.' He was sounding increasingly frazzled. 'And remember, one or two of them will probably try and trip you up. Any questions you don't like the sound of, ignore them.'

'What if they ask about HRT?' Roxanne asked.

Chrissie shot her a furious look.

Susan led them along a series of corridors to the stage where they stepped out into blinding pops of light and shouts, voices cutting across one another. 'This way, Chrissie!' 'Over here, Roxy!' 'Girls, girls!' The women pouted and smiled, giggling together like the best of friends they were meant to be. A voice yelled, 'Chrissie – is it true you and

Roxanne aren't speaking?' Someone else piped up: 'Yeah, tell us about the feud!' Roxy caught hold of Chrissie and planted a lingering smacker on her lips, prompting a flurry of flashes. Chrissie was surprised, to say the least.

When they eventually took their seats the questions came thick and fast. 'What made you want to get back together?' 'How does it feel to be the only female act on the *Rock Legends* bill?' 'Chrissie, is it true you want Scott back?' 'Carly – are you and Dave still together?' 'Roxanne – how do you feel about having a shoe named Killer Heel at New Look in your honour?' 'Anita – after what happened at *Eurovision*, are you nervous about performing again?'

On and on, until Rick wrapped things up.

As they got to their feet, a man in a suit, flanked by two uniformed police officers, stepped onto the stage. Security, Chrissie assumed. They were in front of her, blocking her exit. 'Excuse me,' she said, trying to get past. The one in the suit put up a hand to stop her.

'I'm Detective Sergeant Harry Rose,' he said. 'I'd like you to come with us, Ms Martin.'

The others stayed where they were, watching.

'Why?' Chrissie asked.

'Your husband has been the victim of a hit and run accident,' DS Rose told her.

Chrissie's mouth fell open. 'Oh my God, is he all right?'

'He's in hospital.' He gave her a hard look. 'We'd like to speak to you in relation to the incident.'

Carly was straining to hear. 'What did they say?' she asked Roxanne.

'Scott's been knocked down and they must think Chrissie did it,' Roxanne told her. 'Callous bitch, I wouldn't put it past her.'

Chrissie was indignant. 'The only place I'm going to is my husband's hospital bedside.' She made another attempt to sweep past DS Rose, who put a hand on her arm. She swiped it away. 'Don't touch me!'

DS Rose nodded at one of the uniformed officers who stepped forward and expertly restrained her with a pair of handcuffs. She gasped. 'Pig! Get those things off me!'

The uniforms bundled her off the stage amid a frenzy of flashes.

Rick was waiting for Chrissie when the police let her go. 'How you feeling?' he asked.

She scowled. 'Bastards. Asking me the same questions over and over. Accusing me of driving at Scott, trying to kill him when I don't even know where he is!'

'I had a word with the sergeant, Rose. Nice enough bloke—'

'Ill-mannered pig, you mean. Tried to make me drink tap water – wouldn't even get me a bottle of Evian.'

'—and he said you'd made threats to kill Scott . . .'

Chrissie stared at the floor.

'Is it true? You threatened to kill him?'

No answer.

'He said they've got a recording.'

Bloody Andy. 'That pathetic private eye – the one who leaked the story about Scott leaving. I rang him up and . . . well, I might have said some things.'

'What kind of things?'

'Oh, you know – maybe something about him being . . . toast. Scott, as well.'

'Chrissie . . .'

'I was upset. I trusted him. What did you want me to do – give him a medal?'

'This arrest could've really ruined things for the band.'

'Look, missing a dress rehearsal is bad, and the latest headlines . . . But we can reschedule that and fix the press; we still have a little time between now and the relaunch. If the bastards don't arrest me again.'

'Well, lucky for you I was able to show Detective Rose the Thunder Girls' schedule. He's going to check it out and when he does he'll know you couldn't have been the hit and run driver.'

'*I* could have told him that, if he'd given me a chance.' She shook her head, disgusted. 'Coming for me like that. At *Wembley*, of all places. In front of the world's press. I've a good mind to sue him!'

'It's a serious thing, a hit and run.' Rick waited a moment. 'It might have been better if you'd stayed calm.'

She glared at him. 'He'd just told me my husband had been knocked down. And *you* want me to be calm. Honestly, Rick, listen to yourself.'

He changed tack. 'The main thing is we can prove you had nothing to do with it.'

'I need to see Scott. Will you take me?'

'You sure that's a good idea?'

41

Scott was sleeping when Chrissie slipped into his hospital room. She crept up to him and peered at him. Not a mark from the accident on his gorgeous lying face, which was something. In fact, he seemed unscathed, apart from the cast on his left leg. She looked around the room. No cards, nothing to suggest anyone cared about him. In spite of herself, a smidge of the fury she had felt towards him over the last few weeks began to melt as she looked at the lips that had once declared undying love as he explored her body. Suddenly Scott opened his eyes and on seeing Chrissie standing over him he started thrashing about, feeling for something at the side of the bed.

His reaction snapped her back into reality and she held up a cable with a big red button on one end. 'Looking for this?' she smirked, closing the door behind her.

'They check on me every few minutes.' He looked panic-stricken. 'They'll know if you do something.'

Chrissie moved closer. 'Something like what? Put a pillow over your face? Pull out your tubes?' She looked around. There didn't seem to be any tubes. Damn.

'You ran me down! Tried to kill me!'

She sighed and strutted over to the chair at the side of his bed, picking up the cushion from it, then turned back towards him. 'Wrong. That wasn't me.'

Scott looked at the cushion in her hands intently and turned towards the door. 'The police said they've got you on tape, making threats, so—'

Chrissie interrupted him, walking closer now, holding the cushion in one hand and the call bell cord in the other. 'Oh, I would have happily run you over if I thought I could have got away with it, but one of your other victims obviously beat me to it. Here.' She handed him the call button. 'Press away! The nurses all know I'm here. So I'm not going to do anything.' She pushed the cushion behind his neck. 'I'm just making sure you are comfortable . . . I am your *wife*, after all.'

He looked away. For a moment neither of them spoke.

'Nothing to say?' she hissed, inches from his face. Scott stayed silent. She stepped back and sat in the chair. 'Apart from all my money, don't you think you owe me some answers?'

More silence – but was that a look of shame on Scott's face?

'We were happy, weren't we, or was it all lies? For fuck's sake, Scott, say something! You took every penny I had and now I've been humiliated by the press even further for being arrested, thanks to you too, so I'd like to know why you've done all this to me?' He didn't answer and kept his eyes fixed on the bed cover. Chrissie followed his gaze and felt the rage rise. 'I said why?'

As she spoke she reached out and grabbed his face, digging her bright pink nails into his cheeks.

He looked perplexed. 'We never *had* anything, Chrissie.'

Chrissie stepped back, shocked at Scott's matter-of-fact delivery of such a devastating revelation.

'You said you loved me, that we were for keeps . . . you made promises.'

He gave a shrug. Chrissie clutched the arms of the chair, unsure if she was going to faint or explode with rage.

'That's the standard script, works every time; nothing personal,' Scott went on. 'It's not like I set out to hurt you – it was just business.'

Chrissie's insides steadied. No longer nauseous, no longer faint, but steeled by rage. '*Business?*' she shrieked.

Scott's eyes clouded over with terror.

42

It took all of Chrissie's strength – aided by the very recent memory of handcuffs being slapped on her wrists, and not in a fun kind of way – not to strike a hospital patient. She stormed out of the room, her chest heaving with deep, angry breaths.

She eyed one of the IV drip stands in the corridor. She wanted to tip it over in frustration.

A nurse cautiously approached her. 'Are you okay, ma'am?'

'I'm not a *ma'am*,' Chrissie hissed. 'I'm Ms Martin.'

The nurse blinked.

'Sorry,' Chrissie said. 'It's just so hard . . .'

'It must be awful seeing your husband in such a way,' the nurse said sympathetically.

'Yes, it is awful seeing him.' The nurse watched Chrissie for a moment. 'I'm all right,' she insisted. 'Thank you.'

The nurse patted Chrissie on the arm tenderly before

moving on. Chrissie eyed the door to Scott's room and walked back in.

Scott looked up at her, as startled as when she had first come into his room.

'Let's talk about this "business" you said I was.' In one fluid motion, she kicked the door behind her shut with her stiletto heel and grabbed the red call button from Scott's hands.

'Chrissie!'

She marched over to the window and shut the blinds. She turned back and locked eyes with her husband.

'Babe . . .' Scott's voice quaked.

'Don't "babe" me, you thieving shitbag,' she said, her voice dripping with menace. 'I want my money back.'

Scott sat in silence.

'I said, I want,' Chrissie spoke slowly as she walked towards him. 'My fucking. Money. Back.'

'Maybe we can work something out . . .'

'What drugs have they got you on in here? There's no deal to be done with me, you toerag. I want everything you stole from me back and I want to know why you did this to me!' Chrissie stood tall over him, ready to smother the bastard.

'I needed it! I'm sorry. I'm sorry,' Scott said, almost shaking. 'I never made much money being a model. I'm known for being able to play women which is why I was offered this job.'

'Job?' Chrissie said. 'What job?'

'You. You were the job.' He waited a moment as her face went paler than he had ever seen her, even with thick make-up on and a tan. 'Our whole relationship was a scam: he paid me at the start and you paid me at the end.' Chrissie felt her heart thumping in her chest. 'My job was to get with you. Sweep you off your feet and whisk you down the aisle – take all your money, then dump you.'

The room seemed to be spinning. Chrissie put her hand on the side of the bed to steady herself.

'Who, who put you up to it?' she asked, catching her breath and standing back upright.

'Does it matter? It's done now, and legally there's nothing you can do anyway.'

'Of course it fucking matters. Oh, and isn't there? If I let some really good forensic accountants take a look at the paper trail you left behind, I think you'll find there is. My tax return last year, the one you *insisted* on doing for me, for example. That should show up a few of your sticky finger-prints. You taking my money might technically be legal once we were married, but before – oh no – that's fraud, mate, and you'll do years for it.'

The room was silent as the two stared at each other. Chrissie knew she had him.

Scott finally cracked. 'Look, I don't know what you did to him but he was absolutely clear with me from the get-go that I was to ruin you,' Scott said. 'I've never seen anyone so dead set on taking someone down.'

'Who?'

'Jack Raven at Shine Records.'

Chrissie's jaw dropped.

'Jack?'

'Yes. I never asked why but I got the sense he didn't just want to ruin you, he wants to destroy you. I'm sorry for my part in it but it's what I do, so I've learnt to live with it.'

Chrissie stared at him, cracking under the tension.

'So now you know,' he said, and took a grape from the bowl and threw it into his mouth.

She closed her eyes. She felt faint – how could this be true?

'Look – let's make a deal. I'll tell the police it wasn't you who knocked me down, but you'll have to forget about the tax return money, legally speaking – you know the rest were joint assets as you didn't sign a pre-nup,' Scott said. 'That's a bad move, by the way. Don't do that again. I've seen you in the papers and on the news with the band. You'll earn it all back, but where Jack is concerned, watch out – cos who knows what else he's ordered to happen beyond *my* job, which I've now completed.'

Chrissie's throat was dry. So Scott had never loved her and Jack had set her up. She struggled to take it in. For a second or two the room swayed, then her knees gave way and she hit the floor.

43

'I fainted, that's all.' Chrissie sat in the hospital canteen with Rick. When she had collapsed, Scott had hit the call button, summoning a friendly nurse. Chrissie had got to her feet and fled the room as fast as she could. She wasn't ready to share what she knew with Rick yet – she still had to process everything.

'Are you eating properly?' Rick wanted to know.

She shrugged. 'I've been on a detox. Cayenne pepper and stuff.'

'I'll take that as a no, then.' He looked concerned. 'I thought you were looking a bit peaky. On the skinny side.' She rolled her eyes. The whole point was to look skinny. 'You need to eat, look after yourself,' he told her.

'Why? What's the point?'

Rick was shocked. 'The band's back together, *that's* the point, and the world knows about it now.'

'I suppose I'm all over the internet? I suppose the gutter

press have got me splattered everywhere being dragged away in handcuffs by that sweaty copper.' She sounded huffy.

'Actually, they've all gone for the snog instead.' He chuckled. 'You and Roxy having your Madonna/Britney moment.'

Chrissie winced. She had forgotten about that.

'Jack's thrilled with how it all went, by the way. Not the unscheduled finale with the plods, obviously, but the rest of it was good.'

Chrissie's face contorted. '*Jack*.' She practically spat the word out. 'As if I give a *toss* what that *tosser* says.'

'Well, you should. He's the boss. It was Jack made all this happen, don't forget.'

'Oh, don't worry, I won't forget. Good at *making things happen*, isn't he?'

Rick looked perplexed and pushed a coffee towards her. 'Soya latte, best I could do. No kombucha on the premises. I've put some sugar in.'

'I don't take sugar.'

'Drink it. It's good for shock.'

She sipped it, enjoying the sweet taste, thinking about what Scott had told her. *Watch out*.

'Feel like telling me what Scott said?'

Chrissie paused, thinking over the revelation. About Jack. It was him, all him.

'It's all his fault,' she said softly.

Rick looked sad. 'I know, Chrissie, I know. I know it was hard to hear at first, but I'm glad you're finally accepting it.'

Rick thought she was talking about Scott. It didn't matter. She knew who her real enemy was.

She looked at Rick with eyes of steel. 'I'm going to kill that fucker.'

44

'It's Jack, he's up to something bad,' Chrissie said. She was at home, pacing about the kitchen. Feeling done in. Dark smudges had appeared under her eyes and her face had a hunted, hollowed-out look. Since the Thunder Girls press conference more than twenty-four hours earlier she had not slept at all. All she could think about was what Scott had told her about Jack. His words were on a loop inside her head. What she didn't understand was, why? What would make Jack come gunning for her? She went to the window and peered through a crack in the blinds, checking for paparazzi. All seemed quiet. *Seemed*. Her marriage had *seemed* genuine and yet . . . She chewed her lip, for once devoid of the customary slick of gloss, battling a growing sense of paranoia.

'Is that why you've dragged us over here?' Roxanne rolled her eyes at Carly and Anita and yawned. 'Tell us something we don't know. Jack is *always* up to something bad.

Double-crossing, scheming snake is what he does best. Don't tell me you've only just realized.'

Chrissie's lip trembled. 'This is different. Personal. He wants to destroy me.'

The others at the table, who were tucking into olives stuffed with almonds and were onto their second bottle of champagne – except Carly, who had barely touched her glass – all looked at her.

'Is this anything to do with you getting arrested at the press conference?' Roxanne asked. 'What's happened – you've had a slap on the wrist from the big boss?' She made a sad face. 'Poor you, in the bad books.'

'I did *not* get arrested!' Chrissie spat back.

'You were dragged away in handcuffs – what would *you* call it?'

Anita started to laugh. 'It *was* funny, babe. PC Plod snapping on the cuffs—'

Without warning, Chrissie's face crumpled and tears streamed down her cheeks.

Anita shot a frantic look at Roxanne. 'I was only joking . . .'

For a moment no one spoke, then Carly rushed over and put an arm round Chrissie. 'Hey, come on. Forget about it. The launch was a hit. We smashed it, all of us – so stop worrying.' Chrissie clung to her, shoulders heaving, sobbing, while Roxanne and Anita stared open-mouthed. It was the first time any of them had ever seen Chrissie cry.

No one was laughing anymore.

Carly led Chrissie back to the table and sat her down.

'Take your time,' Carly said. 'And when you're ready, tell us what's happened.'

Anita got a box of tissues. Chrissie grabbed a handful and dabbed at her face. Her eyes were red and swollen, streaks of mascara on her cheeks. When she made no attempt to fix her make-up or at the very least slather on a bit of lip gloss, they were left in no doubt how serious things were.

Chrissie told them about seeing Scott and what he had said about Jack. 'He *paid* Scott to fleece me,' she said, her voice cracking. 'It was all a big set-up. None of it was real. Scott never loved me. It was a scam from the off. Jack set the whole thing up.'

'Oh my God,' Anita said. 'I can't take it in – that's so evil, and how could Scott agree to go along with it when he knew you loved and trusted him?'

Roxanne was pale. 'Bastards, both of them. But I don't get it, though. Why would Jack want to financially ruin you, then offer us as a band a big deal which is going to earn you money? Plus he backed your solo career and finished the rest of us off the first time around – so this makes no sense.'

Chrissie blew her nose. 'I don't understand it either but it's true.'

'You don't think there's any chance Scott made it up?' Anita asked.

Chrissie shook her head. 'No – this time he was telling me the truth, said I needed to watch my back. That Jack is behind my downfall.' She blinked back tears. 'He *hates* me and I don't even know what he thinks I've done to deserve this vendetta.'

'I think I might,' Carly said, her voice small.

They turned to look at her.

'He came to see me, after I'd had my fall. The way he was acting was . . . unhinged. Coming out with all this crazy stuff about how he'd always loved me and we were meant to be together.'

'I know he always fancied you,' Roxanne said.

'It was a bit more than that.' Carly hesitated. 'Jack got me pregnant.'

Chrissie's jaw dropped. 'It was *Jack*'s?' she whispered.

Anita was taken aback. 'Shit, I had no idea.'

'Why didn't you say anything?' Roxanne asked.

Carly looked uncomfortable. 'I thought you'd be angry about me and him and think that was the only reason I was in the band. We were working flat-out, travelling the whole time. The last thing anyone needed was me chucking a spanner in the works.'

There was silence.

Anita was shaking her head. 'It must have been a nightmare, keeping something like that to yourself.'

Carly glanced at Chrissie. 'I wasn't completely on my own. Chrissie caught me in the loo one day chucking up, and we decided the best thing was to have an abortion.'

Roxanne turned on Chrissie. 'And you didn't tell the rest of us.'

'She was embarrassed,' Chrissie said. 'We were just about to go to Japan. And her life was with the band.'

'You could have told us, Carly,' Anita said. 'We wouldn't have judged. I had three terminations myself – sometimes it's just not meant to be.'

Carly placed a protective hand on her belly. She had been about to tell them about the baby. Perhaps now was not the time.

Instead, she touched Anita's arm softly and they all fell silent for a moment before she finally spoke as she stared at the table. 'The thing is, when Jack came to see me, he kept going on and on about the baby. He's got it into his head that Chrissie was to blame.'

'What!' Chrissie stared at her. 'I hope you put him straight.'

'I tried, but he's lost it.' Carly gave her a helpless look.

'If you'd said you wanted to keep it I'd have supported you,' Chrissie said.

Carly nodded. 'I know you would and I told him it was my decision. But the way he was acting, well, it just wasn't what you'd call normal. Saying the two of us would have lived happily ever after if only I'd gone ahead with the pregnancy. I told him it was never on the cards, but . . .' She left the sentence hanging.

'So that's what all this is about.' Chrissie looked shaken. 'He thinks I'm some kind of baby-murderer.'

'That's insane – her body, her choice,' Anita said.

'Actually, he did say we'd killed his child,' Carly said.

Chrissie groaned and covered her face with her hands.

'If we were about to tour Japan when all this happened, that was '88,' Roxanne said. 'We'd just been in the studio, done the Pointer Sisters cover, "I'm So Excited". I remember because it was Carly's birthday and Rick brought a cake in at the end of the session. Candles, the lot.'

Carly nodded. 'We scoffed the whole thing. Then got drunk and went clubbing.'

'*Sixteen* candles,' Roxanne said. 'Which means you were *fifteen* when that pervert knocked you up.' She gave Chrissie a sharp look. 'You should have shopped him back then when you had the chance.'

'I didn't know it was Jack! She wouldn't tell me who the father was.'

'Well, we've got him now,' Anita said, 'filthy creep. You were a *child*, Carls. You've got to report him. Let the police deal with it.'

'No!' She looked sheepish. 'It's not like I was some little innocent. Jack wasn't even my first. I'd been clubbing since I was thirteen, getting off with blokes a lot older than me. It wasn't considered wrong then – look at Mandy Smith and Bill Wyman. I knew Jack was some big record company honcho, and I went after him. He didn't take advantage of me.'

'It doesn't matter,' Roxanne said. 'I don't care how grown-up you thought you were, you were under-age and he shouldn't have gone anywhere near you like that. Anita's right. You need to report him.'

'I can't.'

'You *have* to. Why should he get away with it? I guarantee you won't be the only one,' Roxanne said. 'Look what's going on with #MeToo – women coming forward, calling out men who thought they could do what they liked because of who they were. Women like *you*, being listened to.'

Carly shook her head.

'If you don't speak up he'll keep coming after me,' Chrissie said.

No one said anything.

'Okay, here's what we do,' Anita said eventually. 'From now on, we put aside all our problems and we stick together – the four of us are more than a match for Jack, as long as we've got each other's backs. Agreed?' The others nodded. 'We make sure he gets nowhere near Chrissie, given she's already had such a lousy time, thanks to the shitty stroke he pulled with Scott.' More nods. 'And when we're ready, we take him down faster than you can say "pervert".'

45

Roxanne and Anita were shopping, Anita on the hunt for boots. She had seen a pair that were just right in the *Style* section of the *Sunday Times* but they were Prada and she didn't feel like splashing the thick end of a thousand pounds on footwear. She knew exactly what she wanted. 'Cowboy-style ankle boots. Black patent. Some kind of detail – gold, or rhinestones, maybe.'

After traipsing in and out of what seemed like every shop in London they ended up back in the little boutique that had been their starting point, with Anita buying the first pair of boots she had tried on. Other than being black, they were nothing like what she claimed to have wanted, and were almost twice as expensive as the Prada ones.

Roxanne was exhausted. 'I can't believe you just did that,' she said.

Anita grinned. 'I knew they were the ones, straight away.'

She caught her friend's pained expression. 'Come on, you can't go buying the first thing you see—'

'You just did!'

'You know what I mean. Where's the fun in that?' Roxanne groaned. 'You have to see what else is out there . . . just in case.'

'Can you actually walk in them?'

Anita looked puzzled. 'What's that got to do with it? They're the business. Proper head-turners. I might wear them for the gig.'

She was right, the boots were fabulous. Velvety leather, stretchy and out-there. Unlike anything Roxanne had ever seen. Then again, for a cool two grand, they needed to be special. 'I could murder a drink,' she told Anita.

They headed to a bar tucked away at the back of Regent Street and flopped onto a squashy sofa in a quiet corner.

'I am never going shopping with you again,' Roxanne said. 'It's like a form of torture, being made to walk miles and miles, going round in circles, only to end up back where you started.' She rubbed at her ankle. 'No wonder my poor feet are killing me.'

'If I hadn't made you go to Covent Garden you wouldn't have seen those racy undies on Monmouth Street,' Anita said. 'And, by the way, you still haven't said who the lucky man is.'

Roxanne rolled her eyes. 'Who said they're for a man? Can't I treat myself to some decent knickers if I feel like it?'

'Course you can.' Anita waited a moment. 'So, who is he?'

Roxanne sighed. 'If I tell you, you have to promise you won't breathe a word.'

Anita nodded. 'Cross my heart, or whatever it is people say these days.'

'It's not like anything's happened . . . yet.' Roxanne sipped her drink. 'Maybe I'm getting my wires crossed, misreading the signals, but I don't think so. I mean, you can tell when there's still a spark, can't you?'

Anita nodded. 'Always. So, come on, spill – who's the lucky guy?'

Roxanne took a deep breath. 'Rick.'

'*Rick!*'

'I know, it caught me by surprise too. After what he did, the way he dumped me, all the other stuff . . .' She seemed deep in thought. 'Then, before the night we all got together again that first time at Chrissie's, he turned up, no warning. Said he'd guessed I wasn't planning on going. Well, he was right about that! Honestly, Nita, you won't believe how bitter I felt . . .'

Anita gave a wry smile. 'Oh, I would. I walked in on you and Chrissie half-killing each other, remember.'

'Well, anyway. Rick persuaded me to go.' She shook her head. 'All those years I'd spent being furious with him for breaking my heart, feeling pretty damn sure I'd never forgive him. In fact, I'd spent a fair chunk of time thinking that one day I'd get my own back – and what I'd say if I ever got the chance. That was the plan. I wasn't banking on going weak at the knees the second I set eyes on him.' Another bemused shake of the head. 'Butterflies, the lot. Definitely not what I was expecting. It threw me completely.' She glanced at Anita. 'I swore I'd never go there again. Once bitten, twice shy and all that.'

Anita took all this in. 'So, what changed?'

Roxanne finished her drink. A waiter appeared and topped up their glasses. She waited until he had gone before saying, 'I can't help the way I feel, I suppose.'

Anita looked serious. 'But he really hurt you, Roxy. Would you ever be able to trust him?'

'That's the real question, I guess.'

They were both silent.

Anita was thinking back to Rick coming to the house when Chrissie was doing her ritual bonfire. The two of them staying up late long after Anita had turned in. Taking Chrissie a mug of her yak tea the next morning and finding her in bed with Rick. Beating a hasty retreat before she was seen. She had said nothing to Chrissie and now wondered whether to mention it to Roxanne.

'It's like he's looking out for me,' Roxanne said. 'Making up for what he did – or trying to, at least. I know how sorry he is – I've seen it in his face when he apologized – he means it. A couple of times he's turned up unannounced at the club, wanting to make sure I'm okay. And last time I saw him . . . we almost kissed.' Her eyes shone. 'I know it's mad and if it was one of my friends thinking of getting back with someone who'd cheated and left them in pieces I'd be screaming: *Don't do it!*' She gave Anita a helpless look. 'Tell me, am I being stupid?'

Anita had no idea what to say. The image of Rick in bed with Chrissie refused to go away. Not that she could be sure they'd actually had sex. Or, if they had, that it was anything more than a one-off. All she knew for sure was that Roxanne wasn't the only one Rick seemed to be looking out for. From where she was standing, he was lavishing a fair bit of attention on Chrissie too. After her brush with the law he had sent her flowers, and Anita had clocked the drippy look on Chrissie's face when she'd read the message on the card. *Chin up, Toots*. The fact he was calling her by the pet name he'd used when they were together struck Anita as a bad sign – from Roxanne's point of view, anyway. Worse, almost, than sleeping with her. 'I'm probably not the best person to come to for relationship advice,' she said reluctantly.

'If you were me, what would you do?' Roxanne asked.

Anita couldn't help laughing. 'Probably the wrong thing, every time.'

'You're happy now, though?'

Anita sighed. 'Don't get me wrong, I love Maria. She's amazing and she's been good for me. It's just, I don't know if I'm cut out to be with one person forever. It's a pretty tall order for anyone, if you ask me. And she can be . . . needy. Suffocating. Let's just say it's not a bad thing we're having some space right now.'

'Relationship aside, you're okay, though?'

Anita looked puzzled. 'Me? I'm great, having the time of my life, actually. What makes you ask?'

'You were a bit, well . . . *out of it* at the press conference. I was going to have a word afterwards, then the police arrived and Chrissie got dragged away, and in the commotion I didn't get a chance.'

Anita was quiet a moment. On the day of the press conference her nerves had been jangling. Rick had warned her to expect questions about *Eurovision* and she got wound up, which was why she had broken open the stash of herbal tea Maria had packed for her and had a few cups of it. 'Herbal' was a generous label, as it must have been some kind of hallucinogenic (and probably illegal) brew, it turned out – which was why she ended up all over the place. Fortunately, most of the attention was on Chrissie and Roxanne.

'You're not, you know . . .' Roxanne left the sentence hanging.

'What?'

'Taking stuff again.'

'I had some herbal tea.' She saw the look on Roxanne's face. 'Seriously. Maria put it in my bag and said it was medicinal, fantastic for stress. I think it must be one of the weird ones they use in rituals because it sent me loopy. I've binned it – PG Tips for me from now on. I promise, that's it now. I've learnt my lesson.' That much was true. The press conference had been the wake-up call she needed, enough to convince her it was time to clean up her act once and for all. No more drugs.

'Well, if you need to talk, I'm here – and I won't judge,' Roxanne told her.

'No,' Anita said. 'A small voice in my head was tempted by the thought of a cheeky line or two of coke, once I got back to London. But I couldn't do that to you guys . . . not after *Eurovision*. And my accidental experience with the tea . . . has sealed it for me. That reminded me why I *don't* want to go down that road again.'

Roxanne gave Anita a reassuring hug.

'I reckon Carly's the one we should be worrying about,' Anita said eventually. 'And Chrissie, now we know Jack's got her in his sights.'

'I always knew he was a creep,' Roxanne said. 'And nasty with it. But I never had him down as a child molester. Poor Carly. No wonder he wanted her in the Thunder Girls.'

'To be fair, she was good.'

'I reckon we all need to watch out. It would be just like him to chuck a grenade into the proceedings and wreck everything.'

'Relax, there's no way he'll do anything to jeopardize the reunion. The label's got too much money riding on it.'

46

Anita was having a bad dream. She was backstage somewhere – Wembley, it felt like – completely lost, trying to find the Thunder Girls' dressing room, taking wrong turns. Nothing looked familiar. She called for help but her voice was small and muffled. On she trudged, feeling as if she had walked miles (her shopping trip with Roxanne, no doubt) and could barely pick up her feet, thanks to a ridiculous pair of boots that were impossible to walk in (the shopping trip, again). A sudden ringing in her ears made her jump and she came to, not sure where she was for a moment. The duvet was over her head and she flung it back.

Her phone was ringing on the bedside table. She reached for it.

'Hello?'

Rick said, 'Anita, sorry to call in the middle of the night.'

'What time is it?'

'Late. Early. Just gone three.' Anita closed her eyes and

slumped back against the pillow. She felt clammy, disorientated from the dream. 'I've had a reporter from the *Post* on,' Rick said, 'wanting a comment about a story they're running in today's paper.' She heard what sounded like an intake of breath. 'I'll be honest, I had no warning this was coming.'

Anita was suddenly awake. For one wild moment she wondered if Carly had spilled the beans on Jack.

Rick went on, 'There's a book coming out about the band. A tell-all. No holds barred. Way beyond what I was expecting it to be. The *Post* is running extracts and the rest of the tabloids are all over it.' He sounded exasperated. 'What's so infuriating is that I asked Big Becky what was happening with the book last week and she brushed me off, said she hadn't time to go into it.'

Anita didn't think a book sounded too bad. After all, no one had spoken to them about it. 'They've probably just cobbled something together from the cuttings files. I doubt there's anything much in it that hasn't already been out there.'

Rick swallowed. 'It's horrendous, Niţa. And today, of all days.' The preview gig was scheduled at Heaven & Hell later.

She was on the edge of the bed. 'It can't be too terrible, surely,' she said, although something in Rick's voice told her it was.

'Any secrets you girls thought you had – including the ones we had, and all the rest of the stuff we kept a lid on – it's out there now. *All* of it. With bells on.' He gave her a moment to take it in. 'I'm sorry, there's nothing I can do. I just wanted to let you know before you see it.'

She wasn't sure she wanted to.

'You still there?' Rick said.

'Yes.' Her voice was a whisper.

'I've tried ringing Chrissie but she must have her phone on silent – can you let her know? The online editions are already up, so have a look at what they're saying and, be warned, it's ugly stuff.'

'Can't we sue the bastards for defamation or something? You know what the *Post* is like, it's bound to be a pack of lies.'

'That's the problem – for once, it's all true.'

'But how – I don't understand?'

'We've got a mole.'

It was a 5 a.m. call and a full day of final run-throughs ahead of the gig that had got everyone talking. Carly was first to arrive at Heaven & Hell. Her driver, Danny, spotted the paparazzi at the front of the club and did a quick head count.

'Ten snappers and a couple of camera crews,' he told her. 'Shall I go round the back?'

She shook her head. 'They'll just come after us.'

As soon as the car came to a halt it was surrounded. Cameras pressed to the windows. Flashes going off. Shouted questions. Carly kept her shades on and her expression neutral. She knew what the snappers were after – a picture that would make it appear she was reacting to what the papers were saying about her. Well, she wasn't about to give it to them.

Danny, a former Special Forces soldier, got out and cut through the pack, treading on toes, aiming sharp elbows into ribs with painful precision, using his shoulders. Having an elite military background seemed to be a basic requirement for Shine Records' drivers, Carly thought as she remembered Dale shepherding the girls everywhere back in the Eighties. One of the photographers lost his footing and fell down. Danny stepped over him. He slid open the door of the people carrier, triggering an explosion of light. Carly, in a Roberto Cavalli ocelot-print coat, maintained her composure.

Danny whisked her from the car, through the crowd and into the club in a matter of seconds. The door shut behind them and she took off her shades.

A moment later, another people carrier swung into view and Anita got out, followed by Chrissie. The snappers went crazy. Chrissie was in no hurry to get inside the club. Sod them, she thought. Let them have their pictures. She flashed a brilliant smile, ignoring the shouted questions. Just as she was about to head inside, a tall dark-haired man with Brylcreemed hair rushed towards her.

'Chrissie, Chrissie! It's me!' She looked into a pair of intense blue eyes. Something about him was vaguely familiar. She couldn't quite place him, though.

A bodyguard dragged him backwards as she stalked past him in her high-heeled boots and into the club. The paparazzi captured the whole thing, frame by frame.

Inside, Chrissie whipped off her shades. 'Did you ladies see that guy outside? The one with the bluest eyes you've ever seen?'

Anita and Carly exchanged a look. 'The Mad Fan?' Carly said. 'I saw him at the press launch.'

'I've never seen him before. Have I?' Chrissie said, surprised that they all seemed to know who she was talking about.

'We all know who he is,' Anita said. 'How can you not remember him?'

Chrissie shrugged. She looked around. 'Anyone seen Roxy?'

Roxanne was late. She had read everything she could find online before leaving home. As she scrolled through it all she felt sick. It was bad, worse than she had imagined. Anita's cocaine habit and sexuality laid bare. Chrissie's broom cupboard bonk. Scott walking out on her because when it came to diva strops she made Mariah Carey look easy-going. Carly's affair with Jack. Her abortion.

It was just gone five when she arrived at Heaven & Hell and made her way through the barrage of photographers, making no comment.

Inside, the others were clustered around a table at the edge of the dance floor, trawling through copies of the tabloids. Behind them, the stage and lighting crew were busy creating a set that would be a mini replica of the one at the Brits, 1989, when the girls had performed 'Fire Palace'. Rick had brought in the same pyrotechnics team for the fireworks at the end.

Carly looked up and saw Roxanne coming towards them. She nudged the others. 'She's here.'

'About time,' Chrissie said.

Roxanne slumped into the seat they had saved for her. No one spoke. 'Sorry,' she said at last. She glanced around the table. 'I wanted to be sure what they were saying before I came in. The message boards are going crazy already.'

Carly was shaking her head. 'Unbelievable.'

Chrissie pushed a late edition of the *Post* across the table. 'You won't have seen this. It's not online yet.'

The headline read: *EXCLUSIVE: PLUNDER GIRLS! How the world's number-one girl band stole my thunder!*

Roxanne peered at it. Susan stared out at her from the front page, a look of hurt and bewilderment on her perfectly made-up face. Her hair was shorter, Roxanne noticed. 'What's Susan done to herself? She looks . . . weird.'

'She *is* weird,' Chrissie retorted.

'No, I mean, don't you think she looks like that tabloid hack . . . what's her name?' She frowned in concentration. 'Kristen Kent.'

Chrissie had another look. 'She does a bit.'

Roxanne pored over the spread. Susan was claiming she had been lined up to join the band until one day Rick appeared – waltzed in, was how she put it – with his new girlfriend, Roxanne Lloyd. Without warning, Susan was shunted aside and Roxanne became the fourth Thunder Girl. 'It nearly killed me,' Susan said. 'I didn't want to go on. What was the point? Everything I'd dreamed of was snatched away from me. My life was over.'

Rick had never apologized, she said. Nor had Roxanne.

'It's bollocks,' Roxanne said. 'Okay, she was in the running, but nothing had been decided. Rick was keeping his options open till the end.'

According to Susan, Jack Raven at Shine had saved her life. Taken her under his wing and become her mentor.

'I can't believe Jack comes out of this smelling of roses,' Roxanne said.

'That's nothing. Have you seen the other stuff about him and me?' Carly asked. 'Apparently, I was the love of his life and treated him like dirt. Got rid of his baby – which he wanted to keep, by the way – and broke his heart. Dumped him without a second glance.'

'Have you seen the bit about you being an alcoholic?' Anita asked Roxanne. 'They reckon that's why you run a bar – so you can hide your drinking.'

'I'm not an alcoholic!'

'They know about your stints in rehab – and the fling you had with the therapist, who got sacked and had a breakdown. Still sectioned, apparently.'

Chrissie was hunting in her bag for her lip gloss. 'They

know everything.' She looked up and shot a desperate look at the others, the colour suddenly draining from her face.

'What's the matter?' Anita said.

'I've come out without my lip gloss.'

Anita rolled her eyes in disbelief and dug out her make-up bag. 'Here, have mine. Panic over.'

Carly was leafing through the *Post*. 'It looks as though the book must be by Susan, but I reckon Jack's behind it – the whole thing.'

'What I don't get is, why?' Roxanne said. 'He's brought us back together to do the relaunch gig . . . and play Wembley . . . he's making more money out of us – none of it makes sense.'

Carly looked to be in shock. 'Don't you see? It isn't about the money. He hates us. He wants to see us humiliated. You didn't see the look on his face when he came to see me in hospital. It was . . . evil.'

Roxanne gathered up the papers. 'Right, that's enough of this – whatever he's up to he won't wreck tonight for us. We've got a show to put on, so let's put all his crap behind us for now. Jamie's coming in for final costume tweaks and Lucy's going to be here soon to start running through the routine and make sure everything's perfect. We *are* going to bring the Thunder back. We'll deal with him later.'

Rick was exhausted from fielding calls from reporters. He turned his phone off and headed over to Heaven & Hell, the paparazzi clustering around as he drew up outside the club.

'Is the gig still going ahead?' 'How do you feel knowing Susan Fox almost took her life because of you?' 'Is it true Jack Raven broke up the Thunder Girls because Carly Hughes got rid of his baby?'

He forced his way through the throng and into the club where he ran smack into Susan in a mannish pinstripe suit and white ruffle shirt. Skyscraper heels, toenails painted black. New short haircut. He almost didn't recognize her. She had a look of that hard-faced journo, Kristen Kent. He didn't understand what was going on with that. 'What are *you* doing here?'

She gave him a triumphant smile. 'I'm here to see how the girls are doing. Make sure they've got everything they need . . . or, should I say, *deserve*?'

'What were you thinking? Jack's going to hit the roof.' Rick had been trying to get hold of him for hours. Left countless messages. Jack had not got back to him and Rick had no idea what to make of it. 'He'll probably sack both of us. You for spilling the beans, and me for letting you get close enough to learn all their secrets.'

Susan was gleeful. 'Don't be ridiculous, Jack won't sack me—'

'He'll have to. There's no way back from this.'

She laughed. 'Jack will understand.'

'He'll go bloody mental.'

'He'll *understand*, I said. Blood's thicker than water, you know.'

Rick frowned. What was that supposed to mean?

She gave him a peculiar smile. 'All these years and you've never guessed. You're not as bright as you like to think you are, Rick. Jack's always said that.' She tilted her head on one side and said, 'Have you never noticed we look similar? He's my brother, you idiot.' Rick's jaw fell open. 'That's right. I'm his little sis.' She was still smiling. 'He's looked after me ever since you kicked me out of the Thunder Girls.'

'But . . . but when I told him the final line-up, he never fought for you to even be in the band!' Rick spluttered, bewildered.

'He regrets that,' Susan said. 'He thought you were all going to crash and burn, so didn't really care or pay attention. Probably thought he was saving me from embarrassment, and that he could swoop in and be Carly's safety net when it didn't take off. Then it did. And by then it was too late to put me back in, you were all a hit,' she said sourly. 'Since then, we've been an unstoppable team. Jack and Susan Fox. He just prefers "Raven" as his "working name", like he has his own stage persona. He's funny like that.'

Rick stared at her, slack-jawed at the series of revelations.

'So, whatever comes of all this, I can promise you I'll still have a job – not sure you can say the same.' She winked at him as she walked away. 'Give the girls my best, won't you.'

Rick found them backstage, in their costumes, Jamie fussing and making final adjustments. Rick gave him a nod. 'You've done a great job. They look amazing.'

'I was aiming for warrior-queens meets Mad Max.'

Rick took in the leather and chain mail, the headdresses and thigh-high boots. 'I'd say you've smashed it. You've definitely gone beyond the Thunderdome.'

The atmosphere was subdued.

'Any news?' Chrissie asked furtively.

Rick dug his hands deep into his pockets. 'Jamie, can you give us a minute please?' He waited until he had gone. 'I need to tell you about Susan,' Rick said. 'And Jack . . .'

Carly's face twisted. 'Don't tell me they're together!'

'Sort of.' He looked uncomfortable. 'He's her brother.'

Chrissie looked stunned. '*What?* So where does that leave us?'

A voice said, 'That's a very good question.'

Rick wheeled round to see Jack standing in the doorway.

He swaggered into the room in his biker gear get-up – battered leather jacket, paisley-print scarf knotted at the throat, clumpy boots. All of it phoney since he had never been on a motorbike in his life. Underneath the jacket, his Dixie Chicks T-shirt bore the slogan 'Not Ready To Make Nice'. He rubbed his hands together and grinned, making Rick think of a crocodile closing in on its prey.

'Well, this is cosy. What's going on – bit late for Halloween, aren't you?' Jack threw his head back and laughed. His Adam's apple bobbed about in a violent fashion. He wiped at his eyes. 'I take it you've all seen the papers?'

No one spoke.

Jack frowned. He had stopped laughing. 'You know what? You disgust me, all of you. Standing there in your short skirts, everything on show, like a bunch of hookers old enough to know better.' His voice rose. 'Have you no shame?' He pointed at Chrissie. 'Nothing to say? That makes a change. Look at the state of you, Chrissie. You can't polish a turd – although that never seems to stop you trying.'

'I know about you. I know what you did,' she said, refusing to be intimidated. 'Scott told me everything.'

Jack gave her a horrible smile as he walked closer to her. 'Well, then you have *some* idea of how I feel about you.'

Roxanne cut in. 'Get away from her, you bastard.'

Jack went up to her and put his face close to hers. She kept on looking at him. He sniffed at her, curling his mouth. 'You still reek of booze, Roxy. You weren't bad-looking when you were younger. Not now, though. Alcohol oozing out of every old pore.'

She backed away, glaring at him. 'Go to hell! You think we're scared of you? We're not.'

He folded his arms. 'Well, you should be.' He sought out Anita and put a finger to his nostril. 'Have you got something on your nose?' he mocked.

Anita scowled at him. 'I am *not* back on drugs!'

Jack frowned. 'My mistake. Must be face powder.'

Roxanne said, 'Just get out. Before I call security.'

He laughed again. 'My security, you mean? Try it. I think you'll find they're on a permanent break.' He gazed at Carly. 'You're very quiet, Little Miss Innocent. Have you seen what they're saying about the *baby* of the band on the message boards? How she *killed* her baby?'

Carly gasped.

Rick put a hand on Jack's arm. 'It's time you left.' Jack shook him off.

Roxanne stepped towards him. 'Yes, fuck off, Jack, it's our show tonight, so get lost.'

'Ah, yes, the show. I'd make the most of it if I were you because it's the last one you'll ever do. Wembley is OFF.' He turned and walked away.

47

The women sat in stunned silence in the dressing room.

Carly was the first to speak. She looked dazed. 'We can forget about doing our dream gig, then.'

Roxanne frowned. 'What do you mean?'

'You heard him. Wembley. It's not happening. He'll make sure of it.'

'*He* is in no position to decide anything,' Roxanne countered. 'Not after what he did to you. He needs locking up.'

'She's right,' Anita said. 'If ever there was a time to wipe the sick smirk off that smug, reptile face, this is it.'

'He thinks he can do what he likes. Wrong.' Chrissie was incandescent. She had Anita's lip gloss in her hand and began dolloping it on. 'Let's see how he likes it when we take him down, the evil bastard.'

There was silence.

They were in a huddle in the VIP section of the club. Rick had gone after Jack.

Chrissie double-checked no one else was near the VIP section before she spoke. 'Sneaky Susan . . . Can you believe she's been spying on us all this time? Reporting back to her bastard of a brother.'

'He's no Jack Raven, more like Jack Snake,' Roxanne said.

'Remember how much Susan wanted to be in the Thunder Girls?' Anita said. 'When Rick said he wanted Roxanne for the band, Jack briefly talked about making it a five-piece just to keep Susan in the mix.'

Roxanne looked surprised. 'I didn't know that.'

'The rest of us thought it was a bad idea,' Chrissie said. 'It was obvious you were the best fit. When we met you we all wanted you. Soon as we heard you sing, we were blown away.' It was the first time Chrissie had ever said anything complimentary about Roxanne's voice, which she usually described as 'pitchy'.

'I remember saying I thought Susan was a bit too buttoned-up for the band. I didn't think she'd be much fun.' Carly winced. 'Actually, that's what I told Jack.'

Roxanne was watching her closely. 'You really had no idea she was his sister? Didn't even suspect?'

Carly shook her head. 'He told me he had a kid sister and that his mum had got pregnant around the same time he got his start at Shine. I got the impression they weren't close because of the age difference. I mean, he was a teenager, working in the music business, when she was a baby. And he goes by a different surname to her!'

'I can't get over how sly they were, keeping it quiet,' Chrissie said.

'Oh, he knew exactly what he was doing,' Roxanne said. 'Made sure Susan was always around, part of the furniture. Taking everything in. And it wasn't just us, Rick trusted her too. The number of times he said he didn't know what he'd do without her.' She rolled her eyes. 'We've been taken for a right old ride. We've never cared what she saw or heard and all the time she's been running back to Jack, telling tales.'

'And writing a book in her spare time,' Chrissie said. She jabbed the applicator into the tube of lip gloss.

'It's empty,' Anita said. Chrissie looked panic-stricken. 'Calm down. I've got more in my bag.'

They fell silent again.

'So, what are we going to do about Jack?' Roxanne asked Carly. 'Have you got anything we can use against him – photos, letters?'

Carly took a moment, before having a eureka moment. 'He filmed us together.' She stared at the floor. 'In bed.'

'Bloody pervert,' Chrissie muttered.

'He had a houseboat at Little Venice. He always said he'd never sell it. That's where we used to go. I thought it was amazing, all crushed velvet and satin sheets—'

'Oh, please, not *black* satin,' Chrissie said, disgusted. 'Don't tell me there was a mirror on the ceiling too.'

'Now, thinking back, it was like some awful brothel.' Carly kept her eyes on the floor. 'It was all set up for filming.'

'What did he do with the recordings?' Roxanne asked.

'There was a cabinet full of audition tapes, loads of different girls in alphabetical order. That's where he stashed our sex tape. He wrote my name on the spine and put it between Belinda and Chelsea, the singers who tried out for the band at the same time as me. Said no one would ever think to look for it there.'

Roxanne exchanged a look with Chrissie and Anita.

'You don't think all those so-called audition tapes were actually sex tapes with other young girls he'd picked up?' Roxanne asked.

Carly looked horrified.

'I was thinking the same thing,' Chrissie said.

'We need to get our hands on those tapes,' Anita said.

Roxanne arranged a car to collect Carly from the back of the club. She ditched the ocelot-print coat in favour of Jamie's parka.

'You're sure about this?' Roxanne asked.

Carly nodded. 'Hundred per cent.' She shoved her hands into the pockets of the jacket, so the others wouldn't see she was shaking.

Chrissie walked her to the car. 'Keep your eyes peeled, and don't take any risks. Not in your condition.'

'What do you mean?'

Chrissie lowered her voice. '*Pregnant*.'

Carly stared. 'How do you know?'

'I guessed. That day at my place, after the press

conference and the business with Scott . . . you weren't drinking. I saw you pouring your champers into the gerbera.' She gazed at Carly. 'It didn't survive, by the way, the plant.' Chrissie took her hand. 'Is it Dave's?'

'I don't know.'

'Oh, Carls, why didn't you tell us?'

'I was going to but with everything going on . . . it never seemed the right time.'

'I'm not sure you should be breaking into Jack's houseboat. It's too risky.'

'I want to. I *need* to.' Carly looked determined. 'Don't you see – it *has* to be me?'

Chrissie sighed.

'Plus, I know where to look, and I'm not breaking in, as such. There's a secret panel on deck where he keeps the key.'

48

Carly cut down the steps that led to the towpath. There were more boats than she remembered, neatly lined up all along one side of the canal. She put up the hood of the parka and hurried along, passing an ornate vessel with an impressive roof garden lit by fairy lights. Voices drifted towards her from the open windows of the cabin. She glimpsed candles, a couple at a table drinking wine. Head down, she pressed on.

She was afraid she wouldn't recognize Jack's boat but the instant she saw the gleaming black and gold paintwork she knew it. It was one of the biggest on the water, named *Stairway to Heaven* after Jack's favourite Led Zeppelin song.

She glanced behind her. No one else on the towpath as far as she could tell. Without breaking her stride, she stepped onto the boat and went along the deck to the far side, feeling for the panel where the key was kept hidden. She slid it back and took the key, her heart hammering, crouching for a moment in the darkness, listening. Laughter from the boat with the fairy lights floated across the still night air.

She crept to the door and put the key in the lock. As it turned, she remembered Jack talking about having an alarm fitted after one of the nearby boats was broken into, and her heart rate shot up. Holding her breath, she pushed the door open a crack, expecting a klaxon to go off. When nothing happened, she breathed again and ducked into the cabin. Her back was soaked in sweat, her legs like jelly. She stood completely still, breathing hard, willing herself to keep calm.

She moved stealthily through the cabin, relying on what light there was from the towpath to see what she was doing. The cabinet where the tapes were stashed was in the living room at the far end of the boat. She felt her way through the little galley and dining area, banging her knee on a bench seat, wincing in pain. When she reached the cabinet and found it locked, panic went through her. She remembered now, Jack always kept it locked. Of course he did – it was jammed with incriminating material. She thought back – where had he kept the key?

She dropped to her knees and felt along the cabinet's underside. Nothing. Beside it was a built-in window seat. She removed the cushions and, tilting the seat up, felt around. Her hand touched something ticklish and she recoiled. When she peered inside she saw a glint of metal, fur-trimmed handcuffs. She picked them up. A key dangled from the lock. On the off-chance, she tried it in the cabinet.

'Yes!'

A sudden creaking sound made her freeze. Someone was outside. Carly looked about her in panic. The only way out was the same way she had got in. She could make a dash for it but the chances were she would run slap into whoever was there. Her heart was thudding in her chest, making what seemed like a deafening sound. She put a hand against it, trying to shush it. Bang. Bang. Bang. Whoever was on the boat was bound to hear it. She stopped breathing, waiting for the door to open. She hadn't even managed to get the tapes! Careful footsteps moved about above her. The deck groaned. A shape moved in front of one of the narrow windows a few feet from where she was. She stared at it. Through the window, a beam of light shone into the cabin and she shrank down, flattening herself against the floor, burying her face under the hood of the coat. As she lay, heart pounding, sweat running down the back of her neck, the light swept back and forth through the cabin.

At the club, the waiting was killing the others. Chrissie, unable to keep still, paced about the dance floor, working her way through another of Anita's lip glosses.

In the background, the stage was set. The lighting crew completed their checks and the pyrotechnics team ran final safety tests. In a few hours the club would open to the public. Outside, there was already a queue.

Every few seconds Roxanne checked her phone. No word.

Anita drank endless cups of strong coffee and disappeared to the loo every five minutes, growing increasingly jittery.

'I just ran into Rick – he's still taking calls from the press about Susan's revelations,' she told Roxanne. 'Apparently, the *Post* is running another thrilling instalment from the book tomorrow.' Anita waited a moment. 'Something else. I think Jack's gone. I've looked everywhere and I can't find him.'

'He was at the sound desk half an hour ago.'

Anita shook her head. 'They haven't seen him. He said he had to nip out, apparently. Urgent business.'

'You don't think he's got wind of what Carly's up to?' Roxanne asked.

'No way.' Anita didn't sound convinced.

Chrissie stopped her pacing and came over. 'Has anyone heard from her?'

'Not yet.' Roxanne glanced at Anita. 'And Jack's nowhere to be seen.'

Chrissie's face fell. 'Oh my God, he's gone after her.'

'We don't know that.'

Chrissie threw a frantic look over her shoulder. 'He's probably got the place bugged. What if he heard what we had planned?'

Roxanne caught hold of her. 'Calm down. The club is *not*

bugged. He's not MI5. And there's no way that dickhead knows what we're up to.'

'Urgent business, he said,' Anita offered.

'Pricks like Jack always say it's something urgent, even when they're having a frigging routine dental check-up. Makes them feel important. We just need to hold our nerve and wait for Carly to get back.'

Roxanne caught Chrissie's anguished expression. 'Why are you looking like that – what's the matter?'

'We should never have let her go – she's pregnant!'

49

'We should call the police,' Chrissie said.

Roxanne threw her hands up. 'And say what? Excuse me, officer, our friend's late back from a spot of breaking and entering and we're getting worried . . .'

Anita sniggered. Roxanne and Chrissie sent icy looks her way. 'Sorry, it was funny though, the way you put it.' She got up a little unsteadily. 'Just nipping to the loo – all the coffee.'

'As long as that's all it is,' Chrissie said, suspicious.

'Goes straight through me,' Anita told her.

Roxanne watched her go. 'She's not doing the other stuff. She promised. She knows how important tonight is.'

'I think we need to keep an eye on her,' Chrissie said, watching Anita teeter off, struggling to stay upright in her new two-grand boots.

There was silence.

'We could phone the police and tell them about Jack

having sex with Carly when she was under-age,' Chrissie said.

'We don't have any evidence, not until she gets back with the tapes. Always assuming . . .' Roxanne left the sentence hanging.

'What?'

'. . . that Jack hasn't got her.'

'*Got* her? *Oh my God*, dial 999. NOW!'

The door opened and Anita came back in, eyes bright. 'Look who I found!' she announced.

Carly, pink-cheeked, rushed in behind her. She held up her bag, triumphant. 'Ta-dah!'

'You got them?' Roxanne asked.

Carly nodded. 'I got mine – and some more!'

Chrissie ran at Carly and threw her arms around her. 'Thank God you're safe! We thought Jack had gone after you.'

'I thought so too.' Carly laughed. 'Can you believe, someone showed up while I was on the boat? '

'*Oh my God*,' Chrissie said again.

'I was in the cabin, heard them on the deck above. I tell you, my heart nearly stopped. I was sure whoever it was would come in and catch me red-handed.'

Chrissie whispered, 'What did you do?'

'Lay flat on the floor and hoped for the best. Then I heard a voice. A girl, calling for Jack. Lucky for me, she must have assumed the place was locked up and she can't have known where to look for the key. Or she did, but it was missing because I had it . . . Anyway, she gave up eventually and I got on with helping myself to his stash.' She patted the bulging tote. 'Thirteen tapes, from Ava to Melanie. Doesn't look like he's got past M . . . yet.'

Roxanne shook her head. 'All those tapes. *Thirteen*.'

'Unlucky for some,' Chrissie said.

Roxanne beamed at the others. 'Blinding job, Carls. That's it – we've got him now.'

Chrissie was gazing at Carly. 'I told them – about the other thing.'

Jack returned to the club after dining alone at a new Japanese place where the bento box was second to none, and installed himself in a corner of the office the pyrotechnics guys were using. He was busy fending off angry emails from Kristen Kent, who wanted to know why she had no by-line on the book extracts in the *Post*. And why 'crazy Kimberley' was actually Susan from Shine. Jack had tried his usual tack and ignored her but she wasn't having it and kept phoning, leaving irate messages, threatening to cut off his balls if he failed to sort out her credit. When he didn't reply she upped the ante. *Check the contract, you arsehole*, she had written in her latest email (no *Dear Jack* or *Hi*, or anything remotely polite). Jack was taken aback. He had known she was spiky but hadn't anticipated how overly sensitive she could be. Really. All that fuss over a credit. Just as he was considering whether to email her back and tell her where to go, the door to the office opened.

He looked up as Chrissie, Roxanne, Anita and Carly stormed in. His face twisted into a mean smile. 'Shouldn't you *girls* be getting ready for your final close-up?'

They were already in their stage gear, outfits made from wafer-thin leather that clung in all the right places, the fabric embellished with chains and mesh panels, oversized gemstones. Chrissie and Roxanne had thigh-length peep-toe boots on over their fishnets. Carly was in a pair of Giuseppe Zanotti heels with what looked like crystal flames licking around her ankles. Anita insisted on wearing her new and amazing boots, even though they were killing her. Thigh-high gladiators were on standby in case she changed her mind, although Jamie had warned her he would need a bit of notice if she wanted them as it took forever to do them up.

'You really thought you'd got away with it, didn't you?' Roxanne gave him a look of contempt.

Jack's phone started to ring. Kristen Kent. Again. Couldn't the woman take a hint? He swiped the screen, sending the call to voicemail.

'You should know better than to think you can keep anything secret in this business,' Chrissie said.

'Quite right,' Jack said. 'As you lot already know to your cost. Bet you can't wait for tomorrow's *Post*. I can give you a sneak preview, if you like – there's a great interview with your old dealer, Anita.'

'Arsehole!' Chrissie spat it out. Roxanne put a restraining hand on her arm and Anita looked shocked.

Jack shrugged.

Carly was looking at him intently. 'We've got the tapes.' Jack looked utterly unfazed. 'The *tapes*.' Carly loaded the word with meaning.

Jack's face twitched. 'I don't know what you're talking about.' Sounding unsure all of a sudden. Surely she couldn't mean . . .

'I think you do,' Roxanne told him. 'Starting with Ava.'

'Right through to Melanie,' Carly said.

'And *Carly* in between,' Chrissie chipped in.

Shit. Jack attempted a smile. 'Ladies, ladies, let's not get carried away. They're audition tapes.'

'Auditions for what?' Roxanne asked. 'Child brides?'

He flinched. 'And they're private property.'

'They're ours now,' Chrissie told him.

Jack was anxious. 'Come on, we can talk about this. I think you've got the wrong end of the stick . . .'

Carly stared at him, disgusted. 'We've got you bang to rights and you still can't admit what you've done, can you?'

'Do you know what they do to paedophiles in prison?' Roxanne said.

'I saw a programme about it,' Anita said. 'They have to put them on a special wing but even then they can't stop them from being attacked.' She frowned in concentration. 'I think the guards sometimes turn a blind eye. Some bloke had his cock chopped off in one episode.'

Jack's eyes were wide.

'It's over,' Roxanne said. 'You can't get away with your sort of behaviour anymore. Haven't you heard about Rolf Harris? Gary Glitter? Operation Yewtree?'

Jack swallowed. 'I'm not some kind of pervert.'

'Technically, I think you'll find that's exactly what you are,' Carly told him.

'Please, let's just talk this through.' Jack was pale. 'We can make a deal – can't we?'

Chrissie took a triumphant step forward, her tall-heeled frame towering over the seated Jack. 'Can we now . . .'

'I know I hate the pigs but I can't wait till we call them on Jack,' Chrissie said for the second time in the space of a few hours.

'I want to see what's on the tapes first. I'm not sure I want them seeing everything,' said Carly.

'I still feel bad letting that scumbag walk free for now, thinking he's got away with it,' Chrissie said.

'We had to let him think we'd just blackmailed him,' Anita said. 'That after our new contracts are signed and we perform at Wembley, he thinks we'll give the tapes back. We get our second chance, our second big break . . . and *then* we call the cops, have Jack arrested and sent to prison for being a paedophile.'

'I know you're right,' Chrissie said, then smiled. 'Ruthless. You're learning.'

Roxanne dumped an ice bucket on the table. 'Right now we need to concentrate on the show. No distractions.

Phones in here and let's forget about Jack until later.' There was a moment's hesitation before the phones went in. 'Okay. Let's just do the show and enjoy the party.'

'*Yaaaaaay*, party!' Anita said. She caught Chrissie's look and made a face. 'Sorry – getting a teensy-weensy bit over-excited.' She teetered off to the loo. 'The boots are feeling better, anyway,' she said over her shoulder before disappearing.

'What about you?' Roxanne asked Carly. 'You feeling okay after all the stress of today?'

'I feel great. Like a weight's been lifted.' She looked thoughtful. 'What's bothering me is . . . I don't know for sure whose baby I'm carrying. Dave's? Adam's? Let's be honest, neither one is ideal.'

Chrissie gave her a squeeze. 'Sod the pair of them, you've got us, you know you have.'

Carly smiled. 'Thanks.'

Roxanne said, 'We'll be there for you, no matter what.'

They were silent.

Roxanne glanced at the clock. 'I'd better go and find Nita.'

In the corridor, she bumped into Rick, looking frazzled. 'I was just on my way to see you,' he said. Roxanne felt her heart rate go up. He gave her a long look and whistled. 'You look sensational, Rox. Peachy.' Her stomach did a flip. He reached up and fiddled with a strand of hair. 'There, perfect.' For a moment, as they gazed at one another, Roxanne was afraid she might pass out, then Rick cleared his throat.

'Sorry I've not been around much today. Bloody phone hasn't stopped ringing.' On cue, it rang. They both laughed. 'See what I mean?' The phone emitted a series of beeps and he rolled his eyes. 'I wanted to warn you – Jack's still here.'

'I wouldn't worry about him.' He gave her a curious look. 'He's realized it's in his – I mean, Shine Records' – best interests to support the Thunder Girls.'

Rick looked suspicious. 'Sounds . . . intriguing.'

Roxanne gazed into his eyes. He touched her cheek. She took a breath and told herself now was not the time to lock lips, even though it was what she so desperately wanted, and gave him a friendly pat on the arm instead. 'I need to find Anita,' she said. 'And there's something I want Jamie to do.'

Roxanne and Anita went from the bathroom to peek at the crowd. The club was heaving with what looked like a very lively bunch. Some of Jamie's designer friends were in, already on the podiums, bare-chested, shirts dangling from their belt hoops.

Anita slumped into a chair. 'God, my poor feet.'

'Do you want the other boots?'

She shook her head. 'I am wearing these bad boys if it kills me.'

Roxanne signalled to Carly, who went to sit with Anita.

'I'll be closest to her onstage,' Chrissie said. 'I'll keep an eye on her, check she doesn't trip over herself from post-shopping exhaustion.'

'Good luck with that,' Roxanne said. 'Did you see Rick?'

Chrissie's face seemed to light up. 'Yeah, and he loves the costumes. Your Jamie's a star.'

Roxanne felt a ripple of pride. 'I know. Clever lad.'

'He's a gorgeous kid.'

Roxanne smiled.

'I never wanted children,' Chrissie said. 'Too selfish. I'm beginning to think I missed out.'

Roxanne was surprised. 'It's not too late. In India they do IVF up to sixty. You could still do it, if you wanted. Loads of women our age do.'

Our age. Chrissie gave her a grateful look. 'Never say never, I guess. I mean, after the nightmare with Scott I was sure I'd never want to go near a man again and yet I still haven't learnt my lesson. I mean, I must be the archetypal dumb blonde.'

'Not using words like that,' Roxanne said, amused. 'So, you're thinking you might dip a toe in the water, have another go at a relationship? Or were you just contemplating the occasional meaningless shag?'

They both laughed.

Chrissie glanced across at the others. 'I've realized not all men are bad.' Roxanne raised an eyebrow and Chrissie laughed again. 'I know! But through all the shit that's been going on, Rick's been amazing. I mean a-may-*zing*.' Her eyes shone. 'He's been my rock and I think . . . I think I want him back.'

Roxanne felt her stomach tighten. Before she could speak, Rick popped his head round the dressing room door. 'I hope you girls are ready because the place is packed.'

50

The show was over in a flash. Fourteen minutes and forty-two seconds, to be precise. The time it took to perform three tracks, ending with an extended version of 'Fire Palace'. On the final note, the pyrotechnics erupted in a series of explosions, smoke and sulphur billowing into the air. The girls exchanged huge grins, soaking up the shrieks and applause and thunderous stomping. Chrissie took a microphone and stepped forward to thank the crowd for their support. She caught sight of Jack leaning against a pillar, grim-faced, with that awful hack, Kristen Kent . . . no, it was *Susan* – looking like a psychopathic carbon copy.

'I'm happy to announce the Thunder Girls are back for good!' More cheering. To her astonishment, she spotted Scott in the crowd, hobbling on his cast. Who invited him? 'I hope you'll all come and see us at Wembley!' She aimed a dazzling smile at Jack, knowing his plans to put paid to their dream gig were in bits. As she turned she saw Maria and Dave also in the sea of faces. Everyone was crawling out of the woodwork.

A few feet away, a muscly man with staring blue eyes worked his way towards the front of the stage. She stiffened – oh God, was this a hit man, was she about to be shot live on stage, would this vendetta never end? Her mind was racing before she suddenly realized she knew those eyes. 'Oh, thank God!' she breathed under her breath. It was just the Mad Fan! Bless.

'Look out for the new album, and there's a brand new video coming your way, thanks to our *lovely* team at Shine, who we're proud to reveal have given us a new five-album deal,' Chrissie continued. Another pointed look at Jack. At the back of the room she clocked yet another familiar face. One she had definitely not expected to see. 'And for now, thanks to all of you for coming. *We love you!*'

Backstage, Rick was opening champagne. 'Amazing, all of you,' he said, as the cork flew from the bottle. 'Better than ever. What a bunch of stars.'

Jamie rushed into the room, flushed, beads of sweat on his brow. He had been out front, watching with his mates. 'Well, that seemed to go okay,' he said, grinning.

'Yeah, not bad,' Rick said, keeping a straight face. Jamie's smile vanished and Rick clapped him on the back. 'I'm kidding! It was *incredible* – great work all round.'

Jamie went over to Carly. 'There's a guy trying to get backstage. Says he's your husband.'

Carly shook her head.

As they made their way to the after-show party in the VIP area, Chrissie felt a touch on her arm and turned to find Scott in front of her. Seeing him was almost like a physical blow. She felt suddenly unsteady.

'You were amazing, babe,' he said, giving her a look full of longing.

She stared at him, not trusting herself to speak. She'd barely held herself back from killing him in the hospital. Why was he here?

'You look gorgeous, by the way.' Gazing at her the way he had on their wedding day.

She found her voice. 'What are you doing here?'

'I wanted to see you. I had to.' His hand was still on her arm. 'I miss you. And I feel bad about, you know . . .'

Chrissie held his gaze. She wished he would stop looking at her like that.

'I was thinking maybe we could have a drink.' His thumb stroked her arm. She couldn't take her eyes off him. 'Come on,' Scott was saying. 'We don't have to hate each other – do we?'

She shook her head. 'No, we don't. I don't hate you.' He smiled and she caught his look. Relief. She was better at reading him now, she realized. 'I *despise* you,' she said. 'For being a lying, two-faced shit and letting a creep like Jack pull your strings – for *money*. You make me sick.'

'But, Chrissie, we can really have something—'

'You want another chance to steal all the money I'm about to make now the Thunder Girls are hot again, you mean!

Ha, no chance! I see through you now, Scott. You're not a man, you're a . . .' She searched for the word. 'A *gigolo*,' she said, raising her voice. 'That's you, Scott – and now you're a desperate one – but I do not pay for "it".'

Rick appeared at Chrissie's side. 'Everything okay?' he asked her as he gave Scott a filthy look.

She nodded. 'Yes, he was just leaving.' On the far side of the room she caught sight of Jack. She looked back at Scott. 'Oh look, your chum's over there. You can take him with you . . .'

'He's not my friend,' Scott said.

'Whatever. If you'll excuse us, we've got showbusiness to attend to.' Rick's voice was full of contempt. He nodded at one of the security guys to escort Scott out and steered Chrissie away.

'I'm still your husband!' Scott yelled as she made her way up the stairs to the VIP area. A few heads turned to see what the shouting was about.

Chrissie kept going while shouting her reply. 'No, you're a fraudster, there's a difference – look out for divorce papers in the post.'

Upstairs, Anita was deep in conversation with Lucy, the choreographer. She had an arm slung casually over the woman's shoulder. Chrissie went over, peeled Anita off the girl, and led her bandmate away to a quiet corner.

'Spoilsport,' Anita said. 'All this time I've been good as gold, you could at least turn a blind eye just this once.'

'You're a married woman,' Chrissie said.

'When did you get to be such a prissy missy? What goes on tour stays on tour.'

'We're not on tour.'

'I just want a bit of fun. What the Brazilians call *el rumpo-pumpo*.' Chrissie frowned. Anita roared with laughter. 'I made that up!'

Chrissie got hold of her. Glancing over her shoulder, she lowered her voice. 'Here's something I'm *not* making up.' She waited for Anita to pull herself together and pay attention. 'Your wife's here.' Anita's eyes widened. 'That's right. I spotted *Maria* in the crowd.'

Anita peered over the balcony from the VIP section onto the dance floor below. 'You're sure it was her?' she asked Chrissie.

'Certain.'

Anita looked alarmed. 'But how? I don't understand – what's she doing here?'

'I'd have thought that was obvious. She's come to support her other half.'

Anita helped herself to another glass of champagne from a passing waiter. 'You'll have to keep her away from me.'

'*Me?!*'

'You're the only one she knows. Maybe you could have a scout around, see what kind of a mood she's in . . .'

'No way!' Chrissie stared at Anita, who seemed to have sobered up all of a sudden. '*You're* the one she wants. *You* go and find her.'

On the other side of the room Chrissie spotted Roxanne.

Animated, head on one side – talking to Rick. He said something that made her laugh. Leaned in close and the pair of them dissolved in hysterics. Chrissie felt peculiar. She decided to go over and see what was so funny.

Anita got hold of her, digging her nails into her arm. 'Don't leave me,' she pleaded. 'I've been ignoring her calls, putting off talking to her. Thinking once I get back I'll sort things out properly.' Maria's messages had become increasingly irate, sometimes tearful, often threatening.

'She can't get into the after-show, not without a pass,' Chrissie said, trying to get her arm free, feeling Anita's nails rake her bare skin.

Anita's eyes were wild. 'That won't stop her!'

Carly wandered over. 'There's a chocolate fountain over there, if you're interested.' She saw Anita's panic-stricken face. 'What's happened now?'

Anita shook her head.

'Her wife's here,' Chrissie said. 'In a mad rage, quite possibly. Looking to drag her woman off to her cave in the back of beyond.' Carly's eyes widened. 'Subtlety isn't exactly her strong point.'

'She's not that bad,' Anita said, casting nervous looks in all directions. 'I do love her . . . I'm just confused.'

Carly smiled. 'Dave's here somewhere. He collared Jamie earlier, tried to get him to bring him backstage.'

'Must be something in the water. Scott showed up too. Funny how success can change things.' She glanced over at

Rick again. Now Roxanne was saying something that made him laugh.

Something caught Carly's eye on the dance floor. 'I thought the pyrotechnics were over,' she said.

Chrissie followed her gaze. Smoke drifted across the mass of bodies moving in rhythm to the thumping music. She caught sight of Jamie swan-diving from a podium into the arms of his friends. On the edge of things, the Mad Fan stared up at her as, around him, the throng appeared molten, surging in different directions. Something was wrong. A series of bangs shook the place. The lights at the side of the stage blew. Screams went up, the crowd pitching and rolling. Chrissie registered panic, a girl in a sparkly dress being lifted off her feet and carried along, before disappearing.

'What's happening?' Anita asked.

'It's a fire.' Chrissie could barely get the words out. In the space of a few seconds the smoke had become thicker and was snaking among the crowd. 'Fire,' she said again. 'Dial 999.'

Carly looked stricken. 'I can't. I haven't got my phone. *Shit* – they're in the ice bucket in the dressing room.'

Chrissie felt the atmosphere change. She scanned the room for Rick, but people were already panicking and pushing and making for the stairs. In the crush it was impossible to see anything.

'We need to get out.' She got hold of Carly, who seemed rooted to the spot. 'Now!' The smoke was getting even thicker. A man shoved past, almost knocking her off her feet.

Anita stared at the bodies on the dance floor. 'Oh God, there's Maria!' The women locked eyes, Maria trying desperately to get to the staircase that led to Anita. 'I need to help her!'

Chrissie hung on to her. 'You can't go down there.' People were surging up the staircase, some losing their footing. 'Nita, we *have* to go.'

'No!' Anita was frantic. 'I can't see her anymore!'

Chrissie looked around. No sign of Carly. She prayed she was making her way out. 'Go.'

Anita hung on to the balcony rail. 'Maria!'

Chrissie dragged her away. 'Look at me – we *have* to get out of here, right now.' They were surrounded by people pushing and shoving, sobbing. She pushed Anita ahead. Suddenly they were separated.

Outside, Roxanne raced up and down searching for Jamie among the hundreds of clubbers pouring into the street. She was hysterical, her breath ragged. Rick did his best to keep her calm. 'He'll be okay,' he kept saying, not that he could possibly be sure.

'Oh God, where is he?' She was screaming. 'Jamie! *Jamie!*' Tears streamed down her face. Sirens sounded, a long way off, it seemed; a series of drawn-out, rising whoops amid blasts of something almost musical. Horns blared and she pictured fire engines speeding towards them, jumping red lights. She willed them to get there. What was taking so long?

Anita staggered along the pavement, dazed, and Roxanne rushed at her. 'Have you seen Jamie? Is he in there?' Anita didn't know. She hadn't managed to find Maria either. And in the crush to get out she had lost sight of Chrissie.

A burly shape appeared, moving swiftly. Danny, Carly's driver, with her lifeless body in his arms. He swept past them to the square opposite, where small groups of survivors milled about, and laid her carefully on a bench. The others ran after him.

'She's breathing,' Danny said. His face was streaked with ash. 'I can hardly feel her pulse, though.' He looked around. Still no sign of the emergency vehicles. 'Someone needs to stay with her while I get the car – I'm not waiting for an ambulance.'

'I will.' Anita knelt at Carly's side and stroked her hair. 'You need to tell them she's pregnant.' Danny looked surprised. 'I don't know how far along she is,' Anita told him.

Rick seemed bewildered. 'Are you sure?' he asked.

'She told us tonight.' Anita started crying. Beside her, Roxanne was frantic. 'You go,' Anita told her. 'Find your boy.'

Roxanne caught hold of Danny's arm. 'Did you see him, my Jamie?' He shook his head.

Rick said, 'What about Chrissie?'

Another shake of the head.

'I'm going back in,' Rick told Roxanne. 'I need to look for her.' The sirens still seemed far away.

Roxanne's voice rose. 'Jamie, find Jamie – *please*!' He gave her a helpless look. She was clawing at him. 'You *have* to find him, Rick – he's your son!'

51

Chrissie didn't know where anyone was, and she could barely see.

She was going to die here, in Heaven & Hell. Well, far more Hell than Heaven. Lights were out and people were stumbling about in all directions. There was lots of screaming and swearing.

Someone with strong muscles grabbed her. Maybe it was a fireman. She pawed at the bare torso of the person she couldn't see, trying to get a grip. She felt a thin T-shirt, with a clearly defined, ripped six-pack underneath.

She made eye contact with the figure. The Mad Fan! He took his T-shirt off and threw it over Chrissie's head, as if he was shielding her from the smoke. 'I'll save you, Chrissie,' he said. He stared at her with his incredible blue eyes.

He might be a Mad Fan but, as the others had reminded

Chrissie, he'd been loyal to them for years. If Chrissie was going to die here, she wasn't going to do it alone. She clasped the Mad Fan's face and kissed him passionately.

For Jason Naylor, it was utter euphoria. After all these years, what was meant to be had finally come true. He kissed Chrissie back with passion. He was going to save her from the fire and they would be together forever. He'd been up close to Scott in the club and he definitely hadn't recognized him as the one who had run him over – so he didn't need to worry about being locked up away from his dream girl now she was finally in his arms. He and Chrissie were always meant to be, and now she knew it too.

The feeling of ecstasy built and built. Jason had never felt so alive, so aroused . . . and then it was all over too quickly.

As Chrissie kissed the Mad Fan, and he awkwardly and with no skill whatsoever kissed her back, she felt him shudder against her. She broke off the kiss and looked down. 'Did you just—'

Before she could finish her question, one of the show lights fell from the ceiling and smacked her last kiss on the side of his head. Chrissie screamed in fright as he collapsed to the floor, unconscious.

'Great, now I'm going to die alone.'

The smoke was getting stronger, and she was getting dizzier . . .

'Chrissie!' a voice called from the distance.

She whirled around until she caught sight of what she thought was Jamie. Not wasting time, she followed him along a corridor.

'Sorry, I can't carry you!' she called back to the unconscious Mad Fan.

The further she went in the direction of the voice, the harder it was to see in the thick, suffocating smoke, which was getting worse. She tried not to panic and remembered hearing somewhere that smoke went upwards and to try and stay beneath it, so she dropped to her hands and knees and began crawling along, keeping her face close to the ground, feeling her way. Suddenly, she bumped into something and when she looked up, Jamie was on all fours in front of her, doing the same thing.

'Jamie, thank God,' she said. 'Can you get us out of here?'

'I don't know.' His face was rigid with fear. In front of them a door blocked their way. He put a tentative hand against it and flinched. 'It's red hot,' he told her. 'I daren't open it.'

Chrissie looked over her shoulder. Smoke now filled the space, forming a solid wall. She swallowed.

They were going to die.

It went through Chrissie's mind how peculiar life was, that it would all end for her with Roxanne's son. She put a protective arm around him and pulled him close.

52

Carly lay in a dimly lit room hooked up to monitors. Her head was encased in a bandage. Danny had done the right thing rushing her straight to hospital, getting her there before other casualties started arriving. His soldier's training had kicked in and he had dialled 999 and put his phone on speaker as he drove, telling the operator he was on his way to Chelsea & Westminster and that Carly was unconscious. Breathing, but only just.

He had found her out cold in a heap, slumped over a speaker, one of her arms jutting out at an odd angle. Still wearing her ridiculous heels. The 999 call was the right thing to do and when he screamed up to A&E a crash team was at the entrance waiting to rush Carly away.

A nurse who didn't look old enough to be doing the job had led him to the relatives' room and brought him coffee laced with sugar. His prompt action had probably saved Carly's life, she said. Danny hoped so. When he finished his coffee he went and found the hospital chapel and, for the first time in years, prayed.

She had a swelling on the brain and was taken straight into theatre. The operation had lasted hours but had gone well, according to the surgeon, although it was still too early to say whether she would make a full recovery. 'It's a case of wait and see,' was how he put it.

On top of the head injury, she had dislocated her shoulder and broken her wrist, not that anyone was too worried about her arm. As long as her brain healed, her arm would too.

So far, all the indications were the baby was fine.

Danny was in two minds about whether to call Dave. He had seen him at the club doing his utmost to get to Carly – at one point sidling up to Danny and begging him to get him into the after-show party. Danny had been under instructions from Carly to tell him there was no Payback Prince on the guest list – what that meant, he had no idea, but Dave definitely got the message.

Now, though, he wasn't sure if Carly would want Dave at her bedside. Her being pregnant changed things. What if Dave was the father?

In the end he decided to ring him. He also put in a call to Adam, even though he wasn't sure what had happened between him and Carly – she'd told him everything that had been going on, but clammed up when he asked where Adam was. All she had said was that he had gone back to the States on business. Even if he was too far away to be of any use, he needed to be told. That baby might, after all, be his.

When Dave showed up he told Danny he could go home and take a break. Danny went as far as the relatives' room and had another coffee.

He was going nowhere until he knew Carly was going to make it.

Anita was treated for smoke inhalation and minor burns. She begged the nurse to find out if Maria Rodrigues had been brought in. The nurse said she would check. The demented look in Anita's eyes prompted her to return with a mild sedative. Anita hugged her knees to her chest and wept. She would be to blame if anything had happened to Maria. Oh, *why* had she not just called her when she had the chance? No matter what, she would find her. Make it up to her – let her know how sorry she was, and how much she loved her. Arrange a romantic holiday, where they could renew their vows. *Please, please, let her be okay*, she said to herself.

Anita waited on the narrow bed in the cubicle as patients either side were treated. Someone nearby was crying, noisy great sobs. Anita kept her eyes shut. When the nurse came back in she asked if Maria Rodrigues was a friend. Anita told her she was her wife. The nurse retreated again.

Anita waited what seemed like an age before a kindly man in a pink shirt, sleeves rolled up and a stethoscope round his neck, came to ask how she was feeling. The name on his badge was Dr Andrew Curtis.

'I'm okay,' she said. 'Shaken up. It was horrible.' He was looking at her with such concern she began welling up again. Tears slid down her face. He whipped a fresh tissue from his pocket and handed it to her. 'Sorry.' She blew her nose.

Dr Curtis frowned. 'Is there anyone we can call for you?'

'My manager's here somewhere,' she said. Rick had called in to see her on his way to find out about Carly. 'I'm in a band. We were doing a show at the club before . . . before the fire broke out. One of my friends is in a pretty bad way.'

'You were asking about another patient,' the doctor said. 'Maria Rodrigues.'

Anita brightened. 'Is she here?'

Dr Curtis gave nothing away. 'Just give me a moment,' he said.

Rick was stroking Chrissie's wrist. Her hand was bandaged. She had scorched it hanging on to the handrail on the stairs as she tried to escape the fire.

Rick had found her and Jamie huddled together. Somehow, he scooped both of them up and made it back along the corridor and out into the street where fire crews were on the scene, ambulances parked at angles across the road.

Chrissie glanced at Rick, who seemed deep in thought as he absent-mindedly ran a thumb over her wrist. He had saved her life and risked his own in the process. 'I love you,' she said, so softly he didn't hear.

*

The Mad Fan had concussion and lung damage from the smoke, but he would fully recover. Being knocked out by the lighting fixture had ruined his moment with Chrissie, but he would have another chance to show his love. He was sure she would have tried to pull him out of the building, but couldn't due to all his impressive muscles. At least a fireman had found him.

Susan had burns to her legs. She got a nurse to wheel her to intensive care where Jack lay in a coma, and sat at the side of his bed, alarmed at the wires and drips and machines that seemed to be going off every few seconds. How was he supposed to get any rest with all that going on? She tried talking to him. It would all be fine, she promised. She would make sure he got the best care. She bent and kissed the back of his hand while he lay motionless. The pain of seeing him helpless made her cramp up. Jack had always looked out for her, been her protector.

Well, now she would be his.

Roxanne put a mug of strong tea in front of Jamie. 'I wish you'd let them keep you in overnight,' she said.

He shook his head. 'I'm better off at home.' He'd had a soak in the bath and borrowed one of Roxanne's snuggly dressing gowns. She faced him across the kitchen table.

'I thought I'd lost you,' she said, tears sliding down her face.

'You nearly did.'

They were silent.

'I can't believe Rick came back into a burning building,' Jamie said. 'What a hero.'

Roxanne took a deep breath. 'There's something I need to tell you . . .'

Danny was on his way to check on Carly when Adam stepped off the escalator in front of him.

'I got your message,' Adam said. He looked awful.

Danny looked puzzled. 'I thought you were in New York.'

'I was, I just got back. Thought I'd make it in time for the gig but my flight was delayed.' His face was etched with worry. 'How is she?'

Danny held his gaze. 'They don't know.'

'They must know something.'

He shook his head. 'Not until she comes round.'

Adam seemed dazed. 'I left for the States in a hurry, some bloody crisis at the bank. Didn't even get a chance to say a proper goodbye. I didn't think I'd be gone this long.' He gave Danny an anguished look. 'I've tried calling her so many times.'

'No one could have seen this coming, mate.'

'What if she doesn't . . . you know?' His voice cracked.

'We're not thinking about that.'

They stood for a moment. 'Why don't I take you to see her?' Danny suggested. Adam nodded. 'Just so you know – Dave's in there.'

*

Anita followed Dr Curtis along a series of corridors, past a display of cheery paintings by schoolchildren, to a lift that descended to the basement. He showed her into a small room with bare walls, a couple of armchairs, small side table.

Anita shivered. This part of the hospital felt colder. She stood facing a wall that was painted a very pale shade of green. Almost cream, just the slightest hint of colour. She had heard that green was soothing. The bar in Sao Miguel was painted green, but a lot brighter. Emerald. Everything about the bar was bright, loud. Perhaps they should give it a makeover.

'There's no rush,' Dr Curtis was saying. 'Tell me when you're ready.'

Anita nodded. The hairs on the backs of her bare arms stood up. She hugged herself. 'I am,' she said.

He waited a moment and then slipped out of the room.

It seemed the temperature had suddenly dropped again and she felt icy cold. She gave her arms a rub but couldn't stop shivering.

The door opened and Dr Curtis was back. He touched her shoulder. 'If you're not ready . . .'

'I'm ready,' she told him as she took a step forward and peered through the glass at a woman in scrubs. The woman drew back the sheet from the trolley in front of her and Anita's hand flew to her mouth. Her body shook. She let out a howl.

Maria.

She flung herself at the glass and hammered on it. 'No! No! No! No! Nooooo!' Dr Curtis caught hold of her before her legs gave way.

In the end, Roxanne didn't go to bed. Rick had called to bring her up to date and when he broke the news about Maria she knew she would never sleep. Anita had been given sedatives, he said. She was hysterical. Once she calmed down, he had taken her home to Chrissie's. Roxanne wasn't sure sedatives were a great idea for a former drug addict, but it was already done. Rick was still there, keeping an eye on her in case she tried to do something stupid, as he put it.

'What about Carly?' Roxanne asked.

He didn't answer right away. 'Not good. It's a serious head injury. We just have to hope . . .'

'It's all so . . . terrible.' She felt that was nowhere near a strong enough way of putting things but couldn't think what else to say. 'I don't know what to do,' she told him.

'Me neither.'

She could not get her head around what had happened. How could a fire have started in the club? All those years, nothing had gone wrong. It had to be something to do with the pyrotechnics.

'What about you – are you okay?' she asked. She owed him everything. A man who had gone into a burning building and risked his own life to save her son. *Their* son. 'Rick, I don't know how to thank you. If it hadn't been for you . . .'

Her voice cracked. 'I came so close to losing him.' She wiped away the tears streaming down her face.

Rick was silent. 'How's he doing?'

'Sleeping.' *Alive*, she wanted to say. She wanted to tell him how she felt about him – apologize for all the years she had kept Jamie's existence from him. 'Rick . . .' she began.

'I know.' He didn't, though. He had no idea how she really felt. 'We're the lucky ones,' he said. 'We made it.'

He was right about that.

She had told him Jamie was his son. And now Jamie knew Rick was his father. What happened next? She had expected a reaction – *something* – but so far she had been met with silence from both of them. Perhaps she was expecting too much. It was a lot to take in, after all.

'I've texted Jamie. We're going to have dinner soon. To talk. I hope that's okay,' Rick said.

'Oh. Of course,' Roxanne said. She hung on the line, waiting for Rick to say he needed to see her, that there were things they had to discuss, but instead he ended the call, saying he had to check on Anita.

After he had gone, she stared at the phone, wondering if she had been right to tell him. Now that she had thrown everything into the air she had no idea how the pieces would fall. Perhaps he was angry with her for not letting him know all those years ago he had a child. He had every right. As for Jamie, he might never forgive her for hiding the truth about his father.

When the doorbell went an hour later she was still in the kitchen, cooking eggs she had no intention of eating.

The same detective who had come for Chrissie after the press conference was on the doorstep, an officer in uniform at his side. He held up ID. 'Detective Sergeant Rose,' he said. 'Okay if I come in?'

Roxanne wondered if she was in trouble. Somehow to blame for the fire and about to be arrested.

DS Rose accepted a cup of coffee. The uniformed officer declined. Rose looked worn out, as if he too had been up all night, his suit and shirt grubby.

'The fire brigade's still there, damping down,' he said. After a long pause, he added, 'Three fatalities, so far. I'm very sorry.'

Roxanne felt suddenly tearful. 'One of them was the wife of my friend, Anita.'

Rose looked away. 'Shocking business. Terrible.'

That word again. *Terrible*.

'She's in bits.' How – if – Anita would recover was anyone's guess. Rick and Chrissie were taking it in turns to be with her round the clock.

'Do you know anything yet – what caused it?' It was a question she hardly dared ask.

Rose cleared his throat. 'The fire brigade investigators are still on the scene but the early indications are it started at the back of the stage area.'

Roxanne knew it. The pyrotechnics. She covered her face.

Rose said, 'They found accelerant concentrated where the fire started.'

She looked up. 'What are you saying?'

'It was definitely started deliberately.'

53

'Arson,' Roxanne said. 'That's what the police said. I can't believe it.'

Chrissie took this in. She looked shattered, red-eyed, as if she had been awake for days. Not a scrap of make-up. 'Someone tried to kill us,' she said.

'Us, and everyone else in the place.'

They were at the kitchen table in Chrissie's house, drinking coffee. Upstairs, Anita was sobbing. Rick was floating about somewhere, on the phone. They heard him say, 'There's loads of time – we don't need to decide yet.'

'Jack has to be behind this,' Roxanne continued. 'We were about to bring him down. That's what the police call motive.' She had spoken to DS Rose and told him about the fallout with Jack before the show after he threatened to pull the plug on their dream gig, Wembley. For the time being, she had said nothing about the sex tapes.

What little colour there was in Chrissie's face seemed to

drain away. 'Shit, I've just remembered – the tapes! What happened to them? Don't tell me they went up in smoke!'

Roxanne shook her head. She had got Jamie to spirit them away from the club before the gig and they were safely under lock and key. 'We've still got them,' she said. 'And, whatever happens, we'll use them.'

'What if he doesn't make it?' Jack remained in a coma.

'Let's wait and see,' Roxanne said. 'How's Anita?'

'Blaming herself. Wishing she'd replied to Maria's messages. Feeling awful because she knew Maria was there and didn't want to see her – too scared there'd be some horrible scene.' Chrissie frowned. 'She was probably right about that.'

'Even so, it's not her fault.'

'No, course not, but she keeps saying if she hadn't come back Maria would still be alive.' Chrissie gave a tiny shrug. 'I've tried telling her she can't think that way but I'm not sure I'm getting through.'

'Poor Nita. We always think there's time to put things right and then . . .' Roxanne sighed.

Chrissie gave another shrug and went to make more coffee, the racket of the grinder making conversation impossible. She took her time, standing over the machine as strong black coffee trickled into fresh mugs, frothing up milk, returning to the table with the drinks and a pot of cinnamon. Anti-inflammatory, she had heard. Packed with antioxidants. 'She needs time,' she told Roxanne. 'And a hell of a lot of TLC.'

Roxanne watched her sprinkle a generous helping of cinnamon into her drink.

'At least it's good news about Carly being awake and the baby being okay,' Chrissie said.

'Do we know whose it is?' Roxanne asked.

'I'm not sure *Carly* knows whose it is.'

'So, is she back with Adam?'

'She hasn't decided. Seems they've kissed and made up . . . for now, anyway.'

'Dave's still hanging in there, insisting the baby's his, and Carly's saying nothing on the subject. Seems to think if he keeps sending ridiculous bunches of flowers she'll cave in, even though he was the one trolling her, the evil bastard.' Roxanne nodded in the direction of an enormous bunch of roses on the kitchen counter. 'I see you've got an admirer too.'

'Rick sent those.'

Roxanne felt as if something had got hold of her heart and was squeezing hard.

Chrissie warmed her hands on her mug. 'I don't know how I'd have got through everything without him. He's been incredible.'

Roxanne forced herself to ask the one question she dreaded getting an answer to. 'So, are you back together?'

Chrissie shrugged. The sound of footsteps crossing the hall made her clam up.

Rick, looking harassed, suddenly appeared in the doorway. 'So, now Susan's in charge at Shine.' Chrissie's jaw dropped. 'I know, it's bonkers, but that's how Jack set things up – if anything happened to him, she got to take over.' He looked uncomfortable. 'And that's not all. I've just spoken to her – twenty minutes talking to a frigging brick wall – she's saying there's no future for the band. She's about to pull everything.' He looked from one to the other. 'Including . . . Wembley.'

Susan sat behind Jack's desk at Shine. She had already spoken to the *Rock Legends* people and set up a meeting. She had a few more calls to make before gathering the rest of the Shine team to tell them Project Thunder Girls was dead in the water. She smiled. Something to look forward to. It would cost the business, but Susan didn't care. Her mission was too important. She had arranged the meeting for the end of the day. Six o'clock to be precise, which hadn't gone down well. Big Becky from marketing was the first to object. 'With all due respect, most people are heading home at six,' she told Susan. Hari from the press office said he usually did a spinning session at six and was there any chance of bringing the meeting forward? Susan stuck to her guns, Lazy bunch. She knew exactly who was in the habit of sliding off early and now she was in charge she intended to put a stop to it.

She scribbled Rick's name on the pad in front of her on the desk, then put a line through it. He was on borrowed time, but for now, while Jack was out of things, he still had his uses. Once Jack was back on his feet, though, Rick could be dispensed with. She would sack him on some trumped-up charge for bringing the company into disrepute. That way, he wouldn't get a pay-off. She doubted he would have the means to take on the might of Shine.

She phoned the hospital to see how Jack was doing. Better. Breathing without a ventilator. The night of the fire still haunted her and she kept going over events at Heaven & Hell, thinking about Jack heading to the loo just before the blaze broke out, his back disappearing along a corridor at the side of the stage. It was the last she had seen of him. Once smoke started to billow out across the dance floor she had tried going after him, only to be carried in the opposite direction by a panic-filled crowd. She had made it out of the building with minor injuries while Jack was trapped inside. The firefighters had found him huddled under a desk in the office the pyro crew had been using. Susan couldn't understand how he had ended up there when the loos were nowhere near. He must have got disorientated.

She glanced at the TV, where Sky's rolling news was still showing a reporter outside Heaven & Hell, and watched for a moment before switching channels. Nothing had been said in the press about the cause of the fire. Not officially, anyway, although there had been unconfirmed reports of arson.

The door to the office flew open and Roxanne, Chrissie and Anita burst in. Carly – head still bandaged – brought up the rear.

'We want a word with you,' Roxanne said.

'I take it Rick's broken the sad news?' Susan's lip curled in a horrible smile. 'About Wembley. I'm afraid it's off. Over. No more. Finito. Kaput.' She chuckled. 'Other phrases are available. Take your pick.'

'I think you'll find the gig's going ahead, as planned,' Chrissie said.

'And I think *you'll* find I'm running things here and what *I* say goes.' Susan's voice was harsh. She looked them up and down. 'What a bunch of ragbags. None of you are up to performing at the local community centre, never mind Wembley Stadium.' She glanced at Carly, who had inched her way towards a chair and gratefully collapsed into it. 'You'll get no sympathy from me, baby killer.'

She then pointed at Anita. 'Aren't you supposed to be grieving?'

Anita's face contorted and she lunged at the desk. Chrissie caught hold of her.

'Well, if that's everything, see yourselves out,' Susan said. 'Or would you prefer it if security showed you to the door? I suppose being marched out of the building would bring back memories.'

Roxanne held up a video cassette. 'We're not going anywhere.'

Susan gave her a cold look. 'Sorry, I don't think we have VCR players anymore. It's all digital these days.'

'That's a pity,' Roxanne said. 'Although I'm not sure you'd want to see what's on this – and all the others we've got safely stashed away.' Susan rolled her eyes, unconcerned.

'Did you know your pervert brother had a thing for underage girls?'

'Don't be so—'

'Because we've got the evidence right here. Not just one girl, loads of them.'

'You're making it up.'

Roxanne held her gaze. 'Nope. And he also had a thing about filming himself in action, so it's all on tape. He knows we've got them.'

'We could always just take the tapes straight to the police,' Chrissie said.

Susan's face went white.

'*We're* in charge now, bitch,' Chrissie went on. 'Which means you are finished. Terminated. Done for.' She waited a moment. 'Other phrases are available.'

54

Susan had worked too hard for this. Too hard to be on the cusp of finally having revenge on the Thunder Girls. And it was going to be taken away from her at the last minute thanks to her *brother*? He had failed to protect her thirty years ago when they threw her out of the band, and now his mistakes were costing her justice?

She stood, grabbed her desk lamp and threw it at Roxanne.

The Thunder Girls all screamed. The lamp missed Roxanne, just. 'You stole my career!' Susan yelled at Roxanne.

She then turned to Carly. 'You stole my brother!' She picked up her landline phone and tried to hurl it at Carly's head. But the landline cable wouldn't reach that far, so it fell flat to the floor.

Anita took a step forward, trying to stop Susan. Susan was having none of it. She picked up her laptop and hurled it at her. 'Stay away from me!' The laptop hit Anita in the chest, the impact forcing her to the floor. Roxanne stood over Anita defensively while Carly knelt next to her, checking if she was okay. Susan ignored them and turned to Chrissie. 'You're the worst bitch of them all.'

Chrissie looked right back at her. 'Takes one to know one.'

Susan let off a primal howl and leapt at Chrissie, her hands grasping for her plastic throat.

Before she could have the sweet, satisfying feeling of choking the life out of Chrissie, Susan felt herself hurled to the floor.

'Oh my goodness!' Big Becky exclaimed.

Susan writhed on the floor, struggling against the weight on top of her. She eventually craned her neck to see – it was Hari. Others at Shine must have heard the commotion.

'Let me go. Let me go!' Susan screamed.

'I'll call the pigs,' Chrissie said, whipping out her mobile while Susan screamed and screamed.

55

By the next morning, there had been some very interesting changes at Shine. The staff and the Thunder Girls had all watched Susan being carried off by the police, still frothing at the mouth to kill them all.

'Assault!' Roxanne had cried to the police, pointing at Anita – who was very much okay, just a bit stunned by being smacked by a flying laptop.

'Attempted murder!' Chrissie had exclaimed, pointing at herself.

With Susan locked up awaiting charges, and Jack in a coma, temporary control of Shine Records fell to . . . Rick Davies.

Rick had already opened control of Jack's office to the band members, set up passes so the women could come and go at Shine when they pleased, and given them access to Jack's computer. They were busy scrolling through his emails, on a coffee and kombucha high.

'I knew it!' Roxanne was triumphant. 'Jack was behind that trashy tell-all book. There's a whole file on it here. Bloody Kristen Kent—'

'I *knew* it was her! She *hates* me,' Chrissie said.

Carly fizzed. 'Let's sue the publishers,' she said.

'I don't see how we can – there's nothing in the book that isn't true.' Roxanne looked glum.

'Shine could put out a press release, saying it's a load of bollocks. Unsubstantiated.' Carly looked pleased with herself.

Chrissie was nodding. 'Why not? Rick will do it on their behalf now.'

Carly clapped her hands. 'That's more like it.'

'Wait,' said Roxanne. 'What about Jack's tapes?'

Anita and Chrissie looked at each other. 'We don't need them for blackmail anymore,' Anita said.

'Let's take them to the police before the Wembley concert,' Chrissie said. 'Brother and sister, locked up together, and justice for the other girls on those tapes as well . . .'

Carly nodded.

Later, Roxanne was in her dressing gown. She had finally sat down with Jamie and spoken to him about Rick. Explained as best she could why she had decided to keep Rick out of his life. It had been the right decision at the time, she said, in floods of tears, but she would understand if Jamie couldn't forgive her. Jamie cried too and said he wished she had been honest but he wasn't about to judge her. She was a brilliant mum, the best. And there was still time for him to get to know his real dad.

Afterwards, feeling drained, she'd had a long soak in a rose-scented bath and was just about to apply a face mask, one of those scary-looking sheets that promised to plump skin up overnight, when the doorbell went. DS Rose, she hoped, with an update.

So far, the police had questioned a number of potential suspects, including Scott. A strange chap called Jason Naylor – the girls' Mad Fan – had come forward to say he had seen Scott arguing with Chrissie before the blaze broke out. Naylor was such an oddball the police wondered about looking into him too until Roxanne assured them the Mad Fan would never harm the band. And he had been found unconscious nowhere near the starting point of the fire, for what that was worth.

Jack was responsible, Roxanne insisted. Had to be.

She opened the door to find Rick facing her. At once, she wished she wasn't wearing her tatty old dressing gown.

'Sorry, is this a bad time?' He stepped into the hall without waiting for her answer.

They went into the kitchen, Roxanne hoping her face wasn't bright red from lying in a too-hot bath for longer than was wise.

'We need to talk,' Rick said, looking at her in a way that made her stomach do what felt like a series of somersaults. 'I'm sorry, I should have come before now. I just . . .'

Roxanne wasn't sure she wanted to hear whatever it was

he had to say. Chrissie was in love with him all over again and wanted him back – and Roxanne knew from experience that what her old frenemy wanted she got. Now Rick had come to break the news, she guessed.

'It's okay,' she said. 'Things have been crazy for all of us.'

Rick nodded. 'Chrissie said she'd been asked by DS Rose if she thought Jack could have started the fire.' Roxanne wished he would stop mentioning Chrissie. Each time he said her name it felt like a knife going in. 'Do you think he could have?' Rick asked.

'I think there's every chance. Let's face it, that day at the club, he was jumping up and down with rage. You heard him, what he said to us.' She waited a moment. 'He thought he was calling the shots, then we turned round and kicked him where it hurt – let him know we were ready to bring him down.'

'I knew you had some kind of dirt on him to make him give you back the Wembley gig,' Rick said.

Roxanne smiled. 'You have no idea. You'll see. Soon. Jack's not the type to go quietly. My guess is he decided to burn the club down to stop us.'

Rick whistled. He looked deep in thought.

She went to the fridge and took out an already-open bottle of wine, poured them both a glass.

Rick cleared his throat. 'About what you told me. Before I went back into the club.'

'It's fine, you don't need to say anything, I understand,'

she said, the words tumbling out in a rush. 'I dropped it on you and I had no right to.' She couldn't look at him.

'I'll be honest, you threw me.'

'I know and I'm so, so sorry—'

'Roxy . . .'

'I should have told you when I knew I was pregnant. But you were with Chrissie and we weren't talking and Pete assumed the baby was his so . . .' She gave him a helpless look.

It was a while before he said anything. 'I just came over to say—'

She interrupted. 'You're back with Chrissie, I knew you would be, and it's completely fine, I understand.' It wasn't fine. Her feelings were all over the place.

'Hang on, who told you that?' He looked thoroughly perplexed. 'Oh, Rox, there you go putting two and two together, making about a hundred and fifty.' His hands were on her shoulders and he was gazing at her almost as if . . . as if he felt the same about her as she did about him. She swallowed, not daring to trust what her feelings seemed to be telling her. Hadn't she got it badly wrong in the past, falling madly in love with Rick when it was Chrissie he wanted? It was not a mistake she was about to make twice.

'If the fire's taught me anything it's that life and death are so close,' Rick said. 'That's why I'm here – because I want us to be together.' She could barely breathe. 'I want to get to know my son, for us to be a family. And I want to do it properly. So let's get back together. It's not too late for us to live "happily ever after", is it?'

Roxanne blinked. Was her mind playing tricks? His eyes were on her. She swayed slightly and felt him holding her, keeping her on her feet.

'This is where you say something – yes, I hope.' He was smiling that smile of his, the one that turned her to mush.

She went to speak and a small indistinct squeak came out. Rick frowned. 'What was that?'

'What about Chrissie?' Her voice was croaky.

He held her gaze. 'I want her to be okay, but there's nothing going on between us.'

Neither one spoke.

'Say it again,' Roxanne said at last.

'I swear, it's over with Chrissie. I know I've made massive mistakes, but I would love to try again.'

She started to nod.

'Roxanne Lloyd, will you give me a second chance?'

'YES!'

56

On the day of the *Rock Legends* gig, Jack was sitting up in his hospital bed. On the mend, keen to be discharged. He switched the TV on and caught the build-up to what was being billed as the biggest music extravaganza for decades, some dim woman with blue hair doing a piece to camera about the Thunder Girls. He gritted his teeth. He wasn't finished with them yet, whatever they might think. The woman turned to Jason Donovan, who said he was honoured to be on the same bill as the biggest – and still the best – girl band in the world. Jack felt like chucking the remote at the screen. Irritated, he muted the sound. If one more person called those old has-beens *girls*, he would throw up.

There was a tap at the door. 'Susan, is that you? Where have you been?' he bellowed.

'It's the police.'

Jack scrunched up his face. He was too busy for that. 'I'm resting,' he roared.

The door opened and a man in a cheap suit came in. Two police officers followed.

'I'm Detective Sergeant Harry Rose,' the one in the suit said.

'If it's about the fire, I've already given a statement.' Jack hit the volume button on the remote and the TV came to life again.

Detective Rose moved closer to the bed, took the remote from Jack and switched the TV off.

'Hey! I was watching that!'

'Jack Fox, known as Jack Raven, I am arresting you on suspicion of arson . . .'

Jack's face was ashen. Suddenly, the room was on a tilt. He took in only a fraction of what Rose was saying. *Murder. Attempted murder. Unlawful sexual activity*. Jack opened his mouth to object but nothing came out.

Rose was telling him to get dressed.

They were taking him to the station.

Kristen Kent was cock-a-hoop. She loved it when a plan came together. When the features editor at the *Daily Post* got in touch to say they had a massive Thunder Girls scoop for her she was taken aback. After all, there was nothing she didn't already know about the band. Or so she thought. She was even more dismissive when they said they wanted her to sit down with what they called an impeccable source – then introduced her to a scarily sexy man with the smoothest skin and biggest eyes she had ever seen. Once she got chatting to Jason Naylor – a self-confessed obsessive Thunder Girls super-fan – she was strangely drawn to him.

Jason, it turned out, had an encyclopaedic knowledge of the band, and an undying love for Chrissie Martin – bizarre he would fixate on her and not the younger, prettier Carly, she reflected as she took notes whilst also sneaking a peek at what looked like an eight-pack under a tight white T-shirt.

'Chrissie and I had a moment in Heaven & Hell. I just need another chance,' he said.

Kristen didn't write that comment down.

It was fair to say he had devoted much of his life to worshipping the pop diva – what a waste of abs, she pondered, chewing her pen, feeling oddly turned on by the sort of person who usually repulsed her. She wondered if she had used too much of her HRT cream as she continued to feel drawn into his moon-like pupils.

And he had quite a story to tell.

Before he spilled the beans, though, he wanted to make sure that what Kristen wrote was sympathetic – nothing about how old Chrissie was, or anything negative. As for Scott, he wanted him hung out to dry. To be sure Kristen did as she promised, Jason insisted on final approval of the piece. In writing.

Kristen was impressed and agreed – something she never did.

Her eyes had widened when she listened to Jason's illicit recordings. Scott, on the phone to who she now knew was

Jack Raven before fleeing to Cornwall in Chrissie's new Range Rover. (Later offloaded for a good twenty grand less than it was worth, Jason said, repeating what the indiscreet salesman at the car showroom in Truro had told him.)

Jason wondered if it mattered that he had obtained his information by questionable means. Kristen assured him it was of no consequence. What was Scott going to do – sue? They'd both had a good laugh about that.

He decided not to mention the hit and run business. It didn't seem relevant. Kristen had lovely eyes, he thought as she looked at him, and the lines around her mouth where she was chewing her pen were strangely arousing him.

Kristen said the *Daily Post* was willing to pay him for the story. Ten grand. He didn't want it, he said, but there was something Kristen could do for him . . .

Her exclusive was splashed all over the front page (and several inside pages) on the day of the *Rock Legends* gig. Thanks to Jason, Kristen knew that Scott was on his way back to Cornwall, hoping to disappear under the radar. Some chance! She hoped he would call at a service station on the way and spot the early editions.

Kristen loved what the editorial team had done with the front page. The headline was a single word: *HATED*. Beneath it was a grainy photo, some awful snatched picture of Scott outside Chrissie's house, loading his things into the Range Rover, looking . . . *furtive*. Taken the day Scott had come back early from honeymoon and skipped off, according to Jason. *Fleeing with his ill-gotten gains*, was how the paper put it.

Love rat Scotty! How Scumbag Scott broke the heart of one of the world's best-loved pop icons. An inside page carried a picture of Chrissie managing to look tragic and hot at the same time. *Stunning blonde, Chrissie Martin*, the caption said, *ripped off by a cheapskate conman*.

Not only was Scott getting his comeuppance, Kristen's police contacts had also tipped her off about Jack Raven. *Arsonist. Murderer. Paedophile*. And that absolute creep 'Kimberley' was actually Jack's sister and PA? Kristen heard she had been arrested too. What a pair! It was getting better all the time. She was already working on the piece that would crucify them both.

As for Carly's lush of a husband, Dave 'The Destroyer' Dixon, his exhibition series was in tatters. Kristen had caught a bit of it on Sky Sports – Dave stumbling about, half-cut. Ripping the baize.

The sponsors were up in arms. According to the sports guy on the *Post*, Dave was well and truly finished.

She checked her watch. *Rock Legends* was about to start. Jason Naylor's face had lit up when she told him she had got him into the Golden Circle – as well as a meet and greet with the girls. He reckoned that when Chrissie saw him again without the drama of the fire around them she'd finally be able to tell him how she felt about them being together, that the kiss in the club proved they were meant to be. Kristen suspected Chrissie would make his gorgeous blue eyes fill with tears when she made it clear he'd be getting nowhere near her again, so she said she would come with him – just for support, of course . . .

The girls had made it. Wembley Stadium. Their dream gig. They stood at the side of the stage, arms linked, waiting to go on, as the band played the intro. The noise from the crowd roared around the arena.

'How did this happen?' Carly was wide-eyed. 'We've been battered, bruised . . . had our fingers burned, *literally*, yet here we are – still standing.'

'It was meant to be.' Chrissie beamed. 'We're the world's biggest girl band. We get knocked down, but we get back up again – we will survive, as Ms Gaynor would say.'

Roxanne laughed. Adrenalin raced through her body. 'Let's go out there and put on the show of our lives.' Anita blinked back tears. Roxanne gave her a squeeze. 'For Maria,' she told her. A glance at Carly. 'And the baby.'

'The Thunder Girls are *back*,' Chrissie yelled.

'And better than ever!' Carly gazed at her bandmates. 'God, I love you girls.'

Chrissie pulled a face. 'Hey – no going soppy.'

Carly grinned. 'I *am* soppy.' It was the happiest she had felt for ages. 'Just goes to show – when it comes to friendships, some last forever . . . whether you like it or not!'

With that said, the lights dimmed, leaving the stage in darkness. On their cue, the girls walked out onto the stage.

They assumed their positions. Just before they were thrust back into the spotlight of the world, they all swapped smiles in the dark and held hands.

Then the lights went up, and they were back.

Acknowledgements

Without some very special women, *The Thunder Girls* and my journey here may not have been possible. Firstly the late, great Jackie Collins for showing me that girls can do anything and for giving me the chance to dream of a better life than the one I was born into. Secondly the amazing and much-missed Jackie Hatton for helping that dream become a reality; I miss you every day and hope you will read this on a cloud somewhere with a cocktail. The perfectly poptastic Claire Richards and the wickedly wonderful Claire King, who believed in me long before anyone else did as a manager and gave me the chance to prove myself; you both changed my life and I am proud to still have you as friends so many years down the line – thank you. To my mum, who sadly lost her life to cancer at fifty-two just as she was finally getting to live her own dreams – Mum, I'm living them for both of us and I hope you are somewhere lovely enjoying the ride.

I would like to thank the Joan Crawford to my Bette Davis: Amanda Beckman, who runs our management companies like a true tigress and is quite frankly my sister from another mister. Amanda, you are a true friend and eternal ally . . . Love ya.

Angela Squire – well, what can I say to my partner in entertainment crime! We've been on quite a journey, haven't we, my love. We are as one and you are the fifth Thunder Girl! Here's to a huge year ahead – you've always had my back and I'll always have yours.

To the wonderful, kind-hearted and lovely Coleen Nolan for friendship, loyalty and for allowing me to sail her into the choppy waters of the Nolans' thirtieth anniversary reunion tour, the gig that taught me so much about the dynamics of the music business, alongside equally lovely Linda, Maureen and the dearly departed dynamic Bernie Nolan, who blew the roof off those arenas, leaving me feeling like a proud mother in the wings . . . I'm always 'In the Mood for Dancing' with you fabulous ladies – here's to many more memories to come.

To Saira Khan for her unwavering support, and to the truly fabulous Beverley Callard for believing in me and *The Thunder Girls* play when it was still a babe in arms, and for being such a loyal friend.

It truly takes a village to keep the Blake ship afloat so I'd like to thank some of my special gang who are always there for me . . . My 'takeaway at Mel's' chicks, Moiya Saint and Amanda Bragnoli: I love you girls, thanks for always being there for me, I don't know what I'd do without you – bu keep your hands off my chilli squid!

My fabulous friend Caroline and her lovely husband David – your support and friendship means so much and I hope you are proud of me like I am proud of you. Lesley Reynolds and Dr Aamer Khan for constantly repairing me! My glam squad Anna, Lucinda, Cindy, Chantelle and Sally – you know where all my bits and pieces go! My great pal, lovely Elaine Stoddard, who was the first person to read *The Thunder Girls* and tell me she loved it.

A very, very special shout-out goes to my wonderful team at Pan Macmillan, headed up by my fabulous publisher Wayne Brookes, for adopting *The Thunder Girls* into his literary nursery, feeding them, nurturing them and finally letting them – and me – loose on the world. You got *Thunder* from day one and I hope I've done you proud. So many thanks to Ingrid Connell, also at Pan Macmillan, for years of support when I was on the other side of the fence. You both believing in me having 'my own moment' finally led to this book being born after a twenty-year labour – I think I might call you my hospital team because you certainly made me push to deliver these four feisty girls! Thanks to the tireless sales and communications Pan Mac team as a collective, and also Alex Lloyd, Alex Saunders and Samantha Fletcher, and my PR gurus Shona Abhyankar and Emma Draude at EDPR – thank you so much for spreading the *Thunder* news.

And thank you to Tory Lyne-Pirkis at Midas PR for doing

such a wonderful job on selling out *The Thunder Girls* play and always being there. To Helen Warner, who threw me many a lifeline in the choppy seas of entertainment when others were hoping I'd be washed away by waves – you are a true pal and are much-appreciated; may our adventures continue into new seas. To Caroline Waterston, Alison Phillips, Julia Davis, Claire Higney and Emma Jones – all goddesses of print and great friends who I admire and am grateful to know. And a special thank you to Gary Jones for giving me my first break as a writer by making me a national columnist. I hope I've done you all proud.

Not to forget my wonderful Thunder Boys . . . I'd like to thank my lawyers, Stephen Luckman and Keith Ashby at Sheridans, for taking such good care of me, and Martin Riley at Lion Eyes for being the most brilliant person ever. Nicky Johnston for capturing my essence on camera for all the PR images in the way only he can, and Daniel Cocklin for sharing his creative genius designing all *The Thunder Girls* campaign artwork and always being a calming shoulder to lean on – you rock. An extra special thank you to Jon McEwan for filling the Thunder tank with petrol when it was still parked in the station, and to Dermot McNamara for being such a great support – I'm looking forward to seeing your journey next!

To my *Thunder Girls* stars of the live stage show: you girls amaze me by bringing my characters to life with true passion and dedication and I shall be forever grateful for your support and belief in the journey.

Also a personal special shout-out goes out to all my fabulous friends past and present who have always believed in me, encouraged me never to give up, chatted with me on Messenger in the early hours during writer's block, helped heal the heartbreak that nearly derailed me, and contributed to a hell of a lot of hangovers over the years, especially my darling pals Collette Cooper, Nick Jones, Dee Collins, Davina DeMiguel and Julie Frisbee.